KISS THE DEAD

Anita Blake, Vampire Hunter Novels by Laurell K. Hamilton

GUILTY PLEASURES

THE LAUGHING CORPSE

CIRCUS OF THE DAMNED

THE LUNATIC CAFÉ

BLOODY BONES

THE KILLING DANCE

BURNT OFFERINGS

BLUE MOON

OBSIDIAN BUTTERFLY

NARCISSUS IN CHAINS

CERULEAN SINS

INCUBUS DREAMS

MICAH

DANSE MACABRE

THE HARLEQUIN

BLOOD NOIR

SKIN TRADE

FLIRT

BULLET

HIT LIST

KISS THE DEAD

STRANGE CANDY

eSpecials

BEAUTY

KISS
THE DEAD

LAURELL K. HAMILTON

B

BERKLEY BOOKS, NEW YORK

THE BERKLEY PUBLISHING GROUP
Published by the Penguin Group
Penguin Group (USA) Inc.
375 Hudson Street, New York, New York 10014, USA
Penguin Group (Canada), 90 Eglinton Avenue East, Suite 700, Toronto, Ontario M4P 2Y3, Canada
(a division of Pearson Penguin Canada Inc.) • Penguin Books Ltd., 80 Strand, London WC2R 0RL,
England • Penguin Group Ireland, 25 St. Stephen's Green, Dublin 2, Ireland (a division of Penguin
Books Ltd.) • Penguin Group (Australia), 250 Camberwell Road, Camberwell, Victoria 3124, Australia
(a division of Pearson Australia Group Pty. Ltd.) • Penguin Books India Pvt. Ltd., 11 Community
Centre, Panchsheel Park, New Delhi—110 017, India • Penguin Group (NZ), 67 Apollo Drive,
Rosedale, Auckland 0632, New Zealand (a division of Pearson New Zealand Ltd.) • Penguin Books
(South Africa) (Pty.) Ltd., 24 Sturdee Avenue, Rosebank, Johannesburg 2196, South Africa

Penguin Books Ltd., Registered Offices: 80 Strand, London WC2R 0RL, England

This book is an original publication of The Berkley Publishing Group.

FIRST EDITION: June 2012

Library of Congress Cataloging-in-Publication Data

Hamilton, Laurell K.
Kiss the dead / Laurell K. Hamilton. — 1st ed.
p.   cm.
ISBN 978-0-425-24754-9
1. Blake, Anita (Fictitious character)—Fiction.   2. Teenage girls—Fiction.   3. Vampires—Fiction.
4. Werewolves—Fiction.   5. Kidnapping—Fiction.   6. Serial murderers—Fiction.   I. Title.
PS3558.A443357K575   2012
813'.54—dc23
2012005138

PRINTED IN THE UNITED STATES OF AMERICA

10   9   8   7   6   5   4   3   2   1

To Jonathon, my husband, who understands that the journey is long, but worth the ride. To Shawn for all those calls about police work and for just being that lifeline call over the last two decades. All mistakes in this book are mine and mine alone; there never seems to be time for him to see all of the book. To Jess, who has taught both Jonathon and me that mischief is both fun and damn near necessary in our lives. To Pilar, my sister of choice, who taught me that it's never too late to have a happy childhood. To Missy, welcome aboard, a continuity editor at last. To Steven, who helped me with research I didn't even know I was doing. To Bryan, who managed to inspire and challenge me in unexpected ways. To Mitch, good luck in New York.

I kiss'd thee ere I kill'd thee: no way but this;
Killing myself, to die upon a kiss.

—Speaking to the corpse of Desdemona,
and kissing her, Othello dies

1

On TV, INTERROGATION rooms are roomy and have big windows so that you can watch everything. In reality, the rooms are pretty small, and there are almost never big picture windows; that's why real police footage is grainy and black-and-white, rather than Technicolor gorgeous. The interrogation room was painted pale beige, or maybe it was taupe, I'd always been a little fuzzy on the difference between them. Either way it was a bland color described by real estate agents as a warm neutral; they lied. It was a cold, impersonal color. The small table was all shiny metal, and so was the chair. The idea was that the prisoners couldn't scratch their names, or messages, in the metal like they could have in wood, but whoever thought that had never seen what a vampire, or a wereanimal, could do to metal. There were plenty of scratches in the shiny tabletop, most done with just fingernails, superhuman strength, and the boredom of hours of sitting.

The vampire sitting at the small table wasn't trying to carve his initials on anything. He was crying, so hard that his thin shoulders shook. He'd slicked his black hair back from his face in a widow's peak that I was betting was a haircut and no more natural than the ink-black color.

He was mumbling in a tear-choked voice, "You hate me because I'm a vampire."

I spread my hands flat on the cool metal table. My jacket's jewel-tone blue sleeves looked too bright against the naked metal, or maybe it was the crimson nail polish. That had been for my date the night before; it looked out of place while I was U.S. Marshal Anita Blake. I counted to ten, to keep from yelling at our suspect again. That was what had started the crying; I'd scared him. Jesus, some people don't have enough balls to be undead.

"I don't hate you, Mr. Wilcox," I said in a smooth, even friendly voice. I had to deal with clients every day at Animators Inc.; I had a customer voice. "Some of my best friends are vampires and shapeshifters."

"You hunt and kill us," he said, but he raised his eyes enough to gaze at me between his fingers. His tears were tinged pink with someone else's blood. His putting his hands over his eyes had smeared the tears around so that his face was trailed and marked with the drying pink tears. It didn't match the perfectly arched black eyebrows, or the eyebrow ring that sat dull blue metal above his left eye. He'd probably done it to bring out the blue in his eyes, but at best they were a watery, pale blue that didn't work with the dyed black hair, and the dark blue of the eyebrow piercing just seemed to emphasize that his eyes were too pale, and matched the pink traces of blood way better than the artificial additions. I was betting he started life as a white-blond, or maybe pale, nondescript brown.

"I'm a legal vampire executioner, Mr. Wilcox, but you have to break the law to bring me to your door."

Those pale eyes blinked at me. "You can look me in the eyes."

I smiled, and tried to shove it all the way up into my own dark brown eyes, but was pretty sure I failed. "Mr. Wilcox, Barney, you haven't been dead two years yet. Do you really think your weak-ass vampire mind tricks will work on me?"

"He said people would be afraid of me," and this was almost a whisper.

"Who said?" I asked. I leaned forward just a little, keeping my hands still, trying to be pleasant, and not spook him.

He muttered, "Benjamin."

"Benjamin who?" I asked.

He shook his head. "Just Benjamin. The old vampires only have one name."

I nodded. Old vampires had one name, like Madonna, or Beyoncé, but what most people didn't know was that they fought duels to see who got to use the name. A powerful vampire could demand that another lesser vampire give up the use of a name he'd had for centuries, or fight for the right to keep it. I didn't say that part out loud, because most people, even us vampire experts, didn't know it. It was an old custom that was dying out as the modern vampires kept their last names, and duels were illegal now that vampires weren't. Dueling was looked on the same under the law regardless of whether the participants were alive or undead. I would have bet a lot of money that this Benjamin wasn't old enough to know the history behind vampires having only one name.

"Where can I find Benjamin?"

"I thought you were so powerful that no vampire could resist you." There was a flare of sullen anger in his pale blue eyes. There was temper in there, under the tears.

"I would need a connection with him, someone who was metaphysically joined with him in some way, so I could follow the psychic connection. Someone like you." I let the hint of threat ride into that last part.

He looked sullen and arrogant. "You can't do that; no one can."

"Are you sure?" I asked, and my voice dropped a little lower.

"You're a U.S. Marshal, you're not allowed to do magic on me."

"It's not magic, Barney. It goes under psychic skills, and law enforcement officers are allowed to use psychic abilities in the performance of their duties if they think that is the only way to prevent further loss of life."

He frowned, rubbing one pale hand across his face. He sniffed loudly, and I pushed the box of Kleenex toward him. He took one, used it, and then gave me angry eyes. It was probably his hard look, but as hard looks go, it wasn't. "I have rights. The new laws won't let you hurt me without a warrant of execution."

"And a minute ago, you were worried I'd kill you. Barney, you need to make up your mind." I raised a hand and spread it flat in the air as if I were holding something he should have been able to see. "Am I a danger to you, or"—and I held up my other hand—"not able to hurt you at all?"

His anger sputtered down to sullenness. "Not sure."

"The girl that Benjamin and the others took is only fifteen. She can't legally agree to become a vampire."

"We didn't take her," Barney said, indignant, slamming his hand on the table.

"Legally, she's a minor, so it's kidnapping, regardless of whether she went willingly or not. It's kidnapping and attempted murder right now; if we find her too late, it's murder, and I'll get that court order of execution for you and Benjamin, and every other vampire that may have touched her."

A nervous tic started under his eye, and he swallowed so hard that it was loud in the quiet room. "I don't know where they took her."

"Time for lies is past, Barney; when Sergeant Zerbrowski comes back through that door with an order of execution, I'll be able to legally blow your head and heart into bloody ribbons."

"If I'm dead, I can't tell you where the girl is," he said, and looked pleased with himself.

"Then you do know where she is, don't you?"

He looked scared then, wadding the Kleenex up in his hands until his fingers mottled with the pressure. He had just enough blood in him for the skin to mottle. He'd drunk deep of someone.

The door opened. Barney Wilcox, the vampire, made a small yip of fear. Zerbrowski's curly salt-and-pepper hair fell around his half-open collar, his tie at half-mast with a spot of something he'd eaten smeared down it. His brown slacks and white shirt looked like he'd slept in them. He might have, but then again, his wife, Katie, could dress him neat as a pin and he still fell apart before he reached the squad room. He pushed his new tortoiseshell glasses more firmly up on his face and held a piece of paper out to me. The paper looked very official. I reached for it, and the vampire yelled, "I'll tell you! I'll tell you everything, please, please don't kill me!"

Zerbrowski drew his hand back. "Is he cooperating, Marshal Blake?" There was the slightest of twinkles in Zerbrowski's brown eyes. If he grinned at me, I'd kick him in the shins. He stayed serious; there was a missing girl.

I turned back to Barney. "Cooperate, Barney, because once I touch that piece of paper I am out of legal options that don't include lethal force."

Barney told us where the secret lair was, and Zerbrowski got up and went for the door. "I'll start the ball," he said.

Barney stood up and tried to move toward Zerbrowski, but the leg shackles wouldn't let him get far. It was standard operating procedure to chain vampires. I'd removed the cuffs to try to gain his trust, and because I didn't see him as a danger. "Where's he going?"

"To give the location to the other police, and you better pray that we get there before she's been turned."

Barney turned that pink-stained face to me, looking puzzled. "You aren't going?"

"We're forty-five minutes away from the location, Barney; a lot of bad things can happen in that amount of time. There'll be other cops closer."

"But you're supposed to go. In the movies it'd be you."

"Yeah, well, this isn't the movies, and I'm not the only Marshal in the city."

"It's supposed to be you." He almost whispered it. He was staring into space, as if he couldn't think clearly, or like he was listening to some voice I couldn't hear.

"Oh, shit," I said. I was around the table before I had time to really think what I'd do when I got there. I grabbed a handful of Barney's black T-shirt and put our faces inches apart. "Is this a trap, Barney? Is this a trap for me?"

His eyes were wide, showing too much white. He blinked way too fast; the unblinking vampire stare took decades to perfect, and he hadn't had that much time. The pale watery blue bled over his entire eye, so it was like looking at water with sun shining through it—his eyes with vampire power in them. He hissed in my face, snapping fangs at me. I should have backed off, but I didn't. I was so used to dealing with vampires who wouldn't hurt me that I forgot what it meant that he was a vampire, and I wasn't.

He moved, too fast for me to blink, his arms around my waist, lifting me off my feet. I was fast enough to have time to do one thing, before he slammed me down on the table. Once I would have pulled out my cross, but it was in the locker with my gun, because a new law had declared it unfair intimidation against preternatural suspects. I had a split second to choose between my only two options: Do I slap my hand on the table to take some of the impact, or put my arm against his throat to keep his fangs away from mine? I chose my arm in his throat, and I was down. The table shuddered with the force of the blow, but his arm was between my back and the table and it took some of the impact. I wasn't stunned, good.

The vampire snarled in my face, fangs snapping; only my forearm shoved against his throat kept him from tearing mine out. I was more than human-strong, but I was a small woman, and even super-strong, I wasn't as strong as the man pinning me to the table. He grabbed my wrist where it pushed against his throat and tried to pull it out of the way. I didn't fight him for it; the best he was going to do was turn more of my arm into his throat. He didn't know how to fight, didn't understand leverage, he'd never grappled for his life—I had.

I heard the door slam open but didn't glance at it. I had to stare into those burning blue eyes, those fangs; I couldn't afford to look away, even for a second, but I knew the door meant help was in the room. Arms grabbed him from behind, and he snarled, rising up off me, taking his arm from behind my back so he could stand up and face them. I was left lying on my back on the table, to watch the vampire hitting the men, careless blows with no training behind them, and my knights in uniform went flying. I took the moment they'd given me to roll off the other side of the table and to the floor beyond. I landed on the balls of my feet and fingertips; the heels of my Mary Jane–style stilettos didn't even touch floor as I crouched.

I could see legs: the vampire still shackled, the other legs uniforms and slacks; police. Two of the policemen went flying. One uniform didn't get back up, lying in a painful heap against the wall, but two other sets of legs, one uniform and one slacks, were still struggling with the vampire. The shoes with the slacks were shiny and black like they'd been spit-polished, and I was almost sure it was Captain Dolph Storr.

The vampire popped the chain on his shackles, and suddenly the fight was on. Shit! In the bad old days I could have gotten my gun from the locker where it was stored and shot his ass, but I didn't have a warrant of execution for this vampire. Zerbrowski and I had lied to him. Without the warrant, we couldn't just shoot him. Fuck.

I stood up in time to see Dolph's six-foot, eight-inch frame wrapped around the much smaller body of the vampire. Dolph had his arms around the vampire's shoulders, with his own hands behind the vampire's head. It was a classic full nelson, and Dolph was big enough that against most humans he'd have won, but he was struggling to keep the hold on the vampire, as the uniform struggled to pin one of the vampire's arms. Then the uniform's face went slack, and he tried to hit Dolph in the face. Dolph saw it coming, and ducked using the vampire's trapped head as a shield.

I yelled, "Don't look the vampire in the eyes, damn it!" I went back over the table, sliding to the fight, because it was the quickest way I could think to get to Dolph. One of the other uniforms was struggling with the officer who had been mind-fucked by the vampire. The vampire reared back and bucked against Dolph's hold, and his hands came loose. There was movement by the door, but the vampire was twisting in Dolph's grip, and I was out of time to see what the backup was going to do.

I kicked the vampire in the ribs, the way I'd been taught, visualizing the kick going into the ribs, through the body, and a few inches out the other side. That was the goal I'd been taught in judo, and even now that I was taking mixed martial arts the old training kicked in, and I aimed through the ribs and the wall beyond. I forgot two things: one, that I was more than human-strong now, and two, that I was wearing three-inch stilettos.

The kick drove the vampire stumbling away from Dolph, a hand going to his ribs, as he leapt for me still on the table on my side. I kicked him again, this time aiming for the sternum, aiming to take the breath out of him, as if he'd been human and needed to breathe all the time. In a fight, you fall back on training, no matter what you're fighting.

My foot caught him square in the chest, my stiletto sank into his sternum, and the force of the kick drove my heel upward toward his heart. I had a moment to feel the heel sink home, a second to wonder if three inches of stiletto would hit his heart, and then he reacted to the stab, and I realized there was a strap on my shoe, and my heel was stuck in his chest, because he moved away, and my foot went with him, and the rest of me slid off the table. I was short enough that I had to put my hands on the floor to keep from just dangling from his chest. There was nothing I could do to protect myself, or to keep my skirt from inching down. I had a moment of modesty fail as the thigh-highs and thong were exposed to the room. Shit! But if my modesty took the worst of it, I could live with that.

A bright white light began to fill the room. The vampire hissed and backed up. I had to hand-walk as he dragged me across the room. My heel began to slide out of his chest, my body weight finally too much for it. My foot slid all the way out as someone walked into the room with a holy object blazing white, strangely cool, as if the cold light of stars could be held in your hand. I'd never seen a holy object glow this bright when I didn't have my own glowing along with it. It was even more impressive as I lay on the floor, tugging my skirt down, and watched Zerbrowski walk past me, hand held high, most of his body lost in the bright glow of his cross. I had afterimages of the cross in my eyes when I blinked, as if I needed a welder's helmet. It never seemed this bright when my own cross was shining alone, but we were allowed holy objects in the interrogation room only if the vampire was under arrest for assault or murder. Then we could say we needed the protection of something that couldn't be taken away from us like a weapon could.

Dolph offered me a hand, and I took it. There'd been a time when I wouldn't have, but I understood that from Dolph it was a sign of respect and camaraderie, not sexism. He'd have offered Zerbrowski a hand, too.

We watched Zerbrowski drive the vampire into the far corner with the light of his faith, because a holy object doesn't shine unless the holder believes, or the object has been blessed by someone holy enough to make it stick. There were a few priests that I wouldn't let bless my holy water, because I'd had it not glow for me at critical moments. The Church actually surveyed the vampire executioners around the country asking what priests had failed that test of faith. I'd felt like I was tattling.

The vampire curled into the corner, trying to make himself as tiny as possible, his face hidden between his arms. He was yelling, "Please, stop it! It hurts! It hurts!"

Zerbrowski's voice came out of the shining light. "I'll put it away after you're cuffed."

A uniform had brought in some of the new cuff-and-shackle sets that were designed specifically for the preternatural suspects. They were expensive, so even RPIT didn't have a lot of them. Barney was a new vampire; we didn't think he was dangerous enough to need them. We'd been wrong. I looked at the one uniform still lying against the wall. Someone was checking his pulse, and he moved, groaning, as if something hurt a lot; he was alive, but not because of anything I'd done. I'd been stupid and arrogant and others were hurt because of it. I hated it when it was my fault. Hated it, fucking hated it.

The uniform had wide eyes but he went toward the vampire. Dolph and I both reached out at the same time to take the cuff set with its single solid bar connecting the hands and ankle shackles. We looked at each other.

"I was the one who took off his cuffs to play friendly cop."

He studied my face. His dark hair, cut short and neat, was actually just long enough on top that it was mussed from the fight. He smoothed the hair in place, while he gave me serious eyes.

"Besides, the captain shouldn't be wrestling suspects even if he's the biggest guy here," I said with a smile.

He nodded, and let me go first. Once he would have protected me and gone first, but he knew that I was harder to hurt than anyone in the room except the vampire. I could take a beating and keep on ticking, and he also understood without having to say anything else that I was blaming myself for it all getting out of hand. Protocol was that you left vampires completely shackled. I'd taken his cuffs off so he would talk to me. I'd been convinced I could handle a baby vampire like Barney with his hands free. We were lucky no one was dead.

Dolph understood all of that; he'd have felt the same way, so he let me move forward with the heavy metal contraption. He waved the uniform back and he stayed at my back, just in case. When you have someone who is six foot eight and keeps himself in good shape, I'll take him as backup. There'd been a time when Dolph hadn't trusted me because of my dating the monsters, but he'd worked out his issues, and I'd gotten a real federal badge. I was a real cop according to the paperwork, and Dolph had wanted a reason to forgive me for consorting with the monsters. The new badge had been reason enough, that and the fact that he had behaved badly enough toward me and others that he almost let his hatred of the preternaturally challenged cost him his badge, and his self-respect. Some long talks with the local vampires, especially one ex-cop named Dave, of the bar Dead Dave's, had helped him make peace with himself.

I walked around the edge of the cool, white glow of Zerbrowski's cross. The vampire had stopped yelling and was just whimpering in the corner. I'd never asked any of my vampire friends what it felt like to face a cross like this; did it really hurt, or was it just a force they couldn't stand against?

"Barney?" I made his name a question. "Barney, I'm going to put the cuffs on you so that Sergeant Zerbrowski can put the cross away. Say something, Barney. I need to know you understand me." I was kneeling beside him, but not close enough to touch him. It was still way too close if he went apeshit again, but someone was going to have to get that close and I'd picked me for the job. I couldn't have stood there and watched while he hurt someone else, knowing that I'd given him the space to do it. Arrogance had made me uncuff him; guilt made me kneel there and try to get him to hear me.

There was movement behind us. I kept my attention on the vampire in the corner; I knew better than to look away from one danger to another. I trusted the other policemen to have my back. My world had narrowed down to the suspect in the corner. But Dolph spoke low to someone, and then he leaned over me and said, "We found the location, but we've lost contact with the first officers on sight."

"Shit," I whispered. It could be that the officers were having to stay off their radios to search for vampires, or they could be hurt, or dead, or hostages. We were out of time to mess with this vampire; others had our people. I needed him to hear me. I needed him to do what I wanted him to do. "Barney," I said, "hear me." And there was a thread of power in my voice now, a faint vibration of my necromancy. I was a vampire executioner as a job, but I'd started life raising zombies. My psychic gift was with the dead, or the undead. I hadn't meant to, but my desire to control him had found a part of my own natural gifts that might do just that. Was it illegal to use psychic gifts on a suspect? Not after what he'd just done, and not with a fifteen-year-old girl maybe dying at this minute, and at least two officers gone into radio silence. We were out of time, and we needed any help he could give us. The law did allow for psychic force to be used if it would save lives, or if the suspect had proven uncooperative with more normal means. The same new laws that had made it so I couldn't just shoot Barney also allowed me to do things that would have been iffy before they were in place. The law giveth, and the law taketh away.

Barney whimpered, and then his voice came small and almost child-like: "Don't."

"Don't what, Barney?" But my whisper held that echo of power. In the middle of the fight there hadn't been time to think of it, because it took concentration to work with the dead. I could have put the power back in its box, but I wanted him to let me cuff him. I wanted him to talk to me. I wanted it enough that I was willing to go all "witchy" in front of the other cops.

"You aren't my master," he said, "and your master isn't my master. We're free vampires and we won't let you control us."

He was one of the new vampires, ones that didn't want to follow a Master of the City. They wanted to be free like humans were, free to make decisions and be just people, but no matter how many vampires I might love, and protect, what Barney had done in the few minutes he'd been free proved why freedom from the control of the masters was a bad idea. Sometimes you had a bad master and the system went bad, very bad, but you couldn't let people with this level of strength and power out there without a power structure. They needed someone to hold their leashes, because you give most people this kind of power and you find out that they aren't nice people at all; they'd been nice because they were weak. It takes a truly good person to gain power, strength, and mystical abilities and not misuse them. Most people weren't that good, or sometimes they're just too stupid to not hurt someone by accident. Think about waking up one night strong as a superhero. There is a learning curve, and people can get hurt while you learn. How do you balance one section of the population's right to be safe against the freedom of another? We were still struggling for that answer, but today, this moment, I knew my answer. I would take Barney Wilcox's free will in trade for the safety of a fifteen-year-old girl and the officers that his vampire friends were holding hostage. If I could take it, that is. He wasn't blood-oathed to Jean-Claude; if he had been, then I could have made him behave through my links to Jean-Claude. He was a free vampire with no master to answer to, or no master he knew about. We'd found that most of the "free" vamps followed their group leader. Vampires are just like most other people; they want to follow, they just don't want to admit it.

I called my necromancy and aimed it at this one very young vampire. He pressed himself into the corner, as if he could push himself through the wall. "You can't do necromancy on me with the cross there."

"I raise zombies every night with my cross on, Barney," I said, voice still low and with slightly deeper power. There had been a time when I'd believed my power was evil, but God didn't seem to feel that way, so until He changed His mind, I just had faith that my power came from the right side.

"No," he said, "no, please don't."

"Let me cuff you, Barney, and then maybe I won't have to."

He held his hands out, but the remains of the first cuffs were still on his wrists. I had to lay the heavier cuff set on the floor and have someone hand me a key, because my keys with the cuff key on them were in my purse, which was in my locker with my weapons and cross.

The light from Zerbrowski's cross began to fade. One of the younger officers asked, "Why is the glow fading?" First, he shouldn't have asked that in front of the vampire, and second, he shouldn't have asked until the emergency was over.

Another cop called out, "I'm surprised that Zerbrowski could make it glow at all."

"Yeah, Sarge, didn't know you were that goody-two-shoes."

The vampire in the corner began to be visible again as the light faded, almost as if the glow had made him partially invisible, and he became more solid as the holy fire receded. I had the old cuffs off and was able to see Barney's wrists clearly enough to think that they were both thicker than mine, though still narrow for a man of his height. I had a moment of struggling with the locking mechanism on the new cuffs. It was only the third time I'd put them on anyone outside the practice that we'd all been ordered to attend when they became semi-standard issue. I was up on my knees, concentrating so hard on the metal that Barney leaned close enough so his mouth almost touched my hair, before Dolph put a foot on his shoulder and kept him pressed against the wall. He also had a handgun pointed at him. It would be hell to pay if he died in custody, but Dolph was the boss, and if the boss said it was time for guns, you didn't argue. I couldn't even argue, not really.

I answered the young cop's question, now that I had Dolph there ready and willing. "Most holy items only glow like that when the vampire is using vampire powers; once the vamp quiets down the glow diminishes, or goes out."

I got the shackles off over Barney's boots; they were the big ones designed to go over men's boots. The cuffs were big enough to fit around my neck and have room to spare. The vampire was tall enough that he had to draw his knees up so the single solid metal bar between cuffs and shackles could reach, since Dolph was keeping his upper body very solid against the wall.

"So, it's not that the Sarge lost his faith?" the young guy asked, and the moment he asked I realized we had a more serious problem. I stood up so I could keep half my attention on the newly chained vampire and still see the cop who'd asked. He was a uniform, with brown hair cut too short for his triangular face. His eyes were a little wide still. I didn't get into it in front of the suspect, but I made a mental note later, noting the name tag on the officer: Taggart. If you didn't have faith in God, or whatever, then holy items didn't work no matter how bug-nuts the vampires got. It was the person's faith that made it work, unless it was blessed by a priest or someone equally holy. Blessed items glowed and protected without need of faith, but just regular crosses, not so much. Even blessed items needed to be reblessed from time to time. I would have to see if Taggart was having a crisis of faith, because if he was, he had to be moved to a different squad. This was the monster squad, and an officer without faith was crippled against vampires.

I started to help Dolph get the vamp on his feet, but Dolph wrapped one big hand around the other man's upper arm and just pulled him up. I was strong enough, but not tall enough or heavy enough to have the leverage to do it with someone so tall. The vampire was about six foot three, but Dolph still towered over him. The vampire marks I shared with Jean-Claude made me stronger, faster, harder to hurt, but nothing would make me taller.

Dolph put him back in the chair he'd knocked over. He kept one big hand on the vampire's shoulder, and the gun was very big, and very black, as he held it beside his thigh. The implication was clear: Cooperate, or else. We couldn't actually shoot him now, but no law prevents the police from making threats to get suspects to talk, and the vampire had opened the door for naked guns in the interrogation room. It took two men to help the worst of the wounded officers out the door, but everyone was able to walk out; it was a good night. Now all we had to do was get the girl out before she was murdered as a vampire, and find the officers that had gone radio silent unhurt. Oh, and get them all away from a rogue vampire kiss. Yeah, that's the group name for a bunch of vampires: a kiss of vampires. A gobble of ghouls, a shamble of zombies, and a kiss of vampires; most people don't know that, and the rest don't care. A pretty name for a group of super-strong, super-fast, mind-controlling, blood-drinking legal citizens, who might live forever if we didn't have to shoot them. That last part made them just like any other bad guys; the earlier parts made them unique, and too fucking dangerous.

2

POLICE OFFICERS GO radio silent for a lot of reasons, including equipment failure. It doesn't automatically get SWAT called out, or anything much except more officers dispatched to the scene to check on things, unless preternatural citizens are involved. Words like *vampire, werewolf, wereleopard, zombie,* et cetera, can be an automatic rollout for our special teams. Unless they're already busy elsewhere with a genuine situation, not just a maybe one. Some of them were with my fellow U.S. Marshal Larry Kirkland delivering a warrant of execution on a vampire that had moved into our town with a live warrant from another state. He'd killed the last Marshal who tried to "serve" the warrant, so the warrant had been electronically transferred to the Marshal who was next up in the rotation here, which made it Larry's warrant. A warrant of execution was always considered a no-knock warrant, which meant we didn't have to announce ourselves before coming through the door. I'd started Larry's training, but the FBI had finished it; he was all grown up now, married with a kid, and I'd learned to ignore the tight feeling in my gut when he went off on his own into something dangerous. There was also a more routine warrant on drug dealers, suspected of a string of deaths, so SWAT was going in with that one, too. St. Louis is a smaller city; our SWAT had enough men to field one more team, but we wouldn't get it until we had proof something bad had happened. Until then it was just the officers originally dispatched to the scene and us, RPIT. Frankly, I preferred it that way sometimes. Too many rules with SWAT.

The night was strobed with blue and red lights as Zerbrowski and I pulled up. There were no sirens, just the lights. In the movies there's noise to go with the lights, but sometimes like now, when you get out of the cars, it's quiet, just the colored lights swirling over and over the huge brick buildings and empty brick courtyard. In the 1800s the brewery had been one of the major employers in the city, but it had been abandoned for years. Someone had bought it and was trying to convince people it could be condos and office space, but mostly it rented out for photo and video shoots. The two police cars looked empty. Where were the cops who went with them, and why weren't they answering their radios?

Detectives Clive Perry and Brody Smith got out of their car. Perry was tall, slender, neatly but conservatively dressed. He was African American, but his skin wasn't as dark as the colored lights made it seem; Smith was a natural blond, and he looked paler as the lights painted him blue and red. Perry was almost six feet, Smith not much taller than me. Perry was also built like a long-distance runner, all height and slender frame; Smith's shoulders were broad and he was built like someone who'd muscle up if he ever hit the gym enough. Smith's white shirt was open at the collar, no tie, and his jackets always fit wrong through his shoulders, as if he had trouble finding suits that fit them and were still short enough for his height. They say opposites attract, or at least work well together, and Perry and Smith did. Perry was the normal one of the pairing, and Smith the supernormal—which sounded better than *psychic*, or *witch*. Smith was part of an experimental program that St. Louis was trying in which cops with some psychic ability were trained up so they could use their talents for more than just following their gut. What had surprised the top brass had been how many cops were psychic, but it hadn't surprised me. Most cops talk about their gut feelings, instinct, and most of them will tell you it's kept them and their partners alive. When tested, it turned out most of the "gut instinct" was latent psychic ability. Smith could sense the monsters once they used some sort of ability. When a lycanthropy suspect started to shapeshift, Smith would sense it and warn everyone, or warn the suspect not to do it. He could sense vampires once they went all vampire-wiles on your ass. He was better with the furry than the undead. He could sense when someone was using certain psychic abilities, like when I searched for the undead. As psychics went, Smith was pretty mild, or they hadn't found his true ability. It was sort of a wait and see.

Zerbrowski and I weren't officially partners. U.S. Marshals didn't usually have official partners, and Preternatural Branch, never. But I'd probably worked with Zerbrowski more than any other single cop over the years. We knew each other. I'd been invited over to his house for dinners with his wife and kids, and last cookout he'd let me bring my two wereleopard live-in sweeties. Two men who were "monsters," and I was living in sin with both of them, and he let me bring them to his house with his family and a bunch of other cops and their families; yeah, Zerbrowski and I were friends. We might never confide our deepest darkest secrets in each other, but we were cop-friends. It's like work-friends, but you get each other's blood on you, and keep each other alive. But when I went out with RPIT they did try to pair me with normals. Zerbrowski had gut instinct, but not enough to score on the tests.

We checked the two cars, found them empty, and I just said it: "We have to assume that the officers are hurt, so I'm invoking." Invoking the Preternatural Endangerment Act, that is; it was a loophole in the new, more vampire-friendly laws that allowed Marshals of the Preternatural Branch to use lethal force if they thought human lives were endangered and would be lost waiting for a warrant of execution. At least two officers missing from their cars, maybe more if either ride had two officers apiece, they were either hurt or dead, and there was still the missing girl. If we wanted anyone left alive, we needed to be able to shoot the vampires.

"You're not supposed to invoke until we know for sure someone's hurt, or there's a hostage situation," Perry said. He was all about the rules, our Clive.

"We have to assume the officers are hurt, or worse, Clive," Zerbrowski said. "Anita's within her rights to invoke the Preternatural Endangerment Act, which means she, and anyone with her, can use lethal force to save human lives without waiting for a warrant of execution." Zerbrowski was the highest-ranking officer on site, and he was backing me. Clive did what the rule-lovers do, he followed the rules. Later he could tell himself he'd tried to prevent the bloodshed, but he was technically clean on it. He nodded, and said, "You're in charge, Sergeant."

Zerbrowski let it go at that, and turned to me. "Sic 'em, Anita."

I raised an eyebrow at the phrasing, but let it go. His grin was enough; he'd make a joke with his last breath, and after a while you had to let the smart-ass remarks go, or he wore you down.

"Give me a minute," I said. If we'd been trying to sneak up on the vampires I couldn't have searched for them using my necromancy because they might sense the power, and then they'd know we were coming, but with the marked police cars, it wasn't like we were hiding.

In the interrogation room it had been an accident, a little power leaking out, and only after that on purpose. There was nothing accidental about this. Most people who raise the dead—animators if you're being polite, zombie queens or kings if you're being rude—have to do ritual to raise the dead. They need a circle of power, ointment, ritual tools, a blood sacrifice, and even then, they're lucky to raise one zombie a night. I used a circle of power to keep wandering bad powers out of my zombies, and the blood sacrifice just meant I could raise more and better zombies, but with nothing but my power I could raise the dead. If I used all the accoutrements of the profession I could raise cemeteries. I'd kept that part to myself as much as possible, because no one, absolutely no one, should be able to do that—not even me.

I didn't so much try to conjure up my necromancy as release it. The best I could describe it was like having a fist in my diaphragm, a fist that I kept clenched tight, holding on to my power so it didn't escape. This was unfolding my fingers, spreading my hand wide, letting go that tension that was almost always there just under my ribs. It was like letting out a breath I always had to hold, and finally being able to be free.

Maybe for some it was magic and that was why they needed all the tools and ointments, but for me it was a psychic ability, and all I had to do was unleash it. My necromancy was like a cool breeze flowing outward from me. It didn't actually move so much as a hair on anyone's head, so maybe *breeze* wasn't the right word, but I could feel it seeking outward from me almost like the rings in water when you throw a pebble into it, except I was the pebble, and the power tended to be a little more powerful and directed in the direction I was facing. I could "feel" behind me, but it wasn't as strong. I had no idea why.

Smith shivered beside me, and Clive Perry actually took a step back from all of us. He didn't really feel anything, but I'd learned that his grandmother, like mine, had practiced as a Vaudun priestess, except his had been a bad person and mine hadn't been. It had made him skittish around me, but not have a problem with Smith.

I searched for the undead. My power never even hesitated at a truly dead body. It was as if my power saw it the same as a table or chair: inert. Then I caught a hint of vampire, like something tugged at the edge of my attention, and I'd learned to direct my power so that it was like a scenting hound. I followed that "feeling," that energy, and if the pull got stronger, then it was vampires; if not, it could be ghouls, or zombies, or just a place where vampires had been recently. The feeling got stronger, and stronger, and now my power was being pulled.

"This way," I said. They'd all been with me before on hunts; they knew that once the power found the vampires it was a race. A race to see if we found them before they fled, or found us. We got our guns out and we ran. Running over the brick in the stilettos made me curse under my breath. The men couldn't go first, because I was the only one who knew where we were going. I moved up on the balls of my feet, so the heels didn't touch, and I ran, gun pointed at the ground. I loved Nathaniel, but I was going to have to stop letting my stripper boyfriend dress me for work. I had a moment to realize I hadn't cleaned off the one heel after it went in the vampire's chest. They'd smell the blood on me; they might even know it was Barney's blood. I wondered if they'd think I killed him; I wondered if I cared.

A scream sounded, high and piteous, echoing off the buildings. We ran faster, and somehow I knew the "feel" of vampires would be in the same direction as the scream.

I HATE IT when the bad guys are in upper stories because there are only two ways up, elevator or stairs, and either way they know you're coming and can ambush you. The huge, rickety freight elevator, which was the only elevator in the place, was a metal cage—a kill box, if they had guns. No way.

That left the stairs, which were so narrow, dark, and dank that given a choice I'd not have gone into them. Another scream sounded from above us and there was no choice, so we went up. The steps were so narrow and steep I had to kick the stilettos off, and the moment my bare feet touched the chilled, damp steps, I slipped because of the hose. Shit!

There was just enough room for Smith and Perry to ease past us, while I sat down on the steps and unfastened the hose from the garters. Zerbrowski stood beside me, gun in hand, watching up and down the stairs. He never made one smart-ass flirting remark as I slid the hose down and left them crumpled on the steps. When Zerbrowski missed a chance to make some inappropriate remark, things were serious.

I stood up, my bare feet feeling the grime on the steps, but I didn't slip as I followed Zerbrowski up. Still, I went up with my gun in a one-handed grip, the other hand on the wall, just in case. I smelled blood, a lot of it. I grabbed his arm and moved up beside him, our bodies almost pressed together by the narrow stone walls. I used two fingers to point not at my eyes, but at the tip of my nose. He knew that meant I'd smelled something, and that something was usually blood. He let me ease around him and go first. Zerbrowski also knew that I was harder to hurt than he was, and let me go forward as if I were the big bruiser

of a guy, the meat shield. I was small, but I had become fucking tough thanks to the vampire marks.

Blood was drying on the steps in a thick, darkening pool; at the top of that pool was a uniformed officer I didn't know on sight. I was glad I didn't know him, and felt instantly bad about thinking it. His pale eyes stared wide and sightless, his face frozen in death. His throat was savaged on one side so there was no way to check for a pulse; it was gone, torn out.

Shoe prints marked up the sticky blood; Perry and Smith had gotten past this point. I tried not to step in the blood with my bare feet, but couldn't avoid it all unless I wanted to climb over the dead officer. I wasn't willing to do that, and the blood was thick and squishy. I forced myself not to think about it, but just to think about getting up the steps to help the others. There was at least one more officer on site, maybe two more, depending on whether he'd been riding with a partner. I concentrated on the living and left the dead for later, but it was hard to ignore the blood sticking to the stone with every step I took. Perry and Smith's bloody footprints went up, too. There was no way not to track the crime scene up, no way to avoid the blood, no way . . . Another high-pitched scream sounded and this time I knew it was a girl, and I could hear words: "Don't hurt them! Don't hurt anyone else!"

I didn't look back at Zerbrowski to check, I just started running up the steps. They were so steep, my center of gravity so low, that it was faster to use my free hand to help me run up them. I climbed up the steps like you'd go up a stone hill, so that when I suddenly spilled out the opening into the huge room at the top I was on hands and knees, which was why the gunshot shattered the stone above my head, and not me.

I flinched, but was already turning to find the shot and return fire. I saw the standing figure, gun in hand, and had already sighted and fired at his chest before my mind had caught up to the fact that his other hand held the girl's arm, while she struggled to get away from him. He fell backward, taking the girl with him. I felt movement in time to see another man launching himself at me, but there wasn't time to bring my gun around. Another gun exploded in the room and the vampire fell beside me, a hole in his chest, but still reaching for me. I put a bullet in his head without thinking about it. He stopped trying to grab me, mouth open, so his fangs glistened. Zerbrowski was standing in the doorway, gun pointed at the fallen vampire. I wasn't sure if he'd shot him, or . . . Smith was kneeling behind a huge industrial-sized metal cog that was to one side of the door. His gun was pointed that way, too. I caught a glimpse of Perry lying on the ground beside him. Smith had him behind cover, which was more than Zerbrowski and I had. Another gunshot made Zerbrowski duck back through the doorway, but I was too far away; I turned and found a boy with a gun in his hand. He was standing there, so straight, so tall, so arrogant, as he took his time and aimed at me. I shot him in the chest before he could finish. He crumpled around the wound and then fell to his side. Another teenager rushed forward to grab the gun from his hand.

I slid to a one-knee shooting stance and shot him, too. Smith was yelling, "They're kids, Anita, they're just kids!" He was still behind cover; I wasn't.

I yelled out, "Touch a gun, you die! Hurt anyone, you die! Are we clear?"

There were sullen murmurs of *yes*, *yeah*, and one *fucking murderer*. Some of them looked scared, eyes wide. There were a few more teenagers in the group, but there were also adults. In fact, we had vampires of all shapes and sizes in the large group. "Hands where we can see them, now!"

They raised their hands up, some ridiculously high, others barely out. "Hands on your head."

Some of them looked confused by the request. Zerbrowski said, "Hands on your heads, just like you see on TV, come on, you know how to do it."

I stood up, keeping my gun aimed in their direction, but I was keeping a peripheral eye on the first one I'd shot. The girl was whimpering, trying to get his hand off her arm, but either his hands had seized up in death or he wasn't quite dead. One silver-plated nine-millimeter bullet in the chest doesn't always kill a vampire.

The vampires in the shadows did what Zerbrowski told them. Smith came out from behind his cover, and I saw Perry moving a little. He wasn't dead—good—and he wasn't hurt enough for Smith to feel he needed to keep pressure on the wound, or whatever had happened to him, even better.

I eased toward the girl and the first vampire. She looked up at me, tearstained face, eyes wide. "He won't let go," she said. She was trying to peel just one finger back so she could get away. His hand stayed closed. Vampires died weirder than humans; sometimes they seized up, but . . . I went slow and careful, my bare feet making almost no sound on the dirty floorboards. But he was a vampire; he'd hear my heartbeat. There was really no way to sneak up on them, not yards away, not feet away . . . He sat up, gun coming with him. I put a bullet in his forehead before he had the gun aimed at me. The girl was screaming again, but she was able to get away now and ran away from the vampire into my arms, trying to get comfort, but I needed to make sure he was well and truly dead, and unarmed, so I pushed her away, told her, "Go to the others. Go!" I pushed her too hard, and she fell, but I was moving to the fallen vampire. The gun was still in his hand. I needed it not to be.

I crept up on him with my gun held two-handed. If he'd twitched I'd have shot him again. I kicked the gun out of his hand and he never reacted. His eyes stared wide and sightless like the officer on the stairs. The vampire might actually be dead, but . . . I put a second bullet beside the hole in his head, and another one just a little lower than the other hole in his chest. I could have shot holes through both head and heart with the handgun, but it was messy, and it might eventually go through the body and into the floor beyond. Smith or Zerbrowski would have called for backup by now. It would be bad to accidentally shoot cops on the other floors. Bullets weren't always a respecter of floors and walls. I needed my vampire kit from the car.

Smith was yelling at me, "You shot kids!"

I didn't want to walk away with the vampire's head and chest still intact, so I reached down, grabbed the dead vampire by the back of his jean jacket, and started dragging him over toward the other dead bad guys. Smith followed me, still trying to pick a fight, or something. I let the man drop beside the two teenagers' bodies. Now I could keep an eye on all of them. If they moved I'd shoot them some more.

Smith actually pushed my shoulder, moving me back a little. "You fucking shot them! You shot kids!"

I glared at him, but knelt down by the teenagers and pulled the lips back on the first boy, exposing the fangs. I showed Smith fangs on the second teenager.

"You knew they were vampires," Smith said.

"Yeah."

All the anger just leaked away, and he looked confused. "They jumped us at the door. They threw Perry into the wall."

"How hurt is he?" I asked, standing up from the pile of dead.

"Shoulder and arm may be broken."

"Go see to your partner, Smith," I said.

He nodded and walked away to do that. Zerbrowski joined me, his gun still on the kneeling teenagers. There wasn't an adult face in the kneeling group. Zerbrowski leaned in and whispered, "You told me once that when your necromancy is on full power you can't always tell vampire from human servant in a room."

"Yeah," I said.

"You didn't know they were vampires when you shot them," he said quietly.

"No," I said.

"Were you checking for fangs when you showed Smith?"

"No, I knew they were vampires."

"How?" he asked.

"Look at the wounds," I said.

He did, and said, "What?"

"The blood's wrong," I said.

"It looks the same to me," he said.

"It's too thick. Human blood is a little more watery than that, even heart blood."

His eyes flicked to me, then back to watching our prisoners. "You know, Anita, it's just fucking creepy that you know that."

I shrugged. "If you'd been in front, would you have hesitated because you thought they were human teenagers?" I asked.

"Maybe; they're not much older than my oldest," he said.

"Good that I was in front, then," I said.

He glanced down at the dead kids. "Yeah," he said, but not like he was sure.

I walked away to get closer to our prisoners, one, to help watch them better, but two, to stop the talk with Zerbrowski about my decision to shoot the vampires when I thought they were flesh-and-blood teenagers. I didn't regret my choice in that split second of life and death, but a small part of me wondered how I could be all right with the choice. It bothered me that it hadn't bothered me to gun down two kids neither of whom could have been more than fifteen. It didn't bother me as I looked at the kneeling figures, and I knew without doubt that if any more of the vampires tried to attack us I'd kill them, too, regardless of apparent age, race, sex, or religious affiliations. I was an equal-opportunity executioner; I killed everybody. I let them see that in my face, in my eyes, and watched fear leak through the toughness on their faces. One of the women started to cry softly. What does it mean when the monsters are so afraid of you that you make them cry? That maybe *monster* depends on which end of the gun you're on, or that I was just that good at my job. Looking at the twenty or so frightened faces staring at me, I felt bad that they were afraid of me, but I knew that if they attacked us, I'd kill them. They should have been afraid—of me.

3

THE AMBULANCE TOOK Perry away with his arm as immobilized as they could get it. We'd found the other officer dead with a host of vampire bites on his torn and bloody clothes. They'd take bite impressions of the surviving vampires, and if their bite marks matched the wounds it was an automatic death sentence. They'd be morgue stakings, which meant they'd die at dawn, be chained down, hung with holy objects, staked and beheaded while they were "dead" to the world. They were already caught, so there was no need for a hunt. I wondered if they understood that they were as good as dead; I doubted it, or they wouldn't have given up. They'd have fought, right? I mean if you're dying anyway, wouldn't you go out fighting?

Once we had more police on site than we knew what to do with, I found a spare room to change and put on all my vampire hunting gear. I trusted Zerbrowski to alert me in case the captured vampires got out of hand, but I had to change in order to keep the Preternatural Endangerment Act in effect. Another U.S. Marshal of the Preternatural Branch had ended up on trial for murder because he invoked the act, but then didn't change into his gear when he had the opportunity. The idea behind the act is that the Marshal can, in effect, create his own warrant of execution on the fly in the middle of the action. The act came into law after lives were lost because several Marshals who had been trying to get a warrant of execution, but hadn't been granted one yet, had hesitated to kill vampires for fear of being brought up on charges. They could have faced serious charges, or at least lost their badges, for killing legal citizens who just happened to be vampires without some judge telling them it was okay. With the vampires shooting at us, and a hostage, we would probably have been in the clear on the shootings, eventually, but while the investigation was ongoing we might have had to turn in our badges and guns, which meant that I wouldn't have been able to do any monster hunting or executions for the duration of the investigation.

There weren't enough Marshals in the Preternatural Branch to spare us every time we had to kill someone; it was, after all, our job. But more than that, the Preternatural Endangerment Act covered the police with me just like a warrant of execution. As long as I invoked, and was with the police, then it was green-light city for all the bad guys. They'd tried to enact it so that only the vampire executioner, personally, could kill without a warrant, but that had made local police reluctant to be backup for the Marshals, and since most of us work solo a lot, that got people killed, too. Law is almost always made by people who will never see that law in action in a real-world situation; it makes it interesting.

One of the first cases to test the use of the act in the field had come down to the fact that the Marshal involved had not put on all his gear, which he was legally forced to wear once he was actively hunting monsters with a warrant of execution in effect. The lawyers had successfully argued that if the Marshal had truly believed the situation merited a warrant of execution, then why hadn't he geared up appropriately once he had time and access to his gear? He obviously hadn't felt it was the same as a real warrant of execution; he had simply invoked the act so he could play Wild West and kill everything in the room. The police with him had also been charged, but were declared free before the trial started, because they had acted in good faith, believed the Marshal's judgment to be sound, and didn't have the preternatural expertise to make any other choice. The Marshal had been found guilty and the case was in appeals, but he was in a cell while the lawyers argued.

It did mean that I always had a change of clothes with me—pants, T-shirt, socks, jogging shoes, underwear, and bra. The undies were for those moments when I got enough blood on me that it soaked my clothes to the skin. I had a coverall, too, but that was more for official morgue stakings. I put the protective vest on over the T-shirt, because otherwise it rubbed. The vest had MOLLE attachments, because the weapons came next. The 9mm Browning BDM went to my side with a holster attached at my waist and around my thigh so it didn't move. In an emergency you wanted your gun to be absolutely where your body memory could kick in—seconds counted. I had the Smith & Wesson M&P9c in a holster attached across my stomach, canted to the side so I could grab and pull it smoother and faster. I had a new sheath attached to the back of the vest with the MOLLE grips for the big knife that had enough silver content to slice anything, man or monster, and was as long as my forearm. Wrist sheaths held two more slender knives, again with high silver content. Extra ammo for all the handguns was on my left hip, strapped down like the Browning on my right. I had one AR on a tactical sling. I still had my MP5, but now that I had a badge I didn't have to sweat the barrel length restrictions for carrying, so I had an AR modified to be a door-kicker for close indoor action.

I had warned our prisoners that I was going to change into my full vampire hunting gear, because the law forced me to do it, not because I was upping the violence. The first time I'd had to change at a scene and come out in full gear the vampire prisoner had totally freaked, because he'd thought I was going to kill him then and there. I'd ended up having to do just that, when I probably could have brought him in alive. So many laws sound like a good idea until you try them out in real life, and then you find the flaws, and sometimes people die because of it.

The vampires had wide eyes, and some looked pretty spooked, but they didn't freak. I'd warned them. I'd helped take the first handful of them down in the ancient elevator to the reinforced transport van that we had for preternatural criminals. We had one van that could hold up to the kind of strength vampires and shapeshifters could use to pound their way through metal—one. Which meant we still had fifteen vampires on their knees in regular handcuffs and shackles, just like the ones that Barney the vampire had broken easily in the interrogation room. Technically I was supposed to take the heads and hearts of the four dead vampires in a heap on the floor, but doing it while the other vampires watched was a disastrous idea. It was just asking for them to realize they had nothing to lose, and that now was the best chance they had to fight their way free, so I was waiting. Not everyone seemed to understand why I was waiting.

Lieutenant Billings was taller than me, but then in my combat/hiking boots, so was everyone in the room, except for some of the vampires. I was just glad I had the boots with my vampire kit in the car. They didn't exactly match the skirt suit, but I was still happy not to be barefoot. Billings seemed to think his being six feet and built like a hard, muscular square would impress me, because he was looming over me now, snarling into my face. "I want you to do your job, Marshal Blake!"

"I did my job, Lieutenant," and I motioned at the piled bodies on the ground beside us.

"No, you did part of your job, Blake." He was so close to me that his upper body was actually curving over and down above me. Most people would have been totally intimidated by a guy this big up in their face like this; me, not so much. I spent too much time with vampires and wereanimals snarling up in my face. A human, no matter how angry, just didn't have the same impact. Also, there was a part of me that was attracted to the anger, the way a wine enthusiast could be attracted to a fine bottle of wine. I could taste his rage on the roof of my mouth, like I'd already drunk a bit of it, and all I had to do was move my tongue and I'd be able to swallow it down. I'd acquired the ability to feed on the energy of anger; it was a type of energy vampirism, but the laws hadn't caught up to it, so it wouldn't have been illegal to drink down all that rage, but if any of the supernormal cops in the room had sensed what I was doing, it might have raised questions. And Billings would certainly have noticed that his emotions had been messed with. I behaved myself, but my fascination with anger helped me keep my own temper, and not mind his so much.

My voice was calm, almost matter-of-fact, as I spoke into his reddening face. I gave him back peaceful, because I didn't want to feed into his rage, and I didn't want to be any more tempted to feed on his anger than I already was. Both the dead officers had been his men. He had a right to his anger, and I knew that as long as he was raving at me he could push back the grief. People will do a lot to keep that first rush of true, stomach-churning grief at bay, because once you feel it, it's like it never really leaves, not until the process is complete. There are five stages to grief. Denial is the first stage. When you've seen the bodies dead at your feet, it's hard not to skip that one, but you don't always go to the next step in order. Grief isn't a neat series of stages. You can jump around in the stages, you can get stuck at one point or the other, and you even get to revisit stages you've already finished. Grief isn't a neat, orderly kind of thing. It's messy, and it sucks. Billings wanted to yell at someone, and I was just convenient; it was nothing personal, I knew that. I stood in the face of his yelling and let it flow over me, through me. I didn't buy into it, I truly didn't take it personally. I'd had too many people scream in my face over the years with their loved ones dead on the ground. People wanted revenge, they thought it would make them feel better; sometimes it did, sometimes it didn't.

"I'll finish the job, Billings, but we need to clear out the prisoners first."

"I heard you'd gone soft; guess it's true."

I raised an eyebrow at him.

Zerbrowski left the uniforms that he'd been giving instructions to, so they could guard the vampires. He was the ranking RPIT officer on site. He called out, almost cheerfully, "Billings, Anita killed the three vampires while they were shooting at us. I got a piece of one, but it was her shots that were the kills for all three. How much harder do you want her to be?" His face was as open and friendly as his tone. He understood what it was like to lose people, too.

Billings turned on him; any target would do. "I want her to do her goddamn job!"

"She will," Zerbrowski said, and made a soothing gesture with one hand. "She will, just as soon as we clear out some of the crowd."

"No," Billings said, pointing a finger at the chained vampires. "I want them to see what's going to happen to their friends. I want them to know what's coming! I want them to see it! I want them to fucking see what's coming to each and every damned one of them. No goddamned bloodsuckers can kill cops in St. Louis and not die for it! Not here, not in our town. They are fucking going to die for this, and I want Blake to do her fucking job and show those motherfuckers what they have to look forward to!" He finished the last sentence bent into Zerbrowski's face, so close that spittle got on his glasses.

"Come on, Ray, let's go for a walk." Zerbrowski touched his arm, tried to get him to move away from the bodies and the vampires, and me.

Billings, whose first name was apparently Ray, jerked back from the touch and stalked toward the chained and kneeling vampires. They reacted like humans, recoiling, faces showing fear. God, they were all so recently dead that it was like watching human faces.

One of the uniforms on guard stepped in front of him, a little unsure, but trying. "Lieutenant . . ."

Billings pushed him out of the way hard enough that the smaller officer stumbled. His hand went to his baton, but he couldn't use it on a lieutenant, and with five inches of height and at least fifty pounds of muscle in Billings's favor, short of harsh physical measures the officer was out of options. Fuck.

Billings grabbed one of the closest prisoners in his big hands and dragged him to his feet. It was one of the teenage boys, and Billings didn't believe he was a kid any more than I did. I yelled, "Billings!" If he heard me, he didn't show it. Zerbrowski yelled, "Ray!" There was other yelling, but he didn't seem to hear any of us. His big arm came back, fist cocked, and I was just suddenly there, grabbing his arm. I don't know who was more startled that I'd managed to get there in time to stop the blow—him, or me. I was fast enough to get there before he hit the prisoner, but I wasn't fast enough to get in front of the punch, and I didn't weigh enough to stop him from swinging. I was airborne as I held on to him, moving with the force of his swing the way small children swing on their father's arms. I threw his balance off, so that he didn't hit the boy. He let go of the boy, who fell to the floor, unable to catch himself in the chains. Billings turned, with me still dangling from his arm. His other hand grabbed a handful of my hair as if he meant to fling me across the room, and I just reacted. I let myself do what I'd been tempted to do since the fine, red burn of his rage touched me—I ate his anger. I sipped it through the muscled bunch of his arm under my grip, through the twist of his fingers in my hair, through the bulk of his body, so big and solid beside my so much smaller one. I drank down his anger as he breathed heavy and loud, through the pounding of his heart, the pulse and beat of his blood, and as I swallowed the thick, red fire of his rage, I smelled his skin so close: sweat, and the scent of his fear, which was what lay under all that anger. Beyond that I smelled his blood beating just under the bitter sweetness of his anger, so that Billings was like a piece of cupcake with dark bittersweet chocolate icing that could be licked away, to the warm, moist cake, and then the hot, liquid center where the sweetest, thickest chocolate lay waiting like some hidden treasure that would make the anger even tastier. All I had to do was bite through that sweet, slightly salty skin of his wrist that was just above my mouth, that beating pulse so close to my hands, where they encircled his arm.

His hand let go of my hair, and he lowered me to the ground. His eyes were open wide; his face tried to frown as if he were struggling to remember something. He looked confused as he set me gently on the floor.

"Where are we?" he asked.

I was still holding his arm, though now it was more like holding hands than holding on. "We're at the old brewery," I said, and I didn't like that he didn't know where he was; it made me wonder what else he didn't remember. What had I done to him? I'd fed on anger before and never had anyone forget things.

He wrapped his big hand around one of my small ones, and blinked at the vampire that was crumpled at his feet. "Why are these people shackled?"

Jesus, he didn't remember they were vampires, which meant . . . "Lieutenant Billings, what's the last thing you remember?"

He frowned at me, and the effort of concentration was visible on his face and in the pressure of his hand, tense around mine. His eyes were a little scared, and he just shook his head. Shit.

Zerbrowski was there with Smith and some uniforms at his back. "Ray," Zerbrowski said, "we need to go for a walk."

"A walk?" Billings made it a question.

"Yeah," he said, and touched Billings's arm where he was still holding my hand.

Billings just nodded, but he didn't let go of me.

Zerbrowski pulled on his arm, just a little, to get him to come along, and Billings moved, but he also kept my hand in his. "Can she come with us?"

"Not right now," Zerbrowski said, and he looked at me; the look said, clearly, what had I done to him? I shrugged, and I knew he under-stood my expression, too. He might even believe that I didn't know what I'd done to the big lieutenant.

Billings was reluctant to let go of my hand, and that wasn't good either. I'd done more than feed on his anger, and way more than I'd intended.

Zerbrowski managed to get Billings to let go of me and go with him, but he mouthed, *Later*. We'd talk later, I knew we would. Double shit.

The vampire on the floor said, "Thank you."

I looked down at him. His eyes were blue-gray, grayer at the mo-ment. His short blond hair was almost shaggy, as if when it was a little longer it would be wavy, and was struggling to do it even short, so that his hair looked messy when it wasn't exactly. The hair seemed too big for his face or his face too thin for the thick hair. His jean jacket and rock band T-shirt untucked over jeans and jogging shoes made him look like a hundred other teenage boys, except for the odd haircut, and the strangely too-thin face. I realized it seemed hungry, as if he hadn't been eating enough, and then I realized what it was; he hadn't fed tonight. He was so recently dead that his skin hadn't lost the human tan he'd died with, so he didn't look too pale, but I could feel that he hadn't fed on blood tonight. This one, at least, hadn't had a piece of the cop we'd found eaten by dozens of fangs.

I looked past him to the other kneeling vampires and I felt their hunger. None of them had fed tonight. They were all hungry, and they were all very recently dead, their skins still kissed with the sun. Fresh-risen vampires could look like everything from corpse-like to nearly human. The more powerful the vampire that brought you over, the more human you could look, depending on the bloodline that your master descended from. Whoever had brought these guys over was powerful, very powerful. The vampire that had been holding the girl hadn't been, not even close, and all the vampires were hungry. I could feel it; in fact, I'd been picking it up without realizing it. It had made me feed too strongly on Billings. That shouldn't have been able to happen unless someone connected to Jean-Claude had made them. Was their master being of Jean-Claude's bloodline enough, or had one of our people fully blood-oathed to us done this horrible thing? And it was horrible. Six of the surviving vampires were teens, or younger, tweens. They were all children, all too young for that secondary growth spurt. They'd all been brought over before they finished puberty. It was forbidden to bring children over, and their faces staring up at me were all borderline, and all recently dead. Fuck, and double fuck.

I looked beyond the kids in front and found that the grown-ups weren't much better. Some of the women looked like they should be baking cookies for scout meetings and packing for family vacations, not kneeling here in cuffs with fangs. Some of the people were a little out of shape or overweight. It was a myth that being a vampire made you thin. Some low-level vampires stayed the same size they were at death, frozen in whatever shape they'd been forever, so if you were going to become a vampire you should drop that extra few pounds first. Some lines of vampires could change their body after death. I'd seen them put on more muscle in the gym, but I wasn't sure how much they could change after they were dead. Had these people chosen to be vampires, or had they been forced? If forced, then it was a truly horrible crime. I'd cheerfully kill the vampire that made them.

Then my metaphysics got out of the way of my cop brain, and I realized I was being stupid, distracted by the metaphysics—which was why the cops had started partnering one normal with a supernormal, so you had a mundane double check. Fuck!

I turned from the vampires and hurried to the knot of uniforms with Smith. "The vampires are all hungry! They haven't fed tonight."

One uniform looked at me, with all the cynicism you gain in police work. He was about forty pounds too heavy around the middle, but his eyes held the years of experience that can make up for speed and athleticism if you paired him with a rookie who could run. "They have to have fed. You saw what they did to Mulligan."

Smith said, "If Anita says they haven't fed, she'll be right. She knows the undead."

I checked the nameplate and said, "Exactly, Urlrich; if these guys didn't feed, then we're missing the ones who did."

"I don't understand," the younger uniform said, and shook his head. He had short brown hair, matching eyes, and a slim, runner's build. The brawn for the brains of his partner.

Urlrich understood. He undid the snap on his gun and rested his hand on the grip. "The body was warm; are they still here, Ms. Vampire Expert?"

"I don't know. With this many vampires, my spider-sense is on overload, and they have to have a vampire master with them powerful enough to possibly hide them." In my head I added, *Powerful enough to hide this much activity from Jean-Claude, the Master of St. Louis.* You gained a lot of power over a piece of real estate as master, and over the vampires in it, so at this point the rogue would have to be either fucking powerful, or so good at hiding in plain sight that it was a type of power.

"Is it a trap?" Smith asked.

"I don't know, but they left these vampires here to take the blame for the crimes. Master vamps don't waste this much manpower without a good reason."

"Maybe they thought we'd believe it," Smith said, "and they'd be in the clear."

"Only if we killed them all on sight," I said.

Urlrich said, "You do have a reputation for shooting first, Marshal Blake."

I couldn't argue with that. Was that what the vampires had counted on, that I'd just kill everyone in the building? If that was the plan, then my reputation was even worse than I thought. I wasn't sure whether I was sad or happy about that. You're only as tough as your threat is good; apparently my threat totally rocked.

Zerbrowski came back up as we were talking. "We need to talk about Billings, Anita." He looked very serious.

I nodded. "Agreed, but later." I told him that the vampires hadn't fed.

"Is it like the serial killer who left his wee little vamps to take the blame for his kills, a few years back?"

I nodded. "Maybe, but the laws were different back then; SWAT and I had the green light and had no legal option but to use it. We have options now."

"Tell that to Mulligan's wife," Urlrich said.

I nodded again. "If they helped kill Mulligan and the other officer, then I'll happily end their lives, but I'd like to make sure I'm putting a bullet between the right pair of eyes."

"You don't shoot 'em between the eyes," his partner said.

I checked his nameplate. "Stevens, is it?"

He nodded.

"Yeah, you do, and one in the heart, and then you take the heart and decapitate them."

He gave me wide eyes. "God."

"Would you want to put a bullet in their brains while they were looking at you, and chained up?"

He looked at me, a soft, growing horror in his eyes. "Jesus." He looked past me at the vampires. "They look like my grandparents, and kids."

I turned and looked at the vampires, too, and Stevens was absolutely right. Except for the two male bodies that were with the two teens we'd killed, everyone looked like either a kid, or a grandparent, or a soccer mom. I'd never seen a more ordinary-looking bunch of vampires in one place at one time. Even in the Church of Eternal Life, the vampire church, you didn't have this many older people and children. No one wanted to be trapped forever in a child's body, or an elderly one; it was too early, or too late, to want to live forever in the bodies that were kneeling on the floor.

I leaned in and whispered to Zerbrowski, "I've never seen this many elderly vampires ever, and this many kids in one place, also never."

"And that means what?" he asked.

"I don't know."

"For a vampire expert, you don't know a hell of a lot," Urlrich said.

I'd have liked to argue with him, but I couldn't.

4

IT WASN'T JUST the vampires that watched me as I moved around the room armed to the teeth. Someone muttered, "Who does she think she is, Rambo?" I didn't look around to see who had said it; it didn't really matter. I was a girl and I had the best deadly toys in the room. Gun envy is an ugly thing.

"She's the Executioner," the blond boy vamp said.

"They're all executioners," Stevens said. His partner hit him in the side with his elbow; you didn't talk to prisoners, especially not vampires.

"No, Anita Blake is one of only a handful of the vampire hunters that we've given names to; she was *the* Executioner, years before the rest." He studied my face with those blue-gray eyes of his, so serious. "We only give names to the ones that we fear. She is the Executioner, and along with three others she makes up the Four Horsemen."

I heard Stevens take a breath, and then stop. He obviously wanted to ask, but Urlrich had probably stopped him, so I asked for him. "The Executioner isn't a name of one of the Horsemen of the Apocalypse."

"You are the only one with two earned names," he said.

"Let me guess, I'm Death," I said.

He shook his head very solemnly. "You're War," he said.

"Why?" I asked.

"Because you've killed more of us than Death."

I didn't know what to say to that. I wanted to ask who the other Marshals were, but I was afraid that Death was my very good friend Ted Forrester, and he'd earned that nickname long before we all had badges, and some of the things he'd done to earn the name hadn't been legal. I wasn't sure how much the blond vampire knew, or how much he'd share. He was acting too odd for me to judge what he'd say next.

A woman who looked more like someone's youngish grandma than a vampire said, "Why haven't you killed us?"

"Because I didn't have to," I said.

The blond boy that Billings had tried to hit said, "The other officers want you to."

"You haven't fed, so you didn't take the officers' blood. You didn't kill them."

"We watched it done," he said, "under the law that makes us as guilty as the ones who tasted them."

I frowned at him. "Do you want me to shoot you?"

He nodded.

I frowned harder. "Why?"

He shrugged and dropped his eyes so I couldn't read his face.

"You are evil and your master is evil," said the grandma.

I looked at her. "I didn't just rip the throat out of a man who was trying to keep you from making a fifteen-year-old girl a vampire against her will."

Her eyes showed hesitation for a moment and then she said, "The girl wanted to be one of us."

"She'd changed her mind," I said.

The grandma shook her head, looking sullen. "There was no going back."

"That's the same thing date rapists say: 'She agreed to the date, so it's too late for her to say no to the sex.'"

She looked shocked, as if I'd slapped her. "How dare you compare us to that."

"Forcing someone to be a vampire against their will is rape and murder all rolled into one," I said.

The boy said, "You believe that, don't you?"

"I do."

"And yet, you cohabitate with the master vampire of this city," he said.

"Cohabitate," I said. "You're older than you look."

"Can't you tell my age?" he asked.

I thought about it, just a tiny use of power, and said, "Twenty years dead, that's why the eighties haircut."

"I don't have enough power to grow my hair long after death like the vampires closest to you. Your master steals energy from me, from all of us, and uses it to heal his people, and grow his long, black curls out for you."

I'd known that Jean-Claude took power from his followers, and gave power to them, but I hadn't thought how that exchange of power might affect the other side of the equation. Was Blondie here right? Did Jean-Claude steal power from them just to grow his hair long for me, when they could have used it to heal their wounds, grow their own hair? Was it true?

"You didn't know," he said.

"She knew! She knows!" Grandma said. Her voice was strident with her anger, but under the anger was a thread of fear like a hint of spice in a piece of cake. I looked at her, and something she saw in my face stopped her, and upped the fear in her. Was she really that afraid of me?

Zerbrowski came to me. "Anita, the bus is back. We need to move them."

I nodded, and realized I'd made the rookie mistake. I'd let the bad guys talk me into doubting people I trusted. They say if you listen to the devil he won't lie, but he won't exactly tell the truth either. Blondie wasn't the devil, far from it, but he'd spoken the truth as he saw it, and I'd ask Jean-Claude tonight when I got home.

I addressed the prisoners. "If you try to escape, try to run, we will shoot you."

"Because of the Preternatural Endangerment Act," Blondie said.

"That gives us the legal right to kill you, yes, but the two dead cops, killed by vampire bites, make you all murder suspects. Vampires suspected of murder can be killed if they try to escape."

"If we were people, it wouldn't work like that," he said.

"With two dead cops, it might," I said.

"Not legally," he said. I grabbed him by the arm and helped him to his feet hard enough that he stumbled and I had to catch him.

He whispered, "You're as strong as we are, and I felt you feed on the other officer. You're not human either."

I pushed him away from me, forgot he was wearing shackles to go with his cuffs, and had to catch him again. No one else in the room could have moved fast enough to catch him with barely a pause between the push, the start of the fall, and the catch—no human in the room.

"See," he said.

I got him shuffling along with the others that were being helped to their feet. I wasn't sure if I needed to put him close to me so I could watch him, or far away so he couldn't keep fucking with me. Why was he getting on my nerves so badly? Answer: because I believed what he'd just said. I'd raised my first dead by accident when I was a teenager, saw my first ghost at ten; the dead had always liked me. I wasn't like most of the Marshals; they were humans who just happened to be good at killing monsters. I was one of the monsters.

A girl stumbled in her shackles. I grabbed her arm to steady her, and she mumbled, "Thank you," then turned and saw who was touching her. She let out a little shriek and began to struggle. I held on just a moment, caught off guard by the fear that just radiated through her, from her, down my hand, across my tongue. I could taste her fear the way I could taste it on a shapeshifter or a human. Anything that's afraid of you is food. I let her go, and she fell, unable to catch herself. The other vampires tried to help her up, but they were struggling, too. Zerbrowski finally helped her to her feet.

The vampires watched me and even behind the sullenness, the anger, there was fear. What do the monsters fear? Other monsters, of course.

I caught Blondie watching me, but it was Grandma who spat the word at me. "Monster!"

I said the only thing I could think of. "That's Marshal Monster to you, Grandma."

Zerbrowski said, "Why don't I have any nifty nicknames?"

"No one's afraid of you, Zerbrowski," I said, and smiled at him for trying to make a joke out of it.

"You're just so bad-ass, I can't compete."

"That's what your wife says."

"Oooh," Smith said, "that was low."

Zerbrowski grinned at me. "I don't have a problem with you being the better man, Anita; I never have."

If I hadn't been armed to the teeth, surrounded by murderous vampires, in view of way too many other cops, I'd have hugged Zerbrowski. "Thanks, Zerbrowski." But I tried to show him in my eyes how much it had meant to me, that guy moment where you can't actually say how many emotions you've got running through your brain.

He smiled, not his cocky teasing grin, but that gentle one that let his eyes look tired and sort of tender. He gave a small nod, and I smiled back, and that was it. He understood that I'd understood that he'd understood. It took us one sentence, two looks, and a nod—with another woman it would have been at least five minutes of out-loud talking. Lucky for me I spoke fluent guy.

5

ZERBROWSKI HAD TO take a call from Dolph, so it was Stevens, Url-rich, and Smith who helped me move another seven vampires to the big freight elevator. I decided to keep Blondie near me, because if he was screwing with me this badly, I didn't trust how bad he'd fuck with the others. Besides, to move him away meant to admit he was fucking with me, and that I didn't know what to do about it. The only way I knew how to face anything was head on, so Blondie stayed by me. He wasn't half as disturbing as the elevator. It was a bare, metal cage, one that actually needed someone to pull a lever and drive the thing. It was open to the cool, dark shaft with wooden slats as a door on one side, and then metal mesh as a second door, but the rest of the elevator was truly a cage, open to the shaft. It was a killing box if someone could get above us.

I put Smith on the lever to drive the elevator. He'd driven it last time and hadn't crashed us. I tucked my AR to my shoulder, then snugged my cheek to it and let out a breath, so that I was still as I pointed the barrel upward through the metalwork.

"Why are you pointing up?" Stevens asked.

I kept my attention on the top of the shaft as I answered him, "Some vampires can fly."

"I thought that was just movie shit," he said.

"Not just movie shit," I said. I let my eyes relax, searching the darkness above us for movement, just movement, because there shouldn't have been any.

"Moving," Smith said.

I flexed my knees a little, steadied myself, and kept watching the darkness above us. "Go," I said.

The elevator shuddered to life. It was like trying to get your sea legs, and then it smoothed out, and we started down.

"Most people don't look up," Blondie asked.

"I'm not most people," I said softly; my attention was all on the darkness as it fell away from us. So far, the only movement was us, and the cables. I forced myself not to stare at the cables, but to keep my vision soft and not choose any one thing to look at, like you look for animals in the woods when you're hunting. You don't look for deer, you look for movement at first; once you have movement then you let your brain figure out what made the movement and if there's a shape to go with it. It was actually harder than it sounded to not "look" at any one thing, but to keep your eyes looking for things that weren't there when there was so much solid stuff to look at. The eyes want to look at something; the brain wants certainty, not shadows.

"Almost there, Anita," Smith said.

I braced for it, and the elevator stopped with another shudder, and a bump. I swayed—we all did—and bumped into Blondie. The moment I touched him, I felt his fear. He'd been shielding like a son of a bitch, so close to me, but touching makes all the vampire mind tricks stronger, and I mean my vampire mind tricks, not his. I heard the doors opening; Smith was closer, so he had probably been the one to open them, but I didn't look at him, I looked at Blondie.

We had a moment of meeting each other's eyes. Smith and Urlrich were ushering the vampires in front out of the elevator. "You're afraid," I said softly.

"I'm in police custody for murder; shouldn't I be afraid?" he asked, but his eyes were too wide, his lips parted. If he'd been human his breathing would have been fast, his heart racing. He'd been dead for twenty years; he shouldn't have been showing this many signs of stress, unless he was distracting me from something else?

I looked past him and caught a glimpse of the grandmother vamp, as Smith and Urlrich and another uniform led her out. I looked back at Blondie. "Don't do anything stupid," I said.

"Who are you talking to?" Stevens asked.

We all moved forward, sort of herding the vampires in front of us. "Him," I said.

Blondie smiled. I didn't like the smile, at all.

I grabbed him by the arm and hurried him out of the elevator to catch up with the others, but shackles mean you have to go slow. I didn't want to leave Stevens alone with the last of the vamps in the elevator, but . . . I had a bad feeling.

We got out into the last bit of the warehouse, as Smith and others opened the main doors and started easing the chained vampires out into the thicker darkness outside. They were outside; only Urlrich was left in the doorway. Stevens moved forward with the last of them. I came at the rear, with Blondie going even slower than he needed to be ahead of me.

The grandmother looked back. I looked into her eyes, and I saw it, saw what she was about to do, but I was yards away from her, from the door. I met her frightened eyes, watched her gather her courage. Urlrich had to catch a vampire that fell in his shackles; he helped them out the door, and it was just Stevens and me with the last few. He was closer than I was.

I called out, "Stevens, watch Grandma."

He turned and did what I said, but he didn't bring his gun up, only his eyes. Smith hadn't dealt with enough vampires.

"Don't do it, Grandma," I said, "Don't move."

"Or you'll kill me," she said.

"Escape attempts allow us to use deadly force; don't do it."

Stevens was looking from her to me. "What's going on?"

"She's considering," I said.

"Considering what?" he asked.

"Running," I said.

"How can you tell?" he asked.

"I just can." I wasn't being psychic; it was just years of doing this shit. I just knew.

"What?" Stevens asked.

"Just don't let her run, Stevens," Urlrich said. He'd come back inside, and he hit the slide on his shotgun. It made that thick, meaty sound that raises the hair on your arms, and makes your shoulder blades tighten in anticipation of something bad. The vampires flinched, except for her.

"Don't," I said.

"Stevens," Urlrich said.

Stevens put his gun point-blank against the woman's back. She smiled at me, and the fear was gone. Shit. She turned that smile up to Stevens, and she was suddenly your favorite grandmother. She radiated good cheer; you could almost smell the cookies baking.

"No one move!" Urlrich said, and his voice had that drill sergeant bite to it.

She smiled at Stevens. I would have liked to say it was vampire mind tricks, but she looked so harmless, so human, so like the storybook grandmother. His gun lowered. I think the rookie just didn't have it in him to shoot, point-blank, into a handcuffed elderly woman. She looked so human.

She turned and ran, and Stevens didn't shoot her. Urlrich was blocked by other vampires that weren't running. He couldn't use the shotgun.

I yelled, "Fuck!" and started to run. I yelled for Smith as I went. Guns exploded outside—lots of them.

I yelled, "No!" I don't know what I was saying no to, but I knew that whatever was happening outside, the vampires had wanted it to happen, and if they wanted it, it was bad.

I felt the vampires. Felt their power. They were going all vampire apeshit. I ran to the door, AR up and ready; the darkness blazed with holy fire. Every holy object in the courtyard was glowing with white, cool fire, like stars had fallen to the earth and just kept shining, but stars are just suns, distant, burning suns; they burned now.

There were bodies on the ground. The vampires were screaming, falling to the ground, trying to hide their eyes from the glow. It was so bright that I couldn't look directly at any of it, so everyone was shadows and shapes in the bright, bright lights.

My own cross burst into light. I put my back against the wall on the side of the open door and wheeled around to point my AR at the few vampires left inside. Urlrich was doing the same thing on the other side of the door. His tie-tack cross was blazing. We were both squinting against the light, trying to aim past it. It was the serious downside to the holy objects. If the vampires fell over and huddled from the light, you were fine, but if they didn't, it was hard to shoot at them. Somehow I knew what vampire I'd be looking at.

Blondie had Stevens in front of him, using him as a shield. They were both on their knees. The broken chain from his cuffs to his shackles dangled near Stevens's face.

The vampire's eyes glowed like gray ice with moonlight behind it. "The young officer has no faith in his cross."

Stevens's cross-shaped lapel pin wasn't glowing.

"Stevens," Urlrich said. He had his shotgun to his shoulder, but he didn't dare use it, not with the two of them so close together. If there was a shot to be had, it would have to be mine. I was good enough, if the range was any judge, to hit Blondie's head where it peeked out from around Stevens, but that was at the range. If I didn't hit inside the seven ring, I just adjusted my aim. If I missed this shot, I'd hit Stevens. It would be a head shot, and there would be no second chance for Stevens. But I couldn't aim past the damn glow of my cross. I tore it off and threw it into the corner.

"Blake," Urlrich said, voice low and urgent.

I ignored him and let my eyes adjust to the dimness.

Blondie tucked his head even tighter against Stevens so that it was just the barest sliver of his face, and that one glowing eye half lost in Stevens's short hair. "Don't do it," the vampire said.

I slowed my breathing first, it all begins with the breathing, and then I slowed my heartbeat, timed it. I thought softly, in time to that slowing beat, "Fuck . . . fuck . . . fuck . . . fuck. . . ."

"Even if you can make the shot, you can't make it fast enough."

I kept my voice even, my vision on that edge of face. "Let . . . him . . . go." I stopped looking at Stevens's wide eyes and tried to just see my target.

He ducked completely behind Stevens so that I had no head shot except Stevens. I kept my aim on where his head had been last. He'd peek back out. He wouldn't be able to resist—probably.

He spoke, hidden. "You're talking in time to your heartbeat."

"Yes," I said softly.

"Don't," Stevens said, voice strained with the pressure of the vampire's hand against his throat.

"If I tear his throat out now, you don't have a shot."

Urlrich said, "You kill him, and I'll shoot you through his body."

"I'm already dead; you can't scare me."

"You're . . . not . . . dead," I said. I was having trouble focusing where I thought his head would pop out. You can't focus like that forever; you have to take the shot, or rest your eyes. They give out before your arms give out on holding the shooting stance.

"I am dead," the vampire said.

"Not . . . yet . . ." I said.

I saw an edge of blond hair. My breathing just stopped, everything stopped. I pulled the trigger in a well of silence, where the emptiness waited for my heartbeat.

The blond hair fell back behind Stevens, and I thought I'd missed. I waited for the vampire to tear his throat out as I ran forward, gun to shoulder, yelling, "Fuck!"

Urlrich yelled, "Stevens!"

Stevens fell forward on all fours. I waited for his throat to spill crimson. He got to his feet and stumbled away from the vampire. The vampire stayed on the floor, on his back. I had the AR snugged tight, and suddenly I thought I could aim at that body all damn night. I walked carefully, but quick, up to the fallen vampire.

Urlrich was moving in from the other side, the shotgun tight to his shoulder.

I looked down at the body and found that the corner of his skull was open, the blond hair peeled back, with blood and brains seeping out. It was the brain shot that had killed him instantly. If I'd just hit his skull, he'd have had enough time to rip Stevens's throat out. Fuck.

"Hell of a shot, Marshal," Urlrich said.

"Thanks," I said, and my voice was a little breathy. My arms were tingling down to my fingertips, almost like pins and needles. It was as if my pulse poured back into my body all at once, as if I'd slowed more than just my heartbeat down for those few minutes. I felt a little weak-kneed, and light-headed. I let out a big breath and focused on standing firm.

Stevens was throwing up in the corner, not from fear, but the same sense of relief that made me want to drop to my knees rather than keep aiming at the vampire. I could see brains on the outside; that meant dead vampire, hell, dead anything.

"He dead?" Urlrich asked.

"Yeah," I said, "brains on the outside means dead."

"Then why you still aiming at him?"

I thought about that, and let out another long breath, and forced myself to lower my weapon. Somehow I didn't want to; it just seemed safer. Not logical, but the urge to just keep aiming was very strong. I fought the urge to put another bullet in him, but his brains were leaking out onto the floor. That was dead, until we had to decapitate him and stake his heart. He was dead. He was really, truly dead, but I still moved so that standing with my weapon down kept the body clearly in my sight.

"See to your partner," I said.

Urlrich nodded, and moved to do what I said.

Smith was in the doorway, and there were more cops with him. "Everyone okay?" he asked.

"Yeah," I said, "except the vampire. Who's dead outside?"

Urlrich had moved to see to his partner, who was dry-heaving in the corner.

"Most of the vampires; no cops."

"What happened?" I asked.

"The elderly woman flew, and then our holy items all went off and someone fired."

"And everyone else thought the vampires were attacking," I said, "so they fired, too."

"Yeah," Smith said.

"Shit," I said.

"Hey, no cops dead," he said.

I nodded. "You're right. Bright side."

A uniform ran up to us. "There's a news crew out here."

"Shit," Smith said, "how the hell did they get in?"

I looked down at the dead vampire, and thought of all the vampires that looked like grandparents, children, soccer moms, all slaughtered by police on camera. Fuck, fuck, fuck, fuckity, fuck! I fought the urge to kick the vampire's body. Had they planned it this way? Had they alerted the media, and been willing to die for this? Had they made martyrs of themselves? God, I hoped not, because where there's one martyr, there'll be more.

The elevator clanged to life behind us, and we all turned, guns coming up. I snugged the AR to my shoulder and cheek until I saw Zerbrowski lift the wooden door. He had his gun out; so did they all. He glanced at the dead vampire. "I miss all the fun?"

"Missed the firefight, yes. Media shitstorm, no," I said.

"I can go back upstairs," he said.

"You may be ranking officer on site; I think you get to talk to them."

"Shit," he said.

That about summed it up.

6

I WALKED OUT into the courtyard into chaos. People were yelling, there were lights everywhere, including a chopper overhead, with a spotlight. One uniformed officer was kneeling over a child vampire, holding his hands over her stomach wound, trying to stop the bleeding, trying to save her. A gunshot sounded loud, close, and I turned, gun in hand, pointed and ready. Another uniformed officer was shooting into a vampire on the ground, finishing him off. Another cop with a blond ponytail was yelling at him, "Stand down! Stand down!"

Smith asked, "Do we save them, or kill them?"

That was an excellent question. Legally we could kill all of them. I'd invoked the act, which meant it was a paperless warrant of execution. We could legally do a coup de grace and put a bullet in everyone's head and heart. Some officers were trying to stanch the wounds with their hands or jackets. Some had guns out, pointed at the fallen. If I gave the word, we'd just make sure they were dead. Legally I could do it; a few years back I would have, and been absolutely sure I was right. Now . . . I wasn't sure. What legal options did I have here? What did the law say I could do? When you have a badge, sometimes that's all that's left; you have to follow the law. Problem is that sometimes the law is gray, and not clear, and other times, it's too clear—clear, but not just, not right. Once I'd believed that the law was about justice, but I'd carried a badge and a gun too long not to understand that the law was about the law. It was about how it was written by people who would never have to stand here in the night with bodies bleeding, and men asking them, *What do we do?* Fuck.

Zerbrowski had his phone and came to me, speaking quietly, "Everyone upstairs is getting antsy. Do they shoot the rest, or try to bring them downstairs? And we've got two ambulances outside the kill zone. Do I have them come ahead and try to save the ones they can, or are we going to finish the job?"

"You know the legal options as well as I do," I said. I didn't want to make this call. Why couldn't someone else make it?

"You want us to just shoot the ones upstairs, and send the ambulances away?" he asked, and he was studying my face, as if he didn't know me, or was waiting to figure out who the fuck I was; maybe we both were.

I shook my head. "No, fuck it, but no, I guess not."

"Guess?" he asked.

I shook my head again, and started moving. "Let the ambulances through. Tell the cops upstairs to reassure the vampires that we will get them to safety, but things are too volatile down here to guarantee their safety. Tell them to sit tight; everyone will get out alive, if everyone cooperates."

He did what I said, and I went to help the wounded, and show, by example, what we were going to do tonight. How we were going to handle this would all depend on the next few minutes.

How do you help wounded undead? Smith was kneeling beside a teenage girl vampire. "Is she supposed to have a heartbeat?" he asked.

"Not necessarily," I said, and went to kneel by him because it was as good a place to start as any.

"Then how do we tell if they're dead, or . . . saveable?"

"Good question," I said.

He spoke low. "You got a good answer?"

I smiled, but he didn't smile back. I sighed and dropped some of my psychic shields. I was a necromancer, the first real one allowed to live and mature into their power in over a thousand years. The vampires had killed people like me for centuries, because legend said truly powerful necromancers controlled all the undead, not just zombies. I couldn't control vampires the way I could a zombie I'd raised, but I had power over them . . . sometimes. I looked down at the "girl" with her short black hair and pale, pale skin. She was the most Goth, or emo, of the vampires. The hair so wasn't her natural color. She looked about fourteen, maybe younger, the age when a lot of us rebel. I tried to "see" more than just the physical packaging. I'd been able to feel their hunger earlier; maybe I could do more? I'd saved a vampire or two in my time. There . . . a spark, like a cold flame flickering in the center of her body, about where the sternum and stomach met. The energy that I saw wavered like a candle flame moving in the wind, guttering down to die. I "looked" at the other bodies, concentrating, trying to see. Some of them were cold, no hint of energy. They were gone, truly dead, but three others had flames burning above them, in them.

The ambulances were here, the emergency medical technicians coming with wheeled stretchers. I saw them hesitate, wondering where to start. I called out, "Start with the woman at the edge of the group, near you, she's closest to dying."

They exchanged glances, sort of shrugged, and started hooking the vampire up to plasma. They'd found that plasma, or a rush of blood transfusion, could "save" a vampire and give them a chance to heal on their own. It was about all they'd found to do for vampires in an emergency. I directed the second group of EMTs to the next vampire whose flame was wavering; that left us with two that were still alive, but hurt, but you can hook IVs up only so fast.

I touched the girl's cold skin. Vampires that haven't fed and are less than a hundred years are cold without our blood to make them live. I willed that flickering flame to burn steadier, brighter. It flared enough that I pulled back, as if it were real fire.

"You okay?" Smith asked.

"Yeah, just bring the other live one over here, so I can touch him, too."

"You'll explain why later," he said.

"Yeah."

Smith took me at my word and just went to help carry the vampire to me. I heard a gasp, and a stifled scream from someone. I looked over, and the fire wavered with my concentration. Shit. "What's wrong?" I asked.

"He's awake," Smith said. "It startled someone." He gave one of the uniforms with him a look, but they carried the man's body over to me in a cradle of their arms. They laid him down on the other side of me so I'd have a hand for each vampire.

The man blinked large dark eyes at me, his face grimacing in pain. His short hair was naturally black, to match the slight uptilt of his eyes. I wasn't a good judge of Asian ethnicity. If I'd had to guess, I'd have said Japanese or Chinese, but he could have been Korean. I guess it didn't matter. He was slender, and about my size, so he looked delicate for a man. Like everyone in this group he looked like a victim, or at least not dangerous. The bullet hole in his upper chest added to the whole not-dangerous thing. I reached out to touch his hand. He flinched and did his best to move it away from me.

"Let me help you," I said. I lost concentration on the girl's spark as I spoke, and had to put more energy into that, closing my eyes for a moment, so I could see her flame burning brighter. I could see his more with my eyes closed, too. It was burning better than hers, fueling itself. He was probably the least hurt of any of them.

"Get away from me," he said.

I opened my eyes to see fear on his face. "I'm not touching you," I said, and worked to keep my voice steady, even, so I could keep the girl's energy steady.

"You know exactly what you're doing," he said, and there was anger with the fear now.

Actually, I didn't know exactly what I was doing. I'd done the whole flame/energy hold only once before, and that had been on a vampire I knew really well, and had done energy work with before the emergency. I shouldn't have been able to work this smoothly with strange vampires, and the moment I thought it, my hold on the girl's energy wavered. Psychic ability is like magic; ya gotta believe. I pushed my doubts away and held on, helped her hold on.

The other vampire half sat up, trying to push farther away from me. He gasped and fell back on the bricks, his face contorted in pain. He was suddenly doing much less well.

"Shit," I said, "bullet's still in there, and he's shifted it." The girl vampire's flame wavered as my emotions did, and her spark was a candle in a strong wind, almost out, but now his was guttering in the "wind."

I yelled, "Medic!"

One of them was running our way with his case, leaving his partner to keep the IV going for another victim. Seconds, just seconds, minutes, and there'd be more help.

I grabbed the boy's cold hand. I shoved power into him, and he yelled, "No! No, I won't be another of your slaves!" I was so startled, I let go of him.

He settled back into the bricks, coughing blood the color of black syrup. The EMT hesitated between the two. "Girl, she's fading faster." He took my word for it, kneeling down, beginning to work on the girl. He got one of the uniforms to help hold things. I was left with the man, a boy physically, maybe seventeen when he had died the first time.

"Let me help you."

"No." He coughed harder, and it looked like it hurt.

I put more energy his way, but he screamed, "NO!"

I couldn't concentrate on both of them, because my emotions were getting in the way. I fought to hold the girl's spark steady as the IV went in, and they began to put something in her veins that would help more than my power. I offered my wrist toward his face. "Feed then, if you won't take energy."

"Then I'll be bound to Jean-Claude."

The police didn't really understand how deeply tied I was to Jean-

Claude with the whole human-servant thing, so I had to be careful what I said next. "Would you rather die?"

"Yes." He coughed again, and writhed in pain as Smith tried to keep him still.

"Why?" I asked.

When he could speak past the pain, his voice came thick with the blood spilling from his lips, "Freedom; we don't want to belong to a master. We want to be free, not belong to another council. They're gone; let them stay gone."

The girl's spark clicked into place, the plasma keeping her "alive." I sent all my energy into him. His flame flared so that I had to fight not to close my eyes against the brightness that was all inside my head.

"No." He rolled on his side, and the blood drained faster from his mouth. "I refuse medical or metaphysical aid. I refuse."

The EMT said, "I don't know what you're doing to him psychically, but you've got to stop now. He's refused aid; legally you have to stop."

"He'll die," I said.

"I'm already dead, I'm a vampire."

"You're not dead," I said, "you're undead; it's not the same."

"I die for the cause." His voice sounded rough, almost painfully deep. A gout of black blood welled up and spilled from his mouth.

"What cause?" I asked.

"Freedom," and it was the last thing he said before his eyes glazed over; his body gave one last convulsive movement and I watched his flame flicker and go out, as if some great breath had blown it away.

I grabbed his hand, and it was too late to save him, but not too late to feel him go. It didn't feel the same as a human dying in my arms; there was a difference to what went out of a vampire when they died. Was it a difference of souls? Were they evil? Were they lost like the Church maintained? I didn't know the answers to any of that. All I knew was he wasn't much older than his physical body looked, and he'd forced us to kill him, and I didn't understand why.

7

It was an ongoing police investigation, but these vampires had been willing to die rather than risk being in Jean-Claude's power. If you're willing to die to avoid being part of someone's power structure, it's only a small step to being willing to kill to destroy that power structure. I normally don't share information on investigations with my boyfriends, but . . . if I didn't share and something bad happened to Jean-Claude, or one of my other lovers, or friends, I'd never forgive myself. They could have my badge, if it was a choice between losing it or losing one of the people I loved.

Was I trying to justify what I was about to do? Yes. Was I going to do it anyway? Yes.

I moved to the side of the courtyard, out of the way of the crime scene techs and the dozens of extra cops that always seem to flock to a murder scene. I found a little piece of alley between two of the buildings. Admittedly the "alley" was big enough to drive a beer wagon through, back in the day when the brewery was built for just that, but it was shadowed, and away from everyone. I leaned my shoulder against the cool bricks and had what privacy I was likely to get.

I didn't have to pick up a phone and call Jean-Claude; all I had to do was drop the shields I kept in place between him and me. It was like opening a door that I kept bolted shut, because without real effort to block it, we invaded each other's emotions; thoughts, even physical sensations could be shared. At the most extreme the boundaries between where one of us ended and the other began blurred; it got confusing as hell, and frankly, scary as hell. I didn't like being that far into another person's mind, body, and heart, and I sure as hell didn't want him seeing that far into me.

But it didn't mean that all I had to do was unlock that "door" in my head, and then knock on the shields that kept me from falling too far into Jean-Claude's head, because we'd found that it wasn't enough for only one of us to block. If only one of us did it, then we got echoes back and forth at odd moments. Mostly strong emotions, strong sensations, but not always; it could be very random.

Jean-Claude opened to me, and I knew he was sitting in his office at Guilty Pleasures. I could feel the sweat on his skin as he wiped his naked upper body down with a towel. He'd danced, which was rare, since he was owner and manager of the club. On the nights when he danced, the club would be full to bursting with women and men who wanted to see the sexiest vampire in St. Louis take off some of his clothes onstage. He never stripped down as far as his other dancers. Nothing as common as a G-string for my main squeeze, but he had some pants with enough lacings and holes that they didn't hide much more. I'd learned that most of the time the more dominant personalities liked to keep more clothes on, and the submissive ones were more comfy getting naked. The days when Jean-Claude had been anyone's submissive little bloodsucker were years in the past. Outside the bedroom neither he nor I was very fond of stripping down, or at least not first.

He looked down the line of that long, lean, finely muscled body, so I could see that the leather pants were the ones with the very open ties that went from waist to ankle, so that it was more like he had the fronts and the backs of the pants on, but the sides were sort of missing-in-action. They were mostly the white, perfect skin of his long legs revealed through the black laces of the leather.

Just his looking down his body, so that I could see, tightened things low in my body and made me have to let out a deep, shaking breath. I even put a hand out to steady myself against the cool bricks of the wall. Jean-Claude had affected me that way almost from the moment I'd seen him.

He spoke to the empty office, "*Ma petite*, I love that you react to me so."

I whispered, my face close to the bricks, "You just got offstage; everyone reacted to you that way."

"But that is the lust of strangers, that first flush of desire where all is possibilities and fantasy. To have someone react as you do after seven years of being together, that means more."

"I can't imagine anyone ever not reacting to you like that," I said.

He laughed, and it was that touchable, caressing sound, as if his laughter spilled down my skin, underneath my clothes, and touched all the naughty places.

"Stop that," I said, "I'm still working."

"You do not usually contact me until after work. What is wrong?" We had been dating long enough for him to understand that when I was on the job, I was a Marshal, not anyone's girlfriend. Other men had had a problem with that division of mind-set; not him. Jean-Claude understood compartmentalizing your life, your emotions, and your people. Vampires that are successful at living for hundreds of years are the ultimate compartmentalizers. They have to be, or they'd go crazy. You can't dwell too much on the bad stuff, because after a few lifetimes, there's too much of it. I had found enough bad stuff in just one lifetime that I'd had to do it; I couldn't imagine nearly six hundred years' worth.

I told him the shortest version that I could think of, and added, "Have you heard any rumors about shit like this?"

"Not this precise one, no."

"That means yes, doesn't it?" I said.

"I heard rumors of dissatisfaction at the idea of the ruling council of all vampires being here in America. There are some that fear that the old council members that remain alive will simply set up shop here, and rule as they did of old. To keep that from happening was one of the main reasons that I have been encouraged, by most, to set up an American vampire council. I and the vampires here are more trusted than the old European masters."

"I've met enough of the old council to agree with that," I said.

"I had not heard that some vampires were actually contemplating having no master at all. Only the very young among us would dream of such a thing."

"The vampires here were, and are, young. None of them were over a hundred, most of them between fifty and twenty, and then ten years and under."

"Were all of them American?"

I thought about it. "I think so."

"Americans, living and undead, are an odd lot. They value their ideal of freedom beyond anything the rest of us would dream of."

"We're a young country," I said.

"Yes, in another day and age, America would be in its expansive, empire-building stage, but you came of age too late. The world leaders, and military, would never allow such conquest now."

"It would be nice to start keeping some of the land and resources that our soldiers are dying for," I said.

"*Ma petite*, are you a secret imperialist?"

"Just tired of watching our guys and girls die on the news, and have nothing to show for it except body bags."

"You have the freedom and gratitude of the people you are helping," he said, voice very mild.

I laughed. "Yeah, they're so grateful they keep trying to blow us up."

"It is at an odd moment in history that America comes of age, that I will agree."

"These guys were willing to die rather than risk blood-oathing themselves to you, but I could sense them as if they were already blood of our bloodline."

"That is interesting, and unexpected. Are you certain they are not from our bloodline?"

I took in a deep breath, let it out, and really tried to think about it, feel what I'd felt. I let him feel the memory with me. I just stopped talking and let him get it directly from my mind.

"I will think upon this." He was drawing back away from me, shielding a little.

"You've thought of something, and I'm not going to like it, am I?"

"I have an idea, that is all. I wish to think about it, and ask opinions of some of the older ones that I trust most, before I share it with you."

"Once, you'd have just lied to me," I said.

"And once, *ma petite*, you wouldn't have realized I was keeping anything from you."

"I know you," I said.

"We know each other," he said. "Will you trust me to keep the idea to myself until I think it is ready to share with you?"

"I'd rather know," I said.

"Will you trust me?" he asked, again.

I sighed. "Yes." But I thought, *I want to know*, and I was in his head again, but he pushed me out, gently.

My viewpoint shifted from being almost in his head to being slightly in front and above him. It used to be how I did all the long-distance viewing, before I'd gotten more comfortable with it, but it had been Jean-Claude who pushed me further away now.

He smiled up at me, his eyes that rich, cobalt blue, the darkest true blue I'd ever seen in anyone's eyes. The eyes first, and then the black curls spilling around that glistening, beautiful upper body; the small cross-shaped burn scar on his chest was a slickness under my fingertips when I touched him. The moment I remembered the physical sensation of it that clearly, I was closer in, like doing a close-up with a camera.

He pushed me back harder this time, and he wasn't smiling as he gazed at me. I knew he saw me in the shadowed alley, as I saw him in his elegant office. "You said you would trust me."

"I do trust you," I said.

"But still you push; still you test your boundaries."

I shrugged. "Sorry, didn't really mean to."

"You didn't, and you did, *ma petite*."

I shrugged again. "Can't blame a girl for trying."

"Yes, yes I can," he said. "*Je t'aime, ma petite*."

"I love you, too, Jean-Claude," I said.

He closed down the link between us, shut his metaphysical door hard and tight. He'd thought of something, and if I pushed, he might have told me, but I'd learned that when Jean-Claude told me I didn't want to know something, he was usually right. Ignorance isn't bliss, but neither is knowledge. Sometimes you just know more, but it doesn't make you any happier.

I heard someone behind me, and turned to find Zerbrowski in the mouth of the alley. "He see it on the news?"

"What?" I asked.

"The bodies," he said.

I blinked at him, trying to bring myself solidly back into my own head, my own body. I pressed my fingertips against the cold, rough brick, and it helped.

"You okay?" he asked.

I nodded. "Sure."

"I called Katie, too," he said.

"She saw it on the news," I said.

"No, but the kids did."

I gave him a sympathetic face. "I'm sorry, Zerbrowski, that must be hard."

"The news is showing all the bodies with sheets and shit over it, and they said that two officers had been killed, but they never release the names until the families are notified, which is great, but it's hell on everyone else's families," he said.

I thought about it, but most of my "boyfriends" could feel me alive, or they'd feel if I died, just as I'd feel it if they died. But I was shielding like a son of a bitch to keep them out of my head. I'd made it clear that all of them were supposed to stay out of my head while I was working a crime scene. I did my best to make sure that ongoing investigations weren't shared with any of them. It took real work to stay separate enough to keep secrets from each other, but I had to do it, not just to keep the police work confidential, but because they didn't need to see the horrors I saw on the job. I didn't want, or need, to share that part of my job. Sometimes when I had nightmares, they got glimpses of it if we were sleeping next to each other. When I was working on a really violent case, some of my lovers started sleeping elsewhere. I didn't really blame them, though I found that I did take brownie points away from the ones who hid. I preferred the people in my life who could take all of me, not just parts.

Did I need to call home? Probably. Shit.

"What's that look on your face?" Zerbrowski said.

"I let Jean-Claude know, but I didn't tell him to tell the others."

"Won't he do that automatically?"

"Not necessarily; the older vampires aren't always big for sharing information."

"We need you to come talk to these vampires right now, but if you want to call one of your other guys, make it quick."

"Thanks, Zerbrowski," I said.

"Yeah, might want to call the boyfriend most likely to tell everyone else next time."

"That'd be Micah," I said, and was already fishing for my phone.

"Say hi to Mr. Callahan for me."

"Will do," I said, and had my phone out.

"You didn't have your phone out before," Zerbrowski said.

I looked at the phone in my hand as if it had just appeared there. I realized in the dimness he'd assumed I was talking on it already. If I'd thought, I could have hidden the fact that I wasn't using a phone the first time.

He shook his head, waved a hand. "I don't want to know, because if I actually knew for sure you could talk to Jean-Claude without using a phone, that would sort of compromise the integrity of our crime scene. Just use a phone from now on, okay?"

I nodded, held it up in my hand. "You got it." I hit Micah's number on my favorite's list, and the phone dialed him for me. He was a were-leopard, not a vampire; wereanimals tended to think more like modern people. You'd think it would be the other way around, but it wasn't. Vampires weren't human, or animals; they were vampires, and no matter how much I loved Jean-Claude, I knew that was the truth.

8

MICAH'S RING TONE was "Stray Cat Strut," by Stray Cats; Nathaniel had put it on when he went wild giving nearly everyone personal ring tones on my new phone. It wasn't a perfect ring for Micah, but I hadn't found anything I liked better yet, so I'd left it.

His business answer was always, "Micah Callahan here." Tonight, to me, it was, "Anita," and there was relief in his voice, and then he recovered his tone and was businessier when he said, "I didn't expect a call this early. You can't be done with the crime scene."

That relief at the beginning and his quick matter-of-fact recovery made me start with an apology that no amount of criticism, or whining, could have gotten from me. "I'm sorry I didn't call earlier, but I knew that you guys would know I wasn't one of the dead officers." I regretted using the word *dead* as soon as it left my mouth, and then I didn't regret it, because it was the truth, and then . . . Oh, hell.

I could picture him at his end of the phone, his chartreuse eyes, green and gold, depending on the light. Leopard eyes, because a very bad man had forced him to stay in animal form until he couldn't come all the way back to human. If his deep brown curls were loose, and not back in a ponytail or braid, he'd be pushing them behind his ear so the phone could set better. He was my size, the shortest man in my life, with the delicate frame to go with it, but he'd put muscle over that fragile-seeming body, and like me he made the most of what he had.

"Nathaniel would have let me know if you were hurt," he said, and his voice wasn't as calm now. There was a slight tremor in it. He had moved in with me at the same time Nathaniel did, so we'd been a happy little threesome the entire two years we'd been together. Micah was my Nimir-Raj, leopard king to my Nimir-Ra, leopard queen, and we had an amazing metaphysical connection, but Nathaniel was my leopard to call, just as if I were a real vampire, which meant that if I died, there was a very real chance that he'd die with me. It didn't work as much the other way, because animals to call and human servants, in my case a vampire servant, were meant to feed the master vampire energy, strength, which meant the vampire would feed on the servant's energy first to stay alive longer. It was the way the system was set up, and in fact when Nathaniel almost died from a gunshot wound, I hadn't been that hurt. If I died, though, Micah would almost surely lose us both. I hadn't thought until this moment how that must make him feel. I was a coldhearted idiot. Fuck.

"I'm so sorry," I said.

"For what?" he asked, and he sounded genuinely puzzled.

I shook my head, knew he couldn't see it, and tried again. He did not need me to say out loud what I'd just thought; one, he already knew it, and two, that I'd only just now figured it out would probably not earn me any couple brownie points.

"Ignore me; I just wanted to make sure you told everyone that I'm okay."

"Of course." He still sounded a little puzzled, and finally said, "Do you have a few minutes to talk to Cynric?"

"Maybe; why him in particular?"

"He saw the special report on the news. You standing surrounded by bodies. He's scared for you now, for you and Nathaniel."

My insight was new enough that I understood that last part.

Nathaniel and Cynric were close, maybe because they were closer in age. Cyn had figured out the issue with Nathaniel before I had; I felt slow.

"Shit," I said.

"Yes," Micah said.

"Yes, put him on, but I'm needed to talk to the vampires that are still alive, so I can't be long."

"He just needs to hear your voice, Anita."

I sighed. "Sure." I was dreading the next few minutes for so many reasons. Cynric had been with us almost a year now. He'd turned eighteen, old enough to die for his country, but I still wasn't sure he was old enough to be my lover. Of all the men in my life, Cynric bothered me the most.

He was my blue tiger to call. Theoretically, I now had enough weretigers whose energy I could drain that my near-death might not touch Nathaniel, if I could pick and choose whose energy I took. The fact that I'd trade Cynric's life for Nathaniel's, given a choice, didn't make me feel any better about Cynric being my lover. He was on the list of people that I called and texted when I had to travel for work. Some of the people on my text list could have contacted me mind-to-mind, like Jean-Claude; not as smoothly, but they could feel me, sense me, we could share sensations and emotions, but that could be very distracting in the middle of hunting down a rogue vampire, or questioning witnesses, so they refrained. The compromise was that I texted them, and called when I could.

"Anita, I'm sorry that the news freaked me a little." His voice sounded even younger than usual, not a kid's voice, but not a man's voice either. He was taller than me and Micah, five-nine now and still growing. His hair was a deep, cobalt blue; in low light it looked black, but it so wasn't. Just as his eyes were two colors, the way some cats' eyes could be, with a paler ring of blue and a darker inner ring that was almost as dark a blue as Jean-Claude's midnight blue. All the pureblood weretigers were born with tiger eyes, not human; it was a mark of the purity of their bloodline. There were occasional throwbacks to human eyes among them, but that usually meant they were survivors of an attack and had started life as human, or sometimes it was just a sign of how even the pure tiger clans occasionally married and bred with a human being. They liked to deny it, but when you're lonely enough, you take what you can find. Cynric was the last pure blue tiger male that we could find. The rest of his people had been slaughtered off long ago; in fact, we weren't sure where he'd come from. The white tigers of Vegas had found him in an orphanage.

I fought the urge to squirm uncomfortably and answered him. "It's okay, Cynric; the news doesn't usually get crime scene footage this fresh."

"And they reported two officers dead," he said.

"You knew I wasn't dead," I said, and kept my voice even.

"I know I would have felt the energy drain if you'd died, but you shield really well, Anita. Sometimes so well, it scares me, because I can't sense you at all."

I hadn't known that. "I'm sorry if that bothers you, but I can't let you guys know about investigations."

"I know, but it's still . . . I . . . Shit, Anita, it scared me."

He hadn't cussed when he first came to us, but he'd picked it up from me—or maybe trying to "date" me would drive any man to curse?

"I am sorry for that, Cynric, really, but I have to go question the surviving vampires."

"I know you have to work, solve the crime."

"Yes," I said.

"When will you be home?"

"I don't know; this one is a mess, so it'll take longer."

"Be careful," he said, and again his voice sounded young, fragile.

"As I can be," I said.

"I know you have to do your job." He sounded defensive.

"I've got to go, Cynric."

"At least don't call me that; you know that's not what I like to be called," and he sounded exasperated, and still scared.

I swallowed, took a deep breath, blew it out, and said, "Sin, I've got to go." I couldn't keep the displeasure out of my voice. I hated that he wanted to be called Sin, as short for Cynric. We'd tried spelling it *Cyn*, but no one could spell it, so he went with the actual word *sin*. That the only teenager in my bed preferred to be called "Sin" was just rubbing salt in my already wounded sense of self.

"Thank you. I'll see you when you get home."

"It may be after dawn."

"Then wake me up."

I had to count to ten to keep from snapping at him, but it was my discomfort that wanted to snap, not really him. He was so young he just didn't have the skills to deal with me being shot at yet. Hell, some men decades older than Sin couldn't deal with my job.

"I'd rather let you sleep."

"Wake me," and now his voice sounded older, an echo of what it would be in a few years, maybe. There was demand in those two words, almost like an order. I fought off my knee-jerk reaction to that, too. I was the grown-up; I'd behave like it.

"Fine," I said.

"Now you're mad," he said, and he sounded sullen, and on the edge of anger himself.

"I don't want to fight, Cynric—Sin—but I have to go."

"I love you, Anita," he said.

And there it was, so bold, so out there, so . . . Fuck. "I love you, too," I said, but I wasn't sure it was true; in fact, I knew it wasn't. I cared for him, but I didn't love him the way I loved Jean-Claude, or Micah, or Nathaniel, or . . . But I said the words, because when someone says they love you, you're supposed to say it back. Or maybe I was just too cowardly to let the silence fill up; when Sin said he loved me, I said the only thing I could: "I love you, too, Sin, but I have to go."

It was Micah on the phone, though. "It's okay, Anita, go; I'll take care of things here."

"Shit, Micah, I have to have my head in the game here, I can't . . . Is he all right?"

"Solve the crime, catch the bad guys, do your job; Nathaniel and I will take care of Sin."

"I love you," I said, and this time I meant it.

I could see the smile that went with the tone of his voice as he said, "I know, and I love you more."

I smiled. "I love you most."

Nathaniel's voice came on the phone as if Micah were holding it out to him: "I love you mostest."

I got off the phone in tears. I loved Nathaniel and Micah, so much. There was no guilt there. We made each other happy. Cynric should have been with someone who loved him the way I loved them. The way I loved Jean-Claude. Hell, the way I loved Asher, or Nicky, or even Jason. He shouldn't have had to compromise for a relationship that got him great sex, and even love of a kind, but I didn't think I'd ever be *in love* with Cynric. He deserved someone who would feel for him what he seemed to feel for me, didn't he? Didn't everyone? I wasn't sure I could give that to him, and the fact that he'd stood there and heard the three of us say our cute little trio of *I love you, I love you more, I love you most, I love you mostest*, which was just ours, made my chest tight and my eyes hot with unshed tears. I had crimes to solve, more rogue vampires to find; I couldn't afford to be distracted like this, not by an eighteen-year-old kid who happened to love me more than I loved him. And that was the thought that made me wipe the tears away with the back of my hands, that was the thought that cut the deepest. He loved me, was in love with me, and I didn't feel the same. If he hadn't been metaphysically bound to me, I could have broken up with him, sent him home, but once some preternatural bonds happen, they can't be undone. We were trapped, Cynric and I, and there was no way to undo it. Fuck.

9

SMITH SAW ME come out of the alley. "Your boyfriend making you feel guilty, too?"

"Something like that," I said, wiping one last time at my face. I was glad all over again that I didn't wear makeup to crime scenes.

"I think my girlfriend is going to dump my ass; she can't deal with the job."

"At least she can dump you," I said.

"What?" Smith asked.

I waved it away and we went back to work—to our job, *the* job—and left the shambles of our personal lives for later. The job came first, because if we failed at that, people died. If we failed at our personal lives, only emotions died, but there are moments when it feels like a broken heart is a kind of death, and you'd trade a little less crime busting for a way to fix that part of your life.

I should have probably been more sympathetic to Smith, but I was feeling too sorry for myself to have any sympathy left over, and the moment I realized that, I stood a little straighter and tried to pull my head out of my ass and back in the game.

I turned and said to Smith, "Sorry to hear about the girlfriend, Smith."

He gave a smile that didn't reach his eyes. "Thanks. How long have you been dating Jean-Claude?"

"About seven years," I said.

"When we've got some downtime, I'd love to hear how you manage to have a relationship and do this job."

I smiled, I couldn't help it. "We'll never have the talk if you wait for downtime, and I'm not sure what works for me will work for anyone else, but sure, I'll give it a try when we get a break. Ask Zerbrowski, too; he and Katie have been together for over a decade."

Smith grinned. "I figure that Zerbrowski's wife is a saint. I don't date saints."

I grinned back. "Katie is pretty perfect, but not a saint; they just work together as a couple really well."

"But how, how do they do it?" Smith asked, and that he asked it in the middle of an investigation meant that this girlfriend was special, important. Shit.

I went to him and spoke low. "Every person is unique, Smith, so every couple is unique. What works for one couple won't work for everybody. Hell, what's made Jean-Claude and me work this long is totally different from what makes Micah and me work, or Nathaniel." Smith had met both of the latter at Zerbrowski's house this summer at the RPIT barbecue. It had meant a lot to me that Katie had invited me to bring both of them. Jean-Claude and I were just linked in the tabloids. He was the vampire cover boy, so by just being near him I got my picture taken—a lot. Either way, those were the three boyfriends that Smith knew about. There were rumors of other lovers, but there are always rumors. I neither confirmed nor denied rumors. It was the best I could do.

Smith shook his head, looking serious. "Only Lieutenant Storr and Zerbrowski aren't divorced in the entire squad, did you know that?"

"No," I said, "I didn't know that."

He sighed, and just the woebegone look on his face let me know that he was really serious about this girlfriend.

"Zerbrowski needs me to question the vampires we still have in custody, but later, I'm willing to try to sit down with you and tell you what little I know about relationships."

"You have to be good at it, Anita, or you couldn't have so many of them that last years," he said.

I hadn't thought about it that way, and I started to say that it was the men who made it possible by compromising for me, and then I thought about it and realized that somewhere along the way I'd learned to compromise, too. Being a successful couple was learning what you were willing to compromise on, and what you weren't; learning when to stand your ground, and when to give it up; what was truly important enough to fight over, and what was just you being pissy. You learned each other's hot buttons, the places that hurt, or angered, when you pressed them. Love makes you learn where all the pitfalls are, and how to avoid them, or how to set them off.

"Maybe," I said, "but right now we've got work to do." I patted him on the shoulder and walked away. My phone rang; it was the theme from Charlie Brown, which meant it was Zerbrowski. He didn't know he had his own ring tone, and if asked I would never admit that it was because he was always messy, and his car was worse, like Pig-Pen from the comic strip. "Hey, Zerbrowski, I'm on my way."

"They aren't talking, Anita. They're trying to lawyer up."

"They can't lawyer up," I said, "they admitted in front of other police besides me that they watched the officers being murdered, which makes them just as guilty in the eyes of the law as the vamps that did the bloody deed. Vampires that have murdered humans are automatically executed."

"Bloody deed, fancy," he said, "but you're right. They don't seem to understand that their rights under the law are different from humans' now. If it had just been kidnapping the girl, they could have lawyered up."

"But they can't lawyer on murder," I said.

"No," he said, "I haven't exactly pressed on that, because once they realize they're just going to be executed then . . ." He let it trail off.

I finished for him. "They have nothing to lose, so they could fight, go apeshit. I would in their place."

"I know you would," he said.

"Wouldn't you?" I asked.

He was quiet for a minute. "I don't know."

"Letting someone kill you is harder than it sounds, if you have another option," I said.

"Maybe," he said, and his voice was thoughtful, too serious for him.

"What?" I asked.

"Nothing."

"There's something in your voice, Zerbrowski. What is it?"

He laughed, and it was suddenly him again, but his next words weren't. "Just thinking I hope you never end up on the wrong end of the law."

"Are you implying that I'd be treated as less than human?" I asked, and I was both angry and hurt.

"No, and you're a good cop."

"Thanks, but I hear a *but* in there somewhere."

"But, you react like a bad guy when you're cornered. I just don't want to see what would happen if you felt you were out of choices."

We were quiet on the phone, listening to each other breathe. "You've thought about this," I said.

"Hey"—and I could see him shrug, that awkward version he did in his ill-fitting suit—"I'm a cop; that means I do threat assessment. I wouldn't want to be on the wrong side of Dolph either."

"Should I be flattered by the company?"

"He's six foot eight, you're five foot three—he's an ex–college football player and power lifter who stays in shape. You're a girl. Yeah, you should be flattered."

I thought about it for a moment, and then said, "Okay."

"Why do I feel like I should apologize? Like when Katie gets that silence, that girl silence?"

"Don't know; why should you apologize for the truth?"

"I don't know, but you've got that same tone that Katie gets, so I know I'm in the doghouse for it anyway."

"You can't compare me to Dolph and then compare me to your wife, Zerbrowski?"

"You're my partner, and you're a woman; actually that's about right."

I thought about it for another minute, and then said, "Okay."

"Now that's an *okay* that really means *okay*, not that *okay* that women use when it means *everything but okay*."

I had to laugh then, because he was absolutely right. "What do you want to do to get them to talk?"

"I had an idea. It's going to make me into bad cop, and you into serial killer cop, but we have about twenty missing vampires that have already killed two police officers. They fled, because they do know that they're going to be executed when we catch them."

"Which means we need to find them fast," I said.

"I think they'll give up the others after we're done questioning them."

"What's your plan, Zerbrowski?"

He told me. I was quiet for a few heartbeats. "God, Zerbrowski, that's fucking evil."

"Thank you, thank you very much," he said.

"It wasn't a compliment," I said, and I hung up before he could say something funny, and jolly me out of what I was thinking. Dolph was more physically intimidating and had the worse temper. I was scary in a lot of ways, but Zerbrowski—he hid it better, but the inside of his head could be fucking scary, too. He'd be the last one you'd shoot, but it might be a mistake you wouldn't live through. I filed that thought away, with the thought that he'd been thinking what he'd do if I went over to the Dark Side of the Force. Partners shouldn't think that way about each other—should they?

10

RULE ONE OF trying to break someone down: Isolate them. Zerbrowski separated the vampires, and divided officers up to guard them. SWAT was on the scene now, not the team that had gone to back up Marshal Larry Kirkland, but a second team. Normally I had mixed feelings about having SWAT with me, but tonight I was just glad to see the manpower, and the skill level. I needed some of the vampires alive enough to talk. I spoke with Sergeant Greco and explained what I needed. He passed it on to his men, and I knew that they would do their best to wound and not kill. Not every shooter, no matter how good, can aim to wound when the monsters are coming at them. You've got to have nerves of steel and the marksmanship to go with it; SWAT would have that or they wouldn't be on the team in the first place. There were other police officers in uniform and plainclothes that had what it took, but those were officers I knew had that set of nerve and skill; with SWAT there was no guesswork, they had to have that set of skills or they wouldn't stay on the team.

Zerbrowski had the dead vampires divided up into five rooms, which was how many live, uninjured vampires we had to question. I went to my Jeep for the rest of my gear. Zerbrowski would spend the time it took me to outfit myself looking at our suspects, so he could make a call on which ones might break first. My only job was to scare the hell out of them. I was the threat, the monster in the closet. Zerbrowski would be the good cop, or at least the less scary cop.

To be as scary as needed, I had to get my second bag of gear from my Jeep. I got to walk through the bodies that were lying on the uneven bricks. On TV they cover the bodies with white sheets, but in real life sheets do not magically appear to drift down effortlessly on the dead. We'd had only two ambulances on site when it all went down, and their resources of sheets, blankets, everything had gone to the living and wounded, the ones that could be saved. They'd thrown out a few body bags, but hadn't had time to bag the bodies. Some of the police on site had spread the bags like dark plastic blankets over the youngest-looking vampire dead, the ones that looked like children. Maybe they'd been old enough to be everyone's grandparents agewise, but the bodies looked junior high age, high school at best. The adult-looking dead stared up, sightless, unmoving, as I walked through them. Most of the cops moved through the field of bodies with their eyes averted, as if looking at the dead bothered them. I looked at the dead, because they were dead vampires and I hadn't shot them all myself. I hadn't made certain that every last body was safely dead. Vampires are tricky; even hospitals with full equipment have trouble being certain when final death occurs. Brain scans were the only close certainty, and even that tech was in its infancy for vampire use. How do you tell when the undead are dead?

I stopped beside a man that looked like the perfect grandfather, as if some Hollywood casting agent had picked him to look sad and pitiful dead on the uneven bricks. Maybe I'd feel sympathy for him later, but right that second I was more worried that I couldn't see much damage on the body. The bullet wound on him looked too low for a heart shot, and his head seemed completely intact. What I was seeing so shouldn't have killed a vampire.

"It doesn't bother you to look at them, does it?" Urlrich came to stand beside me.

I answered without looking away from the body. "No."

He gave a low, very masculine chuckle. It was a sound I'd heard before; it was a sound of approval, and surprise. Men never expected me to be able to keep up with them, especially older men. I looked younger than I was; I was female, and petite. It was a triple threat to either men's egos or their expectations. Urlrich's ego was fine, but his expectations had been given a kick in the ass.

"They're saying you're going to cut the bodies up in front of the other vampires; that true?"

I nodded, still watching the body on the ground.

"I'll help you carry your equipment inside."

That made me look at him. What I saw in his face had me turning my head to the side, as if I were trying to get a better view of the shine in his eyes. He was angry, but it was the kind of anger that filled the eyes with light and gave a little color to the face. If he'd been a woman, I might have told him, *You're beautiful when you're angry.*

"Your partner is going to heal, right?"

He nodded, but his eyes had narrowed and now the anger looked like what it was: hatred. He had a hard-on for, or against, vampires, and it hadn't started today. I knew long-standing hatred when I saw it. I debated asking him about it, but it was against the guy code to question it that bluntly. I could do that with officers I knew well—they gave me room to poke at things, to be the girl—but with new officers I had to be one of the guys. Guys didn't ask about emotions unless they had to; I didn't have to, I just wanted to, so I let it go—for now.

"I want to watch their faces," he said.

"You mean the vampires' faces?"

"Yes."

"I don't," I said.

He looked puzzled and frowned at me. "Why not?"

"Because all that fear, all that loathing, will be directed at me. It's not cozy being the monster, Urlrich."

"They're the monsters," he said.

"You try being chained up in a room, and watch me tear out a heart and decapitate a body in front of you, while you know that legally I could do the same to you, and probably will; would you think I was a monster?"

"I'd think you were doing your job."

"You know, legally I don't have to kill a vampire before I start taking out the heart, or cutting off the head. I can do it while they're alive and aware."

"Have you ever done it that way?" he asked.

"Yes," I said, and I left it at that. I didn't tell him that years ago it had been because I was young and stupid and thought vampires were monsters, and didn't realize that I had the right to wait until the vampires died at dawn to take them out. Killing them while they were "alive" had been the beginning of my realizing that maybe there was more than one side to the whole monster question. I'd done it once as a way of getting information out of a vampire, as legal torture; I hadn't done it a second time. Some things you can do and live with yourself, but that doesn't mean they don't leave a stain on your soul.

I started walking for my Jeep again. I'd get my equipment and I'd put a stake through the hearts of any of the dead vampires that didn't have an obvious hole in the heart or brain. I didn't use the stakes much, but legally I had to carry so many with me in my kit. I'd use them as place markers until I had time to remove the hearts from the bodies; as long as no one was stupid enough to take the stake out of the body the vampire would be down for the count, and they'd lie there until I got around to them, or dawn came and the sunlight did my job for me. Though that last was illegal now, ruled cruel and unusual, equated to burning a human alive. I couldn't argue with the cruelty part, but this was a lot of bodies to destroy before sunrise. I was going to need help.

11

HELP WAS U.S. Marshal Larry Kirkland. He was my size, small for a guy, with blue eyes, freckles, and short red-orange hair grown just long enough that it was curling in soft ringlets all over his head. He usually kept it short enough that there were no curls, which meant he almost had to shave it. His two-year-old daughter had his curls, but with her mother's darker brown color. They let Angelica's hair grow into ringlets that touched her tiny shoulders. Larry still looked like a grown-up Howdy Doody, but there were lines around his mouth, as if he spent too much time frowning, or being serious. When he came in as my sort-of apprentice in the execution business, he'd smiled more. I had warned him that this job can eat you, if you let it.

We were standing near the bodies as we talked. "I staked all the ones that didn't have enough damage to be reliably dead. Stake the rest, and then join us upstairs."

"Join you for what?" he asked, and he sounded positively suspicious. He'd learned that on the job, too.

I'd already told him what I was going to do to help break the suspects down. "You can work in one room with one suspect while I do someone else. It'll cut our time in half, and increase the odds that we get usable information before dawn."

His face set in familiar stubborn lines, his mouth turning down at the edges. This was part of where he got his frown lines, this stubborn cynicism. I'd been getting my share of those years back, but the last few years I'd turned any lines on my face into smile ones. I smiled, shook my head, and sighed.

"What are you smiling at?" he asked, and his voice matched the suspicion on his face.

"You, me, nothing, everything."

"What does that even mean, Anita?" The frown softened, but he looked tired, not of hours worked, but just the situation, I think. We were both tired of it.

"It means I can read your face, the set of your shoulders. All we're doing is our job, Larry."

"It's my job to take the head and heart of dead vampires so they won't rise from the grave. It's my job to execute vampires that are legally sanctioned for death, but it's not my job to help the police terrify suspects. It would be like electrocuting a dead body in front of a condemned human prisoner. The body is still dead, so you don't kill it in front of them, but they'd still smell the meat cooking. It's barbaric, Anita. I won't be Zerbrowski's monster in the closet."

I sighed. We'd had similar philosophical disagreements before, not about this particular issue since I'd never done an interrogation like this one either, but . . . "So it's okay for me to be the monster, but not you?"

"If doing this makes you feel like a monster, Anita, then you know it's wrong. If you know it's wrong, then don't do it. It's as simple as that." He looked so serious, so convinced he was right. He always did.

"And if I don't do it, and you won't do it, then who does do it?"

"Don't you understand, Anita, no one should do this. It's a horrible thing, and it shouldn't be done at all, and it really shouldn't have people with badges doing it. We're the good guys, and good guys don't do things like this."

"We need to locate the vampires before they kill again."

"We interrogate these suspects the way we do anyone else," he said.

"Regular interrogation takes time, Larry, and by nightfall tomorrow the vampires will be hungry again. They've killed. They've killed police officers. They know they're dead meat, which means they don't have a damn thing to lose. It will make them even more dangerous."

"There's got to be a way that doesn't make us the bad guys, Anita."

I shook my head, and fought off the beginnings of anger like a warm flush of memory back when everything seemed to make me angry, and I didn't have the control I had now. "If I wasn't here you'd have to do the bad stuff yourself, Larry."

"If you hadn't been here, I still wouldn't have done it." He sounded so sure of himself, so sure he was right.

I counted to ten, forcing myself to breathe even, and slow. "How many times did my willingness to be the bad guy save civilian lives?"

He glared at me, letting me see the beginnings of his own temper. "I don't know."

"Twice," I said.

"You know it's more than that," he said.

"Four times, five, ten, a dozen? How many times do you acknowledge that my shooting or hurting someone saved lives?"

Others would have lied to themselves, but Larry held to his convictions, and still understood the cost of them. It was one of his saving graces. "Twenty times, maybe thirty, where I know you went over the line, but I do acknowledge that it saved lives."

"How many lives saved by my being a monster?" I asked.

"I never called you that."

"How many lives saved by my being the bad guy, then?" I said.

"Dozens, maybe hundreds," he said. He looked me in the eyes and said it.

"So, if I hadn't been here to do your dirty work for you, you'd have just let hundreds of innocent people die?"

His hands clenched into fists, but he held my gaze and said, "I won't torture someone. I won't kill if I don't have to."

"Even if your morals cost hundreds of lives?" I asked.

He nodded. "Morals aren't just for when it's easy, Anita. They aren't morals if you throw them aside every time it's convenient."

"Are you calling me immoral?" I asked.

"No, I'm just saying we have a different standard, that's all. We both believe we're right."

"No, Larry," I said. "I don't believe I'm right. I've done things that give me nightmares. I'll probably dream about this tonight, too."

"That means you know this is wrong; it's your conscience talking to you—yelling at you."

"I know that."

"Then how can you do it?" he asked.

"Because I'd rather have new nightmares than look a family in the eyes because their father, their brother, their mother, their daughter, their grandfather, is dead because we didn't get these vampires in time."

"I'd rather make the condolence call than do something that I know is this wrong, this . . ." He stopped.

"Say it," I said, and whispered it then, "Say it."

"Evil," he said, "I'd rather do the condolence call than do something this evil."

I nodded, not agreeing, just nodding. "Good that we have me here, then, so I can be evil, because I'd rather cut up the bodies, terrify the prisoners, than have to see one more grieving family, or explain to anyone why these bloodsuckers killed again, because we were too good, too righteous to get the information we needed."

"You and I are never going to agree on this," he said, voice quiet but very firm.

"No," I said, "we're not."

"You go be Zerbrowski's bogeyman, and I'll stake the bodies down here."

"I'm not the bogeyman, Larry. He's not real and I am."

"Just go, Anita, just let's stop this."

I shook my head. "Not yet," I said.

"Anita . . ." he said.

I stopped him by holding up my hand. "I'm the monster, Larry, not the bogeyman."

"Same thing," he said.

"No, it's not. Like I said, the bogeyman isn't real, but the monsters are real, so I'm the cop's pet monster."

"You're no one's pet, Anita; if anyone makes you a monster, it's you."

And to that, there was nothing to say. I got my equipment and I went for the building, because when a friendship breaks this badly it doesn't turn to hatred; it turns to pain.

12

THE ROOM LOOKED like a set for a slasher flick, with dirty walls; pale paint that might have started as white had flaked away from the bricks, so that the paint debris lay at the base of the walls as if something big had clawed at the walls. The question was, had it been clawing to get in, or get out? There seemed to be a layer of grit and dust on the floor, crunching underfoot, clinging to the walls, and coating the huge pillars that decorated the room and held up the soaring rise of the ceiling. There were a few windows very high up, almost touching the ceiling, but they were small windows, and probably weren't much good for light, let alone for escape. The room was huge and echoing with only a handful of police and two members of SWAT decked out for battle, holding their AR rifles at ease, but strangely ready, too, that combat ready, so that "at ease" is never really the truth. I nodded to them; they gave a slight nod back. The two uniforms on either side of the prisoner stared straight ahead, their cross-shaped tie tacks visible. Once the police officers had a reasonable fear for their lives, as in dead policemen, we could all wear our holy objects visibly without getting shit about them being an implied threat to the prisoner.

Zerbrowski had picked the vampire he thought was the weakest link, and I trusted his judgment, but it wouldn't have been the prisoner I would have chosen. The vampire was one of the ones that looked like she should be asking Chad to go to the junior high dance. She was thin, body barely starting to have a figure, hands small and very childlike. Her yellow hair was cut short and badly, in one of those feathered cuts that were popular somewhere in the seventies, but her hair was too thick for the cut, so that it didn't quite work. Did she know the haircut looked bad on her, that it made her thin face look even thinner, more childlike, rather than less? If she did, why didn't she cut it? Because if she was like most vampires, she couldn't grow her hair out; once cut, it would never grow longer again. She was dead, frozen forever at that point. Her almost bird-thin arms and legs had stopped at one of the most awkward moments, where you've just hit that growth spurt, and the legs and arms are gangly and your balance is bad, and that was it—forever.

Jean-Claude and some of his vampires could put on muscle, grow their hair out, but I'd learned just a few months ago that it was because he was powerful enough to do it. He was the Master of the City of St. Louis, which meant his power helped all the vampires blood-oathed to him in his territory rise at dusk. His will, his power; and with his death some of them would die at dawn and never rise again, or that was the theory. I knew two vampires that had killed the head of their bloodline and survived. I'd been told that Jean-Claude took power from his lesser vampires and shared it with those he valued. The person who told me had been an enemy, but still . . . I had asked him about it. His answer, "I am Master of the City, *ma petite*; that comes with a certain amount of power."

"You told me once that you wasted power to grow your hair out for me, because I like men with long hair, but Asher's hair is longer, too, and the vampire dancers at your clubs have put on extra muscle in the gym. Are you sharing power with them, too?"

"*Oui.*"

"Do you take it from the other vampires?"

"I gain power from every vampire that is mine, but I do not steal from them. Individually they do not have enough power to grow a single hair upon their heads, or add an ounce of muscle to their backs. I do not change their level of power, but I gain from it, and I can share that gain with those I choose to."

So, like a lot of things about vampires, it was true and it wasn't. The girl vampire prisoner's name was Shelby, and she wasn't one of Jean-Claude's chosen few; she was like most vampires stuck with how she'd died—she'd been about fourteen, a young, skinny, barely adolescent girl. None of the new manacles and shackles fit her, so she was in regular cuffs, chained to her waist, but none of the ankle shackles fit her. She was just too small. Which meant she potentially had enough strength to pop the chains, just as the one back at the police station had done, but his body had been six feet of muscled grown man, and Shelby was a very petite, very fragile-looking young girl. I was hoping that meant she didn't have the strength to break free, especially since I was about to scare her within an inch of her undead life.

She watched me with huge eyes, fear plain in them. The older vampires could hide almost any emotion behind centuries of practice, but when you're only about thirty years dead, you're just like someone who's that age, except you're dead and trapped in the body you wanted to leave behind in junior high. Being a vampire doesn't automatically give you great acting abilities. Just like it didn't give you instant martial arts skills, money, or sex appeal, or make you great in bed—that came with practice, and some vampires never learned how to manage money. Shelby the vampire didn't look like she'd gained much from being undead, or maybe it was a trick? Maybe she was playing to her pitiful exterior, and the first chance she got she'd kill us all? Maybe. One of the scariest vampires I'd ever met had looked like a twelve-year-old girl—she'd been a monster and over a thousand years old.

Urlrich had come with me, carrying the second bag, the one I kept for more official executions. When I was on a vampire hunt I killed them any way I could, and didn't worry about the mess, but when the body is already "dead" and we're using property that belongs to a taxpaying citizen, we have to mind the mess. I unzipped the first bag and took out the big folded tarp with its one plastic-coated side. Urlrich helped me spread it on the floor.

Shelby the vampire whispered, "Please, don't"; the soft words echoed in the big room. It was going to be great acoustics for screams.

I knelt by the bag and started getting out the stuff that the law said vampire executioners had to carry but I almost never used. Since the main point of all of this was intimidating the witness/suspect, the contents of the bag were great visuals. The stakes were first. They were in a plastic carrier that folded over and tied; each of the six stakes had a slot where it rode so it wasn't rattling around in the bag stabbing me every time I rummaged around in it. I unfolded the plastic and took each stake out, laying them bare on the plastic in a sinister row of very pointy bits. I almost never used stakes on anything, but the ones I carried were very sharp hard wood, because if I did need them, I wanted them to be ready. You're only as good as your equipment sometimes, so I made sure mine was good.

The girl vampire whimpered, and said, "You can't do this. I haven't hurt anyone."

"Tell that to the officers your friends killed," I said.

She looked up at the uniformed officers on either side of her, raising her small hands as far as the waist shackle would allow. "Please, I didn't know they would kill anyone. We would have brought the girl over, but she wanted to be a vampire until the last minutes. She got scared. We all got scared."

"Who's *we*?" I asked.

She looked at me again, eyes wide, her fear paling the color to an almost white gray. "No," she whispered.

"No, what?" I asked, and drew out a slender black leather cover. It was tied closed like the stakes carrier had been. I untied it and slowly, lovingly, unwrapped a shiny silver hand saw, the kind they used in surgery for amputations. I'd tried to use it once, and hadn't liked the feel and sound of the blade on the spine. It was supposed to make decapitating the bodies easier, and the law said I had to carry it. I'd never used it for taking the head off a vampire; I never planned on using it, but the sight of it made the girl vampire scream. One brief, piteous sound that she muffled quickly, rolling her lips under, biting on them, as if she expected to be punished for calling out. The automatic gesture made me wonder what her undead life had been like, and how much abuse had gone into it. She'd died when vampires were still illegal in this country, able to be killed on sight, by anyone, just for being undead, so she'd had to hide for decades. It's hard to hide as a child vampire; you usually need an adult to help you pretend. What price had she paid for that pretending?

Did I feel sorry for her? Yes. Would it change what I was about to do? No. The days when my feelings affected my job that badly were long past. Now, if my feelings affected my job it was more serious, but happened less often.

Urlrich knelt down beside me, shifting his equipment belt to one side. He favored one knee as if it were stiff. He spoke low. "I'm not enjoying this like I thought I would."

"She can hear you," I said.

He looked startled, then glanced at the girl and back at me. "Their hearing is that good?"

I nodded and drew out a clear plastic jar of pink rosebuds and red petals, all dried and ready to be made into potpourri.

"Roses, what's that for?" he asked.

"To stuff in the mouth."

"I thought you stuffed garlic in a vampire's mouth."

"You can, and most do, but the garlic makes the bag smell, and the roses don't, and they both work just as well." What I didn't say out loud was that I'd never stuffed a piece of anything into a decapitated vampire head, or into a dead vampire when it was whole. Once I severed the spine, I might burn the body parts separately and throw the ashes into different bodies of running water if the vamp was really old, or really powerful, but as far as I could tell the whole stuffing-crap-in-the-mouth didn't do a damn thing to keep them from rising from the grave. The powers that be had added it as a step in the morgue stakings, but the only thing I'd come up with was that it was quicker and less messy to stuff the garlic, or roses, in the mouth than to stake them. Maybe, if you were close to dawn, the vampire wouldn't be able to bite until they got the plants out of their mouth, or maybe they'd choke? I had no idea, but as far as I knew it didn't do anything metaphysical to the bodies of vampires. But it did make the vampire in the room with us start to cry.

Urlrich leaned in and whispered, "She's the age of my grand-daughter."

"No, she looks like she's the age of your granddaughter, but she's really the age of one of your children if they're in their thirties, and she can still hear you."

He glanced at her again.

I heard the chains rattle, and she said, "Please, please, help me. I didn't know they would kill them. I was too small to stop them, too weak. I'm always too weak."

Urlrich went very still as he knelt beside me. I poked him in the shoulder; when that didn't make him move, I punched him in the shoulder. It moved his body, made him almost fall.

"What the hell, Blake?"

"You were looking in her eyes, Urlrich; she was fucking with you."

The two SWAT team members aimed their ARs at the vampire. "You're the green light, Blake, just say the word," Baxter said.

"Not yet," I said. I knew that Baxter had said it out loud to help spook the vampire, but I also knew it was true. A U.S. Marshal with an active warrant of execution was a walking green-light zone for SWAT. Give the word, it was a clean shoot.

Urlrich looked at me, started to protest, and then got a thoughtful look on his face. "Shit, I was thinking about my granddaughter and how much she looks like her, but she doesn't. My kiddo is dark-haired and younger, but for just a minute there I saw the vampire's face over my granddaughter's, as if she were her." There was just the edge of fear in his eyes when he looked at me then. "Jesus, Blake, that fast, she mind-rolled me that fast?"

"It can happen, especially if the vampire appeals to some issue in your own head, like having a granddaughter about the same age."

One of the uniformed officers said, "Our crosses didn't glow; they glow if she uses vampire powers."

"They glow if she uses enough power, or aims it at you, but she wasn't doing a damn thing to you, and she made it subtle." I looked at her then, gave her my full eye contact, because I didn't have to be afraid of a vampire as weak as this one, not just with mind tricks anyway. "Very nice; I bet that pitiful act works for you almost every time you need a grown-up to protect you, or feed on."

Her thin little face went sullen, and there it was in those gray eyes, the monster peeking out. This was the truth, this was what had lived for more than thirty years, and fed on humans back when if her blood donors went to the authorities, she'd be hunted down and killed. I didn't think she was strong enough to wipe their minds clean; her only other option would have been to take blood and eventually kill them, or make them a vampire, so they wouldn't give her away. Most child vampires weren't powerful enough to make humans into vampires.

"How many humans have you killed, not for food, but to keep them from telling on you? How many have you fed on and then killed to keep your secret?"

"I didn't ask to be a vampire," she said. "I didn't ask to be trapped like this. The vampire that brought me over was a pedophile, and he made me into his perfect victim forever."

"How many years did it take for you to kill him?"

"I wasn't strong enough to kill him," she said, and the voice was still a child's, but the tone, the edge of force, that wasn't childlike at all.

"But you manipulated someone else to do it for you, didn't you?"

"They wanted to save me from him, and I wanted to be saved. You have no idea what it was like."

I sighed. "You're not the first child vampire I've met that was brought over by a pedophile."

"He deserved to die," she said.

I nodded. "No arguments."

"Then please, don't hurt me. I don't want to be hurt anymore." She called up some tears to shine in those big eyes of hers.

"You're good," I said, "I thought you couldn't act well enough to hide your fear, but you wanted me to see it. You wanted everyone to see it. I should have thought that in that body you'd have to be a master manipulator to have survived this long."

"Tears and pity are all I have, all I've ever had to protect myself with."

Urlrich was moving for the door. "I can't watch this, it's too close to home."

"Go, check on your partner, and remember she'd kill you as soon as look at you."

"I wouldn't," she protested.

I looked her in the face. "Liar."

She hissed at me, and just like that no one in the room thought she was a little girl anymore. Her eyes started to drown in that glow that meant she was about to go all vampire on us; she was weak enough that she was going to give us clues before she went apeshit.

"Blake?" Murdock said, settling his rifle very still against his shoulder; his partner followed suit.

"Stop, or we shoot you in the heart, and the head, right now."

"Better a quick death than stuffed full of flowers and beheaded."

"None of this is for you, Shelby. It's for the bodies."

The glow began to leak out of her eyes. "What bodies?"

"The dead vampires; you know, we have to take the head and heart once a vampire is dead to keep it from rising from the grave."

"Why show me all this, then?"

"Help us find the ones who did the killing and maybe you don't get executed with them, but if you don't help us and they kill again, when you could have helped us stop it . . ." I motioned at the stakes. "This will be for you."

"If I tell you where they are, they'll kill me."

"Not if I kill them first, Shelby. I'll have a whole team of SWAT with me; we will kill them. They won't ever hurt you, or bully you, again."

"Someone else will bully me; I'm too weak."

"Join the Church of Eternal Life; they have foster groups for child vampires. You can be with others like you, and it's all legal, and you can go to college, hold a job, and have a life."

"To join the Church I have to drink the blood of your master, and then he'll own me. I don't want to be anyone's slave."

"The blood oath is to keep vampires from doing exactly what you did—kill humans. A strong Master of the City can keep his followers from acting on their blood hunger."

"He's too powerful, and so are you, Anita Blake! It's not like a blood oath to a regular Master of the City; you lose your will. You turn us into humans blindly following our beautiful leader and his blood whore!"

I smiled. "Sticks and stones, Shelby; call me all the names you want, but you watched two human police officers murdered in front of you, and did nothing to stop it. Under the law you're just as guilty as the vampires that sank fangs into them, and you will be executed for it. Help us find them, and the new laws may have a loophole for you to slip through, and live."

"I'm already dead, Anita Blake."

"No, no you're not. You're alive. You walk, you talk, you think, you're still you—undead isn't the same thing as dead." I went to the door, opened it, and said, "Bring it in." Two officers brought a black plastic-wrapped body. The face was pale and still showing. It was the vampire that had tried to hide behind the human girl. I'd shot him, and now I'd get to finish the job.

"Lay it down in the middle of the tarp," I said.

The two officers laid the body down where I directed. One of them half stumbled, and an arm flopped out of the plastic, limp as only true death can make it.

Shelby gasped, and I thought that one might be genuine.

I unrolled the plastic and looked down at the dead vampire. The wounds in his upper and middle chest had dried black around the edges, but the blood was still red enough that it had darkened his button-down shirt to shades of crimson, brown, and then the last color of most blood—black. They can say that death is the big sleep, but a dead body doesn't act like it's asleep; even the unconscious don't have the loose-

boned fall of the freshly dead. Some vampires go into rigor immedi-
ately, but this one wasn't old enough for that; he was just like any dead
body that was less than two hours old, though the blood wouldn't pool
in the body as it did in a human.

"This is dead, Shelby; whatever you are, it's not this."

I got the coveralls out of the other bag, the one that held the equipment I used most often, rather than the government-sanctioned stuff.
The government didn't tell me I had to wear the coverall, but then
the people making the laws had never had to do my job. They'd never
found out how much blood and mess comes out of a body when you
remove its head and heart. Until you've been covered in that much
blood and gore, you just don't understand. Coveralls kept the dry-
cleaning bills down and helped me sleep better at night. There's only
so many times you can scrub blood out from under your fingernails
before you start going all Lady Macbeth and stop believing the blood
is ever gone.

I braided my hair, something that Nathaniel had taught me to
do. With my curls it would never be as neat a braid as his, but it meant I
could tuck the nearly waist-length hair into a skullcap. I'd tried the dis-
posable plastic shower caps, but I was just vain enough that I'd started
to use the cheap skullcap hats; they were more expensive than the
shower caps, but they looked less dorky. It was harder to tuck my hair
under the cap, but the black cap looked more threatening than poufy
plastic, and tonight that counted.

Shelby said, "Why are you putting your hair up?"

"Got tired of cleaning bits of people out of my hair."

"Bits of people." She said it low, like she was testing out the phrase.

"Yep," I said. I slid the plastic booties over my shoes next. I'd gotten
where I could do it standing up on one foot, and I didn't track pieces of
my work home with me. I still hadn't heard the end of the time I had a
piece of brain matter stuck to one shoe and didn't notice until I was
walking across the living room carpet. All right, honestly, I didn't notice
at all. Micah noticed, and Nathaniel said he had no idea how to clean
brains out of carpeting, so please don't get it on the carpet. But it was

Sin's reaction that made me throw the shoes out. You'd think a were-tiger, no matter how young, would be a little more understanding. Asher had totally backed Sin, and thought it was beyond the pale. He was the only vampire that complained. I pointed out that with their all-liquid diet, they didn't have to worry about stuff like this; the were-animals did, so they could bitch. Asher had said, "I don't have to eat flesh to not want brain matter in the carpet." I'd called him a pussy, but I'd thrown the shoes out.

There was another leather fold, tied tight so it wouldn't shift in transport, but this one didn't have wooden stakes in it. I untied the leather thong, laid it on the ground beside the stakes, and undid the flap. Blades gleamed in the dim light, glowing softly silver. They were knives that Fredo, one of our lead bodyguards and a member of the local wererat rodere, had helped me pick out after I'd borrowed one of his knives to cut out a vampire's heart, because his knife collection was better. Fredo liked knives the way Edward liked guns. Fredo taught knife-fighting classes to the guards, and I took the class whenever I could.

I took out a blade and made a show of testing the balance in my hands, letting it lie across my fingertips, and resting on a single finger-tip. I loved the balance of this knife, but balance for fighting wasn't always the best balance for carving someone's heart out of their chest.

"What are you going to do with that?" the vampire asked, in a breathy, frightened voice.

I didn't bother looking at her as I answered, "You know what I'm going to do with it." I slid the knife back into its leather home and took out another one. I didn't bother trying to balance this one on my fin-gertips, because it didn't balance that way. I was never going to try to throw this one, and if I had to fight a "living" target with it, then things would have gone so pear-shaped I wouldn't have to worry about how balanced my knives were ever again.

I put the blade on top of the leather, so that the vampire could see it clearly. So she could watch the sharp edge gleam in the dim light. I fished in the equipment bag one more time, and came out with a pair of paramedic's scissors and a box of plastic gloves.

"What is that?" The vampire whispered it. The tone of fear in her voice made me look at her. Her face was pinched, and strained, not with vampire powers but simple fear. If you've never seen a pair of the scissors, they are a little odd-looking, and you might not call them scissors; you might think they were some sort of metal cutters, or pointy pliers. She didn't know what they were, or what I was going to do with them, and that bothered her. The unknown bothered her more than the knowing. Interesting, and potentially useful.

I didn't answer her. The face shield was next, with its little strap that went around the back of the head. That was government ordered, but I actually agreed with it; again, cleaning blood out of your eyelashes loses its charm after a while. The face shield sent my breath back to me, so that I could feel how warm it was. I had a moment to be claustrophobic, but fought it off. If I did it right, I didn't really need it, but every once in a while the undead bodies acted weird, and they'd squirt at you when you weren't expecting it. I really didn't want this guy's blood on my face.

I got out the thin gloves, and then put the longer rubber gloves over that. They went up past my elbows, which I'd need because of the way I took the heart out of the body. A lot of executioners just destroyed the heart with a stake, a knife, or a gun, but left the remnants of it in place. If I could see daylight through the chest, so that I knew the heart was utterly destroyed, I'd do that, but when I couldn't see into the chest cavity, I didn't trust the heart to be destroyed enough. New vampires like this one, the gunshot wounds I'd put in his chest were probably enough to ensure he wouldn't heal and rise unexpectedly, but I'd never gotten in trouble being overly cautious when it came to making certain a vampire was really, truly, completely, dead.

Of course, it was a little hard to see the extent of the gunshots through the clothes, which was why I had the paramedic's scissors. They'd cut through anything but metal, and even cheap metal would yield to them, but harder things like handcuffs were proof against them—but clothes, no sweat.

I knelt beside the body, tucking the scissors in between the buttons just above the waist of the jeans, cutting to one side so I could parallel the fastened buttons.

"Just unbutton it," she said.

"This is faster," I said, keeping my gaze and my attention on what I was doing.

"But the buttons are right there," she said. It's funny what will bother someone most; you never know what it will be. Things that you would never dream would frighten someone, or creep them out, scare the hell out of them or make their skin crawl. For whatever reason, it seemed to really bother her that I was cutting beside the line of neatly fastened buttons, but not using the buttons.

I usually cut a quick, clean line through a shirt, but now I slowed down, took my time, let her watch, let her think, let whatever it was about it have time to bother her more.

"Just do it," she said, her voice holding an edge of franticness. "Just cut through it, if you're going to, or unbutton it. Why do it like that? Why cut it off like you're enjoying it?"

Ah, I thought, she thought what I was doing looked sensual, like I was enjoying it. I wasn't; it didn't move me one way or the other. The days when it would have creeped me out to cut through the clothes were long past. Cutting clothes off a willing lover who enjoyed that sort of thing was fun, exciting, sexy. Cutting clothes off a corpse wasn't any of those things. It was just cutting the cloth away so I could see the chest and judge how much damage the bullets had done to the heart, so I'd know if I needed to take out the heart, or if the bullets had done the job for me. Baring the pale, cool skin was more like unwrapping a piece of butchered meat, inert, not alive, nothing but meat that you might have to cut up. That was the only way to think of it; the only way to do it, and stay sane.

"Just finish cutting it!" She half-yelled it.

The door opened behind me; I caught the movement out of my peripheral vision, so I was able to see Zerbrowski come smiling through the door without actually turning away from the body in front of me.

"What's all the fuss?" he said cheerfully.

The vampire tried to get up off her knees, where the uniforms had put her. The rattle of the chains made me look at her and see one of the officers put a hand on her thin shoulder, automatically pushing her back to her knees.

"Make her stop," the vampire said.

"Marshal Blake isn't under my command. She doesn't answer to me."

The vampire gave me wide frightened eyes. I looked into her eyes and smiled a slow, tight spread of lips. She actually tried to move backward, as if ten feet were suddenly too close to me. I smiled a little more, and she made a small sound in her throat, as if she were trying not to whimper, or scream.

"Please," she said, and held her hand up to the officer who was keeping her on her knees. "Please, please, I don't want to see her cut Justin up. Please don't make me watch!"

"Tell us where the vampires are that killed the officers and you don't have to watch," Zerbrowski said.

I had cut through the shirt, just the collar being upright and the way it fitted through the shoulders keeping it closed over the chest—well, that and the blood. The cloth was sticking to that. I laid the scissors down and began to peel the cloth off the wounds, slowly, letting the sound of it sucking away from the skin fill the silence. I knew the sound would be so much louder to the vampire than to the rest of us. I made it last, made it peel and hiss as I pried the cloth out of the drying blood and the cooling flesh. Some of the cloth was actually sucked into the wounds in the chest, riding along on the force of the bullets, so that I used my fingertips to pick the cloth from the wounds. I didn't have to; I usually just pulled the cloth away in one big movement like tearing a Band-Aid off a cut, but I was pretty sure it would bother Shelby the vampire to do it this way. I was right.

"Please, please, don't make me watch this." She held her hands out to Zerbrowski.

"Tell us where they are, honey," he said, "and the nice officers will take you out of here."

"They'll kill me if they know I told," she said.

"We discussed this; they can't kill you if we kill them first," I said, forcing myself to look at the wounds I'd put in the body, rather than at her. I was hoping she'd think I was gazing longingly at the dead chest, and since I wasn't sure my acting was up to looking sexy, since I totally didn't feel that way, I kept my expression down where she couldn't see it.

"You can't kill them all," she said.

"Watch me," I said, and I did look at her then; I let her see my expression, because I knew it was cold, and empty, and yet a smile started across my lips. I knew the smile; I'd seen it in mirrors. It was most unpleasant. It was the smile that I had when I killed, or felt justified in it. It was a smile that left my eyes cold and dead. I wasn't sure why I smiled sometimes when death was on the line, but I did, and it was involuntary, and it was creepy, even to me, so I let the vampire see it. I let her make everything there was to make of it.

She screamed a short, choked sound. Her breath came in a choked sob. "All right, all right, just get me out of here before she . . . get me out of here! I don't want to watch. Please, don't make me watch." She started to cry, her thin shoulders shaking with the force of it.

"Tell us where they are," I said, "and then the nice officers will take you away from the big, bad executioner." I made my voice low, and deep, with a sort of purr underneath it. I'd used the voice before. It worked both for real sex and for threats. Funny, how some things worked for both.

Shelby gave up her friends. She told us three different daytime retreats. She told us where all the coffins were, all the places where they hid from the sunlight, and where we could find them once the sun rose and they lay helpless.

I asked her one last question. "Are they all as newly dead as the vampires here tonight?"

She nodded, and then wiped pink-stained tears against her jacket with a swipe of her cheek, as if she'd been chained before and knew how to wipe tears away without using her hands. It made me wonder just how horrible her undead life had been up to this point.

"Except for Benjamin, he's older. He's been dead a long time."

"How long?" I asked.

"I don't know, but he's old enough to remember the council in Europe and to not want that to happen here."

"So Benjamin is from Europe," I said.

She nodded again.

"How long has he been in this country?" I asked.

"I don't know; he doesn't have an accent, but he knows things. He knows about the council and the evil things they did over there, and the things they forced other vampires to do. He says you have no will of your own, and you'll just do what the masters want, and you can't say no. We won't be slaves to Jean-Claude, or you!" She put some serious defiance into that last part.

I smiled at her. "I'll be seeing you later."

She looked confused, then scared. "I told you what you wanted to know. I did what you asked."

"You did, and now they'll take you to a cell while I cut up your friend. You don't have to watch, just like we promised."

"Then why will you see me later?"

Zerbrowski said, "Anita, it's over; we don't need to scare her anymore."

I looked into his serious eyes behind their glasses, and just started back toward the body on the tarp. "Fine, get her out of here."

"No," Shelby said. "Why will you see me later?" The police officers were actually having to drag her toward the door. She wasn't exactly struggling, but she wasn't helping either.

"You wanted to go; go," I said.

"Why will you see me later?" She yelled it.

I looked back at Zerbrowski. We shared a long look, and then he gave a small nod.

I took off the face shield and looked into her pale frightened face, and said, "Because all bad little vampires see me in the end."

She started to tremble, then shake, so that she seemed to be vibrating in place, so scared that she couldn't control her body anymore.

"Why?" and it was the barest of whispers; I'm not sure the others heard her, just saw her lips move.

"Because I'm the Executioner, and you helped kill two men."

She fainted. Knees buckling, head lolling, and only the officers at her arms kept her upright. They carried her through the door that Zerbrowski held for them. The SWAT guys followed them; their job was to keep an eye on the vampire, after all.

Zerbrowski and I stood in the empty room. I turned back to the body, putting the face shield back in place.

"What are you doing?" he asked.

"My job," I said.

"We can transport the bodies to the morgue like normal now, and Kirkland can stake and chop the bodies just as well as you can."

I glanced back at Zerbrowski. "And what am I going to be doing while Larry does all that?"

"You're with us, while we check out the locations she gave us."

"We want to wait until after dawn to raid the places, Zerbrowski. They don't have any other hostages that need rescuing."

"So, we just wait until dawn?" he asked.

"Yes," I said.

"I still want you with us. Kirkland can do this part. I'd rather have you at my back in a fight."

"If we wait until dawn, there won't be a fight," I said.

"Maybe, but just in case, you come with the rest of us. Leave Kirkland to clean up."

I took the face shield off again, and looked at him. "You don't trust Larry in a fight either, do you?"

"Let's just say that no vampire is ever going to faint from fear of him."

"Diplomatic," I said.

"I heard that he refused to help us interrogate the prisoners."

"He refused to cut up the dead while the living watched. He said it was evil, said I was no one's pet monster, and that if anyone made me a monster, it was me."

Zerbrowski looked down, pursed his lips into a thin line, and when he looked up, his eyes were angry. "He had no right to say that to you."

I shrugged. "If it's true, it's true."

He put his hand on my shoulder, made me look at him. "It's not true. You do what the job needs to get done. You save lives every night; don't let anyone tell you different, especially not someone who keeps his hands clean because you do the bad things he won't do."

I smiled, but not like I was happy. "Thanks, Zerbrowski."

He squeezed my shoulder. "Don't let him make you feel bad about yourself, Anita. He hasn't earned it."

I thought about it. "Is that why you don't let him work with you much?"

"You know the answer to that."

I nodded.

"Anita, you are not a monster."

"You said we'd talk later about what happened with Billings," I said.

He smiled, but not like he was happy, and shook his head, letting his hand drop from my shoulder. "You just have to do it the hard way, don't you?"

I nodded. It was the truth, why argue.

"You mind-fucked him," Zerbrowski said.

"I didn't mean to."

"What did you do to him?"

"I sort of absorbed his anger."

"Absorbed?" Zerbrowski made it a question.

"Yeah."

"How?"

"It's a metaphysical ability." I shrugged.

"Can you absorb other emotions?"

I shook my head. "Just anger."

"You don't get angry much anymore; is that why?"

"I'm not sure; maybe. Maybe in learning to control my own anger, I can control others. Honestly, I'm not sure."

"He still doesn't have much memory of the last two hours before you absorbed"—and he made air quotes—"his anger."

"That's never happened before, and I didn't do it on purpose. He startled me and I . . ."

"Lashed out," Zerbrowski said, "like with a fist, just not a physical one."

"Yeah," I said.

We looked at each other for a moment, and because it was me, I had to say, "Still think I'm not the monster?"

"You were the only one in the room fast enough to get to Billings before he hit that vampire. Watching him raise you up on his arm like you were . . . you looked tiny, Anita. We were all moving to help, but you took care of it, like you usually do."

"That doesn't answer the question," I said.

He smiled, shook his head. "Damn it, you are the hardest person I know, on yourself and everyone around you. You push until the truth comes out; good, bad, indifferent, ya gotta push, don't you?"

"Not always anymore, but usually, yeah, I push." I studied his face, waited for him to answer.

He frowned, sighed, and then looked at me. He was studying me back. "You're not a monster. When Dolph was having his issues and trashed a couple of rooms with you in it, you didn't report him. You let him go all apeshit on you; a lot of guys wouldn't have, not without getting his ass in a sling."

"He's better now," I said.

"We're all capable of losing it. The difference is that we get it back; we don't stay in the apeshit place, we regain ourselves."

"Regain ourselves, nice phrase," I said.

He grinned. "Katie's been reading me some of her psychology books again."

I smiled at him. "Good to have a smart spouse."

He nodded. "Always marry someone smarter, and prettier."

That made me laugh, just a little. The laugh sounded odd and echoing in the big room. I glanced back at the vampire I'd killed to save the fifteen-year-old girl he'd meant to make into a vampire. Was I sorry he was dead? No. Was I sorry the girl was still a living, breathing human being? Nope. Was I sorry that I'd scared the vampire Shelby? A little. Was I glad we had the locations of the rogue vampires that had killed the police officers? Yes.

Zerbrowski touched my shoulder again. "Don't let people like Kirkland make you feel bad about yourself, Anita."

I turned and looked at him, and there was something in his face that made me smile again. "I'll do my best."

"You always do," Zerbrowski said.

That earned him a grin, and me one in return.

"Pack up your gear; we've got vampires to hunt."

"Be right there," I said, and pulled the black cap off my hair, but I left the braid in, because sometimes the hair blew in my face and I might be shooting at people. You want to see what you're aiming at when you're trying to kill people. It's important to shoot the right ones.

13

EVERYONE AGREED THAT we'd hit the locations after dawn so the vampires would be dead to the world. We had two dead cops; we didn't need more, so we waited. Waiting is hard. It gets on your nerves. There's a chance to sleep for a few hours, and if you can do it, they'll find you a cot in the back of the station so you can rack out. Almost no one would sleep. We had two of our own dead, and we'd be hunting their killers in a few hours. It either buzzed you or made you think too hard; either way, sleep wasn't happening. Most of us had never known either officer personally, but it didn't matter. If you'd thought one of them was the biggest dick in the world while he was alive, that didn't matter either. What mattered was that he carried a badge and so did you. That meant that if you'd put out a call for help, he'd have come, and he would have put his life on the line for you. Stranger, friend, it didn't matter; you would have risked your life for him, and he for you, and if you had to, you'd have walked into a firefight with him, because that was what it meant to carry the badge. It meant that when everyone else was running away, you ran toward the problem, and anyone else who was willing to run into the shitstorm with you was your brother in arms. Civilians think that cops react like this because they're thinking, *There but for the grace of God go I*, but that's not it, not the major part; we're human, so there is some of that, but mostly it's an acknowledgment that we are the ones who run toward the gunshots. We run toward the trouble, not away, and we trust that if another person with a badge is nearby, they'll start running in that direction, too. They'll be beside us, and we'll hit the big, bad thing together, because that's our job; it's who we are.

The vampires hadn't just killed two cops, they'd killed two men who would have put their shoulders beside ours and hit the door. They'd taken out two of the good guys, and that wasn't allowed. Part of the energy, as we waited, was that we weren't just going to track the bad guys down; we were going to kill them, and it was all nice and legal. We'd hunt them down and we'd execute them. Technically, it was serving a warrant of execution, because now we had an official warrant, but to me it was just a vampire hunt with SWAT backup.

There were three locations, so I was the Marshal at one; Larry would be the Marshal at the second location, and our newest member of the Preternatural Branch, U.S. Marshal Arlen Brice, would go in with the third team. Brice was one of the new breed of preternatural Marshals, one who had been a regular police officer for at least two years and then trained for preternatural work in classrooms, not in the field. I had yet to meet a Marshal who had been trained this way who came from any branch of law enforcement that gave them the skill set they needed for hunting vampires and rogue wereanimals, because badge or no badge, preternatural Marshals are legalized assassins. We kill people in order to save lives, but our main job is killing. Police save lives, and most go their whole twenty without ever drawing their gun in the line of duty. Most Marshals in the Preternatural Branch kill at least one vampire their first month in the field, sometimes more. Anyone who thinks that killing vampires isn't like killing real people should try it for a while and see how it feels. I've killed human beings in the line of duty, and honestly, other than the fact that they're easier to kill, it just doesn't feel that different.

But U.S. Marshal Arlen Brice didn't know that yet.

Brice was five-eight, five-nine, short, but with nicely cut hair in one of those in-between colors that was either pale brown or a really dark blond. When I'd been a little girl I would have called it pale brown, but a girl in my class had hair almost the same color and she had informed me that it was "champagne blond." My stepmother had confirmed it was an actual color, but most people called it "dirty blond." That childhood faux pas had left its mark, so Brice's hair color was a mystery until he told me otherwise. His eyes were a pale, almost amber brown, so even the eyes weren't quite brown enough to call.

The rest of him was standard handsome, with an easy smile that went up a little higher on one side and just seemed to add to his charm, because he was charming. Detective Jessica Arnet and any other female officer who came near him reacted to him in a way that let me know that a more ordinary flavor of handsome worked just fine for them. Arnet had finally gotten over her crush on Nathaniel, my live-in sweetie. She still didn't like me. She felt that my keeping it secret that Nathaniel was my live-in lover had somehow humiliated her when she made a play for him. No pleasing some people.

Zerbrowski and I threaded our way through all the extra people who were hanging around the headquarters for the Regional Preternatural Investigation Team, RPIT for short. We weren't going to sleep so we decided to catch food at a restaurant we both liked. The first hint I had that Marshal Brice was behind us was Detective Arnet's voice, high and lilting: "Hey, Brice, do you want to get a bite to eat?"

"I really appreciate the offer, Detective, but I already said I'd catch food with Detective Zerbrowski and Marshal Blake."

That stopped me and Zerbrowski in our tracks. We looked at each other, and I knew from the look on his face that this was news to him, too. We turned to look at him, giving blank cop face, both of us waiting for Brice to catch up as if we'd meant to do it all along.

Larry was the next to offer food, but Brice just smiled and said, "Thanks, Marshal Kirkland, I'll catch you next time."

Larry actually touched the man's arm and said, "What kind of Marshal do you want to be, Brice?"

The question stopped Brice, made him look more fully at Larry, and then glance back at Zerbrowski and me. Brice smiled at Larry. "One who's good at his job, Marshal Kirkland." He kept smiling, but his eyes changed. The look wasn't directed at us, so from the side it was harder to read, but whatever was in those brown-gold eyes made Larry drop his hand.

"I'm good at my job," Larry said. His words were soft, but they carried in one of those weird moments of silence that happens in noisy rooms with crowds. Everyone goes quiet at the same time and suddenly everyone can hear.

"I never said otherwise," Brice said, but he walked away from Larry.

Larry actually blushed, but it wasn't embarrassment. It was anger. "I'm a good Marshal."

Brice's face was serious, almost sad, but I think only we saw it. He got his smile back in place as he turned around to Larry and the still-silent room. "I'll repeat myself, Marshal Kirkland; I never said otherwise."

"Don't let her make you into a killer."

And just like that our little family feud, Larry's and mine, was suddenly very public. The silence was so thick you could have spread it on bread, but you wouldn't have wanted to eat it. Everyone was straining to hear now, because everyone likes gossip, even cops.

Brice said, "Last I checked, Kirkland, our job description says we execute the monsters. That makes us killers, legal and all, but we're supposed to kill things, Marshal Kirkland; it's our job."

"I know my job," Larry said, voice tight.

Brice smiled a little more, and ran his hand through his well-cut hair; it was an aw-shucks movement. It made him look harmless and charming. I wondered if it was on purpose, or just a habit.

"Well now, I can't speak to that yet, but I know that Blake still has the highest kill count of any Marshal in the service. I know that every officer I've spoken to would take her as backup in a firefight. Even the ones who hate her personal life with a vengeance would still take her into a shoot-out and trust her to keep them alive. If there's higher praise from one officer to another, I don't know it."

If Larry followed both the guy and cop rules, he would let it go, but part of the problem was that he didn't follow those unspoken rules. "Are you saying that people don't trust me to keep them safe?"

"I'm just trying to go get some food with two fellow officers; anything else is what you're thinking, not what I'm saying. I just complimented Marshal Blake. I didn't say a damn thing about you." Brice was still smiling a little, still all aw-shucks-ma'am in his demeanor, but there was something harder now, some hint of steel underneath that handsome nice-guy exterior.

Zerbrowski said, "Come on, Brice, I'm starving."

He turned and looked at Zerbrowski, and there was a smile again, but his eyes held more. He wanted out of this conversation with Larry, but if he couldn't get out of it, he'd finish it. That one look and I knew that Larry should shut the fuck up, before he made it impossible for him and Brice to ever be friends. They wouldn't be enemies, but if Larry forced it, they'd never be more than coworkers—hostile coworkers.

Brice started walking toward us, and Larry let him go, but he gave me the hard look, not the man's back as he walked away. Why was everything always my fault?

Brice caught up to us and moved past us, saying quietly, "Let's go before Kirkland says something I'm going to regret." And just like that, Brice was with Zerbrowski and me.

14

WHEN WE GOT to my Jeep, Zerbrowski riding shotgun beside me and Brice in the backseat, I said, "Not that I'm not flattered that you came to my defense, but what's going on, Brice?"

"Thank you, Blake, and you, too, Zerbrowski, for not saying you didn't know what the hell I was talking about, and that you didn't want me to go eat with you."

Zerbrowski turned in the seat as far as the seat belt would allow. "You're welcome to eat with us. After putting Kirkland in his place you can sit by us any time, but why did you want to eat with us this bad? I mean, I know we're charming and all, but with all the offers you've got for dinner and more, why us?"

I glanced back in the darkened car quick enough to catch Brice smiling. He leaned between the seats and I realized he wasn't buckled in. "Buckle up," I said.

"What?" he asked.

"Seat belt. I'm pretty fanatical about it, buckle up."

"It's hard to talk from back here," he said.

"I can stop this car and turn it around," I said.

"Is she joking?" Brice asked.

"No," Zerbrowski said.

Brice frowned, but slid back and buckled himself in for safety. "Okay, now what?"

"Yeah, I'd rather see your face while we talk, but my mom died in a car crash, so seat belts make me feel better."

"I'm sorry to hear that."

"It was a long time ago," I said, pulling out into traffic.

"Doesn't mean it stops hurting," he said.

I used the rearview mirror to glance back, and he was looking at me as if he knew I'd be looking. I looked back at the road. "You lose someone?"

"Yes." He said it soft, and didn't offer to elaborate.

I let it go, but I knew that his loss was more recent than mine. You get better at talking about it casually after a decade or two.

Zerbrowski said, "So, how'd we get to be your pick of dinner dates?" We'd go back to talking about something less painful, by the guy rules. Girl rules are different, they poke at things; guys do not.

"Well, first off, I meant what I said back there. Even officers who don't approve of your lifestyle choices would still take you as backup over Kirkland, or most anyone else. They'd say how you're bad for shacking up with vampires and wereleopards, but in a firefight they'd take your vampire-loving, furry-fucking ass over most anyone else's."

"Did they actually say 'furry-fucking'?" I asked.

He laughed. "Not exactly."

"So you want to learn the ways of the force from Anita," Zerbrowski said.

"Somethin' like that," he agreed.

"Do you have a preference on food?" I asked.

"I've been on the job for eight years."

"Which means you're just glad to have a chance to sit down and get a hot meal, whatever it is, right?" I asked.

"Yes, ma'am." Again, I caught that lopsided grin in the mirror, before I went back to looking at traffic.

"Let's go to Jimmy's," Zerbrowski said.

I nodded. "Works for me." I took a right at the next light and we were there. I found a parking spot, turned off the motor, unbuckled my seat belt. Everyone else followed suit.

Brice said, "Can we talk in the car for a minute?"

Zerbrowski and I exchanged glances, then nodded, and turned in our seats so we could see him more plainly. I thought we were about to find out how we got to be Brice's dinner dates.

"I do want to learn the job from you and not Kirkland, but I didn't expect to have Detective Arnet be so . . . persistent in her attempts to . . ."

"Date you," I offered.

He nodded.

"It's not just her," I said. "You are at the top of the female officer and female employee who-can-date-the-new-guy-on-the-force-first pool."

"I'd gathered that," he said, but he was looking at his hands. He had his fingers tangled together, almost clenched. We were about to get to something he didn't like.

"Smith thought *he* was the hot new thing until you showed up," Zerbrowski said.

"He's dating someone seriously, isn't he?" Brice asked.

"Yes," I said, "but that doesn't always stop some women." In my head, I added, *It didn't stop Arnet from pursuing Nathaniel*, but I didn't say it out loud. It sounded petty out loud; in my head it didn't sound as bad.

"No, it doesn't," Brice said, and he was looking at his hands where they held on to each other between his jean-clad thighs.

"You married?" Zerbrowski asked.

He shook his head, then looked up, and I saw a look in his face, something serious and unhappy.

"What's wrong, Brice?" I asked.

"Rumor says that some of your boyfriends are . . . bisexual?"

I gave him a not entirely friendly look. "A couple, but most are more just heteroflexible."

"Heteroflexible?" He made it a question.

I shrugged. "Nathaniel explained the term to me. He's one of my boyfriends. He explained that it means someone who is predominantly heterosexual, but has an exception with one or two people of the same sex, or someone who will cross the line, like at a party occasionally."

"I've never heard the term," Brice said.

I shrugged again. "Like I said, my boyfriend explained it to me." What I didn't add out loud was that the new label was one that fitted me now; there was a girl in among all my boys now. Her name was Jade, and we'd rescued her from a sadistic master vampire that had abused her for centuries. She'd been his tiger to call, and now she was mine; my black tiger, my Black Jade, which was what her Chinese name translated to. I honestly tried not to think about the whole thing much. When I was with her, I felt protective, and God knew she was fragile from centuries of being basically an abused wife of the vampire that had been her master, but to say I wasn't entirely comfortable with having a woman in my bed was an understatement of gigantic proportions.

"Most people think bisexual is just gay-light," Brice said, "but heteroflexible . . ." He shook his head, smiling.

"I'm not saying some of the men in my life aren't bi, but not as many as I thought. Let's just say that it's been brought to my attention that my issues of not wanting women in the bed made them not suggest it."

"So they'd have more women if you'd be okay with it?" he asked.

I said, "Yes . . ." and then I stopped myself and said, "You know, this is way over your pay grade for my personal life."

"I'm loving it," Zerbrowski said, "more than you usually tell me."

I frowned at him.

He held his hands up, as if to say *Don't shoot*. "Hey, just saying."

"Put a girl in the middle, and it's not gay, right?" Brice said, but he sounded more bitter than some theoretical discussion should be.

"You fall afoul of some couple thing?" I asked.

He glanced back down at his big hands. "You could say that."

Zerbrowski made a small noise.

I glared at him. "Say it, before you hurt yourself."

He grinned. "Just picturing you all heteroflexible."

If he only knew about Jade, the teasing would be merciless, but I shook my head. "You don't mean it. You haven't thought about me that way in years, if ever. You're one of the most happily married men I've ever met."

"Don't ruin my image, Anita. I'm the office lech."

Brice laughed. It made us both look at him. "I figured that if you were okay with Anita's home life, maybe you'd be okay with mine, and I figured Anita wouldn't give a damn."

"What's your home life like?" Zerbrowski said. "You got a harem of cuties waiting at home for you, too?"

Brice hung his head. "I wish."

"It's harder to date this many people than you think," I said.

"Trouble in paradise?" Zerbrowski asked.

I frowned, and then sighed. "Let's just say that I'm beginning to wonder if there really can be too much of a good thing."

I waited for Zerbrowski to make another smart remark, but he didn't. I glanced at him and his face was serious, not like him.

"What?" I asked, and even to me it sounded suspicious.

"I've never seen you as happy as you've been the last couple of years, Anita. Whatever you're doing, it works for you. It makes you happy."

"And?" I asked.

"And I don't like hearing you poke at it."

"I'm not poking at it, Zerbrowski, I just had one of the newest boys get all panicked about seeing the bodies on TV. It's like he didn't realize how dangerous my job was until now."

"I hadn't thought about that; you have to explain the job to every new boyfriend. That makes me tired just thinking about it. It's hard enough with just Katie." He took his glasses off and rubbed his eyes. There were fine lines that I hadn't noticed with the glasses on.

"Just dreading having the talk again with the new one," I said.

"Understandable," Brice said.

We both looked at him, as if we'd sort of forgotten he was still in the car with us. It wasn't like us. "Why are we getting all warm and fuzzy in front of you, Brice?"

"I don't know," he said, "but thank you."

"For what?"

"For letting me in, I guess."

"What do you want?" Zerbrowski asked, putting his glasses back in place. Push a cop, and you get cynical back, eventually.

Brice smiled. "I'm gay, and I'm not out."

Zerbrowski made a snorting sound, and then finally laughed. We both looked at him, and they weren't friendly looks.

"Oh, come on, it's funny. Arnet has done everything but slip her panties in Brice's hand, and Millie down in tech services has found a dozen reasons to be anywhere he is; every woman in the place is after him, and he's gay. Come on, that's funny."

"Not every woman," he said, and he looked at me.

"Nothing personal, Brice, but my dance card is way beyond full."

He smiled. "If half the news reports are true, you've got your own harem, hisem, whatever. But it's more than that, you aren't attracted to me."

I shrugged. "Sorry."

"No, it's not bad, it's good."

"Wait," Zerbrowski said, "you wanted to go to dinner with the one woman in the entire department who isn't attracted to you?"

Brice nodded.

Zerbrowski frowned, and then grinned. "Sorry, Brice, you're a doll and all, but I don't think you're attractive either."

Brice grinned, then chuckled. "Good to know."

"Your sexual orientation doesn't have a damn thing to do with the job," I said.

"No, it doesn't, but if it comes out I'm gay, it will."

"Maybe," I said.

"I'd just like to come out in my own way, not be outed, that's all."

Would I have been less sympathetic if I didn't have Jade in my life?

Maybe, but I did, and I hadn't been out in public with her yet; part of that was that I didn't enjoy shopping, or most of the girl stuff she wanted to do. "That's your choice," I said.

"Since you're not attracted to either of us, doesn't really matter," Zerbrowski said.

"Thank you," he said quietly.

"But now what?" I asked. "You didn't just want to come to dinner to tell us your big secret."

"I'm looking for some advice on how to handle the women at work without getting them pissed at me. Detective Arnet is being particularly persistent."

I sighed. "I'll need food if we're going to talk about girls."

Brice smiled. "What does that mean?"

"It means I had some problems with Arnet wanting to date one of my boyfriends, and I need food before we get into it."

"Fine with me," Brice said.

Zerbrowski just reached for the door handle.

We all got out and just headed for the lighted windows of the restaurant. Straight, or gay, or being a girl, it didn't matter; we were all just cops eating food and passing time while we waited. I'd tell Brice a short version of Arnet's crush on Nathaniel, and then we'd pass time talking about Brice's personal life. Fine by me, it beat the hell out of talking about mine.

15

ZERBROWSKI SURPRISED ME by getting a salad with grilled chicken on it. "You're not getting a burger?" I asked.

"Had my cholesterol checked. No burgers for a while." He looked glum as he said it.

"So, no more fast-food burgers?" I asked.

He shook his head.

I patted his back. "Dude, I'm sorry."

Brice said, "Am I missing something? You're acting like he's lost a relative."

"When you ride in Zerbrowski's car, you'll understand. He lives on fast-food burgers, and throws the wrappers into the backseat."

"Will there be room in the backseat for me to sit with all the fast-food wrappers?" Brice asked, laughing.

I looked at Zerbrowski. He shrugged. "I can clean out the back."

"I was joking," Brice said, looking from one to the other of us. "Are you serious that the backseat is so full of fast-food debris that no one can sit in it?"

"We're serious," I said.

"I'll clean it out. The smell of the wrappers will just make me hungry." Zerbrowski picked up his tray with its healthy salad on it; he looked sad.

There were plenty of tables to choose from, because we were late for dinner and hours too early for breakfast. We needed plenty of seating choices, because we were all cops and that meant that none of us wanted our backs to a door, or to the restaurant in general, and especially not a busy area where people would be walking back and forth behind us. We didn't really like windows where people on the outside could just walk up to where we were sitting, especially not if we had to put our backs to the windows. Yeah, the chances of someone walking up and just starting to shoot at us was small, but small wasn't the same as not ever happening. Police aren't paranoid because of some psychological disorder, they're paranoid because real bad things have happened to them, and in our job paranoia was just another word for staying alive.

So, where to sit?

There was a booth that sat back in a corner with a wall that backed the kitchen so there were no windows, and as many as four could sit comfortably with enough room to get to weapons without crowding each other. We also had a clear line of sight to the door. It was perfect. We slid into the booth, with me in the middle, which would have trapped Brice or Zerbrowski, but I was small enough that if I had to, I could go under the table and be shooting at people's legs and be shooting them in the chest and face as they dropped to their knees, because that's what happens to most people if bullets shatter their leg bones. Yes, that is how cops think, that's how anyone who lives by the gun thinks. We don't talk about it, but we are totally into preplanning our survival.

We got settled into the booth, portioned out our food, and started eating before we started talking, because we could talk in the car, but we couldn't eat most of the food we'd gotten in the car while driving. Have you ever tried to eat a salad in a car? Of course, I hadn't ordered a salad, I had a burger, but you can't eat Jimmy's burgers in a car either unless you want to be wearing all that yummy condiment goodness.

"Red meat is bad for you, you know," Zerbrowski said, sort of forlornly.

"My cholesterol is fine," I said, stacking the bun higher with all the layers of vegetables on the burger.

"Mine, too," Brice said, as he took his first bite.

"You should have said something when we were ordering, if you were going to pout, Zerbrowski."

"Would you have ordered a salad to keep me company?"

"No, but I would have felt guilty about it." I took the first bite of the burger. It was juicy and cooked to perfection. The veggies were crisp, ripe, and yummy. I tried to keep the look of bliss off my face, but I think I failed, because Zerbrowski looked like something hurt.

Brice and I ate in happy silence for a few minutes, and then I said, "Sorry, Zerbrowski, but I eat salads at home because Nathaniel decides the menu; when I'm not at home, I eat what I want."

"Nathaniel is your live-in boyfriend?" Brice asked, after he'd swallowed another bite of burger.

"Yep," I said, and took another bite of burger.

Zerbrowski gave me a pained look.

I ignored him.

"You said he does the menus; what does that mean?"

"He does most of the cooking, as either head chef or sous chef to one of the others."

"You make it sound like a restaurant," Brice said.

I shrugged. "The men started it; whoever is the main cook for a meal is designated chef and the others are sous chefs. It's their system and it works, so I just work with it. I figure if I'm not doing the cooking, I shouldn't bitch about how they want to do it."

"Very reasonable," Brice said.

I shrugged again and took another bite of my burger.

"She usually is," Zerbrowski said, as he took a small bite of his salad. He chewed the lettuce as if it were the opposite of yummy.

He was only about nine years older than me; would I have to give up burgers someday? Of course, I was as lean as I had been in college, but more muscular. Zerbrowski had started getting a little thicker around the middle, nothing bad, but he had put on weight. With two kids and a wife, he had more trouble finding time to hit the gym. Kids seemed to make things a lot harder; good thing I'd probably never have to worry about that particular complication.

"Earth to Anita," Zerbrowski was saying.

I blinked at him. "What?"

"What were you thinking about so hard just now?" he asked, and he looked suspicious.

"Nothing," I said.

"Liar; women are never thinking nothing."

"When *you* say you're thinking nothing, I believe you," I said.

"I'm a man, I really *am* thinking nothing."

I gave him an exasperated smile. "What the hell does that mean?"

"It means I want to know what you were thinking about so hard just now."

"And I said, nothing, so I'm not going to answer you."

He grinned. "See, you were thinking something."

I frowned at him. "Drop it, okay?"

"No," he said.

"You enjoying your rabbit food?" I asked.

"That was low, Anita," he said, and he stirred his salad with his fork, not really eating it. Maybe that was how you lost weight on salads; you just didn't want to eat them, so you didn't eat, and voilà, you lost weight.

I ate my first French fry. It was crisp, salty, and yummy, too.

"If your lovers are all shapeshifters, then why do they eat rabbit food?" Brice asked.

"You mean when they should be eating rabbits?" I asked.

"Did I offend you?" he asked.

I thought about it. "Sorry, I'm just grumpy. Most of them are exotic dancers, and eating too much meat will make you bloat sometimes, get a little meat tummy. When you take your clothes off professionally, you want to look your best doing it."

"Again, very reasonable," he said.

"You sound surprised," I said.

"If you'd been listening, Brice was saying that you have a reputation with the other cops for being unreasonable."

I looked at Brice. "That true?"

He studied my face as he said, "They say you have a bad temper and bust their balls a lot."

Zerbrowski snorted and almost choked on his soda.

I frowned at him. "I don't back down, so if that busts their balls, then so be it."

"They're jealous that the itty-bitty woman is better at their job than they are," Zerbrowski said, when he could talk again without coughing.

"Itty-bitty?" I said.

"Argue if you can?" he said.

I started to frown, and then just smiled. "I'm short, what the fuck of it?"

Brice laughed.

I looked at him.

He held up his hands in a little push-away gesture. "Hey, I got no problem with anything."

"Fine; weren't we supposed to be discussing you, not me?"

He nodded. "How can I discourage Arnet without pissing her off?"

"I'm not sure you can," I said.

"What do you mean?"

"Nathaniel Graison was my live-in sweetie but I wasn't telling everyone at work, so Arnet saw him a couple of times, thinking he was just a friend of mine. She decided she wanted to date him, and then felt like I'd made a fool of her by not saying up front that he was mine."

"He's a wereleopard, right?"

I looked at him; it wasn't a friendly look. "How do you know what kind of wereanimal he is?"

"He's on the website for Guilty Pleasures. They list the animal form of all the strippers, I mean dancers, who shapeshift."

"Were you checking up on my men?"

"I can look at the men at Guilty Pleasures and pass it off as research, getting to know the local wereanimals and vampires, and no one questions why a male cop would like looking at male strippers."

I had a moment of feeling a little odd that Marshal Brice might have looked at Nathaniel's picture, or Jason's, or Jean-Claude's, and lusted after them. Was it that he was a guy? I didn't think so. I think it was just that he worked with me and you're not supposed to lust after the sweeties of the other cops, or at least you're not supposed to let the cop in question know that you lust after his sweetie. It's just not cricket, somehow.

"Makes sense," I said.

He smiled. "Thought you were going to get weird about me looking at your guys."

"Its not the possible lusting after my guys; I know how yummy they are. It's the idea that you might be checking up on them for future hunting purposes that would piss me off."

He looked genuinely shocked. "I would never do that to a fellow officer."

"Jessica Arnet has; she damn near told me that someday Jean-Claude would go apeshit and we'd have to do something about him."

"She did not," Zerbrowski said. He looked genuinely shocked.

"She threatened your boyfriend?" Brice asked.

I nodded. I was suddenly not nearly as hungry.

"What did she say exactly?" Zerbrowski asked.

"She told me that Jean-Claude was just a pretty monster and if he wasn't around that Nathaniel would be free to have a life."

"She said exactly that?" he asked.

I nodded.

"When?" he asked.

"Three days ago."

"Why didn't you tell me?"

"I was trying to decide if this was something I should handle between Arnet and me, or if it was something to shove up the food chain."

"And?" Zerbrowski asked.

"And I think she went too far by threatening my boyfriend. She's gone to the club on nights that Nathaniel works. She's told him that she would rescue him from me and Jean-Claude. She's told me pretty much the same thing, but that was like over a year ago, almost two. I thought she'd let it go, moved on." I looked at Brice. "Nothing personal, Brice, but if she can obsess about you instead of my sweetie, I'd feed you to her."

"Gee, thanks, Blake," he said.

"If I'd told her that Nathaniel was my lover from the beginning, would she have fixated on him? I was embarrassed that I was living with two men, and I was trying so hard not to love Nathaniel. God, I was so in denial about how I felt about him back then."

"You really did poke at anything that made you happy, didn't you?" Brice said.

"You have no idea," I said.

Zerbrowski laughed. "I do, and no one fucked up their own love life weirder than you did."

I glared at him, but the look of sympathy and real concern on his face made it impossible to hold. I finally just sighed, and poked at my cooling French fries.

"You're not going to argue?" he asked.

I shook my head. "It's the truth, why argue?"

He stood up, leaned over the table, and tried to feel my forehead. I jerked back, batting his hand away. "What are you doing?"

"Checking for a fever," he said, "because you just gave in, and said, *Why argue?* You have to be sick."

I glared at him now.

He grinned. "That's my grumpy partner; I knew you were in there somewhere."

I fought it, but finally grinned back. "Damn you, let me be in a bad mood for a minute or two."

"I'm your partner. I'm supposed to keep your mood up so you can continue being the biggest, baddest bull in the damn shop. You like knocking stuff off the shelves and letting the pieces fall where they may.

You like being the bad-ass, and that rubs people the wrong way. I help rub them the right way."

"You make me sound like a bully."

"No, never that," he said.

"Are you really as good as your reputation?" Brice asked.

I gave him the full attention of my big, brown eyes. "Yes," I said.

"I'd accuse you of bragging, but if half of what I've heard is true . . ."

"I don't know what you've heard," I said.

"That you have the highest kill count of any Marshal."

"True," I said.

"That you've got some kind of super lycanthropy that makes you faster, stronger, harder to hurt, impossible to kill, but you don't shape-shift."

"Everything but the impossible to kill; I wouldn't bet my life on that rumor," I said.

"That you're a living vampire."

I shrugged. "Not sure what to say to that one. I don't drink the blood of the living, if that's what you mean."

"How about the blood of the dead?" he asked.

Zerbrowski and I both stared at him. "Are you serious?" I asked.

He nodded. "Rumor says that you feed off vampires the way they feed off us."

I shook my head. "Not true."

"That you're some kind of succubus and feed off sex with vampires."

"I hadn't heard that one," I said, and it was true I hadn't. I'd heard that I was accused of feeding off sex, but not that my "victims" were exclusively vampires. I was really trying to never admit out loud that I actually did feed on sex, thanks to sharing Jean-Claude's *ardeur*, which translated roughly to fire, passion, and was the blood right, extra-special gift of the bloodline of vampires descended from Belle Morte, Beautiful Death.

"I take it that's not true either."

I was giving him blank cop face, because I'd known that one was coming and it was almost true, except that I could feed off sex in general; it didn't have to be with vampires. "Let's cut to the chase," I said. "Sum up the rumors, I'm bored with the list."

"That your ability to raise zombies from the grave gives you an edge with all the undead, including vampires. That being a shapeshifter that doesn't shift gives you the best of being human and animal. That the reason you're better than the rest of us is that you're better than any human could ever be, and stay human."

"I'm sensing a theme," I said to Zerbrowski.

"Don't say it," he said.

"I'm better at killing the monsters, because I'm one of them, is that it?"

"I never said that."

"But that's what some of the others are saying, right?" I asked.

He sort of shrugged, and looked uncomfortable.

"Remember that some of the people saying that are jealous of my success rate, and others are just plain jealous like Arnet."

"Some of them are scared, Blake," he said.

"Scared of me," I said, and I pushed my food away. I was so done.

"Not of you, of becoming you. They're afraid that the only way to get as good as you is to become like you."

"You mean become one of the monsters," I said.

"You were on the case where Marshal Laila Karlton caught lycanthropy."

"Yes." It had been Laila's first vampire hunt, and it could have been her last. She survived the werewolf attack, but she became one of them.

"She fought for her badge, and she's still a Marshal. She's the first one who was ever allowed to stay after they shifted."

"I was the first they let stay who tested positive," I said.

"But you don't change form," he said.

"There is that."

"Some people say you encouraged her to fight for her job."

"It could have happened to any of us, Brice. The only reason I'm not in the same boat is that I don't change forms."

"That's why she still has a badge, because it could be any of us next. They're afraid if she sues that she'll win. Right now she's riding a desk, but if they put her in the field again, then that opens the way for people who are already wereanimals to try to join up."

I nodded. "I think it's a great idea. I know some ex-cops and military people who are only ex- because they got attacked on the job and that's an instant medical discharge."

He looked at me, and then at Zerbrowski. "Would you partner with someone who shifted completely?"

"If it were Anita, sure."

Brice looked at his plate; there wasn't much left of his food. He ate like a lot of male cops, like he was inhaling. "Just how good are you, Blake?"

I glanced at Zerbrowski. He used his hands to make a little tell-him gesture, like an usher uses to guide people to their seats, but what was I guiding Brice to: the truth, a lie, what?

"I'm a good cop, if you don't make me follow orders too closely."

Zerbrowski laughed into his water.

I didn't bother frowning at him. "But when it comes to killing, it's one of my best things, and my best is very, very good."

"Anyone else I might accuse of bragging, but it's not bragging if it's true," Brice said.

"She's not bragging," Zerbrowski said.

I glanced at him. We exchanged one of those long looks that men are so fond of, and most women are puzzled by—the one that said everything we needed to say about working together, being friends, holding each other's lives in our hands. I had literally held his internal organs inside his body after a shapeshifted and very non-Wiccan witch had gutted him. When you've literally held someone's life in your hands, it's more than the word *friend* can hold, but a look, one look can hold it all.

"Then I want to learn how to hunt monsters from you, not Kirkland."

"You can tag along some of the time," I said.

"Sure," Zerbrowski said, "the more the merrier."

"Now, how do I keep Arnet from obsessing about dating me?"

I shook my head. "I have no idea."

Zerbrowski said, "I only ever understood one woman, and she was kind enough to marry me so I didn't have to decipher anyone else."

Brice nodded. "Fair enough." Then he smiled that lopsided charming smile, and it blossomed into a grin. His teeth were white and even like a commercial for dental care. He was strangely perfect in a down-home sort of way. "I'll date Arnet, and see if that takes the heat off you and your men."

"Won't that make her obsess about you, which you were trying to avoid?" I asked.

He shrugged. "I'll date her and a few others. I can date around for a few months and sometimes by then I've been moved to another state, but maybe Arnet will get jealous enough that I'll have to swear off dating anyone at work, and then it will be her fault, not mine."

"Not a bad idea," I said.

"And maybe it will stop her obsessing about your Nathaniel, and the rest of your men."

"You volunteering to take one for the team?" I asked.

He gave me that smile of his.

"You know the smile doesn't work on me, right?"

The smile faltered around the edges, which let me know he knew just how charming it was to have it aimed at someone. "Sorry, I'll remember not to waste smiles on you."

That made me smile and Zerbrowski shake his head. "You just can't help but try to flirt with women, can you?" Zerbrowski asked.

"I like flirting. It's fun, and if I flirt with women, people think that's all I'm interested in."

"It's a way of hiding," I said.

"Yes," he said, and there was no smile now.

"It's exhausting hiding who you are, and who you really love," I said.

He looked down at his hands on the tabletop. "Yeah." There was absolutely no smile as he said that one short word.

I don't know what made me do it, but I reached across the table and put my hand over his; my hand looked small trying to cover his, but it made him look up at me with those sad brown eyes. "I know about having to hide who you love."

That made him smile, a gentle, more "real" smile. He turned his hand in mine, and we were holding hands when Detective Jessica Arnet and most of the rest of the women from work came through the door and saw us.

Never had I ever wished not to have a perfect line of sight between me and a door more than in that moment. Brice looked at my face and whispered, "It's Arnet, isn't it?"

"Yes," I said.

"If I'm dating you, that keeps me safe."

I said, keeping my mouth very still, "If you use me as a beard, I will hurt you."

He squeezed my hand and let go so he could turn his shoulders and smile at the women as they came toward our table. Their faces ranged from cold to outright angry. The angry wasn't from the policewomen, but from some of the office staff. Cops hid their emotions better by the time they got to be detectives. Arnet's face was hard to read, but it wasn't a good look. Her triangular face that looked delicate and pretty most of the time looked harsh, as if her emotions had honed her down to the bone structure underneath. Her eyes were the darkest color I'd ever seen them. Dark eyes get darker when they're angry; pale eyes get paler.

The other women came at her back like a Greek chorus of disapproval. "Are you dating Marshal Brice now, too?"

"No," I said.

Brice stood up, and I knew he was wasting that great smile on them. The other women stared up at him as if the sun had broken through the clouds, and it was a handsome, yummy, bright sun. Arnet kept looking at me.

Brice said, "I was just asking Marshal Blake here, and Detective

Zerbrowski, which of you had boyfriends and such. I had a bit of trouble at one of my posts with a beautiful woman who failed to mention she had a fiancé. I don't poach other men's girlfriends, or fiancés."

"Why ask Anita?"

"Well, I wanted a woman's opinion, because they pay more attention to that sort of thing than men do, and it needed to be a woman that I wasn't interested in, so there'd be no conflict of interest."

Arnet looked at him then. "Did she warn you off some of us?"

"She said you were all available, and charming."

Arnet looked at me. "You didn't say I was charming, did you?"

"No, but it's not me that's standing in front of a handsome, eligible bachelor and getting all pissy at another woman in front of him. That's all on you, Arnet."

That seemed to get through to her, because she blinked and looked at Brice as he moved around her and started talking directly to some of the other women. They let him flatter them, and flattered right back. Arnet watched them for a moment as if she couldn't figure out how to join in, and then Brice turned and looked at her. He smiled and said, "Was wondering if you would do me the honor of being my first date here in St. Louis, Detective Arnet?"

"I'd be happy to," she said, but her voice didn't sound happy. I could no longer see her face, but I was betting she didn't look as gaga for him as the others.

"Let's get these bad guys and we'll talk about details."

She gave him her cell phone number. He took her hand and actually kissed it, and made it all seem charming. The only man who'd ever been able to do that without looking like a fool to me had been Jean-Claude, but he was over six hundred years old, and had come from a time when kissing the hand of a lady was a lot more popular. Most modern men couldn't pull it off.

"You ladies enjoy your food, and we'll see you back at the squad room."

Zerbrowski and I took that as our cue and got up to follow Brice. Arnet caught my arm as I went past her. I fought the urge to push her hand off me. She whispered, low and harsh, "Stay away from this one, Blake."

"Happy to," I said, and kept on walking. She had to either let go, or hold on tighter. She let go. Zerbrowski and Brice were looking back at us, waiting for me to join them. I caught up with Zerbrowski and we followed Brice through the tables to the parking lot.

"What did she say to you?" Zerbrowski asked.

"I've been warned off Brice." I moved toward the Jeep and the men followed me.

"Have I made your problem with Arnet worse?" Brice asked.

"I don't know," I said, as I beeped the keys. I took a deep breath of the fresh late-spring air, and let it out slow.

Brice spoke over the roof of the car. "I'm sorry, Blake, I didn't mean to make it worse."

I climbed behind the wheel. Zerbrowski was already in the passenger seat, buckled up and ready to go. Brice got in the back. "You have to go on a date with her; that's punishment enough," I said, as I started the car.

"How did I start the evening trying to avoid Arnet, and end up having a date with her?"

"Welcome to my life," I said, "though it's usually men for me."

"What do you mean?" Brice asked.

I backed up slowly, waiting for someone behind us to vacate their parking space and not hit us. "Most of the men I've dated have been ones I tried not to date. The ones I love the most, I fell in love with kicking and screaming."

"Really?" Brice said.

"Really," Zerbrowski and I said together. We looked at each other, and then he grinned. I smiled back. "Zerbrowski said it earlier: I used to hate being in love."

"Why?" Brice asked.

I finished easing us out past the idiot driver behind us. They couldn't seem to decide if they were parking or leaving. "Not sure, something about giving up too much control, fear of being hurt, pick something."

"I like being in love," Brice said.

"I like being in love with Katie," Zerbrowski said.

I smiled and eased out into the late-night traffic, which was pretty sporadic in St. Louis. "I like being in love with who I'm in love with now," I said.

"Too many men to list?" Brice asked.

"No, just can't honestly list all the men that are living with me on the *I love you* list, so I'd rather not say the names, in case I hurt someone's feelings."

"We won't tell," Zerbrowski said.

"Neither will I," I said.

"How did you end up living with men you aren't in love with?" Brice asked.

"I don't know you well enough to answer that question, Brice."

"Sorry; have you answered it for Zerbrowski?"

"He hasn't asked."

Zerbrowski held his fist out sideways to me. I touched it gently as I drove. In all the years I'd known Zerbrowski, he'd never asked as many questions as Brice had asked in one evening. I wasn't sure Brice was going to stay on my top-ten list of people I wanted to hang out with, not if he was always this nosy. My life worked, it made me happy, but I didn't owe anyone a diagram of how it worked. Especially not a brand-new U.S. Marshal who had just ridden into town days ago. I realized that it wasn't just Arnet I didn't know much about backgroundwise, but I could fix that. Was Brice just being friendly, or was he fishing? I realized that just by his saying he was gay, I'd let down a lot of my defenses. Zerbrowski and I both had. What if he'd lied? Was I being overly suspicious? Maybe, or maybe until I saw Brice in bed with a man, I'd never really know if he was lying to me, or to Arnet. The only thing I knew for certain was he was lying to somebody.

16

ZERBROWSKI'S PHONE RANG. It was a twangy country song, the kind I didn't think they made anymore. He picked it up and cut the down-home song mercifully short. "Hey, Dolph," he said.

Brice and I listened to Zerbrowski say, "Hostage situation?" The rest of his end was mostly *ums*, and *Shit*, and *SWAT is en route*. "Okay, give me the address." He repeated it out loud to me, and I looked for a side street so I could turn us around without asking questions. If Dolph and Zerbrowski wanted us at a crime scene, there'd be a reason. Zer-browski hung up and said, "They need us sooner than later."

I hit the switch under the dash, and I suddenly had flashy lights. It was a recent addition to my car, and I kept forgetting I had had it in-stalled. It still felt weird to be able to have lights and even sirens. I wasn't too fond of the siren option. I did the lights but would hit sirens only if Zerbrowski insisted, or the traffic got stupid about getting out of the way.

"Why are we doing hostage negotiations?" Brice asked.

"Vampire or lycanthrope involved," I said.

"She's right," Zerbrowski said, "but Keith Bores is also one of the vampires that Shelby gave up when we questioned her. This vamp is so recently dead he's got an ex-wife, a name, a last known address, and two kids under the age of ten."

"Is that where we're going, to their house?" I asked.

"Yes."

"How long dead is Bores?" I asked.

"Less than two years," Zerbrowski said.

"Good," I said.

"Why good?" Brice asked.

"The younger the vampire, the less powerful it is, generally," I said.

"Generally, so not always?"

"No, not always. I know one vampire that's nearly a thousand who will never be a master vampire no matter how long he lives as undead, but then others that hit master vampire power level at around a hundred years."

"Why the difference?" he asked.

"Strength of will, character, dumb luck, no one knows for sure." I had us going in the right direction.

"Are all the vampires we're looking for holed up with him?" Brice asked.

"It looks like it's just Keith Bores, the vampire ex-husband. He and his wife divorced over domestic abuse charges. She has a restraining order against him."

"Had he stayed away from her up to this point?" I asked.

"Looks like," Zerbrowski said.

"Shit," I said.

"What?" Brice asked.

"The vampire doesn't have anything to lose now. He knows he's wanted for murdering the police officers, and that means no trial, no jury, and no lawyer, just one of us hunting him down and killing him. We can't kill him more than once, so he can finally kill the ex-wife and know that he doesn't get punished for it; he's already going to die for killing the cops."

"So he'll take the ex with him," Zerbrowski said.

"Yeah," I said.

"Do any of the other missing vampires have police records, or a history of violence? If Keith Bores has nothing left to lose, then neither do the rest of them," Brice asked.

Zerbrowski and I exchanged a look. He called Dolph back. I started to pray, silently, *Dear God, don't let the rest of them have the same idea.* Because if they did, they could all choose different people to kill, take hostage, or just decide to do the great-bad-thing that they'd always wanted to do, but never did, because they were afraid of getting caught. Now it didn't matter; there was nowhere to go, nothing they could do to save their lives. Once a vampire killed someone, they were the walking dead in so many ways.

17

I PULLED UP at the staging area, which is almost always blocks away, well out of the danger zone, and prepared to wait and be briefed. Brice and I were at the back of the Jeep suiting up when Hill came jogging up to us. "Blake, as soon as you're suited, I'm taking you up."

"What about me?" Brice asked.

Hill looked at him, just a flick of dark eyes. "We know Blake, and what she can do. We've got a spot for her. Don't know you." Under less tense circumstances Hill would have been friendlier to Brice, but we were in the middle of the shit; there was no time.

Zerbrowski said, "Don't feel bad, Brice, she gets all the cute guys."

Brice frowned at him, but let it go.

"Brief me," I said, as I fastened the vest in place and made sure it was tight enough that once I strapped on weapons and ammo they'd be where I left them, not an inch to one side, but exactly where I strapped, holstered, or slid them.

"Keith Bores, thirty when he died, two years past that. He's taken his ex-wife and family hostage. Says he's going to kill her. Says he's got an order of execution on him, so he has nothing to lose, is that true?"

"It's true," I said. "The hostages?"

"Emily Bores, twenty-six, five months pregnant. Her doctor says a sudden shock, being shaken, hit, being dropped to the floor, and she could lose the baby."

I muttered, *Shit*, but kept putting everything in place. At times like this there seemed to be too many guns, too much ammo, too many blades, but later I might need it all.

"Is it Bores's baby?" Brice asked.

We both glanced at him, and then I went back to strapping everything into place. Hill answered for me. "Doesn't matter."

"He'll be less likely to hurt her if it's his," Brice persisted.

"Second husband's baby, but still doesn't matter."

"But . . ."

"Shut up, Brice," I said. To his credit, he did.

"Boy, seven; girl, four; one small dog. Everyone is in the kitchen at the back of the house. He had the wife close the drapes."

"So you're blind, except for infrared," I said.

"Yeah, and he hasn't fed, so he's not showing up well."

"You need me to spot him."

"Yes," Hill said.

"Spot him how? How can Blake see better than the infrared?" Brice asked.

"Explanations later," I said to Brice; to Hill I said, "Has he got control of the hostages using vampire mind tricks?"

"Doesn't seem to; we're hearing crying and some small screams from the wife and kids. They sound aware and unhappy."

"Good that they're not on his side, so they won't fight us, but shooting him in front of the wife and kids is going to be traumatic. She could lose the baby; the kids could be fucked up."

"It's a last resort."

"Why isn't he controlling them with his eyes and mind?" Brice said.

Yes, I'd told him to shut up, but that wasn't the most diplomatic thing to say, so I answered a question as I tightened the last few straps. "It doesn't work automatically, and extreme emotion can keep you safe from mind tricks. She probably hates and fears him. He's a baby vamp; he can't control the situation."

"But . . ."

"Enough." To Hill I said, "I'm suited up, let's do it."

Hill didn't bother to question; he just trusted that I had everything I needed, and he trusted in something else. He started out at a jog down the street. I paced him easily. We were both carrying between twenty-five and fifty extra pounds of equipment, depending on the kind of operation, the speed at which you needed to move, and dozens of variables. He glanced over at me, smiled, and started to run. That was why they'd sent Hill. They were all in damn good shape, but Hill was in exceptional shape, and he ran, not just for exercise, but for endurance. If I'd been human, just human, female and my size, no matter how good a shape I was in, I probably couldn't have kept up with him, but I wasn't human. I was one of the monsters, and my jogging partners were were-animals. Hill was good, but he was only human. My pulse and heart rates were still even, a bit faster, but not much. We ran down the lighted street together, me having to push my pace only because his legs were inches longer than mine.

Hill led me into the first yard. I just turned with him, following the minute tells his body gave for the movements. It was the same way a lion follows a gazelle on the plains, or the way a fighter knows that the next fist is coming at his head; you see micromovements that tell you what the next big movement will be. The grass was harder footing than the road, but I dug in and kept with him. There was a light in the yard, but the yards beyond were more shadows than light. He vaulted the first fence, one-armed. I used two, and had plenty of breath to say, "Show-off."

He gave a low, growly laugh. It wasn't a beast rising, but the testosterone rising. He was male, and he was in an adrenaline rush, and he was finally able to really push his body physically and expend some of that waiting energy. There are things besides lycanthropy and sex that make a man's voice go lower. He hit the fence on the other side of the yard. We went over it, and we kept going over them. We left the lights behind and ran, and climbed, in the suburban dark. I trusted that this was the best way in, and that Hill knew any obstacles, and that we could handle any surprises. I trusted that SWAT had cleared all the houses that needed clearing. I trusted that everyone had done their job before I got there, and all I had to do was mine.

18

HILL AND I arrived behind the house, pulses in our throats, hearts beating, slow and thick, bodies slick with sweat. Sutton and Hermes were waiting for us, lost in the blackness of underbrush and night. I didn't see them in the dark, but I smelled the oil on Sutton's big fucking gun. He'd brought the Barrett .50-caliber, good for stopping charging rhinos, stray elephants, and any kind of preternatural that bullets could harm. In a neighborhood packed this tight with houses I wouldn't have wanted to use it, because if the big bullet missed its intended target, it would keep traveling until it hit something. A .50-caliber bullet would take out most of the chest on a vampire or wereanimal; on a normal human it would take out the upper part of the entire body. To bring the big gun here said something about Sutton's arrogance about his own abilities and his teammate's confidence in him. He'd already put the Barrett on its little tripod stand, so he didn't have to hold the six-foot barrel. He was kneeling on the spread blanketlike surface of the drag bag that he'd carried the gun in; now it was a nice little shooting plat-form thick enough you didn't have to worry about twigs, rocks, broken glass, or whatever. It was like a picnic blanket but without the basket of edible goodies.

Hermes had put some sort of liniment on a joint, probably his knee, because the scent was lower down than the arm. It was a faint, sharp undersmell. Would I have noticed the scents of Sutton's gun oil or Hermes's bum knee if Hill hadn't told me the sniper would be waiting for us? I wasn't sure; maybe not. Hill and I knelt with them in the planted tree line that bordered the Bores yard and the one behind us. There was no light in either yard. It was the thickest dark that I'd seen in any yard. I had a moment to wonder if SWAT had helped the lights to be out, but it didn't matter. We knelt in a pool of darkness and second-growth bushes and small trees, with Sutton, and were as hidden as if we'd been in deep woods. Even if the vampire looked out the window he would miss us. It wasn't his eyes we had to worry about.

I was almost shoulder to shoulder with Hill, so the fact that I could hear his heartbeat, his pulse thudding faintly in his throat, was almost to be expected. I tried to hear Sutton's and Hermes's bodies, and it was more that I could feel the vampire like heat in the dark. I just knew he was there, but again, would I have been so certain of it if I hadn't known it? I hoped not, because that was the real problem with supernaturals; they had other, better senses than normals.

Lincoln's voice whispered in my ear, "Kids and dog are coming out."

Sutton asked, voice low, "Did perp send the dog out, or did the kids insist on taking it?"

"Perp sent it."

"Shit," Sutton and Hermes said together.

Hill said, "Crap."

"What's wrong?" I asked.

"He either sent the dog and kids out so they won't see him kill Mom, or didn't want the dog to bite him," Hill said.

"Either way," Sutton said, "it's not good."

"Spot him for us, Blake," Hermes said.

I didn't argue; I just looked at the side of the house and lowered my control. I used to say that I lowered my metaphysical shields, but I could keep my shields that protected me in place and still strike out through them. It was like having a shield and sword; you could use the sword and still hug your shield to your body. I tried to do that now, with my necromancy. To use my ability with the dead, but not open myself up so that the vampire inside could spot me metaphysically. I'd only recently learned how to use my power and stay more hidden from the undead in a given area; before this it had been like lighting a bonfire every time I used my abilities. Great as a distraction, an attraction, or if I was positive that I could take out whatever was coming to get me. Being able to do it quieter made my psychic gifts way more useful for police work.

I reached out toward the vampire; toward that particular vampire. Again, I used to just reach out to the dead, but now I could "aim" better at vampires that weren't tied directly to me metaphysically. If a vampire was tied to me in some psychic way I could reach out to them pretty easily, but strange vampires were harder. I reached out toward the house, and as silly as it sounded, reaching out with my hand toward the wall of the house helped me aim. It wasn't like pointing and shooting with my finger, but more like my hand was a line of sight so I could look down it, and follow the line of it toward the house. It was just a visual help, something that helped my eyes get out of the way for my mind.

I felt a vampire in the house, but with one I'd never met before I couldn't honestly tell you that it was *the* vampire that we were looking for; I had to rely on the fact that Lieutenant Lincoln had just been talking to him over the phone, and that everyone else told me this was the right vampire. I had to trust that the intelligence was accurate, because even though it wasn't me pulling the trigger, it was still my warrant of execution. It was my presence as a U.S. Marshal with an active warrant that got us a green light for this vampire. Sutton's shooting on a warrant of execution meant there'd be no investigation into the kill. He could fire, kill, and not lose an hour off the job, or a minute talking to

Internal Affairs or anyone else. The snipers loved working with me, because it was always a clean, no-muss, no-fuss kill.

I couldn't really see the vampire. I could feel him, not like touching something with your fingers, but more as if you could touch something with your thoughts, as if thoughts were fingers, hands that could wrap around the vampire, so that I could feel the edges of him.

"He's pacing," I whispered. I closed my eyes so that my real vision would get out of the way. It didn't matter what the side of the house looked like; it didn't matter that there was a scattering of stronger light to one side. What mattered was inside the house. What mattered were things the real, hard eyes couldn't see at all.

"How fast?" Sutton asked.

"Fast." I didn't realize I was moving my hand in time to the pacing until Hill said something.

"Is that his speed?"

I stopped moving my hand, eyes opening wide and glancing at Hill. "I guess so."

"Hermes, spot the woman for me," Sutton said.

Hermes raised a pair of binoculars that were a little too bulky to be "normal" ones. "She's by the floor, sitting with her back to cabinets, not flat enough to be wall."

"Good," Sutton said, and his voice was already going quieter, a little deeper, as he began to slide away into the mind-set that would let him make the shot. He was already lying on the mat that the drag bag unfolded into, snugged up against the big rifle. It was so big that it mounted on a bipod, to help with the weight. Sutton was about to fire a .50-caliber projectile through a wall, into a moving target, and he needed to not just hit it, but hit it square and true, because the last thing we wanted was a wounded vampire inside the house with a hostage, or for that matter a wounded one coming out at us. The fact that there was even the slimmest doubt that hitting the vampire with the Barrett might not bring him down was exactly why Sutton had been given the yes on bringing the big gun in the first place. We hadn't had it happen, but other units in other cities had had vampires and wereanimals keep coming after anything less than a .50, and a couple of nightmare stories about them coming with half their chests missing. It had just been the wrong half of the chest, like the half that didn't contain the heart. Sutton had to take the heart, or head, or both with one shot. Not just damage it, but take it the fuck out; it was the only surety for a true kill.

Lincoln's voice came over the earpieces. "Boy says suspect has a handgun. Repeat, vampire is armed with a handgun."

"Fuck," Hermes said.

"Blake," Sutton said.

I tried to reach out carefully, but the gun changed things. Up to that point I'd thought the vampire would have to get close to the woman to hurt her; now he could stand farther away and kill her. Shit. The spurt of adrenaline brought my shields further down, but it helped me see the vampire better; no loss without a gain.

"He's slowing, turning," I said, and my voice was lower, careful. If the vampire had been older, more powerful, he might have felt my power touching him, looking at him, but either he was just that weak, or he was too emotional to sense anything but his own immediate crisis.

"Turning which way?" Sutton asked, voice squeezed down with concentration.

I used my finger to point. I could never have explained how I knew which way the vampire was looking, but I was sure of it; knew it.

"That's toward the woman," Hermes said.

"Is he aiming?" Sutton asked.

"I can't tell that," I said, "but he's stopped moving. He's still, very still."

"Sight it for me, Blake," Sutton said.

I opened my eyes and did maybe the hardest part. I had to use real, solid, visual landmarks on the house to pinpoint what the inside of my head that would never see anything solid was sensing. I fought to hold on to the feel of the vampire, as I looked with my eyes, and said, "Edge of window, five feet to my right."

"Aiming," Sutton said.

The side of the house was white siding; he needed marks. Fuck! I described a discoloration on the side of the house. "His head's in line with it."

"Can't see it," Sutton said, "my color vision at night isn't as good as yours, Blake." His voice was losing that edge of calm. You could hear the adrenaline tightening through his words; not good.

"Woman has her hands thrown up, like she sees something bad coming. What's the vamp doing, Blake?" Hermes said.

"I think he's moved closer to her."

"You think?" Hills said.

"This isn't like seeing with eyes, damn it." I reached out to the vampire a little further, like the metaphysical equivalent of standing on a ledge, and just a little farther out in space is what you need, so you stretch out your hand toward it, but it's still out of reach. You stretch a little bit farther and . . . anger, rage, such rage. It was like a red fire, blazing, consuming, filling my brain for a second. It was the vampire. I was feeling his emotion. "God, he's so angry," I said.

"Blake, give me something!" Sutton said.

There were no landmarks to give him. If I could have touched the vampire, maybe I could have eaten his anger like I did to Billings, but from a distance, I didn't know how to do that. I did the only thing I could think of; I dropped my shields and called the vampire. It was like I was still on that ledge, but the thing just out of reach was so important that I leaned too far, and if you lean too far, you fall. I hadn't allowed myself to drop shields like this in months. I called the dead, and I felt that vampire turn and look at me. He was too young, too weak—my necromancy could call really old shit—and he turned and looked at me, because I willed him to see me. Vampires used to kill necromancers on sight, and there was a good reason for that, because all the dead like us, respond to us at some level.

"He's looking at us," I said, "but I can't hold him like this forever."

"Give him to me, Blake," Sutton said.

"Laser-sight him for Sutton," Hill said.

I was concentrating so hard on the vampire in front of us that it took me a second to come back to myself and realize that he was right; I had a laser sight on my AR. I looked down at it as if it had just appeared in my hand.

"Can you hold concentration on the vampire and use the gun?" Hill asked.

It was a good question. I could feel the vampire motionless in the house, feel him struggle a little as I split more of my concentration between him and the reality of the gun in my hands. "We'll find out. I'll know if I lose him, and he's moving again."

But sighting for Sutton wasn't as simple as me aiming at the vampire with my gun while I was standing. That wouldn't help the prone officer aim; I needed to be in his physical space to aim right for him.

Hill said it. "You're small enough, and he's big enough; just lie across him and sight your gun down his barrel."

It was the best idea we had, so I put my body on top of the big officer where he lay on the ground. I held the vampire in my head but had to move my body more, so my concentration was less pure on the vampire. He started to struggle free of me; his rage, that I could have eaten if I'd touched him, now acted like a pry bar to work me away from him. I fought to concentrate on the inside of my head, and the outside with my body, and hold both together. Sutton was so much bigger than me that most of my body was on just his upper body when I lay down, but I couldn't get the angle I needed to aim along the long barrel.

"I can't hold the shot with you on me like this," Sutton said.

"It's not working for the spot either," I said. The vampire was struggling now; I threw a little more concentration his way and he quieted, but I couldn't keep this up forever. I had a smart idea. "Tell the woman to try to leave the room while I hold the vampire. Maybe we don't have to shoot to save her."

Hill didn't argue, just spoke into his mike. Hermes said, "She's up, and moving."

The vampire's rage flared like gasoline thrown on a fire. "Stop," I said, "stop moving her. It's pissing him off. He'll break free of me before she can exit the room."

We were back to our original idea. "Sit up," Hill said.

I tried sitting at Sutton's waist, but I was too short to reach what I needed to with my gun, so finally I ended up half-kneeling, half-sitting on Sutton's lower back and leaning over his shoulder.

"Put less weight on my shoulders if you can," Sutton said.

It was like leaning on him, and not, a careful balance of being so close, so that the heat and rhythm of him was just below me, and yet not touching too much, not putting too much weight so I didn't fuck with his hold, his aim, his sniper mojo. It took too much concentration. I leaned over his shoulder, sliding my AR down his Barrett, but not directly on top; there was too much on the bottom of the AR to make it a smooth slide.

The vampire was almost free. I fought to hold him, and hit the AR against the Barrett. "Don't do that," Sutton said in a tight voice.

"Sorry," I muttered. I called out to the vampire, threw my power into him like a spear. I felt it stagger him, but I also knew that I'd have to let him go to do the other part. Fuck. I hit him one more time; all that necromancy aimed at him staggered him, so that I think he had to grab the kitchen cabinets to stay upright, and in that split second I leaned over Sutton's body, married my gun along his as close as I could, and aimed where I knew the vampire's head would be. Sutton's point of light followed mine like a red-and-green game of tag on the side of the house. I held my red dot steady, and breathed, "There."

Sutton's green dot covered mine. I held my breath, willed my body still, even as I felt his go still underneath me. We held our breaths together, and in that moment of sinking stillness and concentration at that one bright dot, the vampire ripped himself free of me. Sutton fired, and the recoil moved him enough that I slid off, tumbling to one side. I got to my knees, sighting at the house, to find a surprisingly small hole in the white siding.

I could hear the woman screaming inside.

"Did we get him?" Hill said, almost yelling.

"Blake," Sutton said.

I reached out to the vampire, and found . . . "Dead, down, done."

And they accepted that. They gave the all clear, and let officers enter the house from the front, and the only confirmation they had that the vampire was dead was me and my psychic abilities. There were other police officers in St. Louis and elsewhere who didn't trust me or my abilities, but this team did. Sutton, Hermes, and Hill trusted me enough to send the rest of their team into a house with a rogue vampire, with only my say-so that it was no longer a threat.

I heard the other SWAT team members over the radio moving through the house room by room, calling "Clear" as they moved. Hill started up the yard toward the house with his gun at his shoulder. I put my AR to mine and followed Hill, because when your team moves, you move; when they put their guns to their shoulders and start into a house, you go with them. Sutton and Hermes brought up the rear, because they'd packed the Barrett up, and the four of us moved toward the house, guns up, watching for threats. Over the radios we heard, "House secure. Hostage secured . . . Suspect down."

There were no other bad guys in the house. The pregnant ex-wife was being taken out to the waiting ambulance. The vampire was dead. It was a good night.

19

DAWN HAD WASHED the world in soft, golden light by the time I started driving for home. I had texted before I got in the car, letting Nathaniel and Micah know that I was headed their way. I got a typed "kisses" back from Nathaniel, and a "Putting on coffee now." I'd sent "kisses" back, and started driving.

Micah's ring tone sounded. I actually had a Bluetooth earpiece; it made me feel all high-tech. "Hey, my Nimir-Raj, I'll be home in about thirty."

"Good morning, my Nimir-Ra," and there was that edge of smile and just happiness that his voice had held for so long when he called me his.

"You guys should still be asleep. I texted instead of called, so I wouldn't wake you." I was driving on old Route 21 with the early-morning light streaming through the late-spring trees. The leaves were still that tender green, fresh, with its undertone of golds and yellows. It made me think of a poem. "Nature's first green is gold," I said out loud, too tired to just think it.

"What?" Micah asked.

"It's a poem; the trees made me think of it. 'Nature's first green is gold, Her hardest hue to hold. Her early leaf's a flower; But only for an hour,' and I can't remember the rest."

Micah said, "I can. 'Then leaf subsides to leaf. So Eden sank to grief, So dawn goes down to day. Nothing gold can stay.'"

"How did you know the whole poem?" I asked.

"My dad's favorite poet is Robert Frost. He used to read Frost poems to us, and quote him a lot."

"I thought your dad was a sheriff."

"He was, maybe still is."

"A sheriff who loved poetry and quoted it in his everyday conversation, that's nifty."

"Hey, you quoted it first," he said softly, and again there was that edge of happiness in his voice, contentment maybe.

"True; you know, there's no reason you can't get in touch with your family now."

"What do you mean?" and the happy tone was gone, replaced by suspicion. Crap; I wished I'd kept my mouth shut, but I'd been meaning to say something for a few months, and . . .

"You estranged yourself from your family because Chimera used the other lycanthropes' families against them, but he's been dead a few years now."

"You killed him for me," he said, voice quiet, but still without that happy undertone.

I took a deep breath, let it out, and plowed ahead. I was nothing if not relentless. "And then you wanted to make sure you were safe here in St. Louis."

"And then the Mother of All Darkness started trying to eat us all," Micah said.

"But she's gone now, Micah. There's no one left to hurt your family if you show that you care about them."

"There will always be more bad guys, Anita; you've taught me that."

Just hearing him say that made me sad. "I hate that it's something you learned from me."

"Not just you," he said.

"It's just that you seem to like your family, and miss them. I don't see mine, because I don't get along with my stepmother or stepsister."

"I'll get in touch with my family after you take us to see yours," he said.

"Us?" I said.

"Yes, Anita, I love you, but who would you take home to meet your dad? One of us, both of us, more?"

"I wasn't planning on going home," I said.

"But if you did, who would you take as your boyfriend?"

"No vampires; my Grandmother Blake is a little crazy. She'd go apeshit around Jean-Claude."

"Okay, then who?"

"You, Nathaniel, I think."

"And who would I take home?"

I sighed, and wished I had left the entire topic the fuck alone. I was too tired for this kind of conversation. "Are you saying that you don't want to take Nathaniel home to meet your family?"

"No, I'm saying that if I go home to my family I need to take you and Nathaniel. The three of us have been a couple from the beginning, and it's been two years. Two years that have been wonderful, and that wouldn't have been as wonderful if Nathaniel hadn't been with us."

I said the only thing I could to that. "Nathaniel is part of our . . . coupleness. I mean, our ménage à trois, or trio, or whatever you call it."

"Exactly," he said, "so how can I go home without both of you?"

"Are you saying you don't want to take both of us?" I asked.

"I'm not sure how my parents would take me bringing another man home, especially after the horrible things I said to them to convince Chimera I didn't give a damn about them."

I drove in the growing light, and the bright spring trees, and felt vaguely depressed. "I love you, and Nathaniel," I said.

"Me, too," he said.

He said he loved Nathaniel as often as he said he loved me, but for the first time I wondered if he loved us the same way. Did he love me more because I was a girl and he was heterosexual? Okay, technically because of Nathaniel he was heteroflexible, but still, the point was the same. Did Micah love me more, because I wasn't a boy? Did he love Nathaniel less because of it? I knew that Nathaniel love-loved Micah, just like he did me, but I had never asked my oh-so-once-straight boyfriend how he felt about having a male "friend." Had he ever introduced Nathaniel as his boyfriend? No. He'd kissed him in public, but . . . It was too confusing for me tonight. I was too tired to wrap my head around the complexities of it.

I finally said, "I just want to come home and wrap the two of you around me and hold on."

He was quiet for a moment, and then said, "You aren't going to push? You aren't going to make me declare undying love for both of you, or something like that?" He sounded surprised.

I was a little surprised, too, but out loud I said, "I don't think so."

He laughed then, and said, "Are you that tired?"

"I got called a monster by someone I thought was my friend once, and people died, cops died, and . . . I just want to come home and climb into bed between the two of you, and drown in the feel of your hands on me for a while, and sleep."

"That sounds perfect," he said, and his voice was relieved, as if he'd been dreading my pushing the topic.

"Good," I said, and knew I sounded relieved, too.

"But I'll warn you that Sin is awake and upset," Micah said. "You'll have to talk to him before you can do much of anything else."

I tried to not be angry about it. "Cynric knew what I did for a living, Micah. He met me as a U.S. Marshal on a job."

"But he's never seen fresh bodies on the ground and known that you were part of the firefight. It's hard the first few times, Anita, and he's terribly young."

"He's eighteen," I said, and now I sounded defensive.

"I'm not saying he's too young for . . . dating. I'm saying he's too young to cope with seeing you striding through a bunch of freshly dead vampires without freaking out a little, that's all."

"You weren't going to say *dating*, were you?" I sounded almost sullen, and I couldn't seem to help it.

"You know how you don't want to push about how I feel about Nathaniel meeting my family?" he asked.

"Yeah," and sullen turned into wary in my voice, and in my stomach.

"I feel the same about your guilt over having someone this young in your bed. You didn't set out to make him yours, any more than I planned on being part of a threesome with you and Nathaniel. Sometimes things happen, but just because you didn't plan them doesn't mean they aren't good things."

I sighed. "You're right, I do feel guilty about Sin, and I so hate the nickname."

"His full name is Cynric, and he doesn't want to be Rick."

"I know, but I'd send him home if I could."

"You can send him back to Vegas, Anita. He's your blue tiger to call and he obeys you."

I had to focus on the sharp turn between all the morning-lit trees, almost like I'd lost concentration on the driving for a second. He'd surprised me again. "I thought you were one of the ones who told me it would be cruel to send Sin back?"

"I did, but just because I disagree with it doesn't mean you can't do it," Micah said.

I thought about the wording of what he'd just said. Was he hinting that if I did something stupid and all guilt-ridden about my youngest lover, he might do the same about his only male lover? Or was I over-thinking it? Well, yeah, I was overthinking it, but Micah tended to overthink, too, so maybe I was thinking just enough? God, that was too convoluted.

"Truce," I said.

"What do you mean?" he asked, and he sounded cautious, maybe even suspicious.

"No issues that will implode any parts of our personal life tonight, okay?" I said.

I could almost hear him smile over the phone. "That sounds good,

Anita; that sounds very good." He sounded tired, too, and I realized that while I'd been out catching bad guys, he'd been home calming down a teenage weretiger and being the rock of calm for Nathaniel and anyone else who had stressed about the danger in my job tonight.

"Thanks, Micah," I said.

"For what?" he asked.

"For being you, for being there, for being my sweetie, for being in my life."

"You're welcome, and I wouldn't want to be anywhere else, or with anyone else."

"Even with the danger and the preternatural politics?" I asked.

"I dragged you into the preternatural politics the first time we met."

"I was already pretty deep into them before you came along," I said.

"Maybe, but I'm good at the politics, and you help me be better."

"I could argue that you help me be better at them, but okay."

"Hurry home," he said.

"I am," I said.

"I love you," he said.

"I love you, too," I said. We did that couple thing where neither of you wants to hang up, but it finally felt silly and I hung up first. I loved Micah and Nathaniel. I loved us as a "couple." We worked. We worked better than any relationship I'd ever tried. Hell, the two of them helped my other relationships work better. Micah donated blood to Jean-Claude, and let him be on his short list of men he was willing to be naked with, and in bed with, though only Nathaniel was allowed to cross certain barriers. Nathaniel was Micah's exception as Jade had become mine. My life had become something that I could never have planned even a year before, but as Micah said, just because you didn't plan something didn't make it a bad thing. It was just a thing, and one of the unintended things in my life was an eighteen-year-old weretiger who was having his first how-could-you-risk-your-life-and-scare-the-hell-out-of-me moment about my job. I was not looking forward to trying to reassure him, because Micah was right, I had serious issues about Cynric, Sin, God, what a nickname. It just drove home everything that bothered me about the kid, and that was the problem. I still saw him as a kid, and yet he was my lover, so I guess I didn't really see him as a kid, but he was so young. Not just young in years, but sheltered, inexperienced . . . young in that wet-behind-the-ears, haven't-seen-enough-or-done-enough way. I'd been his first lover, and yes, we'd all been mind-raped by the biggest, baddest vampire of them all. It had been done in a cold bid to keep me busy while nefarious plotting went on, but whatever or whoever had done it, I'd still taken Cynric's virginity as part of a metaphysical orgy. It still embarrassed me to think about it, what little I could remember of it. It had been like being blackout drunk, with only glimpses remembered even now.

I'd been his first, and I hated it. No, I felt guilty, because I didn't love him. Even after almost a year of him being with us, I still didn't love him. I liked him, and I had sex with him often enough, so I guess I like-liked him, but I didn't love him. I didn't come close to caring for him the way I cared for others in my life; a long list of others in my life were ahead of him in my affections, and that was why I felt guilty. I'd been the white knight riding in to rescue him and give him all his firsts, which meant I was supposed to ride off into the sunset and live happily ever after with him, but I'd done that once with Nathaniel, and that had worked out really well. Come to think of it, I'd worked really hard to not love Nathaniel, too. He'd made me feel guilty for other reasons, but still I'd fought long and hard against loving him. Hadn't I fought against loving Jean-Claude, too?

I was almost at the driveway to the house. Crap, did I always fight before I loved someone? No, not always. I'd tried to love Richard from almost the beginning, and I had loved Micah from the beginning. Two men out of how many? Too many. Crap, I wished I hadn't thought of it that way, because now I felt guilty and stupid. Was Cynric just one more guy that I'd fight against caring for and eventually I'd feel for him what I felt for Nathaniel, or Jean-Claude? Crap, crap, crap, crap! I soooo wished I hadn't thought of it like that.

20

I GOT OUT of the Jeep, which was second in the line of cars behind the already filled garage. When we were all home, and the bodyguards had their own cars, it was a lot of cars. The guards tried to keep the cars down, and changing, so no one watching could figure out how many, and who was guarding us at any given time, but it was still a lot of vehicles.

I had a sense of movement to the side of the house and made eye contact with Bram for a second; his skin was dark and almost truly black, but in leopard form he was spotted. Since others with paler skin were black leopards, I'd asked, and learned that your animal's coloring had nothing to do with your genetics as a person, but everything to do with the genetics of the line of beasts you descend from, so if you come from a line of leopards that run high to spotted yellow leopards, that's what you'll be, no matter how pale or dark your human form may be. I didn't nod at that brief glimpse of him, as he melted back out of sight; there was just the "seeing" of each other. If someone was watching us, it was unlikely that my acknowledging him any more than what I'd just done would give him away. Bram was ex-military and had been a combat vet before a wereleopard attack had ended his military career for "health" reasons. He and his usual guard partner, Ares, a werehyena and ex-military sniper, had broken all of us of nodding, waving, or acknowledging the guards on duty in any way. They'd pissed and moaned about it, until we all learned better. I wouldn't have waved, but once I would have given the smallest nod.

I tried the door handle before trying the key, because not everyone locked the door. It opened and I stepped into my house. The living room was dim, curtains still pulled, but laughter, talking, and bright morning light spilled through the open archway that led to the kitchen. It was a happy murmur of voices, not that fake murmur you get at a party sometimes where people are struggling to have a good time, trying to find things to talk about; no, this was a group of people who knew and liked each other and had things to share. I put my equipment bags down by the door. The smell of baking bread and bacon filled the air.

Micah stood in our bedroom door across the living room. He was on the phone. He waved, smiling, his green-gold leopard eyes shining in the dimness, catching what light there was and magnifying it. He was my height, built so delicate that almost any clothes hid that there was muscle underneath, and only the athletic set of shoulder to slender waist and hips hinted how much he worked out. He was wearing a T-shirt that fit us both; we even had a few pairs of jeans that we could share. I'd never dated anyone as tiny as I was; I sort of liked it.

I started to go to him, for a kiss, but what he said into the phone stopped me. He was going to need to concentrate on the call. "Stephen, you are not your father. You will not abuse like he did." Micah pushed his dark brown curls back over his shoulder, frowning. Stephen was a werewolf, so he should have been making this comfort call to his Ulfric, wolf king, but Micah had become de facto leader for almost the entire furry community, because he actually led, and wasn't pretending to be anything but who and what he was; the Ulfric, Richard Zeeman, was still trying to have a Clark Kent life and hide that he was also Superman, um, wolf, so he was at school teaching college students about biology. At least he wasn't at the junior high anymore, where being outed as a werewolf would have certainly cost him his job. The college would have a harder time with it.

Stephen and his twin brother had been horribly abused by their father, so he was terrified that his fiancée wanted to have a baby. Stephen was convinced that he would abuse a child, as his own father had done. Therapy can get you only so far with exorcising your childhood nightmares; after that it's willpower, and you, and people you can trust to hold your hand along the way. "I have faith in you, Stephen," Micah said. "If you don't want to have a child, that's your choice . . ." He listened for a minute, and then said, "Vanessa is set on children, I know that. I'm sorry she's given you the ultimatum, Stephen, but that's her choice, too." You think being leopard king and queen, Nimir-Raj and Nimir-Ra, would give you power to rule, and it does, but you also end up being part parent, part therapist, part carrot, part stick, part cheerleader, and part disciplinarian. I did my best, but Micah was really good at it.

I blew him a kiss; he pantomimed one back and went into the bedroom and closed the door. He'd be talking Stephen down for a while. I was honestly beginning to believe that Stephen wasn't going to work through his issues in time to save his relationship with Vanessa, and that was sad, because they loved each other to pieces, but anyone who ever said love conquers all was a fucking liar. Love is a good place to start, but it's a start, not an end.

I washed my hands in the hallway bathroom before I went into the kitchen. You didn't go to breakfast with the possibility of blood under your fingernails. There wasn't any blood on my hands, but . . . there had been in the past, and washing my hands when coming in from work had just become a ritual, like I was cleansing myself of more than just germs and potential crime scene schmutz.

Nathaniel was half bent over, taking something out of the oven. His auburn braid curled on the floor, because it was just that long, falling nearly to his ankles. He was wearing only a pair of jeans so worn they were almost white, and his dark purple chef's apron across his muscular upper chest. I knew the apron made his lavender eyes look very close to true purple. He'd been my live-in sweetie for nearly three years. I knew what his eyes looked like in the new apron, or the old ones.

Nicky was at the stove in a T-shirt that strained over his massive, muscular upper body. He had jean shorts on that had been cut down from an old pair of jeans, so they accommodated the swell of his thighs. He was tall enough to carry the extra muscle at just about six feet. He had a kitchen towel tucked into the front of his shorts, because aprons were not his thing. That he'd put on a shirt to protect himself from the bacon he was frying up in a pan was all the concession I'd ever seen Nicky make to domesticity. He didn't live with us, officially, but he was with us a lot. We always had bodyguards, and he was one of the best we had. He was also my werelion to call, and my lover, though not exactly my sweetie.

Nathaniel lifted weights because he was an exotic dancer, so only to a point. Nicky lifted because he was a bodyguard, and he liked lifting. His body showed how much. His blond hair was cut short in the back and halfway down the sides, a skater's cut, but the bangs were actually a wedge shape, one part in a straight, yellow triangle of hair that trailed halfway down his face. It looked very anime, but it wasn't just a fashion statement; it hid his empty eye socket from where he'd lost his eye long before he became a werelion, or my bodyguard.

Cynric—Sin—was the last one at the business side of the kitchen. His dark blue hair had grown long enough that he usually put it in a pony-tail to cook. I got a glimpse of the blue-on-blue of his tiger eyes. Most people didn't catch that his eyes weren't human, because they didn't think that tigers came with blue eyes, but the clan weretigers were dif-ferent from all the other wereanimals, because they were born with tiger eyes and hair that wasn't always human-normal, like Cynric's deep, almost navy blue hair. He was wearing dark blue jeans; he'd grown four inches in the last year, so we'd had to buy him new pants, so he had no old jeans that still fit. That tended to happen when you were eighteen. He was taller than Nathaniel, and almost the same height as Nicky, though his shoulders didn't have Nathaniel's spread, and he looked damn near willowy beside Nicky, but then most of the men did. I realized that with all three of them turned away from me, Sin didn't look like a little boy anymore. He'd filled out in the weight room and thanks to the new preternatural football league and track. He was Missouri's quarterback, and we had coaches from some serious schools scouting him. A preternatural college league had started last year, and the amateur preternatural adult men's league was one of the top money draws on pay TV, so the colleges had gotten on board, and we were probably only a few months away from a professional league.

Gina was setting the table. Her dark, nearly black hair was short and curled sort of artfully around her face. When my hair was that short, it wasn't artful, just messier, but then some curls are better behaved than others. Gina was tall, nearly six feet; her dark gray eyes were looking more at her husband and baby than at the dishes, so the settings were a little crooked as she moved around the table, but I didn't care; perfect place settings were overrated and the happiness on her face as she watched them was worth it.

Zeke was in half-man form, which meant he looked like most of the movie werewolves you've ever seen, except that his eyes were human. Usually when someone was stuck in animal form their eyes were the first things to go animal, and stick, but for some reason Zeke had done the opposite. His blue human eyes were trapped in the face of a movie monster. The baby in his lap looked up, laughing, and he had his father's eyes, except it was a very human face, with short dark hair just beginning to get long enough to prove he was going to have his mother's curls.

They were living with us because the baby hadn't been getting enough sunlight underneath the Circus of the Damned. The baby had started getting agoraphobic when he was outside the underground, like some kind of post-apocalyptic survivor. They'd been here two months and it had made a world of difference in Chance. He was getting some color in his cheeks and was just a much happier kid.

Nathaniel gave me a brilliant smile as he turned bread in his mitted hands and saw me. He put the bread on the cooling racks by the sink, and took the mitts off as he moved toward me. Sin turned from stirring something and smiled; some thought or emotion chased across his face so fast that I couldn't read it, but it wilted his smile around the edges for a minute, whatever it had been. He finally said, "Hey, Anita. Glad you're home."

There it was, a simple sentence that stood in for a whole bunch of words that might get said later, or might never get spoken out loud. At least he'd know not to say out loud, *I was worried about you*, or *How could you scare me like that, or risk us*, or . . . Richard Zeeman, my onetime serious boyfriend, had been the only one currently on the edges of my life who had said those kind of things out loud. It was why he was on the edge of my life, and not in the kitchen helping with breakfast.

Nicky started taking the bacon out of the pan with tongs. The bacon looked very crisp, just the way I liked it. He glanced back at me and said, "Breakfast is almost ready."

Gina and Zeke said hello, and the baby laughed, that low gurgly laugh that some boy babies have, and girl babies never seem to.

I said hi to everyone, but walked to meet Nathaniel in the middle of the kitchen floor. He'd tossed his oven mitts on the kitchen island, and rolled toward me in that sexy, swinging walk that he used onstage, the roll of his lovely hips that made the customers at Guilty Pleasures scream with delight, but this show was all for me. It was also the real deal. It was hard to explain how it was different, but there was a difference, or maybe what was different was what happened next.

I smiled and he smiled back. His lavender eyes were darker and not just from the purple apron that covered his bare chest. His eyes showed his emotions; richer color meant happy him, though truly purple dark eyes were angry him. It would be three years together in about a month; I knew his face the way I knew my own, maybe better. I didn't spend much time gazing into my own eyes. The smile he gave me was one you never saw at the club; it was a smile that filled his eyes with . . . love. That he loved me was there in his eyes, in his face, and I knew my face reflected it back like water reflects the sun back at itself, in a blinding dazzle of happy light.

My arms slid around his waist, hands sliding over the rougher fabric of the apron, to the smooth, muscled glide of his bare waist and back. God, he felt so good, just that much, and it made me close my eyes for a moment. He pulled me into his body, so that we touched from chest to groin. He didn't press me too tightly, just touching, so to truly feel if he was happy to see me I'd have had to grind myself against him. I didn't, because we weren't alone, but he had a smile on his face that let me know that he knew I'd thought about it. The smile was mostly mischievous, with an edge of wicked fun, and in his eyes was a confidence that he knew exactly how he affected me, and just how beautiful he was. Once he'd believed that only his beauty and his ability at sex made him worth anything, but he knew he was so much more to me than just that; it had given him a confidence that he hadn't had when I first met him.

"Kiss," Cynric said, "so the rest of us can have a turn."

I gave him an unfriendly look, but Nicky added, "Food's getting cold, Anita."

Nathaniel just leaned his extra height downward, curving his body toward me. I would have argued with everyone, but Nathaniel just went with it, which made me rise up on the balls of my feet and lean my face up toward his.

We kissed, a brush of lips that became a caress of mouths, but chaste by our usual standards. I drew back from the kiss, my hand behind his neck, gazing up into his eyes at that startlingly close distance. I wanted to push my tongue between his lips, to do so much more with my hands, but we had an audience, and especially the baby. There was a time when I wouldn't have worried about a baby that young, assuming he wouldn't pay attention, but Matthew, who was now three, belonged to a widow of one of Jean-Claude's vampires, and we babysat Matthew sometimes. He insisted that he get a kiss from me every time I saw him. But what creeped me was that he wanted a kiss on the mouth, like the other big boys, because all the big boys kiss 'Nita. His mother, Monica Vespucci, thought it was cute. I didn't. Matthew had obviously formed very firm opinions of grown-up behavior, at what I thought was too young an age to care.

Nathaniel and I had discussed how bothered I was about the toddler's attitude, so he just let me go with a smile, raising my hand up to lay his lips against my knuckles, and then moving back to start cutting the cooling bread into thick toast-size pieces.

Nicky and Cynric came forward at the same time. They looked at each other. Cynric was nearly as tall as Nicky now, but Nicky was still almost three times as broad across the shoulders and chest, which meant the younger man looked almost fragile beside him.

"I'm her blue tiger to call," Cynric said. His hands were in loose fists at his sides. He was visibly fighting to keep his shoulders from hunching up, or to keep from giving any of those secondary clues that men do before a fight starts.

"And I'm just her Bride of Dracula, her cannon fodder," Nicky said, but there was nothing in his voice that said he thought that was a bad thing, or a lesser thing.

"Exactly," Cynric said.

"If we were doing some formal vampire thing, you'd go first, but this is just us in our kitchen, and by shapeshifter rules I can still beat the shit out of you."

I must have made some involuntary movement, because Nathaniel said, "Anita." It made me look at him where he stood across the kitchen. He shook his head. I was supposed to let them work it out. I trusted Nathaniel's opinion in that moment, but if it came to a fight I was stopping it.

"Almost everyone in Micah's pard can beat him up, but they let him lead, they respect him as their Nimir-Raj." Cynric didn't sound angry, just trying to understand.

Nicky nodded. "True, but you don't just earn leadership by beating up people; it's one of the reasons I wasn't the Rex of my old lion pride. I probably could have won the fight with our king, but he was a better leader than I was, and I knew that without having to fight him."

Cynric frowned, face going all serious. "But your old Rex was a fighter and a mercenary; Micah isn't."

It was Gina who spoke; her face wasn't happy now. Her dark eyes were haunted as she moved toward them. "Micah saved me; he saved us all. He offered himself to Chimera in our place. He was powerful enough that Chimera couldn't force him into animal form as a punishment like he could Zeke. Micah changed into his leopard form and took the punishment, even though he didn't know if he'd ever come back to human form again. That's why his eyes are leopard eyes. His eyes were brown before." The tall woman hunched in on herself, hugging herself as if she were cold in the warm kitchen.

Zeke spoke in that gravelly deep voice from where he sat at the table. "You have no idea what it's like to be trapped for weeks in animal form. You think you will go mad, and then you hope you become all animal, because then at least you won't know, won't remember being human."

The baby in his lap had stopped laughing and was watching his father's face in that solemn baby way, as if he were filing it all away.

Cynric went to Gina and hugged her. "I'm so sorry, Gina, I didn't mean to make you sad." He hugged her tight, stroking her hair like you'd soothe a child. He looked at the werewolf. "I'm sorry, Zeke, I won't bring it up again."

Gina hugged him back, and turned, wiping tears away, and went back to her husband and baby.

Cynric motioned to Nicky. "You get your kiss first, and not because you'd win a fight with me. You're right, dominance isn't just about who's stronger, sometimes it's about being smarter, and I so am not today. I knew better than to bring all that up in front of them."

Nicky gripped his shoulder. "You learn a lot faster than I did at your age, Sin."

Cynric grinned and rolled his eyes. "Is that a compliment, or should I be insulted?"

Nicky gave him a little push with his hand, grinning back. The small push moved Cynric back by inches. Nathaniel was smiling at both of them. Our eyes met across the kitchen and his seemed to say, *See, I told you they'd work it out.* I could only smile back.

Nicky turned to me, face still shining with humor. He wrapped me in his big arms, pulling us close together. I had other men in my life who were taller than Nicky, but no one as muscled up. Truthfully, it was a little too much of a good thing for my preference, but it had just become Nicky, and I knew how to wrap my much smaller body around him, cuddling in among all those muscles, all that strength. Every man in my life had his own feel, his own taste, his own style of . . . most things. Nicky was like a muscle sandwich of manly goodness.

I went up on tiptoe to meet him, his body and chest wrapping around me, so it was like sliding up between all that muscle to reach his lips, and kiss. The kiss was gentle, and then he turned us so that his broad back was all that Gina, Harold, and little Chance would see. Nicky changed the kiss from gentle to something with tongue and teeth, until my fingers tensed in his back and I fought against digging nails into him where they'd see. I drew back, my voice breathy. "Enough, Nicky, enough."

He grinned down at me. "I may never be your main honey-bun, but I love that you react to me like that."

My vampire powers came through Jean-Claude, and he was descended from the bloodline of Belle Morte, Beautiful Death, and her power was seduction and sex, but something had changed between her and Jean-Claude, so that his power wasn't just sex, but had love in there somewhere, and my power went further in that direction, like some kind of vampire dating evolution. Belle had been able to make her "victims" obsessed with her, addicted to her, and she felt very little in return, but Jean-Claude had to be careful not to care too much when he used his vampire powers, and Nicky had been one of the last of my victims where I hadn't had enough control to save myself completely. It felt good to touch Nicky, good to have his arms wrapped around me. If you hadn't had anything to compare it to, you'd think it was love, as in True Love, but it wasn't. It was more a kind of obsession, and no matter what the movies and books say, obsession isn't love, though as he held me, face shining with the kiss, my heartbeat still rapid from the touch of his lips, it was kind of hard to tell the difference. I didn't feel about him the way that I felt about Nathaniel, or Micah, or Jean-Claude, but did that really make it not love, or just love of a different kind? I tried to stop poking at what love was, and wasn't, but . . . sometimes you just gotta poke the badger with the spoon; I'd just learned not to poke it too often. Badgers get pissy when you poke them too much.

Part of the power of the *ardeur*, the fire of Belle Morte's line, was that you could control someone only as much as you were willing to be controlled, only force them to love you as much as you loved them, only make them lust for you as much as you were willing to burn for them. Belle Morte hadn't had that side effect, but Jean-Claude had an edge of it that he could control; I had more problems, but then I was still alive, still human. Maybe that made it harder for me to be cold enough to force someone to want me, love me, without risking my own libido and heart?

Nicky moved out of my arms and Cynric moved into them. I was suddenly looking up into his blue eyes with their circle of navy blue around the pupils and the pale sky blue in its outer ring of color. The morning sunlight made his hair in its loose ponytail very blue. In dimmer light you could pretend it was that shade of black that had blue highlights, but the light was too bright. There was no pretending that that thick, straight hair wasn't a rich, deep shade of blue. It wasn't dyed, but the mark of his other form, his blue tiger.

I wrapped myself around him, the feel of him familiar so that we both knew where our hands went, our arms wrapped, our bodies touched. We'd spent a year discovering how it all worked between us, but . . . I looked up into that handsome, but too-young face, and was still almost as conflicted as I had been a year ago.

"What?" he asked softly.

I shook my head. "You just seem fragile after hugging Nicky."

Cynric laughed, and glanced at the other man. "Everyone's fragile after hugging Nicky."

I nodded. "Truth," I said.

Cynric hadn't been my victim of choice. The Mother of All Darkness had bound us together because she'd had a plan that needed me distracted and powerful, and the fact that he was sixteen and a virgin, and we didn't know each other, hadn't mattered to a being that wanted to drown the world in blood and death. What was one person's innocence compared to all the death and terror she'd brought over the thousands of years of her existence? If you thought about it that way, what she'd done to Cynric and me was almost kind—almost.

He turned back to me, face still shining with the laughter of joking with the other two men. I hadn't even heard what they were saying, until he said, "I'm young; I still have growing to do. I'm already taller."

"Enjoy the height, kid," Nicky said, "because that's all that's going to be bigger."

"So not," Cynric said.

"So too," Nicky said.

Nathaniel walked laughing between the men, carrying the freshly cut and richly scented bread on a serving plate. We all followed the wonderful aroma of the bread like lions scenting a gazelle. My stomach suddenly let me know just how hungry I was.

Zeke joined in the masculine laughter, and even Gina laughed, that higher, pleasant woman's laugh. The baby joined in, totally not getting the joke, but Chance had already learned that when everyone laughed, you laughed. He'd had a lot of practice at laughing living here. I smiled up at Cynric as he turned back to me. He laughed a lot more here than he had when he first came from Vegas. That was a good thing.

He studied my face, still smiling, but his eyes were trying to read mine. "What?" he asked, and even his voice held that edge of happiness.

I shook my head. "Kiss me, so we can eat."

He grinned, and it made his face look even younger and less perfect in some ways, but there was the faintest edge of smile lines beginning around his mouth. There was a grown-up in there beginning to carve its way out of the boy; I liked that it was laughter that was beginning to paint its way across his face, not sorrow. I'd had enough of that in my life a few years back. I liked standing here in the kitchen with the smell of breakfast all around, and the sunlight streaming bright and warm, and the man in my arms smiling down at me, while everyone else's laughter filled the air like some kind of happy perfume.

Cynric bent down that extra height that he'd been teasing Nicky about, and I went up on tiptoe to meet his kiss with mine. Was he taller than he had been last week? It seemed like I was higher up on my toes as his lips found mine. It was a gentle caress of lips, that never quite involved tongue, but there was some body English to it, and *chaste* was not a word I'd have used for it. I broke the kiss first, letting myself fall back to flat-footed. Cynric blinked at me, his eyes a little unfocused. "Wow," he whispered. I loved that he was still young enough to say it out loud. It made me smile.

"Good morning, Cynric."

"Anita," he said, and he gave me the look, it was his you-know-better look. It wasn't nearly as good as my look, or Micah's, but it was getting better.

I gave a little nod, smiled, shook my head, and said, "Good morning, Sin."

He grinned, and hugged me, tight, fast, not sexual, just—happy. We went to the table, and everyone knew where they sat at breakfast when it was just the eight of us. Chance's high chair took up the space of a chair, so we were eight, or would be when Micah joined us. I had a moment of wondering if Ares and Bram could smell the food outside on guard duty, and knew they could, but they'd eat after when their replacements clocked in. Micah came into the room smiling, bending over to kiss me, quick, chaste, squeezing the hand that I raised up to him. The sunlight flared in his eyes, bringing out the yellow and shrinking the green around the pupil so his eyes were golden for a moment. The look in those eyes promised that later there'd be kisses that weren't so chaste. He took his seat beside me, and we held hands under the table. Nathaniel sat on the other side of me, and I gave him my hand under the table, too, so that for a moment the three of us all held hands. Now, we were eight. It wasn't a bad number to be.

21

MICAH, NATHANIEL, AND I retired to our bedroom. Admittedly, we had a California king bed now, which meant a longer than normal bed to accommodate all those over-six-feet-tall lovers. The length certainly wasn't for any of the three of us; we were so not over six feet. So, there was room for more than just us, but I didn't want extra company today and everyone seemed to sense that. Maybe it was the giant-sized dose of tired that hit me after we finished breakfast. I just wanted to wrap my two main squeezes around me, and have them as close to me as possible. Something about seeing so much death makes you want to celebrate life, or drink heavily, and I didn't drink.

I put my equipment bags on the far side of the bedroom by the big chair that held some of my stuffed toy penguin collection. There was a chance I might get called up if they found the other daytime retreat of the rogue vampires, and I'd have to grab and go. So I didn't lock the weapons up in their various safes and lockers. The Browning BDM stayed in its bed holster at the headboard for me to grab, and there were actually a couple of other hideaways in the bedroom, but I didn't usually keep the whole arsenal out like this. There was barely room for the two bags on the far side of the bed and walking room.

I had a choice of stepping on some of the penguins that sat on the floor, or the weapons in the bags. I stepped on the penguins, but I didn't like doing it. I finally gave up going around to the side of the bed I usually got in on, and decided to go over the footboard, rather than step on any more of the penguins. I know it was silly, and they were just stuffed toys, they couldn't feel me stepping on them, but . . . the penguins had been my only comfort objects for years, and they still meant something to me. I had more in storage, because there just wasn't room for all of the toys once we got the bigger bed, not unless we wanted to be wading through toy penguins, or stepping on them, which upset me, or tripped us, so . . . I'd given up some of my penguins for a bigger bed and more real people. I never regretted the trade.

Sigmund, my penguin sleeping buddy for years, had pride of place on the chair, but he didn't sleep in the bed anymore. I had enough living, breathing comfort objects; I didn't need stuffed animals anymore, now that I had the real thing.

That real thing was already in the bed, one of them lying with the sheet modestly at his waist and the other totally and comfortably naked on top of it. Once upon a time I'd made Nathaniel get under the sheet, but he'd worn me down, or maybe I enjoyed the sight of him so naked, so beautiful, on top of my sheets, in our bed, with Micah tucked in beside him hiding some of his amazingness with that thin bit of sheet. It was just so them.

I stood at the foot of the bed looking at them, and even after three years I still had that urge to say, "Wow, this is all really mine?" Some days I felt luckier than I deserved, and some days I felt just lucky enough.

Micah had taken the tie out of his hair so that it fell in loose, tight curls around his face and shoulders. His hair was that color of brown that starts life as a pale blond and darkens as you get older. He'd confirmed that he'd had a head full of nearly kinky blond hair as a toddler, but now it was a tiny bit less curly and a rich, dark chestnut brown.

Nude, his upper body showed the muscle that he fought to put over a bone structure that was almost as delicate as my own. The muscle was there in the swimmer's wedge of his shoulders, the arms, the chest, down that slender waist where the white sheet made his summer tan look darker, though not too dark. Micah tanned to a point and then just stopped. It was like his skin loved running outside, shirtless. He ran at the indoor track some of the time, but he preferred to run outside, even in temperatures, both cold and hot, that made the rest of us go for the nice, even, no-ice, no-heatstroke indoor track.

He blinked those chartreuse eyes at me. Most of the cats had a neat line of demarcation between the colors in their eyes, like Cynric did between his two shades of blue, but Micah's leopard eyes were more "human" with the green-gold of them shifting, mingling, changing in the light, depending on what color was close to his face, his moods. It was closer to what hazel eyes do on some people than the kitty-cat eyes most had. In that moment his eyes were very green, but it was a rich, olive green, with that undercurrent of gold like leaves shining in sunlight.

Nathaniel made some small movement, snuggling down into the bed beside Micah, and suddenly I was looking at my second yummy boy. His hair was still back in its long, serpentine braid, but though having sex with all his hair unbound could be done, it also tended to tangle around things like body parts, and one of us was forever putting a knee, arm, back, ass, on all that hair and trapping him in midmovement, so at least for the beginning of sex he'd taken to keeping it braided. Sometimes the point was to play with the hair, and then he'd undo it, but for sleeping and a lot of the sex, you wanted all that auburn goodness bound in some way. He liked hair bondage, too, which I was a little puzzled by because it so didn't work for me, but it worked for him, and sometimes kinky sex isn't about understanding your lover's kinks, but just about honoring them.

He was lying on his stomach so I could see the long, bare line of him from broad shoulders to the muscled spread of his back, V-ing down to his waist; the rise of his ass, which managed to be tight and round and lush; the swell of his thighs, the muscles of his calves, and his feet, where he had pushed his toes under the blanket that was folded at the foot of the bed. He did that a lot, just part of his feet under covers, but nothing else. I'd asked him why he did it, and he'd said he didn't know, he just liked doing it. Answer enough, I guess.

He blinked those big, lavender eyes at me, and smiled that smile. It was part mischief, part happy, and all sex. The look caught my breath in my throat, and things low in my body tightened enough for my breath to shudder out between my lips when I finally remembered to breathe.

Seeing the two of them in my bed, knowing I could touch any part of them I wanted, with pretty much any part of me I wanted to, just made me happier than I could say.

"What's that look on your face?" Micah asked, smiling slightly.

"Happy, I'm just happy."

The smile widened, and then he got that almost-shy look in his eyes, ducking his head, but with the eyes coming back up so you saw that a part of him knew his own worth. I was never sure if the shyness was an old habit, or if the shyness had always been intermingled with that dark, almost predatory look, and I wasn't talking about his beast. It was just the look that some men have in their eyes, their faces.

Nathaniel smiled at us both in a happy, possessive look. There was nothing shy about him when it came to sex, or knowing just how beautiful he was; his problem when he came into my life had been that those were the only parts of him anyone had valued. I was the one who learned to love him without sex. It had been a first for him that Micah and I loved him for other things; the fact that he was gorgeous and great in bed was more icing and not the whole cupcake. Though it was very sweet, yummy icing, and honestly if a cupcake doesn't have icing on it, what's the point?

"You're overdressed," he said.

I looked down at the oversized sleep shirt that fell nearly to my knees. It had Christmas penguins on it, and wasn't the most attractive look, but I didn't have a robe that didn't look like lingerie here, and somehow with Gina, Zeke, and baby Chance staying with us, the sleep shirt seemed better for that last trip to the bathroom than the short red robe that was on the back of the door.

"I need a robe that won't scar the kiddo's psyche," I said, looking down at the ice-skating penguins.

"We need another bathroom," Micah said.

"I like the idea of a master bathroom off a master suite," Nathaniel said.

"We talked about this; if we do that, then we have no bedroom while the remodeling is going on," I said.

"We stay with Jean-Claude, and let Gina and Zeke continue to stay here so Chance can have his sunshine, and they can oversee the remodeling," he said.

I frowned at him. "You've been thinking about this."

He smiled. "Yep."

I don't know what I would have said, because Micah said, "You are still overdressed."

I looked at him, frowning still, then smiled. "Hey, at least my legs are showing; you're the one under the sheet."

"You're both too covered up," Nathaniel said. "I'm the only one who's naked." To prove it, he sat up on his knees, and I got a view of things that no customer at Guilty Pleasures ever got to see. He grabbed a handful of sheet, jerking it off Micah, as he crawled toward me. He bent over the footboard, grabbing me around the waist, lifting, and putting his other arm under my thighs as he did it, so he picked me up at the same time, scooping me over the footboard and half-tossing, half-falling to the bed, so that I was suddenly between the two of them. We were all laughing as Nathaniel's hand slid underneath the sleep shirt. He stayed on the outside of my thigh, then the outside of my hip, my waist, and moved slowly higher. I wasn't laughing when his hand caressed my breast, but I was still smiling, and so was he.

Micah moved onto his side beside me, and his hand traced up the other side of me, to mirror Nathaniel's movements, until they both had a breast apiece, and the smiles began to slip to something more serious, but no less good.

It was Micah who tugged on the shirt and began to lift it up my body. It was Nathaniel's turn to mirror him. I raised my butt up so they could wiggle the shirt up higher and finally pull it over my head and arms. Micah tossed it on the floor and gazed down at me. "That's better," he said, voice already going deeper, not with inner leopard, but simply maleness.

I was suddenly lying there naked, staring up at both of them. They stared back, the green-gold eyes and the lavender. There was a growing darkness in both sets of eyes. That look that all men I've ever been with get in their eyes. A look that is certain of you, certain you won't say no, and that in this moment you are theirs. Maybe not forever, maybe not exclusively, but theirs, nonetheless, because even in the most submissive man there is something primitive that makes him want to possess you, even if it's just a night, an hour, a moment. Women may have their own version of *the look*, but if they do, I'm not near a mirror at the critical moment, and my very limited experience with women hadn't shown me the same look in their eyes. I'm not saying it's not there, just that I haven't seen it.

Micah kissed me, and this time he didn't have to worry about scarring anyone's psyche, so it was lips, tongue, and finally teeth, set delicately into my lower lips until I cried out for him, and a low purring growl trickled out from between his human lips, and into mine, so that I drank the sound of his purr down my throat as if the sound had taste, and substance. What did Micah's growling purr taste like? Cinnamon; he tasted like hot and sweet. I knew it was the new mouthwash, but it made his mouth taste like candy.

Nathaniel smelled like vanilla, always, to me, and as he pressed himself to me, that sweet scent mingled with the cinnamon, and the two of them together, Micah's mouth, and Nathaniel's skin, were like Christmas sugar cookies, vanilla, with that sprinkling of cinnamon on the top, red hots melted into the sugar—sweet and spicy and warm in the mouth.

Nathaniel licked across my nipple, a light flick of tongue, and then began to suck, harder, until it was hard enough for me to cry out softly. Micah kissed me again, while Nathaniel brought small sounds from me as he sucked one breast, and played with the other. It was as if Micah ate the sounds from my mouth, as Nathaniel sucked hard, and harder, his hand squeezing, rolling the nipple between finger and thumb, and finally pulling on the nipple, as he bit my breast. I cried out and Micah's kiss acted like a gag, muffling the sound. I felt his hand slide over my hip as he continued to eat the sounds of pleasure from my mouth. Nathaniel opened his mouth wider, taking as much of my breast into his mouth as he could, before biting down; his hand cupped my breast, digging his fingers in, as his teeth dug into the other breast. When I made small, eager sounds, he did it harder. The feel of his teeth pressing hard and harder into the flesh of my breast bowed my back; his fingers bruising made me writhe into Micah's kisses, and then Micah's hand slid over my thigh and between my legs.

His fingers brushed me, and I spread my legs wider, so he could reach more of me. He played his fingers over and around me, not just going for that one sweet spot like it was a button, but exploring me with his fingers the way his lips explored my mouth.

Nathaniel set his teeth into my breast, his fingers almost crushing into the other breast. I was on the verge of having to safe-word on the breast play, but Micah's deep kisses kept me from saying anything, just as his fingers found that one sweetest of spots and began to play with it. The growing sensations between my legs kept the pain of the breast play on that thin line between amazing pleasure and actual pain. Every time I started to make too much noise, or sound as if I were going to say a word, Micah plunged his tongue into my mouth, caressing deeper, biting at my lips, and then turning it back into a gentler kiss, so that I knew he wouldn't let me safe-word. His kisses were my gag, and the thought that I couldn't tap out, couldn't say no to what Nathaniel was doing at my breasts, upped the sensation of it, helped me begin to slide into that place where what would hurt like hell becomes thrill and pleasure, and an intensity that nothing else seemed to touch, and all the time Micah played between my legs, never losing his rhythm now that he'd found it, even as he kept me muffled, helpless to say *Stop*. If we'd never done this before, it might have been too much; he and Nathaniel wouldn't have known my body, known my reactions even without words, so they could play right on the edge of what I could take, what I would enjoy.

Nathaniel worried at my breast with his teeth like a terrier with a bone, his fingers almost meeting in the flesh of the other breast. I might have forced a stop then, but Micah's hand pushed me over the edge, to a sudden orgasm that the breast play had hidden in an edge of almost-pain. The orgasm flowed from between my legs, up and over my body in a warm, joyous rush. Nathaniel bit harder, fingers crushing, and the pain mixed with the orgasm so that it grew together, making it all so much more. I screamed into Micah's mouth, body writhing, bucking, held down by Nathaniel's body at my chest, and Micah's mouth and body against my side. When my eyes fluttered in my head, my body liquid and helpless with pleasure, Nathaniel stopped biting, stopped bruising. Micah stopped kissing me, and then moved his hand from between my legs. I felt the bed moving, but I couldn't focus my eyes, or even open them enough to see what they were doing.

I felt Nathaniel between my legs, but he wasn't using his fingers. I felt the head of him rubbing against the parts that Micah had just finished playing with, and he made me cry out again, my upper body coming up off the bed, like a puppet pulled abruptly to life, and then the strings were cut again, and I lay boneless, half-blind with the afterglow of the orgasm. Then Nathaniel began to push his way inside me, one exquisite inch at a time, until he was as deep inside me as he could go, his body pressed tight and solid.

I fought to focus on him as he rose above me, his hands bracing his upper body so that he arched over me. I gazed down the line of our bodies and he began to pull himself out of me, and then in, before he'd finished the first stroke.

I whispered, "Oh, God!"

He found his rhythm, in and out, slow, deep strokes, but not too deep, until I felt that warmth begin to grow again, and then he brought me again, and I writhed underneath him, my hands grabbing for his arms, ready to paint my pleasure in scratches, but Micah caught my hands and gave me his arms to push my nails into, but he partially pinned them, so I couldn't rack my nails down his skin, just dig the tips into his arms.

Then Nathaniel began to move faster, sliding in and out. I gazed down our bodies, watching the long, smooth shaft of him working in and out of me, and just the sight of it made me cry out again. I marked Micah's arms again, and then Nathaniel angled his hips, and now at the end of each stroke he touched as deep inside me as he could, hitting that one spot deep inside, and it was yet a different kind of orgasm, one moment all strokes and depth, and then suddenly impact that pushed me over the edge again, and this time the writhing was more of a fight, so that Micah held me down so that I couldn't scratch Nathaniel. He enjoyed nails and teeth, but he was supposed to be onstage that night, and my nail marks lasted on his skin. He needed to be unmarked, and we'd learned that I enjoyed being held down, so Micah held me down and let me paint his arms in little bloody half moons.

Micah's head was turned away, his curls across my face, so that I saw Nathaniel's face through Micah's hair. I watched the concentration on Nathaniel's face, that distant internal look as he fought his body to last, to keep going, to give me as much pleasure as he could, before his own body reached its limit. Then his eyes opened wide, and his hips began to do more than just in and out, adding a sort of sideways motion to each stroke like the difference between throwing a pitch hard and fast over home plate and a curveball. He didn't last long when he started doing that, but that was okay, because neither did I. He brought me with that extra bit of movement, and while I was screaming at the headboard, his body thrust one last time as deep inside me as he could, and the first orgasm hit the second, and I held on to Micah's arms, as if my nails in his flesh were an echo of Nathaniel's body pinning me to the bed.

Nathaniel pulled himself out, which made me shiver, but I was too far gone in afterglow to do much more. I was back to eye-fluttery blindness. He collapsed beside me, breathing hard and laughing softly. "That . . . was . . . amazing."

I could only nod.

I felt Micah's mouth against my face, and thought he was going to kiss my cheek, but he didn't; instead he spoke in a voice gone growling deep. "My turn."

22

THERE WAS A reason that Micah had gone second. Most of the men in my bed were well endowed, but Micah was more than just well endowed. He'd had women in his past actually refuse to have sex with him, because they were afraid of his size. I'd had one man in my bed who gave him a run for his money, and that was Richard, but even he wasn't actually as big. Micah could touch his belly button with the tip of himself, which meant that all of him didn't actually fit into all of me in some positions; I wasn't deep enough. They always said that you stretch to accommodate; well, you do, but there is a limit. Women vary in how deep and wide they are, just like men vary in length and width. He was thick around, too, but thankfully he wasn't the thickest I'd had in my bed; if he'd won on width as well as length, I might have had to call the whole thing off. One of the reasons Micah loved making love to me was that I really did orgasm from deep, hard lovemaking. Nathaniel had already proven that today, but Micah was about to prove it better.

He was in almost the same position as Nathaniel had been: upper body angled upward, only his groin and hips pinning me to the bed. He started slow, keeping his stroke shallow so that I could feel the head of him just touching the end of me, but Nathaniel had done the prep work, and I said, "Harder."

Once, Micah would have argued with me, but now he just did what I asked. He began to pound himself into me; the thickness of him started to fill me up, not just with his body, but with that warmth, that thick, growing hint of pleasure, but it was the tip of him hitting deep that put me over the edge, that brought me screaming, and set my nails in his arms, digging into his upper arms, so I painted my pleasure the length of his arms, as he brought me screaming and writhing underneath him.

He pulled out, abruptly, his body still long and thick and hard. He said, in a voice gone breathless, and growling deep, "You need to feed the *ardeur*, Anita. You didn't even try to feed."

I panted up at him, and finally managed to say, "I forgot."

Nathaniel laughed that deep guy chuckle. "He'd make anyone forget."

We glanced at our other half, and he lay on the bed on his stomach, watching us with those eyes, face alight with emotion, pleasure, just the watching. Nathaniel was both an exhibitionist and a voyeur. He liked seeing me with other people, and he loved watching Micah and me together.

Micah said, "Over."

"What?" I asked.

"Turn over," he said.

My lower body wasn't really cooperating, and Nathaniel helped me over on my stomach. Then Micah put his knees on my thighs, pinning me, which I liked, but I think it was incidental to the fact that the angle was deeper now. He'd spent most of his adult life with women who were always telling him it was too much, too deep, *fucking ow*; the fact that I liked it, orgasmed from it, made positions possible for him that most women would have tried to endure, but they wouldn't have enjoyed it.

"If it's too deep, tell me," he said. He said that before any new position.

"I will," I said, my cheek pressed to the bed. The pillows were gone; Nathaniel had moved them out of the way when Micah put me face-down on my stomach.

He didn't just hit the end of me; the tip of him rolled over, caressing the deepest part of me more than hitting it, and I had to ask, "Is the tip of you bending over, like folding over?"

"Yes," he said. Which meant from this angle he was a couple of inches too long for me now, maybe more.

"Does it hurt you?" I asked.

"No, does it hurt you?" he asked.

"No, it just feels different."

"Different good?"

I thought about it for a moment, and then said, "Yes."

He found a rhythm then, a stroke that carried him into and past the end of me, so that at the end of each stroke I could feel him rolling over, as if he were able to caress me with the tip of himself. It was like he hit the end of me, and then caressed over me, and then stroked upward, and that was at the end of each movement.

"Harder," I said.

"Are you sure?" he asked.

"Yes."

He took me at my word, and began to move faster, harder, but each stroke ended in that caressing roll of his body, as if he were petting, massaging deep inside me. It was an amazing sensation. I felt him hesitate, and looked back over my shoulder to see his face. He had his eyes closed; one, so he could concentrate on his body, feel his way inside me, but the other reason was so he could last. Most men are visual, and without being able to see himself going in and out of me, he was able to fight off that last moment a little bit longer. I watched the concentration on his face as my body rocked and moved against the bed under the push and power of him. I had a second of warning, and then the orgasm caught me. It dug my fingers into the bed, it screamed its way down my throat, and out my mouth.

In a voice thick with strain, Micah said, "Anita, feed!"

I dropped the metaphysical leash on the *ardeur* and let myself feed. Micah could feel when I dropped my shields and released my hunger, and he released himself. He stopped fighting to last, and finally let himself go. He pounded himself inside me, hard and fast, caressing, and then as the tip of him rolled upward with that last extra bit of stroking pleasure he went, and because of the *ardeur* I could feel it. I could feel him hot and liquid inside me, because my body fed on it, fed on the feel of him thrust so deep inside me; he bent himself a little back, and if he'd been a different kind of man, that might have hurt, instead of feeling so very good, and if I'd been a different kind of woman, having him so deep inside would have turned from pleasure to not, but we were ourselves, we liked it deep and hard, and all the extras that went with it.

He shuddered above me, and I fed on his energy as he collapsed on top of me. I fed on the sweat on his chest, the frantic thudding of his heart against my back, the weight and feel of him in me, on me, with me—I fed on it all. When we could breathe enough to talk, he said, "Every time I think you can't get more amazing in bed, I'm wrong."

I wanted to say something profound, to let him know how exquisite he was, how delicious, but what came out was, "Right back at you, babe." Not exactly poetry, but it made him push back my hair until he could kiss my cheek and say, "I love you, Anita."

"Love you more," I said.

"Love you most," Nathaniel said, as he cuddled in beside us.

I smiled, and we said the next part together, all three of us: "I love you mostest." And we did.

23

THE PHONE DRAGGED me from a deep, dreamless sleep. There was the tiniest thread of sunlight in the dark room, proving we hadn't shut the blackout curtains quite right. If they were closed, the room was cave dark. Micah moved beside me, groping on the nightstand for my cell phone. The ring was loud and harsh, an old-fashioned phone ring. Nathaniel made a protesting wiggle on the other side of me, his hand trying to hold Micah in place even in his sleep.

Micah's voice came with only a hint of sleep to it, "Hello."

I lay in the dark of the blackout curtains, with Nathaniel curled around me; he'd pulled me in even tighter to his body, his front to my back, but there was a tension to his body that let me know he was awake.

"Just a moment, Marshal Brice." Micah had said the name out loud so I'd know who I was talking to and have a chance of knowing what it was about. He rolled over and handed me the phone. The line of sunlight slashed across his upper body, so that it looked like it was cutting him like some sort of golden blade. I took the phone but shifted the covers over Micah, so that the line of light didn't touch his skin.

Maybe it was years of dating vampires and knowing what sunlight did to them, but the sight of that line of sunshine across his skin had unnerved me. Micah was a wereleopard; sunlight didn't hurt him, but . . . it was almost as if I'd dreamed something bad and didn't remember it, but it had spooked me just the same.

"Hey, Brice, what's up?" I said, and my voice sounded normal. I'd had time to wake up for the phone.

"While you and Zerbrowski went home to the family, I found a clue."

I leaned higher up on my elbow. "What?"

"Neighbors saw the same van between the locations we have, but the plate is registered to an address that our vampire snitch didn't give us."

I sat up; Nathaniel's arm slid down around my waist, his face snuggling into my bare back and ass. He nuzzled a little, and I did my best to ignore it. "Where?" I asked.

"Out near you, which is why you get invited to the party, otherwise I'd just grab SWAT and you'd hear about it afterward. We can pick you up as we drive past."

Nathaniel was kissing softly against my body. It wasn't exactly distracting me from what Brice was saying, but it wasn't exactly helping me focus either. I put a hand behind me between him and my body. I frowned at the clock on the nightstand. "Crap, Brice, we've only got two hours until sunset, and there could be as many as twenty vampires to execute. We are going to be cutting it close."

"If we use guns, we can do it," he said.

"If they're all out in plain sight and we don't have to play *hunt the vampire hiding place*, maybe."

"What choice do we have?" he asked.

"None. Get your asses out here; if you're late, I go in without you."

"I don't remember giving you the address," he said, "just that it's out by you."

Shit, I was more tired than I knew. "Give it to me."

"Nope, Captain Storr and Kirkland both warned me you'd go all Lone Ranger if I did, and they were right."

I cursed silently. "Are you really picking me up, or will you give me the address when you're closer?"

"I'll pick you up; it really is on the way."

"I'll be ready; hurry, Brice. You do not want to be inside the place when that many vamps wake for the night."

"No, I don't," he said, and hung up.

Nathaniel hugged me tighter around the waist, nuzzling past my fingers to kiss along my hip. He knew better than to say, *Don't go*, but the tightness of his arm said it for him.

Micah looked at me and took my hand in his. "Be careful."

"I will be."

We had a moment of them holding me, and me not wanting to go. I'd have much rather snuggled back down into the warm nest of sheets and body heat. Once I'd enjoyed hunting the monsters, taken a lot of pride in being the best at killing them, but lately, I just wanted to go home and be with the people I loved. Zerbrowski said I was having the ten-years-on-the-job moment. I told him I hadn't been on the job that long. His reply: "You work what amounts to serial killers, or sex crimes, violent crimes; everyone burns out on those details, even you."

I sat there in the dark with that thread of sunlight across the sheets, giving enough light for me to see Micah and Nathaniel by, let them wrap me round with the warmth and strength of them both, and I didn't want to go. Twenty vampires minimum was a lot to kill in less than two hours. I was pretty sure that Jean-Claude could keep my death from dragging any of my other metaphysical sweeties down to die with me, including Nathaniel, but . . . I'd never been as happy as I was right now. Does happiness make us cowards? If someone had threatened the people I loved, I would have been ruthless to protect them, but there was no threat to me and mine. I was about to leave this warm bed, these warm arms, this happy family, and the rest of our family that stayed mostly at Circus of the Damned, for my job.

It was great to get the bad guys. Wonderful knowing I'd saved them from killing other innocent victims, but Nathaniel was so warm cuddled against me, his lips so soft on my skin. Micah felt solid and real, and so good in my arms. I snuggled against them, and we held each other, and for the first time ever, if one of them had asked me not to go, I might have done it.

I let myself think in the front of my head what I must have been thinking in the back for a while. Maybe the world would be safe without me being Marshal Anita Blake. Maybe new Marshals like Arlen Brice could save the day and I could find a different way to . . . live.

24

I HAD TIME for coffee, which is usually a good thing, but it turned into a trap, as if the coffee were the goat the hunter had staked out to lure the leopard into firing range. I stood in my kitchen with the fresh cup of perfect coffee in my favorite baby penguin mug, and was so not happy. Cynric had made the coffee, and it was perfect, but it was a trap. I knew the feel of "the talk" in the air, and I didn't want to have it. Whatever it was, I didn't want to do it, or talk about it, or deal with it. I especially didn't want to deal with it when Brice and SWAT could be outside in just moments. I'd even said that, and his reply had been, "There's never a good time to talk about us, Anita. You're always ass-deep in alligators." It was hard to argue with that, so I didn't try. Arguing when someone says something so very true just makes you look stupid.

I fought not to be sullen about it, and to be a reasonable grown-up. In that moment the grown-up in the room wasn't me. I leaned my back against the cabinet, leaning back on my butt, so it was a type of reclining. Cynric stood in front of me. He'd let his hair grow out in the year and some change he'd been with us, so that now it touched his shoulders. He usually brushed it out when it was wet and tied it back tight in a ponytail. His hair managed to be thick and luxurious rather than just soft. I think he had the thickest straight hair I'd ever touched. He had it back in a ponytail, not quite tight enough to hide the fact that there was a lot more hair behind him. His face had thinned down, letting nice, triangular cheekbones come out of what I could only have called baby fat, though no one called it that now. He was leaner from gaining extra inches of height and hitting the gym in a serious way. Nathaniel worked out because he was a stripper, and when you take your clothes off for customers, you need to look good. I worked out so I could fight bad guys. The bodyguards who stayed at the house with us, and at the Circus with Jean-Claude, worked out to stay in shape to protect our asses. Richard was Ulfric, wolf king, and occasionally you had to fight to keep the title, so he worked out to make sure he could do that. Micah worked out because I, his leopard queen, did, and because occasionally the leopard king had to fight for the right to keep his title, too, though it was a lot rarer among the leopards than the wolves. Wereleopards were more practical creatures than werewolves, as a general rule. Micah didn't work out as much as I did, but then neither did Nathaniel. I was the one most likely to be depending on my body to save my ass on a regular basis. It was a serious incentive to exercise.

I'd insisted that Cynric take fight practice with me and the guards, because I preferred my people to be able to defend themselves. I couldn't be with everyone all the damn time, so fewer victims was a good thing. Cynric had gotten his ass kicked at the hand-to-hand and non–gun weapons practice, so he'd started lifting weights and running with us, so he'd be in better shape for practice. It had probably helped give him that extra height and widen his shoulders, fill out his upper body, and just put muscle on what had been a slender, softer frame. Now he was lean and had more muscle. He didn't bulk up as much as some of the other men; Nathaniel had broader shoulders and put on muscle easier. Cynric muscled up not much better than Micah did, which meant he fought for every ounce of it, almost as much as Micah. Micah looked amazing out of his clothes, lean, muscled, strong, and so very male, but in clothes, especially anything that wasn't tight, it was harder to see the workout. Cynric had some of the same problems. It meant that in the new preternatural high school football league, he was quarterback. He didn't have the bulk to be much else, and he had a good eye, good hands, lightning-quick reflexes, and dead-calm nerves even with kids three times his size barreling down on him. He also could run like a son of a bitch and would have made a good running back or wide receiver if he hadn't been so good at quarterback. Considering he'd never played organized sports in his life, it was pretty impressive. His couch bemoaned all those years of lost opportunity.

He was also running track again, in a preternatural league, and there he excelled at anything that required speed and agility. He was a sprinter, not a distance runner, but within his distances he was almost untouchable. We actually had college coaches sniffing around, because there was talk of a college preternatural league, and there were already amateur adult leagues across the country, with some talk of a professional one starting up, at least in football.

There weren't enough preternaturals between one school and another to have more than one team between states right now. Which meant the St. Louis team was really a Missouri team. We were doing well in football, and a lot of that was due to the guy standing in front of me.

Nathaniel loved going to the games and meets, and they introduced themselves as brothers, which left me in the interesting situation of having a few parents at the games wondering exactly what I was doing with Nathaniel and his younger brother. I didn't really care what strangers thought about me, but Cynric bothered me, personally, and always had.

Cynric was wearing jogging shorts and no shirt, so he'd either worked out already or been about to when he heard me get up. He wasn't sweating, so he'd been getting dressed to run, and just stopped in the middle to come out to me. The shorts left his upper body bare in the last of the late-day sun, so that the dying gold of the light painted his muscles in amber highlights, giving them even more depth and shading. At least he was wearing the bottoms; a lot of the wereanimals went around nude unless my modesty protested—though Cynric had come with his own share of modesty and rarely went around buck naked, come to think of it.

"Would you just stand there and say nothing if I didn't start?" he asked.

"Yeah." I sipped the coffee; it was hot, and Nathaniel had taught Cynric exactly the way I liked it, but today, even good coffee couldn't cheer me up.

"Why?" he asked.

"You're the one who made everyone else leave the room, Cynric. You wanted the talk, not me, so you get to talk."

"God, you are so much the dude."

I shrugged and sipped my coffee; maybe if I just kept drinking it, I'd enjoy it eventually. It was a shame to waste good coffee on such a bad mood.

He ran his hands through his hair, but in the ponytail he couldn't finish the gesture, so he pulled out the tie and let the thick, straight hair fall loose. It fell around his face like a dark blue curtain, making the ring of pale blue in his eyes richer, closer to cornflower blue, and the darker ring of midnight blue, almost as dark as Jean-Claude's eyes, look richer, more blue, a navy bordering on something less deep.

He ran his hands through his hair, now that he could, and started pacing a short, tense circle in the largest piece of unobstructed floor in the kitchen. That just happened to put him directly in front of me, pacing, like one of those big cats in the zoo that forever paces, miserable, and eventually they go mad. His thick hair spilled forward around his face, so that as he turned it fell in disarray around his face. The morning light had made his hair oh so blue, but this was a darker shade of light, thicker, holding shades of gold so deep, it was like fire as it fades, so that some of his hair was rich, deep blue, but some of it looked black, so that the highlights and lowlights of his hair were . . . heart-stopping.

He stopped in front of me, at last, his chest rising and falling as if he'd been running. The pulse in the side of his neck pounded against his skin, already darkening from running shirtless in the spring practices. He tanned, did our Cynric. He stared at me, eyes a little too wide, lips half-parted in that triangular face, hair in that artful disarray.

I had the urge to push it back from his face, out of his eyes, but stayed leaning against the cabinets. I would lose ground if I moved toward him, and I would lose a lot of ground if I touched his hair. If we were going to fight, I didn't want to do it with my fingers remembering the warm silk of his hair.

"I'm worried about you," he said, at last.

"I'm sorry," I said, and started to sip the coffee again, but realized I didn't want it. I set it on the cabinet beside me.

"Sorry about what?" he asked.

I shrugged. "Sorry my job upsets you, I guess." For Micah, or Nathaniel, I would have taken this, owned it, maybe even agreed, but Cynric hadn't earned this yet; he wasn't the boss of me.

"I'm a weretiger, Anita; I can smell your emotions and you're not upset."

"Now you're telling me what I feel," I said.

"You want this to be a fight. I don't want to fight."

I crossed my arms under my breasts and settled against the cabinets again. "I don't want to fight either, Cynric."

"Please, at least, call me by my name."

I sighed. "Sin; fine, I don't want to fight either, Sin. You know I hate the nickname."

"I know you do, but then you hate a lot of things about me."

"That's not fair," I said.

"Maybe not, but it's true." He took two more steps toward me, so that if I'd unfolded my arms I could have touched his chest easily. "I can't help being this young, Anita. It's not permanent; I'll get older."

I hugged my arms around myself, because I wanted to touch him. It was one of the up/downs to him being one of the animals to call. It felt good to touch the type of animal you could call, and it felt especially good to cuddle your very own animal to call, and Cynric was one of mine. The fact that I had a record number of animals to call didn't seem to make any difference; I wanted to touch them all when they were near me. It was damn hard to fight when you wanted to wrap your arms around someone so you could breathe in the scent of their skin.

"I'll get older, too," I said.

"Older in years, but as Jean-Claude's human servant, you won't age."

"I haven't taken the fourth mark from him."

"But you and Damian shared it, and he's a vampire, too."

"He's my vampire servant; we're not sure if that will change the dynamics."

"I know that there's a chance you shared your mortality with Damian rather than him sharing his immortality with you, but so far you both look great. I think you just don't want to accept that it's not an age thing."

"I'm sorry if it wigs me to be sleeping with a high schooler."

"I graduate this year, Anita; then what will your excuse be?"

"I don't know what you mean by that." I held myself very tight, because I was afraid that Cynric—Sin—was about to say some very grown-up things that I didn't want to hear.

"Nathaniel was only nineteen when you met him; Jason, too. That's just a year older than me. It isn't just my age, Anita."

I looked into those eyes, those almost frantic blue-on-blue eyes, and couldn't stand it. I couldn't stand the thought of him knowing that I didn't love him. I couldn't bear to hear him say it out loud, and yet part of me wanted someone to say it, if it meant he'd go back to Vegas and I'd have one less person to take care of in my life. I was tired in a way that had nothing to do with police work, and everything to do with the fact that no one person could date this many people. You could fuck them, but you couldn't have a relationship with them. Maybe I'd been ready to jettison Cynric out of my bed and life, not because of him, really, but because I had to find a way to thin down the people in my life, and concentrating on how young he was seemed a reasonable excuse to thin the herd. Was my issue with Cynric not him personally, but just being overwhelmed with all my lovers? I collected them the way a crazy cat lady found strays to bring home, except I could afford to feed and take care of all of them, I was just running low on emotional resources, or so I told myself.

Was I really ready to send a whole person away, just so I could date the leftovers more easily? Put that way, it seemed a shitty thing to do. Hell, it didn't sound good to call the men I loved and slept with the "leftovers." If I was going to get rid of Cynric and risk Nathaniel losing yet another brother, I needed a better reason than being emotionally tired; didn't I?

I reached out, touched his hair, and smoothed it back from his face. His hair was so soft, softer than Nathaniel's, but not quite as thick; almost, though. I wanted to say, *It's not you, it's me*, but it sounded so fucking cliché. Maybe the reason it's a cliché is that it's true, so much more than people want to believe. You can be a perfectly good person, wonderful lover, great friend, and it can still not work. Fuck, fuck, fuck.

He put one hand over mine, holding it against his face. His eyes closed, and he leaned his face into my palm, rubbing his cheek against me, scent-marking me as his, like cats will do. Was I his? Was he mine? Fuck, I didn't know. How could I not know after more than a year? How could I not know the answer to this? What the fuck was wrong with me? What the fuck was wrong . . . with me? With . . . him and me, with us? No, with me. With me. What was wrong with me?

His other hand went around my waist, drawing me in against his body. It was a possessive gesture, one that marked territory if other men were present. *This is mine, not yours*; mine, just by that arm around me, that drawing me into him. I just didn't think it was true.

I stared up at him, studying his face, trying to see something that would help me know what the hell I was feeling.

He drew me in tighter to his body, and I put my hands on his waist, just at the top of his hips, not holding him, but keeping that last fraction of a distance between his body and mine. I knew what was under the silky jogging shorts. I knew what he had to offer, and I knew my reaction to being pressed against it, even through clothes. It wasn't just love that made me react to the men in my life, and somehow if I reacted to Cynric the same way, it would mean something. I wasn't sure what, but something, something I didn't want it to mean.

He tried to pull me closer, but I stiffened my arms and kept the small distance. He didn't fight me. He just let me go and stepped back a few inches, so we weren't touching at all.

I reached out to him, but the look on his face made me drop my hands to my sides. It wasn't the anger that I'd earned, but the disappointment in his eyes, the pain; I hadn't wanted to see that. It made my chest tight, and there was a lump in my throat that I couldn't seem to swallow around, as if I were choking on something more solid than words.

"I'm not jealous," he said, "but after what I heard and smelled you doing with Micah and Nathaniel, and you won't even let me hold you close . . ." He shook his head, making a little push-away gesture with his hands. He turned and went to stand by the sliding glass door, as far from me as he could get without leaving the room.

I didn't know what to do. If Nathaniel hadn't adopted him as a brother, if Jean-Claude didn't seem to take such pride in his accomplishments, if he didn't try so damn hard to do everything that was asked of him, if . . . how would I feel if I never saw Cynric here in the kitchen again? What if I never saw him painted in dark squares of amber light and shadows again? He was beautiful standing there with the light making his shoulder-length hair rich blues and blacks, as if someone had painted him with the color of dark ocean water, but . . . but I could live without him. I'd miss him, but I couldn't wrap my head around helping him pick out colleges and fucking him. It felt too much like a conflict of interests. Could you finish raising someone, kiss him and send him off to school every day, and be sleeping with him, and have it be okay? I didn't think so.

I decided to try for honesty. I wasn't sure it would help my chest and throat loosen up, but it was all I had. I went closer, but not close enough to touch him. "I'm sorry."

He didn't look at me as he said, "Sorry for what?"

"That there's not enough of me for everyone."

He turned to look at me then, frowning. "What does that even mean?"

I opened my mouth, closed it. I wasn't sure how to put it into words.

"See, it's not a real reason, Anita. You just want an excuse to say no."

I shook my head. "It's not that, damn it."

He turned around, crossing his arms over his bare chest. "Then explain it." He threw the words down like a gauntlet. It was my turn to pick it up and accept the challenge, or leave it lying there, sad and cowardly.

"I don't know how to send you off to high school, hug you good-bye, attend parent-teacher conferences, and be having sex with you. It feels wrong, like I'm doing something wrong. No one else in my bed makes me feel like I'm doing something immoral."

The frown was replaced by a puzzled look, and then a half-smile. "You're serious, aren't you?"

"Absolutely," I said.

"I really am only a year younger than Nathaniel and Jason when you met them."

"But I didn't sleep with them at nineteen, and I was three years younger, too."

"I'm only five years younger than Nathaniel," he said.

I fought a serious urge to put my fingers in my ears and go *La-la-la-la*. I hadn't really thought of it that way.

He gave a short, harsh laugh. "You hadn't done the math, had you?"

I tried not to squirm uncomfortably, and said, "I hadn't thought how close in age you two are, so no."

"Does everything only work for you because you don't think about it too hard?"

I didn't know what to say to that, and said so. "I don't know."

"You're seven years older than Nathaniel, right?"

I nodded, and shrugged. I fought to not look away, because honestly, that had bothered me at one point, too.

"The age difference really does bother you, even just the seven years?"

I nodded. "Yeah, it did, and I was taking care of him, keeping him safe. I thought it was a conflict of interest trying to get him to stand on his own two feet, and sleep with him at the same time."

"He was a pet when you met him, not just submissive but someone who had no ability to protect himself. He said, before you insisted on him getting therapy and being more independent, he was just a victim waiting for the right killer to come along and finish the job."

I couldn't keep the surprise off my face as I said, "He said that, really?"

Cynric nodded.

"I think if I hadn't lost control of the *ardeur* around him, I'd have kept my distance, Cynric."

"Sin." He said it automatically, with a note of tired-of-saying-this in his voice.

I sighed. "Sin, fine; you know the nickname doesn't help me get over this whole taboo thing, right?"

"What taboo?" he asked.

"You're a kid that I'm supposed to be taking care of; I think it was the parent-teacher conferences that really capped it for me, Cynric—Sin." I put my hands on my hips and finally had a solid glare on my face; it felt good, justified even. "You shouldn't be going to parent conferences for someone *and* fucking them, Sin, okay? There, that's the truth, that's the problem. It's just wrong."

He laughed then and leaned against the glass of the door, arms still crossed. "Then stop coming to the parent-teacher conferences."

"What?" I asked.

"Stop coming to the parent things; I don't think of you as a parent, Anita. The closest thing I've had to a mother was Bibiana in Vegas, and she's not exactly motherly to her own sons, but trust me, I have never thought of you that way." He frowned, unrolling his shoulders enough to put more of his back against the glass, his arms back against it, putting his hands flat against the sun-warmed glass, so that his upper body was suddenly framed against the light, and I realized that the pale blue silk of his shorts wasn't exactly light proof.

I looked away, so that I wouldn't keep looking harder to see how much I could see revealed in the sunlight. Wanting to see him silhouetted against the light made my whole protest about feeling parental toward him seem either stupid, like the lady was protesting too much, or incestuous. I felt myself begin to blush and wished, so wished, I could stop doing that.

"You don't think of yourself as my mom." His voice was a little lower as he said it.

I shook my head, because he was right. I didn't, I just . . . "But by going to the parent conferences and things, it puts me in that . . . role. Don't you understand? I can't do stuff like that and still . . ." I waved a hand vaguely toward him. "This!"

"Jean-Claude is my legal guardian, and he enjoys going to the parent stuff. Nathaniel likes it, too. All big brother on me," and there was real happiness in his voice when he said the last.

I looked at him then, and the happiness was there plain on his face. He leaned against the door in that fall of sunlight and was happy, relaxed, himself, more himself than when he came to us. I didn't have to fight not to look lower on his body, because I liked seeing that look on his face. He'd done more than just grow taller and more muscled since he got to St. Louis. I enjoyed watching him grow into himself, become the person he could be. That part I liked, the same way I'd enjoyed it with Nathaniel, or Jason, or . . . or Micah. We'd all grown more ourselves.

"You're right; Jean-Claude does enjoy the whole parent thing."

Sin laughed. "He's a little puzzled by the sports, but he enjoys coming."

"He's proud of you," I said.

Sin grinned. "I think he is."

"I know he is."

Sin looked at me, his blue eyes going more serious. "That's right, you can feel what he's feeling if you're not shielding tight enough, even more so than with one of your animals to call."

"It's harder to shield against Jean-Claude."

"Than against Nathaniel, or Damian?"

"Damian, yes; Nathaniel is harder depending on what we're doing."

"You mean sex," Sin said.

I smiled, and shook my head. "Sex with Jean-Claude is pretty full of abandon, too, but Nathaniel doesn't control his emotions as well as the vampires do."

"They've had centuries more practice," Sin said.

I nodded. "True."

"Just stop coming to the parent things, as my parent, Anita." He held his hand out to me.

"Just like that," I said, "and that'll make it okay?"

"I don't know, but I'll certainly trade you sitting there all uncomfort-able, and half-defensive, for being your lover." He waggled the hand he was holding out in the air.

I went close enough to take his hand. We stood there holding hands. Neither of us tried for anything closer. We just stood there, him still leaning against the door, me fighting the urge to pull against his hand, and looked at each other.

The smile slipped a little, leaving a much more serious look behind. The happiness remained like the glow that lingers pushing against the dark when the sun has gone below the horizon, but you know that true night is only a thought away—night, when the monsters come out to play.

I didn't want to be the monster to Cynric, the way I was to Larry. It wasn't a fair analogy, but I was tired; not physically, I'd slept, but emo-tionally. I was just tired of the shit, everyone's shit. I was also wondering where Brice was, not because I wanted a rescue from Cynric's talk, but because we needed to get these bastards before nightfall.

Cynric squeezed my hand and shook it a little. "You're thinking too hard, and it's not about me."

I had the grace to look embarrassed, but didn't lie. "I'm wondering when the other cops will come and give me a ride to the party."

"You know it scares me every time you leave for work with the police."

I nodded. "I know." We had another moment of just looking at each other, still holding hands from a little distance.

"Nothing I can do would make you not go," he said.

I sighed. "No," I said.

"Can I hug you?" he asked.

I looked at him, startled. The change in conversation was too fast for me. "Hug me, yeah. I mean, why not?"

"Because I think we're fighting, and you've gone all work serious."

"I don't think we're fighting."

"We were both thinking about having a fight," he said, smiling.

I smiled a little. "Yeah, we thought about it."

"But we're not going to," he said, and made it a question with the uplilt of his voice.

"I don't think so."

He frowned and pulled on my hand, bringing me closer to him. "Don't take this wrong, Anita, but why aren't we fighting?"

I realized he'd stopped pulling me closer, leaving me a few inches of distance, so I could decide if I wanted to close the distance or not. Cynric had learned what not to do in the last year. It was figuring out what to do that was the problem with dating me, or so one of my ex-boyfriends had said.

I went to him, closing the distance between us. I was left standing almost the same as before, looking up at him, his arms around me, but my hands on his waist and upper hip, keeping that last bit of distance.

"I don't want to fight," I said.

"Me either," he said.

I nodded. "Good."

"You'll stop coming to the parent-teacher stuff."

"Yeah," I said.

"And you'll stop being weirded out by our age difference?"

I laughed then, and shook my head. "I'm twelve years older than you are, Sin."

"I know."

"But it's not just the age difference; it's the when of the age difference. You're eighteen and I'm twelve years older than you are. I'm thirty, and you're eighteen; that is a big age difference."

"You said I could hug you," he said.

"You can," I said.

He glanced down at my hands where they held us apart. "Not without forcing the issue, and you don't like that, at least not from me."

I moved my hands around his waist, slowly, reluctantly, feeling the firmness of his body and the softness of his skin, so that I wasn't sure whether to say his body was muscled and hard, or soft and tender. He was both, all of it.

His arms slid slowly tighter around me, drawing me in against his body. I let my fingers play up his back, tracing the edge of his spine, the muscles of his lats where they traced under his skin like the faint shape of wings, as if with more weight lifting the angel wing shape would spring out of the skin and rise like a white feathered dream above his back. One of my lovers, more a fuck buddy really, was the Swan King, the leader of the swanmanes. I knew what it was to have sex surrounded by feathers and the strength of wings, but Sin didn't need wings to be special. I wrapped myself around his upper body, laying my cheek against his bare chest, so I could hold the warmth of his skin against me, and just like that it wasn't enough. He was my tiger to call, my blue tiger, and it wasn't just him that was tied to me; because of a lot of metaphysical things I could tie people to me only as tight as I was willing to be bound to them. My power was a double-edged sword, and I could cut someone only as deep as I was willing to be cut.

Sin wrapped his arms around me, curled me in against his body, and I let him do it. I let myself be small, and curl against the front of his taller body, so that he could hold me tight, and enjoy the fact that no matter how in charge I was, in the end he was bigger than I was, and no amount of years would change that. One day he would be twenty, but I'd still be six inches shorter than he was, and I could admit, at least silently in my own head, that it wasn't always bad to be smaller.

He held me tight, and laid his mouth against my hair, and asked, "Can I kiss you?"

"Why ask? Why not just try?"

"Because you're in one of those moods where what you want changes every few minutes."

"God, am I that hard to deal with?"

"Challenging," he said.

"Oh, that was diplomatic," I said.

"I want to kiss you."

"Yes," I said.

"Yes, what?"

"Yes," I said, and went up on my tiptoes, balancing against his chest. He took the hint, and leaned over to bring his face next to mine. We kissed, a soft touching of lips.

He drew back, studying my face. I started to ask what was wrong, but whatever he saw on my face must have pleased him, because he kissed me again, sliding one hand through my hair, so that he cupped the back of my neck and head, and the kiss grew from something chaste to a caressing of lips and tongues, and then a small sound escaped him, and his hands were suddenly eager against my body. He reminded me that he was more than human-strong, and there was a reason that lycan-thropes weren't allowed to play with humans. They were fragile. The fingers of one hand dug into my upper arm, bruising, and if I'd been human-fragile I might have been more than bruised, but I wasn't human, and sometimes I liked it rough. The bruising, the pain, tore an eager sound from my throat and made me press myself against him. His body was hard, and it made me cry out again and press harder against him.

"Anita." He growled it almost against my lips, and the first trickling rise of his beast flared across my skin like a spill of something warm, almost hot, sliding everywhere along my skin.

"God," I said, and got that first glimpse of tiger inside me, that great blue-and-black beast that rose to him.

There was a loud throat-clearing and a knock on the doorway. We both turned, startled, toward the sound. Nathaniel looked apologetic. "You guys are fun together."

"How long have you been watching?" I asked.

"Not long, but the police just pulled up outside."

"Shit," I said. I looked back up at Cynric. "I have to go."

"I know." And then he smiled. "But I know you're sorry to leave me now, and that helps."

I wasn't sure how to take that, so I ignored it and went for the door, adjusting the weapons and straps as if the make-out session had mussed them, but I think it was more to get back into work headspace. I touched the weapons, made sure they were all where I could grab them if I needed them, and went for the door. I gave Nathaniel a quick kiss. Micah was at the door, standing with one of my equipment bags in his hand. I kissed him, too, but neither he nor Nathaniel tried to get more than a quick kiss. They knew my head was already moving ahead, already settling into the mind-set I needed to do my job. When you're thinking about killing people, you don't want to think about kissing your sweeties, or at least I didn't. It was a way to separate that part of the job from the warm, happy part of my life.

"I've got to go," I said.

"We know," Micah said.

"We're scheduled with Jean-Claude tonight," Nathaniel said, reminding me of the time split.

"Thanks, I'd have forgotten and wondered where you guys were." I started out the door. Micah let me take both bags from him. You didn't let the other cops see your guys carrying your bags; you just didn't.

"Do whatever it takes to come home safe to us, Anita," he said.

I looked into those eyes and said, "Always." And I had to go, but now that Brice was calling at me from his SUV, and the SWAT van was already pulling away, there was that edge of excitement in me. I loved my guys, but a part of me still loved this, too. How do you divide yourself between killing people and loving them? The best I had on that one was just to kill the bad guys, and love the good guys, and hope the two lists never crossed.

25

I THREW MY gear in Brice's truck and had barely buckled in when he spun gravel and away we went. I caught movement by the woods near the house. It was Nicky, barely visible in the green of the leaves and trees. It must have been his turn on guard duty. I didn't wave, didn't do anything to draw more attention to him—he and the others had taught me that—but I watched him as we drove away, until the first curve hid him from view. I hadn't kissed him good-bye, and I hadn't thought about him until I saw him in the woods. When I could forget about someone as yummy in bed, and as dangerous, as Nicky, it just confirmed that I had too many men in my life. The trick was, what the hell to do about it?

"Would you be insulted if I said that those are two of the most beautiful men I've ever seen?" Brice said, as we skidded around a corner trying to keep up with the SWAT van.

"Say anything you want, just don't put us in the ditch!" I held on to the oh-shit handle for dear life.

"Sorry!"

"And thanks for the compliment," I said.

"Was the one in the woods one of yours, too?" He braked sharply around the next curve and I thought we were going in the ditch, but he managed to pull it out with a spray of gravel and a whish of leaves catching in the windshield wipers.

"Shit, Brice," I said. "And yes, he's mine."

"Sorry," he said again. "I can't find one gorgeous boyfriend to live with me; how did you manage this many?"

"I was just thinking that," I said.

"What?" he asked. The windshield got another slap of tree limbs, and I yelled at him, "Slow down or I will hurt you!"

He gave a quick darting glance at me, then slowed down; maybe it was the look on my face, or maybe the fact that I had a death grip on the oh-shit handle and my Browning BDM. I wouldn't have shot him, not while he was driving, but by the time we skidded up behind the SWAT van I was motion sick. I never got motion sick.

"I am so driving the truck home," I said, as I got the last of the gear from the back.

"You look a little green, Blake," Hill said.

"Brice's driving sucks," I said.

"Hey," he said.

I just looked at him, and he finally nodded. "Sorry, I'm not used to hills."

We split into two teams, to take the two entrances to the house. Brice would go with one, me with the other. We'd clear the house by shooting things, and if there was anything in the house that was awake in the daylight, if it ran, it would have to run toward one group or the other. SWAT normally liked more time to scout, plan, but the light was dying, there was no time. Our choices were to go in after dark with the vampires awake, or go in early with less planning. Hunting monsters is full of moments when you have bad choices, and worse choices, and no choices. I wanted our bad choice, before it turned into no choice, and the team had worked with me enough to trust my judgment. We geared up, we divided up, we had a plan, and we'd work the plan, until something big and bad changed the plan. I glanced up at the darkening sky and prayed, "God, let us be done before the vampires rise for the night." I didn't believe God would slow the sun in the sky for us, but just because you probably won't get something doesn't mean you shouldn't ask for it, because you never know, sometimes the angels hold hands.

26

I ENTERED THE house behind Hill's tall black armored figure, with Killian, only inches taller than me, and Jung, a bit taller than that, behind and to the side of me. Saville, who towered over all of us, had used the battering ram to open the door, and brought up the rear. I didn't glance behind and see him; I just knew that he'd be there. I trusted everyone in the room to do their jobs. His job was to cover the whole room, so that nothing came running into the room and surprised us while we executed the vampires. Jung and I, our job was to divide the ten kills visible in the room between the two of us. Hill stayed at my shoulder with his AR-15 covering me, in case one of the "kills" got too lively. Killian stayed at Jung's side to do the same for him.

The living room was just a normal living room with a couch, a love seat, and a beanbag chair deflating in front of a small television set, except for the vampires lying in a row. Most of them were in mummy bags fastened up completely over the body shapes. Two of them were just wrapped in sheets. In the movies it's all Dracula, Prince of Darkness, all coffins and candlelight, but most modern American vampires' lairs are more like slumber parties than dungeons. There was just no sense of presentation.

Saville opened the big drapes of the picture window behind us to let in the late-day sunlight. Most of these vampires were probably too young to move until full dark, but if any of them were old enough to move before that, sunlight in the room would prevent it. One, sunlight hitting the "coffin" substitute would simply keep them dead to the world. Two, if they were powerful enough to wake with the light hitting the outside of their hiding places, then feeling the heat of the sunlight would make them think long and hard about coming out early. Of course, once we started shooting them they might risk it, but it was the best precaution we had. When you hunt vampires, sunlight is always your friend.

The thick afternoon light filled half the room, letting us see that the sleeping bags were all different colors, as if they'd bought them all together at some kind of sale, or just wanted not to match so no one would use the wrong bag by mistake. One set of sheets was covered in cartoon characters. I hoped the sheets had been on sale, but worried that it was more than that. The figure underneath them looked small, but it was the fourth one on my side and fifth on Jung's side; we had a lot of shooting between us and it. I snugged my rifle to my shoulder and nodded at Hill. He knelt at the top of the mummy bag and opened it. It was a two-handed job to open most good mummy bags; that Hill was willing to have no active weapon in his hands and trust me to cover him was the highest praise that any of these men had for anyone. I concentrated like a son of a bitch and did my best to be worthy of that praise.

The hair was pale, but not as pale as the face. The face was young and probably female, but it didn't matter, and honestly I tried not to think about it. Hill snapped a picture of the face with a point-and-shoot camera; I sighted between those blessedly closed eyes, and pulled the trigger. The impact rocked me back a little, but it turned the vampire's face into a red ruin. It wasn't decapitation, but it was damn close, and with just one shot. Jung's rifle echoed mine. Sounds of distant rifles came from farther into the house: Brice and the others clearing the back bedrooms where the rest of the vampires were nesting.

Hill and I moved down to the next bag. Dark hair, pale skin; bang! African American, bigger, male; bang! Long blond hair, female; bang! Bald, older male; bang! The cartoon sheets were next.

Hill tried to just pull them back, but they were wrapped too tight. Jung was to his own sheet-wrapped figure, and Killian knelt beside Hill as they both tried to unwrap the little undead bundles.

Hill got ours unwrapped first, and the face was so young. No more than eight or nine when he died. Vampires that young are illegal; it's treated as child molesting, and bringing over someone that young will earn a vampire a death sentence. Most vampires would kill anyone that brought over a child this young themselves; no human laws were needed to tell them how wrong it was to do this shit. I had to believe this body had been dead for decades, long before the new laws, but as Hill snapped the picture, we didn't know that. This could be someone's missing child. Some little boy on a milk carton somewhere right there under my gun. Vampires are still the people they were before they died, for good or ill, so if this was someone's lost child, then they could have him back, but he'd never age, never grow . . . I'd never met a vampire that was under twelve at death that didn't eventually go mad.

Hill said, "Blake."

I blinked, and I pulled the trigger on that dewy, fresh, dead face. It exploded in a red ruin, as if it had been an overly ripe melon, except melons didn't bleed, or leak skull and brains. Jung's vampire was older, at least in its teens. He pulled the trigger, and her head just became a fine red mist.

I prayed that both the kids had been the oldest vampires in the room. I did not want the photos we just snapped to be the last image the parents had of their darlings.

I looked down the line and every one of them was bloody. The sunlight behind us was fragile, and almost gone. We could go back down the line and put a bullet in each chest, but if they rose early now none of them had eyes to do vampire gaze shit with, or mouths to bite with, and just like that the vampires' main weapons were gone.

Jung and I started where we were, Hill and Killian peeling back the sheets and bags so we could see what we were aiming at. I was pretty secure with the heads blown to hell that they were dead enough, but when you're taking out a vampire's heart, it's better to see exactly what you're aiming at. It's *always* better to see what you're aiming at.

We went body by body outward, taking out the hearts this time. Even through the special earplugs my ears were ringing by the time we finished. The sun went down a breath later; I felt it go, like a hand through my heart, and a second after that I felt a vampire. I felt it wake.

"We've missed one!" I yelled.

Hill looked at the bodies. "They're dead."

"Not this room."

Killian got on the radio and said, "Blake says you missed one."

"Everything's dead over here but us," Derry said.

Then the yelling started, and fresh gunshots. We fell back into formation, Hill first, me, Jung, Killian, Saville. We did it without asking, or needing to question each other. We fell back into the plan, except now we ran for the other rooms, our other men, toward the sound of guns and screaming, because that was our job, to run toward the trouble.

27

HILL DUCKED INTO the first small bedroom but was barely in the door before he yelled, "Clear!" which meant we all did our best to back up, turn on a dime, and go for the last bedroom. The yelling was coming from there anyway, and if SWAT hadn't been with me I might have just gone for it, but there was method to the madness of not leaving the chance of a bad guy behind us. If Hill said the first room was clear, it was, and we just had the mess in the second room. I'd have still gone for the second room first; right, wrong, truth.

Hill and I entered; he peeled off right, and I stayed with him. Jung and Killian tried to come in at our backs, but there wasn't room for anyone else in the bedroom. The three men had to stay outside, because every inch of floor space had an armed man already standing on it. Derry was actually kneeling on the bloody bed, on top of two gory body shapes, because there was no room. Brice was at the foot of the bed, in front of a pile of bloody sleeping bags. Hill had taken us right, because Montague's broad back was standing left, rifle to his shoulder. We aimed where they were aiming, but it was Hermes, standing in the corner between closet and nightstand, that everyone was pointing at, because he was aiming at everyone else. What the hell?

I caught movement behind the big guy, caught a glimpse of pale hand, and knew there was a vampire behind him. In the movies Hermes's face would have been bare so I could have seen his eyes and known he'd been mind-rolled by a vampire, but in real life the face is covered, and the helmet sits low. He had his rifle snugged up tight like the rest of us did, so his face was pretty much invisible, but he was aiming at his teammates; he'd been mind-fucked.

I wanted to ask what had gone wrong. How had this happened? But there'd be time later for questions; right now, we needed solutions. Solutions that didn't end with any of our people dead.

Montague was trying to talk calmly. "Hermes, I helped you build your kid's swing set. Do you remember?" Protocol was that you tried to help the bespelled person remember himself, on the idea that he was still in there somewhere and fighting to break free. It wasn't a bad idea.

"Why'd you shoot this woman, Monty?" Hermes asked, and he sounded genuinely puzzled.

"She's a vampire," Montague said, making his words slow, calm. The time for yelling was over; we needed to de-escalate the situation.

"No, you're wrong. She's human and you shot her." He sounded confused, which was good. Hermes knew something was wrong; maybe he was in there somewhere?

"Hermes, you know me, you know all of us, we would never shoot an innocent woman."

"No . . ." Hermes said slowly, "no, you wouldn't."

She spoke from behind the shield of him. "Please don't let them kill me! Please!"

"You wouldn't, but someone shot her," Hermes said, and his shoulders moved just a fraction. "I don't know him." He was aiming at Brice.

"He shot me," the woman said, and there were tears and trembling in her voice.

Brice's barrel wavered, and I heard him say, "I'm sorry . . ." and then the holy objects flared to life. She'd used her voice, and that was fresh vampire powers. The eye trick didn't always flare the holy objects except on the one being targeted, but voice, voice with ill intent did.

Brice's gun came back up, aimed solid, except that there was nothing we wanted to aim at. None of us wanted to shoot Hermes, and none of us had a shot at the vampire behind him. Shit.

My cross flared white and blue with that holy flame that was never really hot until vampire flesh touched it, but it was bright. I was glad the bedroom lights were on, because otherwise it could be blinding, but now it merged with the light in the room, and I could squint past it, except that the only thing I could really se was Hermes.

There was no holy glow from him. She'd persuaded him to take off his holy object, or torn it off of him before she mind-fucked him. If he'd still been wearing it, she wouldn't have been able to roll him, if he believed. Had Hermes had a moment of doubt? Later; I'd worry about his possible crisis of faith later.

The vampire was screaming now. "Help me!"

I had a moment to see Hermes tense; I moved, driving my body with everything I had. If I was supernaturally fast, I called it up and drove my body low into Brice. The rifle shot hit as Brice and I were still falling to the floor. I was on top of Brice's side, with him lying on the bloody sleeping bags. The bed hid us and the action from view.

Hill said, "Blake!"

I said the only thing that came to mind. "Here!"

"Same thing, to the front of me!"

It took me a second, and I hoped I understood the cryptic message, because if I didn't . . . I trusted Hill, he trusted me. I slid off Brice and crawled for the corner of the bed, got down on one knee, rifle held across my body, set my rear foot into the carpet the way you do on the track, fingertips of one hand down to help with the spring. I breathed a prayer, and visualized putting Hermes through the wall, the way you do in judo; you don't aim a throw at the mat, you aim it inches below the mat. I came up off the floor and launched myself at him, trusting that I was faster than Hermes could move to aim at me, or that the other men would shoot him before he could do it.

It was like magic; one moment I was on the floor, the next slamming low into Hermes's body, driving with everything I had. It was like a giant hand smashed him backward. There was a sharp crack, crunching sounds, and a woman's scream. I had a moment to feel Hermes's body give under my push, saw a pale arm sticking out behind him, and then there were men at my back, hands grabbing Hermes's rifle, grabbing him. I was bringing my rifle up to find the body that went with that pale arm when another rifle barrel appeared in my line of sight. I dropped to my knee and turned my head just as the rifle sounded so loud next to my head that I was deafened.

I'd protected my eyes from the muzzle flash, but my ears behind the special earplugs had been on their own. The inside of my head was a mix of strange quiet and muffled-almost-noise. My head rang with the nearness of the shot, and I fought to look around and see what was happening.

The vampire's head was gone, blown away by Montague's bullet. Her body was smashed into the wall, in a crumpled outline like a cartoon. I could see her chest wound clearly now and knew part of what went wrong. The wound was too high and far to the left. Yeah, someone had shot her chest open, but the heart had been missed. There was a larger outline around her body, and I think it had been from Hermes hitting the wall.

Hermes was on the bloody bed with two of the other men on top of him, using twist ties on his wrists. If the vamp wasn't dead, then the mind-fuck was still happening. Montague was bending over me. He was holding my arm and probably saying something, but I couldn't hear him. It was like all sound was on the other end of some cotton-filled hallway, echoes, bits, but nothing I could actually understand.

He ripped off his face mask, and I could see his mouth move. I recognized my name but could only shake my head and try to shrug through all the equipment. I raised a hand and waved it next to my ear, shaking my head at the same time.

I caught him mouthing, "Sorry." He pulled me to my feet, and I let him do it. He screamed next to my ear, "Are you hit?"

Hit, not hurt; it meant shot, or hurt more than just partially deafened. I shook my head. He left me standing there and started using twist ties on the wrists of some of the dead vampires. It was standard to bind everything in a house, even the dead, just in case dead wasn't as dead as it appeared. They'd taken Hermes out of the room, but Hill was kneeling at the foot of the bed. Oh, shit, Brice. Please, God, don't let him be dead his first night out.

Hill was putting pressure on Brice's shoulder, but he was sitting up, blinking—alive. Yay, fucking yay! The distant wail of sirens made it through the lack of clear sound. My hearing was coming back, and I started to get snatches of sound almost as soon as I thought it.

"Ribs broken," and I turned to look down at Hill and Brice.

Brice's voice came tinny, but clearish. "Thanks for saving my . . . but did you have to . . ."

I finally got that he was grateful I'd saved him from getting shot in the chest, but that the force of the "save" had probably broken some ribs. I called him an ungrateful baby. We laughed, he winced, and then two men in different uniforms came in with a stretcher and equipment. The medics were here; my job was done. It wasn't my job to heal the sick, only to make the dead lie down and stop moving.

I looked at the bloody bed, the gory pile of sleeping bags beside Brice and Hill. I'd done my job. I moved out of the room and gave the EMTs room to do theirs.

28

IF I'D BEEN on my own, or just with another Preternatural Branch Marshal, I could have gone home, but working with SWAT meant that I had to give my version of events, since we had wounded officers.

I sat at the little table, huddled over my umpteenth cup of really bad coffee, feeling the dried blood on my pants crinkle as I shifted my weight in the hard metal chair. Two men in nice clean suits sat across from me, asking the same questions for the dozenth time. I was beginning to resent them, just a little.

Detective Preston said, "How did Officer Hermes get his leg broken?"

I raised my eyes from the tabletop to look at him. He was tall, thin, balding, and wore glasses that were too small and round for his long angular face. "Are you asking the same questions over and over because you think you'll wear me down and I'll tell a different story, or do you guys just have nothing better to do?"

I rubbed my fingers across my eyes. They felt gritty, and I was tired. "Ms. Blake . . ."

I looked up then, and I knew it wasn't a friendly look. "Marshal, it's

Marshal Blake, and the fact that you keep forgetting that is either deliberate, or you're just an asshole; which is it? Is it a tactic, or are you just rude?"

"Marshal Blake, we need to understand what happened so we can keep it from happening again."

The second detective cleared his throat. We both looked at him. He was older, heavier, as if he hadn't seen the inside of a gym in a decade or more. His white hair was cut short and precise to his soft face. "What I don't understand, Marshal, is how you moved fast enough and with enough force to break the ribs on both Marshal Brice and Officer Hermes, and break Hermes's leg? Why did you attack your own men?"

I shook my head. "You know the answer to all of that."

"Humor me."

"No," I said.

They both sort of stiffened in their chairs. Owens, the shorter, rounder one, smiled. "Now, Marshal Blake, it's just procedure."

"Maybe, but it's not my procedure." I pushed back my chair and stood up.

"Sit back down," Preston said.

"No, I am a federal officer, so you guys aren't the boss of me. If I were SWAT, I might have to sit here and take this, but I'm not, so I don't. I've answered all the questions, and the answers aren't going to change, so . . ." I waved at them and started for the door.

"If you ever want to work with SWAT again, you will sit here as long as we want you to sit here, and you'll answer any question we ask," Preston said.

I shook my head, and smiled.

"I fail to see the humor," Owens said.

"Last I heard, Brice and Hermes are both going to heal up just fine."

Preston stood up, using that tall, gangly height to look down on me. I so didn't care. "Hermes is over six feet tall, and you shoved him into a wall, left a fucking imprint of his body, and shoved a vampire halfway through the wall by throwing Hermes into her. That's not standard operating procedure, Blake. We want to understand what happened."

"You have my blood tests somewhere. I'm sure that'll help you figure it all out."

"You carry six different kinds of lycanthropy, but you don't shape-shift, which is a medical impossibility."

"Yeah, I'm just a medical marvel, and I'm taking my marvelous ass home."

"Which home?" Owens said.

I looked at him, eyes narrowing. "What?"

"Your house, or the Circus of the Damned and the Master of the City of St. Louis; which home are you going to tonight?"

"Circus of the Damned tonight, not that it's any of your business."

"Why there tonight?" he asked.

I was tired, or I wouldn't have answered. "Because we're scheduled to sleep there tonight."

"Who are *we?*" Owens asked, and something about the way he said it made me suspect that it was my personal life more than my professional life they were after.

I shook my head. "I don't owe you my personal life, Detective Owens."

"There are people on the force who believe your personal life compromises your loyalties."

"No one who's ever put their shoulder next to mine and gone into a dangerous situation with me questions my loyalty. No one who went in to that house today with me questions my loyalty, and frankly that's all I care about it."

"We can recommend that you are too dangerous and unpredictable to work with SWAT here in St. Louis," Owens said.

I shook my head, shrugged. It was easier to do now that I wasn't in the vest and all the weapons. "You're going to do whatever the fuck you want to do. Nothing I say will make a damn bit of difference. You've obviously decided to use my sexual orientation against me." I said it that way deliberately; I knew the rules, too.

"We haven't questioned your sexual orientation, Marshal Blake," Owens said.

"I'm polyamorous, which means loving more than one person, and what I heard was you saying that the fact that I wasn't white-bread, missionary-position monogamous compromised my loyalty. Isn't that what they used to say about homosexual officers, too?"

"It's not the number of men you live with that we object to, it's that they're all wereanimals and vampires," Preston said.

"So, you're discriminating against my boyfriends because they have a disease?"

Owens touched Preston's arm. "We aren't discriminating against anyone, Marshal Blake."

"So, you aren't prejudiced against vampires or wereanimals?" I asked.

"Of course not, that would be illegal," Owens said. He pulled on Preston's arm until the taller man sat down.

I stayed standing. "Good to know that you aren't prejudiced on the basis of illness, or sexual orientation."

"Poly-whatsit isn't a sexual orientation; it's a lifestyle choice," Preston said.

"Funny, I thought it was my sexual orientation, but if you're a psychologist with a background in sexuality, by all means, you're right."

"You know full well I'm not," Preston said, and the first hint of real anger was creeping into his voice. If I kept poking at him, maybe I could get him to yell and that would be on the video, too.

"I have no idea what your areas of professional expertise are, Detective Preston. I thought since you were speaking like an expert about my sex life, you must know something I don't."

"I did not say a damn thing about your sex life."

"I'm sorry, I thought you did."

"You know damn well I didn't."

"No," I said, and gave him the full unhappiness in my eyes, and the beginnings of anger in my cold, controlled voice, "no, I don't know that at all. In fact, I thought I heard both of you question my loyalty to my badge and my service, because I'm sleeping with monsters, and that must mean I'm a monster, too."

"We never said that," Owens said.

"Funny," I said, "because that's what I heard. If that's not what you meant, then please, enlighten me. Tell me what you actually meant, gentlemen. Tell me what I misunderstood in this conversation."

I stood there and looked at them. Preston glared at me, but it was Owens who said, "We would never question your home life, your sex life, or imply that people who suffer from lycanthropy, or vampirism, are less worthy of the rights and privileges accorded to everyone in this country."

"When you run for office, let me know, so I won't vote for you," I said.

He looked surprised. "I'm not running for office."

"Huh, usually when someone talks like a politician they're running for something," I said.

He flushed, angry at last. "You can go, Marshal. In fact, maybe you better go."

"Happy to," I said, and I left them to be angry together, and probably still angry with me. They could recommend that I not be allowed to go out with SWAT anymore, but it would be just that, a recommendation, and the other officers didn't like these guys any better than I did. They could recommend all they wanted; they could go to hell for all I cared. I was going home.

29

WHAT I WANTED was a shower, a good cuddle, food, good sex, and sleep. What I got was two of my lovers arguing so loudly that I could hear it through the curtains that made up the living room walls in the underground of the Circus of the Damned. Nicky was behind me carrying one of my equipment bags; Claudia had the other bag. She was taller than Nicky by inches, one of the tallest people I'd ever met, and definitely the tallest woman. Her long black hair was back in its usual high, tight ponytail. It left her face dark and bare, and strikingly beautiful. It wasn't the beauty of dainty female things, but one of strength and high, sculpted cheekbones. She was a knockout with not a touch of makeup, dressed in the black pants and black tank top of the guards' unofficial uniform. The shoulders and arms that showed were muscled and ripped, so that doing the smallest motion made her arms flex and ripple with muscle. Nicky was broader through the shoulders, but Claudia didn't look small beside him. She looked tall, strong, and dangerous. The shoulder holster and guns were almost not necessary, like an extra rose on top of your birthday cake when the icing was already thick and deep. The fact that she was a wererat, which made her faster and stronger than I was, meant looks were totally accurate. Claudia was dangerous, but she was on our side, so it was all good. Besides, she had a conscience, unlike Nicky, who had to borrow mine. A conscience will get in the way of you being as deadly as you could be.

We stood just inside the heavy, dungeon-looking door that led into the underground. The gauzy curtains started just feet inside the doorway. The gold, crimson, and silver of the cloth was a bright surprise after the bare stone of the entryway and the long stairs that led to the door. I stood there looking at the pretty curtains and didn't want to go any farther. If Nathaniel and Micah hadn't already been staying here for the night, I might have turned around and gone back up the stairs and home.

We could all hear Mephistopheles and Asher arguing. Asher was upset that Devil, Dev, Mephistopheles' nickname, wanted to sleep with someone else. Then I heard the voice of Kelly, one of the other female guards: "Stop it, both of you, it's over, okay? I won't sleep with him, Asher; he's yours, all yours."

"I have a right to sleep with women," Dev said. "That was our agreement."

"Asher may have agreed you could sleep with women, but he's going to cause you so much grief about it that you won't be able to do it."

"Kelly . . ."

"No, Dev, sorry. You're cute, but no one's cute enough for this kind of grief; besides, I don't poach other people's men, and you definitely belong to Asher, or you wouldn't put up with this."

Mephistopheles' voice: "I'm bisexual, not homosexual; that means I like women, too. I'm not giving them up, not even for you."

"It's all been a lie, then." Asher's voice, and his voice held despair and anger like hot ashes against the skin. His voice held negative emotions the way Jean-Claude's could hold sex and love.

My heart dropped into my stomach, so that it hurt from chest to gut. They call it a broken heart, but it's not your heart that breaks, it's more like your insides are carved out from chest to gut, so you feel hollow. I loved Asher, but I was also beginning to hate him just a little. This insecure, almost insane jealousy of his was driving us all crazy.

The curtains were jerked apart and Kelly strode through. She was only a few inches taller than me, long yellow hair back in a high, tight braid; the black T-shirt and black jeans were a little too harsh for her coloring, making her look as if the fight had paled her out with anger, but I knew that wasn't it. Kelly didn't pale out; she flushed when she was angry enough.

She snarled her words, a trickle of her inner lioness growling through them. "They are so yours, Anita. I don't know how the hell you put up with all of them."

"The sex is really good," I said, and shrugged.

She shook her head, making her long, tight braid bounce. "There isn't a sex trick in the book that could make me put up with this level of shit from anybody."

I said the only truth I had. "Love makes you do stupid things."

She looked at me. "You love them all? How can you love them all?"

I thought about it. I thought about trying to explain that I loved them, but not all the same kind of love, but I sure as hell knew it was more than just lust, or friendship. "Yeah, apparently, I do."

She waved a hand sort of vaguely in the air, as if erasing something I couldn't see. "Well, I'm not touching another one of your men. They are way too complex for me. None of them know how to just fuck and leave it alone."

"I think Dev does," I said.

"Yeah, but he's in love with Asher, and that is one screwed-up dude."

"I can hear you," Asher called.

"Good," she yelled back at the curtain. "I hope you fucking can. Dev and I would have just fucked, just fucked, you insecure bastard, but no, it has to be about emotion, because you are more of a freaking girl than I will ever be!"

Jean-Claude said, "Mephistopheles does care for you, Asher, you know that he does."

"As you do, but the first bit of pussy that comes along and you chase it like a dog after a bitch, and I know you are there, Anita."

I sighed and just pushed the drapes aside. Apparently, Asher was going to pick a fight with all of us. "As one of the bitches in question, I think I resent that," I said, as I stepped through with Nicky and Claudia at my back. I didn't want to fight, but that didn't mean I wouldn't fight.

I got a glimpse of Dev as he strode through the curtains on the other side, going toward the bedrooms, the kitchen, everything else. Apparently, he was leaving the fight to us, or maybe he was simply too angry to trust himself, or maybe too puzzled. I knew that Asher confused me more than any other lover in my bed, and that included Cynric. At least with him I knew what my issues and his were, but with Asher . . . I knew some of his issues, and Jean-Claude knew others, but honestly, he was like an emotional minefield; you never knew when you'd step in it again, or how much of your relationships it would blow up. I realized as the first real anger stirred in my gut that I was tired of it.

He turned around, his hair flaring around his shoulders and face in a foam of golden waves. It spilled over one half of his face, leaving one perfectly beautiful half bare to the light, so that only one of his ice-blue eyes showed. He was angry, but not so angry he had forgotten to use his hair to hide the scars on one half of his face. When he was happy, sometimes he forgot to hide the scars, but most of the time I saw his face through a veil of his hair, like a golden cobweb between him and the world. His jacket was a pale blue that brought out the color of his eyes, and was cut at the waist so that it emphasized the broad shoulders narrowing down to slender waist, and the curve of his hips in a pair of painted-on satin pants that matched the jacket. The shirt that showed in a line at his waist was white, and probably silk. He was still dressed in the clothes he'd worn as ringmaster in the Circus above us. There would be a matching top hat around here somewhere, all blue satin and white ribbon band. He didn't always wear the same outfit, but I'd seen him perform in this one, so I knew it was for work, not just because he looked yummy in it, but he still looked yummy in it.

Was it shallow to say that some of my anger vanished because he came through the curtains looking heart-stoppingly beautiful, or just true? Even as I thought it, I felt Jean-Claude in my head, and knew it wasn't just my seeing him as lovely that made me patient, that unmanned me in front of his beauty. It was Jean-Claude who loved him more than I did, and had for centuries. They didn't always get along, and they'd been estranged for more than a hundred years at one point, but Jean-Claude was almost helpless before the beauty of the man in front of me.

Asher's eyes bled to pale blue fire, the hidden one gleaming like iced flame through the waves of his hair. His power rode down my skin like a cold chill.

Nicky and Claudia were at my back, the curtains closing behind them. I heard my bags hit the floor as they dropped them to have their hands free. Asher and I never came to blows, but I wasn't the only one tired of his shit, and neither of the guards was getting sex out of him, or had Jean-Claude's happy memories. It made them crankier than I was, made them sort of ache to smack some of the shit out of him.

I felt rather than saw other movement farther into the room, blocked by Asher's tall figure, and Nicky looming up at my side. But I knew the movement was Jean-Claude's bodyguards. We both had at least two of them with us most of the time. I had no memory of Asher ever hitting anyone he loved, and thanks to Jean-Claude that memory went back a few hundred years, but there might have been more than one reason that no one got physical with us.

Asher turned those glowing eyes to me then, and I felt the push of his power like an invisible wall was trying to move through me. Once his power would have just rolled over and through me, but that was then; this was . . . different. I hadn't had him try his luck against me since the Mother of All Darkness had died. Asher had nearly killed me once, by accident, because I was so vulnerable to his particular flavor of vampire wiles. Now I stood there, and his power did not move me. His beauty moved me. The memory of great sex and bondage moved me. But looking into that amazing face from feet away, with all that potential that I knew was hiding under the fancy clothes, I felt cold, as cold as the power that rolled off him and tried to cloud my mind. He was trying to calm me down, or make me not care about his bad behavior by using vampire wiles. It was so cheating.

"How many times have you used vampire wiles on me to win a fight?"

He blinked, his eyelids coming down over the fire of his eyes, so that his golden lashes were framed against the bright blue, and for a second it was like looking into the hot heart of some demonic oven with the door half closed.

"If your holy object does not glow, then I'm not harming you, isn't that what you said?"

I nodded. "I did, but maybe I was wrong, or maybe if I want to be fooled hard enough romantically, my cross just lets me do it; free will and all that."

"Are you saying your cross is intelligent enough to make judgment calls?"

"No, I'm saying the power that my cross is hooked up to, that I believe in, is intelligent enough to make judgment calls."

"Or perhaps your God sees no harm in me."

I shrugged. "Maybe."

Asher moved closer to me, so that my vision was full of all that gold hair, that heartbreaking face, and the glow of his eyes. His mouth was still the same pouting perfection that it had been when Jean-Claude first fell in love with him. The Church fathers who had used holy water to try to burn the devil out of Asher so long ago had skipped that full mouth, as if even they couldn't bear to ruin the angelic beauty of his face. The scars on his face that he was so self-conscious of actually touched only a small part of his right cheek. Only one long, white line of scar reached out toward the perfect curl of his mouth. It was as if when they'd seen what the holy water had done to his face, they hadn't been able to bear what they'd done. Sometimes when you do evil, you have a realization so bright, so harsh, that you mend your ways. I'd always wondered if the priests who tortured Asher had been converted to a better brand of Christianity, or if their faith had died as they trailed the burns down the right side of his body?

Asher took me in his arms, and the moment he touched me that much, his vampire wiles got a boost of power. Most vampire powers got a boost through touch. He held me and it was as if he were my Prince Charming. I gazed up at him and I couldn't "see" that his eyes were still glowing, or feel the cold march of his power. He was just suddenly perfectly gorgeous. There was no stop in my head, no cautionary statement, no warning. He kissed me, pressing those full, soft lips to mine. I kissed him back, falling into that kiss with my lips, mouth, tongue, and teeth, until it was more a tasting than a kiss. My hands, arms, body, entwined, pressed, wrapped—I couldn't get close enough, and when his hands started to pull my shirt out of my pants I reached under the back of his satin jacket and pulled on his shirt, too. Pressing bare skin to bare skin sounded like such a good idea. Pain, and I tasted sweet, copper pennies. It took me a second to realize I was tasting blood, but once I knew what I was tasting I started swimming up through the mind games.

I pushed at Asher, trying to stop the kiss, but the blood that had made me want to stop had him pulling me tighter, his mouth locked on mine, as he kissed me deeply, thoroughly. If his fangs hadn't been bleeding me, it would have been a great kiss.

I pushed harder, trying to pull away from his painful, sensuous kiss, trying to unlock his arms from behind me. I was making protest noises as if his mouth were a gag, keeping me from telling him, *Stop, don't.* One of the reasons I didn't like gags during bondage sex was that it stole your safe word away. You couldn't tell whoever was topping you, *No.* A gag meant you trusted the person to behave themselves, or, you wanted your *no* taken away. You wanted to leap off the cliff and let the dominant do whatever they wanted to you. Nathaniel found that relaxing somehow; I didn't.

If he'd been human I could have struggled free without hurting him. I was more than human-strong, but if he'd been only human, there wouldn't have been dainty fangs to cut my mouth. If he'd been human I wouldn't have loved him, because he wouldn't have been Asher.

He was holding me too close, too tight, so the only options I had to get away were things that would injure him permanently, or injure parts of him that I might want to play with afterward. He tightened his arm against my back and moved one hand to the back of my head, grabbing my curls tight. In the right head space, the right moment, it was enough to switch me to a submissive mind-set, but this wasn't the right anything. Asher deepened his kiss and drove those dainty fangs into my lips again. I made a pain sound, yelling against the tender gag of his mouth on mine. I stopped trying to push farther away from him, and pushed my body closer to him. He seemed to think that meant I was enjoying myself, because his hands loosened on me, not so much trapping me as holding me. I put my leg behind his, hooked his knees, and drove him toward the floor, but he didn't let go, so we both fell, but if I was falling, and he was going to keep kissing, I should have made sure my knee went into parts of him he wouldn't enjoy, but I liked those parts of him. I didn't want to hurt Asher. It's hard to get away from someone who's stronger than you are, if you don't want to hurt them. Shit!

I felt a trickle of warm energy before a hand grabbed my shoulder, and Asher's. I had a moment to smell the hot, burned-grass smell that meant lion; a second to know it was Nicky, and then Asher's power swatted outward like a slap, but it wasn't aimed at Nicky, or me.

Other hands were on Nicky, and I saw a flash of blond hair and summer-tanned skin, enough to know that it was Ares, and then the fight rolled away from us. Asher's animal to call was hyena. He'd reached out to the nearest one, and Ares's loyalty of paycheck or preference hadn't been enough to overcome the magic of Asher's power over him.

I was still armed to the teeth, had more hand-to-hand training than Asher, but if I wasn't willing to hurt or kill him, it was all useless. The sounds of snarling, snapping, and grunts of effort let me know that Nicky was fighting to get back to my side.

Then different hands grabbed a handful of Asher's hair, and my shoulder. I felt the energy rise and knew it was Cynric before I smelled the scent of his skin.

Asher tightened his hands on my back and hair. I felt him laugh into the kiss. He didn't think Cynric would know what to do next. He was wrong.

Cynric let go of my shoulder, but jerked the vampire's hair tight and hit him in the side of the face hard enough that it jarred me. I tasted fresh blood, but it wasn't mine. Asher stopped kissing me, stopped biting me, and one moment he was underneath me on the floor, and the next I was rolled to one side. I had time to spit blood, and then Asher came up off the floor, swinging. Cynric was strong and athletic, and was training with us in hand-to-hand, but he'd never fought for real. Training doesn't prepare you for a real fight, not completely. Asher had fought for real, for centuries. It wasn't martial arts; it was just a good old-fashioned punch to the bottom of Cynric's jaw. The punch lifted Cynric off his feet and sent him careening backward. He fell flat on his back and didn't get up.

Asher was just suddenly standing above him, his hair like golden fire, eyes blazing, skin almost transparent like crystal as he let himself be consumed by his own power. His humanity was folding away as he stood above the fallen man.

I spat blood on the floor and got to my feet, but wasn't sure what to do. I could draw a gun, but I wouldn't shoot him, he knew that. Asher reached for Cynric, but Nathaniel was there, kneeling between them. I'd never seen him move like that, a blur of almost magical speed.

Nathaniel said, simply and clearly, "No."

He didn't yell, but somehow that one word was louder than any scream. That one solid *No* seemed to reverberate through the room.

Asher stood up, straight and proud, all shining power and fearsome beauty, and was stopped, not by violence, but by a different kind of strength. One that women have understood for centuries, that the strongest man is weak in the face of the determination of someone they love. Nathaniel was kneeling in front of Asher, but somehow he was the stronger of the two. Kneeling between the vampire and his prey, Nathaniel

suddenly wasn't anyone's kitten anymore. He was on the floor, not raising so much as a finger toward Asher, but you just knew he wouldn't be
moved. Nathaniel had drawn his line in the sand with Asher, and if the
vampire crossed it, it would cost him things that wouldn't heal with a
bandage. I couldn't explain how I absolutely knew, but Asher saw it, too,
because he just stood there, and let Nathaniel stop him.

Nathaniel said, again, "No."

The sounds of fighting had stopped. I glanced and found Nicky on
his feet; Ares was on the floor in a broken heap, bleeding and hurt
worse than Cynric looked.

Jean-Claude knelt beside me, touching my face, coming away with
blood on his fingertips. "Enough!" His voice did echo in the room,
bouncing around the stone, and the curtains, so that the shadows
seemed to repeat the word back and forth, "Enough, enough, enough!"

Asher turned to look at the love of his undead life. "The boy hit me
first."

Jean-Claude raised my face to look at him. I was suddenly looking
into those midnight-blue eyes, the black lace of his eyelashes, that painfully beautiful face, the black curls that trailed down his shoulders and
halfway down his back. He didn't fight to keep the concern off his face,
or maybe he fought to let me see how worried he was for me. "How
hurt are you, *ma petite*?"

I shook my head. I wiped blood away from my lower lip and said,
"I'm okay."

He wiped his thumb across my lip and came away with fresh scarlet
on the white of his skin. "You are not all right."

"Better than Sin, or Ares," I said.

He nodded, and kissed me on the forehead. "I am sorry, *ma petite*."

"For what?" I asked, but he called to Claudia. "Help her to a chair."

Claudia was there, helping to my feet, and I seemed to need the help.
Maybe Sin had jarred me a little more than I thought when he hit Asher,
or maybe getting gnawed on had been more of a shock to the system
than I thought.

Jean-Claude was standing, facing Asher. "You make me weak, Asher.

I cannot be the master you need, because I love you too much to be as harsh as you need. Anita would not have taken such treatment from anyone else."

Claudia helped me into one of the new overstuffed chairs. I sat down, feeling shaky, and I wasn't sure it was just from being bled.

"She does not love me more than all the rest, Jean-Claude, that I know." His voice was so harsh; it was ugly as he said it.

"The modern term is polyamorous," Jean-Claude said. "We are polyamorous. It means to love more than just one person, Asher."

"Anita was here before I returned to you, but the weretiger, Envy, she was not. You and your wolf king, Richard, show me a glimpse of paradise, and then next I know you are both fucking a second woman. I was not enough in your bed, Anita was not enough, none of the other men are enough, it always has to be a woman with you."

"I love you, we are lovers, what more do you want from me?"

"I want you to have only Anita and me."

"That's closed poly," I said, "Nathaniel explained it to me. It's like monogamy with only one other person added." I had to cough to clear my throat, and the taste of blood was fresh and strong. Shit. If I'd been truly human I might have needed stitches inside my mouth.

"Jean-Claude and Richard fuck Envy. Why aren't you enraged by that?" He yelled it at me.

Envy was one of the new golden tigers who had moved into the underground. She was Dev's cousin, and as tall, statuesque, and gorgeous as he was handsome. The golden tigers were all pretty easy on the eyes.

"And I fuck about fifteen other guys. It wouldn't be fair for me to bitch about them having Envy in their beds," I said. My voice sounded harsh, so I coughed and tried to clear it, and tasted fresh blood. I had a choice of swallowing it, or finding a place to spit. I'd been where I could spit on the stone floor, but now I was surrounded by carpet. I just couldn't spit on the new carpet.

"Fair, love isn't fair, Anita. Love is one of the least fair things in the world. Don't you ever wonder if Envy is better in bed than you are?"

I frowned at him and shook my head. "No."

"Oh, that is arrogant to not even consider that she might be better in bed than you."

"There's only so much of me to go around, Asher. Richard is dating other women in his mundane life. It wouldn't be fair to make Jean-Claude sit around and twiddle his thumbs waiting for me, when I'm dating other people, too."

"If you truly love, you will wait."

"Who made that rule?" I asked.

"Dev wants to sleep with other women, when he has you; doesn't that bother you, at all?"

I thought about it and just shook my head. "He talked to me about it a couple of weeks ago. He's got a high sex drive, and I'm giving most of my attention to Jean-Claude, Micah, Nathaniel, and you."

"Oh, no, include the boy. He takes up more and more of your time."

I studied the beautiful arrogant face. "You hit him harder on purpose. You're jealous of Sin."

"It would be ridiculous of me to be jealous of a boy."

"Yes, it would," I said.

"Envy is jealous of you," he said. "She hates that Jean-Claude drops her the moment you appear."

"If she has a problem with the way Jean-Claude is dating her, she needs to talk to him about it."

Asher looked at him. "Well, Jean-Claude, has the fair Envy spoken to you?"

"She has not."

Asher turned back to me. "Cardinale, Damian's girlfriend, hates that he leaves her side if you so much as crook a finger at him."

I shrugged again. "Cardinale and Damian talked to me about that, and I haven't slept with him since then. If they want to try monogamy, more power to them."

"Why doesn't it bother you? Why aren't you jealous?"

"I don't know," I said, and that was the truth. I was so far outside the relationship parameters that I'd been taught to expect growing up that I just didn't worry about it. "It works for us, Asher."

"It doesn't work for me."

Jean-Claude moved into the room, not stepping between us, but drawing our attention to him. "I love you, Asher. Anita loves you. Mephistopheles loves you. Nathaniel loves you. Narcissus loves you."

Asher made a harsh sound low in his throat.

"Yes, you do not love Narcissus in turn; the leader of our local werehyenas would love you as obsessively as you seem to desire, but you do not want him, not like that."

"Narcissus loves the attention he gets from me, Jean-Claude."

"Of that, I have no doubt, but he cannot love you enough, I cannot love you enough, Mephistopheles cannot love you enough, Anita cannot love you enough, Nathaniel cannot love you enough. It is never enough for you, Asher. In the end, the fact that you do not love yourself defeats us all."

"Very philosophical," Asher said, and made sure the words were sneering.

"I have found a city in need of a master where werehyenas are the major animal group. I think you need to visit the city and see if it is a good match," Jean-Claude said.

Asher stood there, staring at him. "What does that mean, Jean-Claude?

"I thought I was very clear."

"Are you banishing me from St. Louis?"

"No, I am telling you to go and see if a new city will suit you and your powers better than here."

"You would cast me out because I hit the boy?"

"I let you bleed the woman I love, my human servant. It should have been my fist, not Sin's, that tore you away from Anita." He never called me by my real name unless he was furious. I was just glad he wasn't that angry with me.

Asher looked at him as if he didn't believe him. "I have hurt her worse than that when I top her and Nathaniel in the bedroom."

"That is with her permission; this was not."

"What if I do not like the new city?"

"Then call us; if we are done being angry with you, perhaps I will allow you to come back home."

"You mean to exile me?"

"I mean to send you away so you can think on what it is you value. Your jealousy always ruins your happiness in the end, Asher. I had forgotten that about you." He shook his head. "No, I had made myself forget it, but you have reminded me that this part of you, this terrible insecurity, destroyed almost every love you ever had."

"Tell me truly, Jean-Claude, were you and Julianna planning to leave me before she died?"

"I swear to you now, as I have a hundred times, no. We spoke of your jealousy, and your demands on us both, but we loved you. She loved you."

"She loved you more," Asher said.

"And there it is: your weakness."

"What weakness? That I want someone to love me more than they love you, just this once?"

"Belle Morte did not love me more, Asher."

"Liar."

"Pack for your trip."

"How long will I be gone?" Asher asked. His voice was angry, but there was something else underneath the anger; I think it was fear.

"At least a month."

"Don't send me away," Asher said.

Jean-Claude motioned at Sin, who was making small noises as he came to with Nathaniel still kneeling by him. Nicky was checking Ares's pulse, as if he thought for a moment he'd hit him too hard.

"Everyone is alive, but it is no thanks to you, Asher. You are my *témoin*, my second-in-command, and yet you have done this. It is beyond childish, beyond careless; it is spiteful. The kind of spite that got us run out of town after town centuries ago, because you grew jealous of the very men and women you sent Julianna and me to woo. You wanted to part them from their money, or their blood, but you didn't want us to enjoy our work too much."

"I wooed my share," Asher said.

"You did, but no matter how many men or women you seduced, you always worried more about the ones who were your beaus, your girl-friends or boyfriends."

"Jean-Claude . . ." Asher said, reaching out to the other man.

"Go, pack, and tomorrow night you will leave for your tour of the other city."

"Please . . ."

"Did you think I would take this behavior from you forever!" Jean-Claude yelled it at him. "Did you think that I would do nothing to stop you from hurting us?"

Asher let his hand drop slowly back to his side. "Who will run the Circus for you? Who will be your ringmaster?"

"I will be the ringmaster while you are gone."

"Who will run Guilty Pleasures for you? Who will take your place on stage there?"

"Jason is my assistant manager, he runs the club well."

"He is not you onstage."

"*Non*, but he is very good at being himself onstage, and that will be good enough."

"You will lose business at Guilty Pleasures if you are not onstage," Asher said.

"Perhaps," Jean-Claude said.

"No," I said, and got to my feet. Claudia had her hand out, but I glared at her until she stepped back.

"No, what, *ma petite*?"

"Nathaniel and Nikki will go onstage this week." Nikki was my stage name that Nathaniel had come up with for me, before our Nicky came to us. The few times that Nathaniel and Jean-Claude had persuaded me to go onstage, well, let's just say the club wouldn't lose money. I had inherited Jean-Claude's *ardeur*, and with Nathaniel's help we could use it to make the audience participation into something that left the Guilty Pleasures website inundated with messages asking for Nikki to make a return performance.

"You hate being onstage at the club," Asher said.

I shrugged. "I don't hate it, I just don't like it, but to give us all a cooling-off period, I'll do it."

"Implying that I do not do my duty for master and country, but you do?"

"I'm not implying anything; I'm stating that you are beautiful and amazing, and a big fucking baby." I wiped fresh blood on the back of my hand.

"I didn't mean to hurt you," he said.

"You've said that before. If you really meant it, Asher, you wouldn't have to keep saying it."

Nicky said, "And I gotta say, you've hurt Anita badly enough that no one will get oral sex from her until she heals. She's not just yours. You can't damage her so that it interferes with the rest of us having sex with her, and just expect that to be okay."

"You are just a guard, muscle, and Anita's Bride. I do not have to take chastisement from you."

"But you do from me," Jean-Claude said. "Nicky is right. You have spoiled fun for all of her lovers, and it is not your place to do so. I am her master."

"You aren't Anita's master; that implies control, and you have none over her."

"I do not need to own her to love her, Asher. You always treated lovers like a pet to be spoiled, abused, but above all—owned."

"Why is it wrong to want to be certain of love?" Asher asked.

"I am certain that Anita loves me, as she is certain that I love her."

"But she loves Nathaniel more, and Micah, and the boy adores her."

"I love Anita," Nicky said.

"But she doesn't love you," Asher said, and he spat it at Nicky. He meant it to hurt.

"I can feel Anita's emotions most of the time," Nicky said, "I know what she feels for me. I'm secure in my place in her life. How about you?"

Asher took a step toward Nicky where he stood over Ares's still-unconscious body.

"Asher, you will need the hours until dawn to pack," Jean-Claude said. "Go, and make use of your time."

Asher looked from Jean-Claude to me, and then finally back to Nathaniel, who was helping Sin sit up. "I am sorry."

Nathaniel said, "Jean-Claude is right. It doesn't matter how much the rest of us love you; if you hate yourself, the self-loathing destroys everything."

"Nathaniel . . ."

"Sin is my brother, Asher. I won't lose him because you don't feel loved enough."

"I didn't hit him that hard."

Nathaniel cradled Sin against him, and the younger man still looked out of focus, as if he wasn't quite sure what happened. "Your Master of the City told you to go do something; go do it," Nathaniel said. He sounded as coldly angry as I'd ever heard him.

"Go," I said.

"Now," Jean-Claude said.

Asher started to say something, and then stopped himself. He nod-ded, and then turned and walked back into the underground toward his room, his clothes, his suitcases, and to do what he'd been told to do—it was about damn time.

30

I SAT ON the edge of one of the examining tables in the infirmary area deeper in the underground. Doc Lillian's rubber gloves tasted like stale balloons as she fished around in my mouth. Her short gray hair was long enough to cover her ears now, but she was still the same smallish, thin, and terribly competent woman she'd been when I first met her. She'd thrown a white coat over her dress and hose. It was easier to trade the coats than to keep changing clothes. Lillian had a thriving medical practice in the human world, but that was because they didn't know she was a wererat. Humans didn't want to be treated by someone they were afraid would give them lycanthropy of any flavor, but rats had a double problem of not being "romantic" like werewolves, or were-leopards, et cetera . . . If you were going to be a shapeshifter, everyone wanted to be a big, sexy predator, not a scavenger.

"If you were human you'd need stitches," she said, as she took her fingers out of my mouth. She took the gloves off and tossed them into a large trash can that had biological hazard stickers all over it: Blood from almost anyone here was usually either shapeshifter, or vampire, and though you couldn't "catch" vampirism from being exposed to blood on gloves or bandages, it was still considered a contagious disease. You couldn't become a vampire from touching dirty hospital waste, and come to think of it . . .

"Dr. Lillian, has there ever been a case of someone catching lycanthropy from hospital waste?"

She looked startled, then thoughtful, and finally smiled. "Not that I'm aware of, but we do hospital protocol anyway."

The curtains parted, and Jean-Claude stepped through. He still looked perfect in his black leather pants and matching jacket, only the white shirt in the middle of all that leather was his typical lacy shirt. It was like an echo of his original century, though I had enough memories of that time through him to know that the shirt was modern material and sewn tight to the body, rather than loose and billowy. It looked antique in style, but it wasn't. It was like a lot of his clothes, touches of olden days, but they were all actually sexy club wear, or at least sexy everyday wear. I'd never seen Jean-Claude in anything that wasn't theatrical and/or sexy.

"Anita," Dr. Lillian said, voice sharp.

I startled and turned away from Jean-Claude and looked at her.

She made a little unhappy mew of her lips, then turned to Jean-Claude. "She's a little shocky. I think it's a combination of the police work earlier, then the fight, being injured, and worried about Cynric, and . . ." She paused, looked down, and then said softly, "I'm sorry about Asher. I know he means a great deal to both of you."

"Thank you, Lillian; I know that you do not care for him."

"I try never to question who my friends fall in love with, Jean-Claude."

"I'm happy that you think of me as a friend," he said. His voice was lovely to listen to, but unemotional, as if he could have used the same tone to say almost anything. It wasn't necessarily that he wasn't happy about Lillian thinking of him as a friend, but more that it was the voice he used when he was being very careful not to show any emotion. It was his version of a cop voice and face, except that where my cop affect was hard to read, a little brittle and cynical, his "cop face" was beautiful, almost seductive. You had to know him like I did to realize that it was as empty and meaningless as the smile I could pull out of the air for customers at Animators Inc., when I had time to raise zombies. Lately, police work was taking all my time.

Lillian smiled, but studied his face, as if trying to see behind the pleasant mask. She was harder to fool than most people. "Take Anita to that big bathtub of yours and help her clean up. Enjoy the fact that she's bleeding, before the wounds heal."

"How many stitches would she have needed if she had been more human?"

Lillian looked down, then up, and met his eyes. No, I was wrong on that, she was staring steadily at the corner of his jaw, and not meeting his gaze. It was standard practice with vampires not to meet their eyes, unless you had natural resistance to vamp gaze like I did. Being a were-rat didn't keep you from being bespelled by a vampire, it just made you a little harder to "magic" than a standard human. Even though she considered Jean-Claude a friend, she still wouldn't meet his eyes full on; interesting. But it was interesting in an almost disinteresting way; Lillian had said I was shocky, and she was right. Everything felt a little distant and unimportant.

"Ten, maybe fifteen stitches," she said, as if she hadn't wanted to answer the question. "Don't let that make you angrier with Asher, please."

"Why do you care how angry I become with him?"

"Because you've been fair, and just, and haven't overreacted. I like that about you. It's part of what makes you such a very good leader."

"You flatter me, to try and get me to do what you want."

She smiled, and all the lines in her face suddenly showed themselves as smile lines. It was a glimpse of a younger Lillian before sixty got so close. She was suddenly pretty. I hadn't thought about her one way or the other, until that moment. I realized she was blushing, just a little. Jean-Claude did have that effect on most women.

"My feminine wiles aren't up to your standards, but yes, I want you to keep being patient and fair, and the leader we need."

"As you say, *ma petite* will heal. There is no permanent harm done." But his voice was still that pleasant, empty charm. I couldn't blame Lillian for wondering what he was really feeling.

"Exactly," she said.

Jean-Claude came to me and took my hand in his. I didn't really need help down from the table, but I'd learned to be gracious about the men in my life wanting to be gentlemen. It was rare enough these days that it needed encouragement, not discouragement. I hopped off the table with his hand in mine.

"How's Sin?"

"He is fine. Nathaniel and Micah will take turns staying with him to make certain he doesn't have a concussion."

"Good," I said, but my voice sounded distant. I squeezed his fingers, as if touching him helped the world be more solid.

He swept the curtains aside and led me out. I let him lead. I was ready to follow someone, and Jean-Claude wasn't a bad choice for it.

Nicky and Claudia fell in behind us. Nicky had a small butterfly bandage near his eye, and a bruise starting around it. "How's Ares?" I asked.

"Concussion, broken arm and leg," Nicky said.

I stopped walking, which made Jean-Claude have to stop, too. I looked at Nicky. "Ares is a special forces sniper, and you did all that in just a few minutes?"

"Like you said, he's special forces, I'm not. I had to end the fight hard and fast, or I'd be the one in the hospital."

"I'm not arguing that part, Nicky. I just . . ." What was I supposed to say? "It's just that Ares does better than you in sparring practice, that's all."

"That's practice, Anita. We're not allowed to hurt each other for real in the ring here, and the army doesn't like you disabling each other in practice either."

"I guess not. What's your point?"

"I'm a werelion, Anita. Ares is a werehyena. Hyenas are a rough bunch, but they don't fight each other the way lions do. It's expected that males in a pride will challenge the leaders, and they have to be put in their place, or killed."

I realized something and felt stupid for not thinking of it sooner. "I thought Payne and Jesse were away on assignment like the wererats send their mercenaries away to earn money for the group, but that's not it, is it?"

"What answer do you want?" he asked.

"The truth," I said.

He shook his head. "No, you don't. Because you'll get all self-righteous about it, and then you'll feel guilty because you made me the Rex of the St. Louis lions, and so you'll blame yourself, and me, but you'll take it out on me, and I don't want that."

"So, you killed them."

"To keep them from killing me, yeah, I killed them, but not by myself. Kelly and some of the other werelions helped me. If the majority of the dominants in the pride had sided with Payne and Jesse, then I'd be dead, but they sided with me. They thought I was a better leader, and had stronger ties to you and Jean-Claude, so the lions would be better protected."

I thought about Payne and Jesse dead. It should have meant more to me, but it didn't. I felt numb, and distant with everything. My mouth was beginning to give me small, sharp pains. The fact that I'd gone shocky and it was only now hurting meant I was really hurt.

"So, if I'd been sleeping with Payne, then they would have sided with him and killed you?"

"It's not the fucking, it's the fact that I'm your Bride, and you're fucking me. That makes me more important to you."

I nodded. "What happens if someone I'm tied to metaphysically turns out to be a bad guy?"

"They all trust you to take care of it, like you did with the old Rex before me."

I had shot the old Rex point-blank in the face after he killed one of the other werelions, and tried to kill Nathaniel. Haven hadn't been able to share me with the other men. He'd wanted me to himself, and when he couldn't have that, he'd tried to kill the men I loved. His jealousy had made him do really bad things, and in the end I'd had to kill him to keep everyone safe. It had been a fight that had gotten out of hand, sort of like this one.

I tugged on Jean-Claude's hand, squeezing his fingers. "I don't want to have another moment like with Haven, Jean-Claude."

"None of us do, *ma petite*."

"Asher could have really hurt Sin, Jean-Claude. It takes a lot to knock the weretigers silly with one blow."

"Devil wouldn't have been knocked for a loop," Nicky said.

I looked at him. "What do you mean?"

"Devil is a lot stronger, he's got more muscle around his neck, so the blow wouldn't have hurt him as much, and he's a more powerful were-animal. That helps protect you, too."

I looked at Claudia. "How strong is Sin compared to the rest?"

She shrugged. "He's clan tiger, so that's a step up in metaphysics, but I'd say he's one of the least powerful of your tigers. The only one weaker is Jade, and I think her problem is she's afraid of the power."

I thought about the only woman tied to me metaphysically. She was tinier than me, fit under my arm like I did with most of my men. She was all pale skin, and long black hair, with those big brown eyes that uptilted in her face. She always made me think of words like *delicate*, *dainty*, and not a lot of women made me think that.

"She was her vampire master's punching bag for centuries; it makes her think like a victim."

"She's got these wicked skills when she practices by herself," Nicky said, "but when we try to put her in the sparring ring, she freezes."

"He made her into his victim," I said.

"But she's got these ninja skills, and I'm not making a racist remark on that; all the Harlequin are beyond special-forces good at some things. They're like movie ninjas, almost magical."

"Her master trained her up like the rest of the Harlequin, but he abused her so badly that she had the skills but never got to use them," Claudia said. "As if he crippled her at the same time he trained her."

"Accurate, I think."

"Why would the Harlequin waste all that training?" Claudia asked.

"I still wish you would not all say that word so casually," Jean-Claude said.

"The Harlequin aren't the bodyguards of Marmee Noir anymore. They work for us now, Jean-Claude," I said.

"And you were right to have me change the law about mentioning their name. It was excessive for that to be a death sentence."

"Excessive, you think?" I asked.

He smiled at me. "But they are still the greatest warriors, assassins, and spies that have ever been known," he said.

"Yeah, but they should never have been forced to hunt someone down and kill them for just saying *the Harlequin*."

"The Mother of All Darkness was the ruler of the Vampire Council for thousands of years, *ma petite*. She was the first vampire, the creator of our culture and most of our laws. She was beyond queen or empress to us. She was our dark goddess."

"We killed the Mother of All Darkness; that means we get to change her crazy-pants laws."

"The queen is dead, long live the king," Nicky said.

I looked at him.

He shrugged as much as all that muscle would let him. "It's what all the vampires and older wereanimals are saying. You killed her, so you get the spoils by wereanimal society rules, but you're Jean-Claude's human servant, so he gets credit for it by vampire law."

"I know the vampires consider me just an extension of Jean-Claude's power, like a gun, or a bomb."

"I do not think of you that way, *ma petite*, you know that."

I leaned into the hug, putting my head on his chest. There was no reassuring heartbeat against my ear. His heart beat more than most vampires' did, but it didn't have to beat, and it didn't beat all the time, and it certainly beat slower than human or wereanimal normal. I hugged him tighter, because I missed the beat of his heart. I preferred furry to vampires, still. I loved Jean-Claude and a few other vampires, but I bedded a lot more wereanimals than vampires; there was a reason for that.

"I fed on a human tonight at the club, not one of our wereanimals, and I have not been near enough to you for your presence to warm me."

"We'll fix that," I said, with my head tucked against the ruffles of his shirt. The ruffles and lace were never as soft as they looked, but tonight I didn't care. He'd actually stopped wearing as many of his signature shirts because I didn't like the stiffness of the cloth. But tonight I didn't care; I just wanted him close to me.

He held me close and whispered, "Yes, we can fix that."

"I have to clean up first. I'm still all sweaty and stuff from the crime scene." I realized he was wearing a white shirt and I might have dried blood on me. It made me draw back and look at the front of him.

"What is wrong, *ma petite*?"

"I may have dried blood and things on me, and you're wearing white."

He drew me back into his arms. "I would rather hold you close than worry about my clothes. The shirt will wash, or we can throw it away. I do not care."

I pushed back just enough to turn my face up, resting my chin on his chest so that I gazed up the line of his body, and he looked down so that our eyes met down the line of his chest. "I know you love me, but when you don't care about your clothes, I know it's true love for you." I grinned as I said it.

He laughed, abrupt, surprised, and for a moment I got to see what he must have looked like centuries ago before being a vampire had taught him to control his face and show nothing for fear it would be used against him by those more powerful than him.

I smiled up at him, held as close to him as I could with clothes and weapons still on, and loved him. I loved that I could make him laugh like that, loved that he felt safe enough to show me this part of him, loved that even when we were ass-deep in alligators, being with each other made it better. The alligators would be chewing on our asses either way, but with each other it was more fun, and we were more likely to be able to make a matching set of alligator luggage out of our enemies rather than end up as their dinner.

I gazed up at him as the laughter filled his face, and just loved him. The day had sucked, but Jean-Claude made it suck a lot less, and that was what love was supposed to do. It was supposed to make things better, not worse, which made me wonder if Asher truly loved anyone. I pushed the thought away, and enjoyed the man in my arms, and the fact that I had made him laugh.

31

JEAN-CLAUDE AND I were almost to the bedroom door when God came down the hallway looking unhappy. God was short for Godo-fredo, but he was tall enough, muscular enough, and just big enough that the nickname didn't seem entirely funny. He was darkly His-panic, and we had only one guard more massive than he was, Dino, but whereas Dino moved like a slow but immensely strong mountain, God was as fast as he was big. Dino would hit you harder, but God would hit you faster and more often.

"Sorry, Jean-Claude, Anita, but Asher is requesting to see Jean-Claude before he leaves."

Jean-Claude sighed, and squeezed my hand. "I can deny his request, if you like?"

I looked at him, trying to read his face. I should have known better. "If you want to see him, see him, but I'm still too pissed."

He gave a slight uptilt of lips that was almost a smile, but seemed sadder than a smile should be. The almost-smile was enough. I shook his hand gently. "Go to him. It's okay. I'll clean up and wait for you in the bed."

"I am sorry I won't be able to join you in the tub."

"It's depressing to use the bathtub without company. I'll hit the showers and do a quick cleanup."

God cleared his throat. We looked at him. "Sorry, but handling Asher may take Jean-Claude a while. Just saying, in case that would make a difference to what Anita does."

I looked at the big man. He looked uncomfortable. "What aren't you telling us, Godofredo?" I asked.

He looked at his feet, obviously unhappy. He mumbled something.

"What?" I asked.

He looked up frowning. "I'm pretty sure that Asher wants more than just a talk with Jean-Claude. He seems to feel that once he's exiled you may not allow him back and he wants a good-bye . . ." He spread his big hands out, gave a sort of shrug.

I frowned back at him, not exactly sure I understood, but thinking I might have a clue. I hoped I was wrong.

Jean-Claude raised my hand up and laid a kiss on the back of it. "I am sorry, *ma petite*, I may be gone some time."

I looked up at him. "Asher wants good-bye sex, doesn't he?"

"I believe so."

I looked at him harder. "He hurt Sin and me tonight. I know you're angry with him."

"I am, but if it is to be the last time I would not pass it up."

"Last time? He's only going to be gone a month, right?"

"Perhaps longer; the city is needing a new master vampire and has petitioned me to recommend one."

"You mean Asher might not be coming back?"

"Perhaps it is time he had his own territory."

"Maybe, but . . ." I thought about never making love to Asher again, never seeing him top Nathaniel, or having him top me, or bottom to Richard, or be in the bed with Jean-Claude and me, or . . . Just no more

Asher. It made me sad to think about it, but . . . "If it was the last night ever, I'll regret not being there, but I'm still too mad." Then I realized, "Besides, he didn't ask for me, did he?"

Godofredo shook his head.

"I would say this good-bye, in case it truly is good-bye, but I will give you the choice, *ma petite.*"

"Go," I said, "say good-bye. You've loved him longer than the rest of us have been alive."

"You will need to feed the *ardeur*, to heal yourself," he said.

I fought not to look behind me for Nicky, as I said, "I'll manage."

Claudia said, "If you're thinking about feeding on Nicky, then I need another guard to partner me."

"You want a red shirt, or another black?" God asked. Nicky was wearing a red shirt, Claudia a black; Nicky was willing to feed the *ardeur*, and Claudia wasn't. Red meant food; black meant they were just bodyguards. Though Nicky would feed the *ardeur* for me, but not for Jean-Claude, and he preferred not to donate blood to anyone, though if I told him to do it he'd do it, because he had no choice. I tried very hard not to make Nicky do things he didn't want to do.

"Any time we guard, Anita, we're supposed to be mixed, in case of emergencies," Claudia said.

"I think Domino and Ethan are the only ones on the clock right now?" Domino, like Nicky, preferred to just be my food, but Ethan was more flexible and would let some of the vampires feed on him.

"Either," she said.

"I'll send one of them your way." He looked at me. "Where do I tell them to meet Claudia?"

"Showers," I said.

"The room you share with Micah, Nathaniel, and Sin, or the group showers?"

It startled me that God listed Sin like that. He didn't always sleep with us. He had his own room at the house, and here, too, but he didn't use it much. Was that what Asher had meant? It wasn't always about sex, sometimes it was just the big warm kitty piles, but if God had noticed then everyone had. God wasn't the most observant of the guards when it came to personal stuff.

I thought about what God had asked, and said, "Micah might actually be asleep, so I guess the main showers."

"That's where I'll send the backup then," he said. He looked at Jean-Claude. "Are you ready, sir?"

"Yes," Jean-Claude said, and he gave me a quick kiss, and followed God's longer stride down the hallway. He never looked back, as he went to give Asher his good-bye. I watched him walk away in all that black leather, his long curls almost lost against it.

Nicky moved up beside me, his hand finding mine. We stood there holding hands and he asked, "Am I joining you in the shower, or you want me to wait outside and we find a bed?"

"Jean-Claude won't be using his bed tonight," I said.

"That's true, and he's okay with Micah, Nathaniel, Asher, even Sin, using the bed with you, without him, but I'm not on his favorites list."

I looked at him. "You don't feed him, the others do."

He gave that half-shrug around all the muscle. "And Jean-Claude doesn't like any of the men who won't at least donate blood to him sharing his bed with you when he's not there."

I honestly hadn't noticed, but now that Nicky said it, I realized he was absolutely right. "Then I guess you join me in the showers; that way we don't have to worry about messing up anyone's sheets."

Nicky grinned. "Shower works for me."

I grinned back. "Me, too."

32

CLAUDIA WAITED OUTSIDE against the hallway wall, keeping an eye on both the entrance and exit. The original design for the group showers had been to have only one way in and out, but I'd vetoed that. Yes, it was two entrances that had to be watched, but one way in and out meant trapped. Jean-Claude had pointed out that if anyone got far enough past our defenses to attack the showers, then a second way out of them probably wouldn't help. He had a point, but so did I, and the bodyguards voted with me. Paranoia was our friend.

There was a locker area complete with restrooms for both the men and the women. We actually had enough women living down here that it wasn't as silly as when we'd first had it put in. It was nice not to be the only girl. When we were in the locker area Nicky reminded me of another reason it was nice to be a girl. He took me in his arms, and kissed me.

The kiss was soft, and then he pulled back, and looked at my face with that one blue eye and the fall of his hair over the other side of his face. "Did that hurt?"

"No," I said.

He grinned, a fierce baring of teeth, and kissed me again. This time it wasn't soft. He pushed his mouth hard against mine, and it did hurt.

I drew back. "That hurt."

"I want to taste the blood in your mouth, before the sex helps heal you."

"You aren't a sadist. You don't enjoy causing pain."

"No, but I'm a lycanthrope. I enjoy the taste of blood and meat, and right now your mouth will taste like both."

"Some shapeshifters would lose control doing something like that." I studied his face, searching for a clue as to what it meant to him. Was this a bit of kink that he'd always enjoyed, but it had just never come up before, or was it a test of how much I trusted him?

He was my Bride, so he could feel what I was feeling, but Brides were different from any other metaphysical tie that I had. I couldn't feel his emotions; it was all about his feeling mine, and catering to me. It meant he was, in some ways, a mystery to me.

I realized I was a little spoiled that I could just peek, or share emotions with almost everyone else. I used to hate the intrusive psychic connection; now I counted on it.

"Don't you trust me?" he asked.

Ah, the trust tests. "You're my Bride; I thought you couldn't cause me pain, that it bothered you to do that."

"You like a little pain mixed with your sex. I think it'll translate to pleasure for you, and I know I'll enjoy the blood, meat, and sex."

I nodded. "Yeah, the whole prey-predator-chase thing gets confused with sex for most shapeshifters."

Nicky grinned. "If we weren't kinky before the change, we are after."

I smiled. "Can't argue that."

"Can I kiss you the way I want?"

"Let's take the weapons off first," I said.

"Why?" he asked.

"Because once you get the taste of blood and meat, and if the pain flips my switch, we may forget the weapons and I don't want you tearing the custom-made holsters off me just so you can get my clothes off."

His grin got even wider, filling that blue eye with a shining joy. "Okay." He let go of me and stepped back, hands going to his own holsters and guns. I started with the wrist sheaths and the two silver-edged blades. It would take me longer to strip weapons because I carried blades and guns. Nicky did guns, and kept one folding blade for utility purposes. He didn't actually see the knife as a weapon, though I knew he could fight with a blade if he had to, but it wasn't his forte. He preferred guns or hand-to-hand. He'd proven just how good he was without weapons in the fight with Ares.

"You're all serious," he said, "and not thinking about sex. You're almost sad, what's wrong?"

"You're that finely attuned to my mood, wow."

"You know I live to make you happy."

"I'm sorry that you actually mean that and it's not romantic rhetoric." I paused in taking off the waist holster and the Browning BDM. I'd already put the knives in one of the little open lockers that came with its own key and lock.

"I know you're sorry that you took most of my free will. I appreciate that it bothers you, but I would have killed you, and Micah, Nathaniel, Jason, all of you, if my old Rex had given the order. I'd have done it without blinking."

I was left looking into his face again, trying to figure him out. It was like looking at a wall: smooth, untouched, blank. He was handsome, but his face gave nothing away, and I didn't think it was the blankness Jean-Claude had fought to master, or my cop face. It was more than that, or less. Sociopaths don't have to show emotion; they do it most of the time because they've learned to ape what "normal" people show them, but they never really understand the emotions they act like they have; they are the ultimate actors. It's how they blend in, and most of them assume that the rest of us are pretending just like they are; many never realize that the rest of the human race is feeling emotions that either they never had, or were abused out of them. Nicky was an abuse survivor—that was how he'd lost his eye—so he'd had emotions once; maybe he understood them better because of that, or maybe not?

"That's one of the reasons I rolled you so completely, Nicky. Socio-paths don't help anybody but themselves."

"You're as ruthless as I was, Anita, but it costs you. It makes you feel bad, makes you doubt yourself. I didn't have that problem."

"Because you were a sociopath," I said.

"You say that like it's changed, Anita; it hasn't. I'm still a sociopath, I just can't act on it most of the time because you don't want me to, because it would make you feel bad if I did the things I think about sometimes, and I can't bear the thought of you feeling bad."

"So, what, I'm like your version of Jiminy Cricket?"

"Nathaniel showed me that movie so I'd understand what the hell you meant by that, so yeah, you're my Jiminy Cricket. You tell me when I'm being bad. You make me be good."

"But you still don't have any desire to be good?" I said.

He shrugged, put the last of his weapons in his locker, and closed the small metal door. He didn't lock it; he didn't bother. No one who was allowed in the underground of the Circus would have dared touch any-one else's weapons. People died over misunderstandings like that.

He worked his T-shirt out of his jeans and started lifting his shirt up. He did it slower than normal so that he revealed the flat stomach, the spread of his lats on the side of his lower chest, then the upper chest, and the shoulders swelling with muscle, and last his arms, bare and mas-sive. I looked at his bare upper body, and it caught my breath a little in my throat. I looked up to his face, that yellow, yellow hair that was actu-ally his natural color, with that V of bang that fell across his face in a haircut that should have gone on someone who went to anime conven-tions, or dance clubs and raves. Nicky could dance, which had surprised me for some reason. If he hadn't been so terribly good at hurting and killing people, he'd have been great as a dancer at Guilty Pleasures. The women would have loved the packaging, and he could be charming as hell when he had to pretend. He probably could have danced there for a weekend just to prove he could do it. He was competitive enough for that, but he wasn't temperamentally suited to make it his permanent job.

"You looked at me and were thinking everything I wanted you to think and feel for a second, and now you've gone all serious." He moved toward me, slowly, as if not sure what I'd do when he got there. "What are you thinking?"

"What am I feeling?" I asked.

"Suspicious, you're suspicious, as if you don't trust me."

"I trust you, because my vampire head games make it so that you are utterly trustworthy to me, but if I hadn't mind-fucked you, you would have killed me, and now you live with me. We've been lovers for almost two years, but I'm not sure you feel anything for me."

"You're wrong there," he said, and he was in front of me now, so that I had to look up at an angle to see his face. He put his hand on the side of my face, and slid his fingers into the edge of my hair. He was warmer now, as if he were a little feverish, but that wasn't it. It was his beast stirring inside him.

"What am I wrong about?" I asked softly.

"I want to touch you. I want to strip off and put as much of my body against as much of your body as I can get. I always want to touch you. I feel bad if you're too far away from me. It's like the sun is missing from the sky. Without you I feel cold, lost." He whispered the last, as he leaned down toward me.

"That's the mind-fuck talking," I whispered back as his lips hovered over mine.

"I know," he said, and he rested his face against mine, holding us just barely away from a kiss.

"Doesn't that bother you?" I breathed the words into his mouth.

His lips touched mine as he said it, so that each word was like a small caress mouth to mouth. "I want to kiss you more than I've ever wanted to do anything. I want to fuck you more than I've ever wanted anything, or anyone."

"You're addicted to me." I moved my mouth a little to the side to say it.

"I'm your mind-fucked bitch," he said, and he moved my face back so our mouths were touching barely again.

"Doesn't that bother you?" I asked.

"No," he said. "Does it bother you to know that I want to lick the blood in your mouth, that the smell of it excites me?"

My breath came out in a shiver as I said, ever so softly, "No."

"I want to trap you in my arms, I want to kiss you so deep, and so hard, that you can't tell me stop. I want to feel your body react to the pain I'll cause you, and taste your blood while I do it."

I shivered and it wasn't from fear, or mostly not fear. There was always that edge when playing with a shapeshifter that things could go too far, but that edge was part of what I enjoyed. It was the truth and I tried to own it. I breathed the words into his mouth, against the warmth of his mouth, "Yay!"

"Is that a yes?" he said, his hand sliding around my head to the back of my neck. His hand was so big.

"Yes," and I kissed him first, but then his hand tightened on the back of my neck, and he kissed me so deep and so hard that I couldn't say anything, not even no. His arm was like muscled steel at my back, trapping my upper body against him, my arms at my sides, so much more trapped than Asher had managed. I'd chosen not to hurt Asher, but Nicky . . . he made sure I couldn't hurt him. He trapped me as he kissed me, tongue tracing every wound, as he kissed me and licked the blood from the inside of my mouth. The pain was sharp, and I didn't usually like sharp pain, but about the time I might have protested if I could have said something, Nicky would move off the wound and just kiss me. He knew how to kiss me, and I kissed him back, though he held my head so tight I couldn't move into the kiss, and he was in control even of that part. He touched the deepest wound and I tasted fresh blood.

He made a low inarticulate sound, straightening up. Standing, he lifted me off the ground. My feet were suddenly dangling in the air, but my body was pressed so tight against his that there was no way to fall. I was safe, and at the same time trapped. I couldn't decide if I liked it, or it scared me. I hesitated, and because I didn't feel bad about it, the next noise he made into my mouth was a low, purring growl. It seemed to fill my mouth, to vibrate down my body, until it found that deep, deep center of me and there was a stirring inside me. A tawny, gold shadow rose from the dark, and I visualized my lioness padding through tall shadowy trees. It wasn't really what was happening, but it was what my mind "saw," so that I had some reference for the sensation of a lion moving inside my human body. I saw it as the lioness moving through jungle trees, gliding toward the growling heat that Nicky offered. My beast rose up to meet his, warmth for warmth, heat for heat, until my skin ran fever-hot, and so did his.

He drew back from my mouth enough to show me that his blue eye had drowned to lion amber. A growl that should never have come out of a human throat trickled from between his lips, as he held me.

I growled softly back.

Nicky roared, a great, coughing blast of sound that I'd never heard from any werelion. The sound was stunning this close. I was so startled that he had set me on my feet before I reacted.

I said, "What . . ."

He grabbed the front of my jeans and ripped them open, tearing through the zipper and most of the cloth around it. The strength was startling. He turned me around, roughly, making me stumble a little. He bent me over the bench so that my hands had to catch me on it, or I'd have hit my knees on it. He ripped my jeans open, tearing them down to my thighs. He put one hand around the back of my thong and ripped it off of me in one pull. Did it hurt, or did it feel good? That moment where rough and pain turn to sex and pleasure had switched in my head. I loved the sensation of him ripping my clothes away; the force of it, the eagerness of it, tightened things low in my body.

Nicky slipped his hands around my hips, and growled, "God, I love your ass."

There were other men in my life who whispered sweet nothings during sex, even quoted poetry. I loved them for it, but I loved Nicky for other things.

He kept one hand on my hip, but ran his hand over my ass, stroking, tracing, petting, and finally slid a finger inside me. I was tight enough that even that drew a small sound from me.

"You're wet," he said, in that hoarse whisper-growl of a voice.

"I know," I said, and my voice was hoarse, too.

He slid two fingers inside me, and began to push them in and out like a preview of what he planned to do later. He moved faster and faster, and it felt good, it felt very good, but it wasn't going to hit the mark.

"The angle's wrong," he said, in a voice a little less growling.

"Yes," I said.

"Lie on your back on the bench."

I glanced over my shoulder at him. "It's too narrow to have sex on."

"Just do it," he said, and it was at moments like this that I both enjoyed Nicky being less flowery than most of the other men, and wondered just how blunt he would have been if I hadn't mind-fucked him from the beginning.

I gave him a look the idea deserved, and stood up. "Not with my jeans around my thighs."

"Fine," he said. He knelt, and I had a second to realize what he meant to do before his hands balled into my jeans and jerked downward. I had nothing to hold on to, so it staggered me. He caught me with one hand, while the other one ripped the last of my jeans off. I was left in my shirt with the bra under it, and the ankle-high boots I'd worn in the field. They weren't club boots; they were police/military boots, not exactly sexy.

"I would have said you couldn't get jeans off over these boots," I said, and was half laughing.

He licked one of my cheeks, a long, slow taste of tongue, and I stopped laughing. Then he set teeth into my cheek, and I said, "Ow, too much teeth, too soon."

He licked over where he'd bitten. "You'll like it later," he said.

"Probably, but not yet."

"Lie down, on your back, on the bench."

"It's a really narrow bench," I said, and turned enough so I could look down at him. He looked up at me, his blond hair falling over his face, that one blue eye staring up at me. His face already held that darkness, that surety that most men's eyes get at some point when the clothes are coming off and the sex is happening. It's not exactly possessive, but yet it is, but it is predatory, and it wasn't just because Nicky was a werelion. It wasn't a shapeshifter look, or a vampire look, it was a male look. Maybe women had their own version, but I rarely saw my own face in a mirror during sex, and I had only one other woman to compare to, and she didn't have a look like this one.

I stared down into Nicky's face, and he stared up at me and let me see in his face what he wanted to do to me. "Get on the bench, Anita."

I didn't argue again.

33

THE BENCH WAS narrow, but Nicky pointed out, "You do ab work on the incline bench, just hold on." I put my hands behind me next to my head and held on. Our clothes had ended up in a pile on the floor. He did me by hand, using his fingers to find that sweet spot that was possible from the undignified angle of me on the bench, legs up and half bent, him holding one leg so that he could put one knee on the bench and get the angle his fingers needed to stroke over and over, fast and faster, that sweet spot inside me. He brought me screaming, fighting my body to hold on to the bench and not forget that if I let go, I'd fall.

He moved his fingers out of me, and between my legs to find that other sweet spot that was outside. My words came out breathy, as I said, "Fuck me."

"Not yet," he said, and his voice was growling deep again.

"Why not?" I breathed.

He stroked over and around me, staring at my face as he did it. "Because I've seen what the other men in your bed do to you, Anita. I want you to want me, and that means I have to bring my *A*-game, because anything less and you don't have to fuck me. If I don't put effort in, you'll go to someone who does."

It was hard to think with his fingers playing with me, but I tried. "I enjoy you. You're . . . great."

"You've got at least two lovers who are better at oral sex than I am. You've got two who are bigger than I am."

I started to try to comfort him, but he said, "I'm okay, I don't have to be the biggest boy in your bed." He started moving his fingers faster, a little harder. The pleasure began to build between my legs, and my face must have shown it, because he grinned. "Yeah, that's it. I love that look on your face."

One moment the weight was building, and the next, that wave of pleasure burst over me, poured through me, danced over my skin, my body, as if every muscle, every piece of me had become nothing but the joy, the sensation of it. I shrieked, head back, back trying to arch against the bench. Nicky called out, "Anita!" His hand was suddenly pressing against my sternum, pressing, holding me to the bench, while I rode the orgasm, and his fingers kept it going, until I lay boneless, eyes fluttering, and blind with the pleasure of it.

He was laughing, that deep, masculine chuckle that men have inside them when they are particularly pleased with themselves, usually about sex.

I tried to see me, tried to force my eyes to work, and the world not to be soft-edged and blurry, but another aftershock made me writhe on the bench, and Nicky's hands were wrapping around me, lifting me.

I had time to try to make my arms work enough to hold on to his arms. He moved both his hands down to my thighs and lifted me slightly, and then he sat me down on top of him, and slid the tip of him inside me. It stole the breath from my throat, too soon after the last orgasm, so that the sensation of him sliding inside me, his hands controlling how slow he entered me, was almost overwhelming. It felt so good, so . . . my eyes fluttered shut again, my hands convulsing on his arms, trying to hold me where he wanted me, while he guided our bodies together.

When he was as deep inside me as he could go, he said, "God, that feels so amazing."

I managed to gasp, "Yes, oh, yes."

Then he bent forward, pressing me back onto the bench with his body still buried as deep inside me as he could go.

"We'll fall," I said. The thought was helping clear my head a little.

"Hold on to my arms, I've got this."

I did what he asked, and the happy after-fog was drifting away on my very real fear we would fall off the narrow bench.

He raised my hips a little, angling my legs up and to either side. He steadied me while I found the angle I wanted with him on top, and then he put his hands on either side of me, wrapping them around the edges of the bench, in a reverse grip of what I'd done earlier. He stayed sitting up, his legs on either side of the bench, my legs on either side of his hips and waist, and he began to move himself in and out of me.

"On the bench," I said, eyes a little wide and not just from afterglow.

"On the bench," he said, and he raised his hips a little, lengthening out his upper body above me like a roof of muscle and flesh. His arms were moving with the rhythm of his body inside mine, and I transferred my grip back to the bench, one careful hand at a time. Once I wasn't holding on to him, he changed his angle and started finding a serious, quick, deep rhythm. I watched his body work above mine, only his hips and that long, hard piece of him touching me at all. Technically with the man above me it was supposed to be missionary position, but this was as far from that as you could get and still have the man on top.

The long fall of his bangs began to swing forward at the downstroke so that I could see the smooth, creased scar tissue where his other eye would have been. It was only when he was on top, and only at certain angles that I got to see his whole face above me. I'd come to value those glimpses of all of him. I watched the concentration on his face, that distant inward looking, which was his version of trying to last, trying to prolong the amazing things his body was doing inside mine.

He glanced down at me, truly seeing me. He gave a fierce smile and said, in a voice breathy with strain, "You are way too in control. I'm not doing my job."

I don't know what I would have said, because he sped up what he was doing, driving himself faster, harder, but the bench was too narrow, too hard, too something for pounding. He changed to a rolling, stroking rhythm of his hips, proving that he could dance, even with me on my back. It was a softer orgasm than it would have been if he'd just pounded me thoroughly. It built more like a clitoral orgasm, so that I could feel it getting closer.

My voice showed the strain of holding my position on the bench, keeping my arms tensed and holding, while he danced in and out of me, but I managed to say, "Getting close."

"Good," he said, but his eye was closed, he wasn't watching me anymore. His face had that deep, internal look again, but closing his eye meant he was fighting his body, fighting to keep the wonderful rolling, dancing rhythm, to hold us on the bench, to hold on until I came underneath him, fighting to keep everything moving, and not to lose his concentration now, not now, when he'd done so much work to get us to this moment.

Then from one stroke to another, the orgasm caught me, flung me screaming, writhing underneath him. My hands on the bench jerked and fought with the rest of my body, because my hands wanted to rise up and mark his body with my pleasure.

His voice growled over me, "God, God!" He shoved his body one more time so hard and solid that it made me cry out again, and I couldn't decide if it was a new orgasm, or if it was just an extra ending for the first one.

He growled at me, his face wild with it, and his eye lion-orange, his humanity slipping away as he shuddered and growled above me. One last shudder ran through his body from shoulders to hips, making me cry out again, because he was still shoved deep inside me as he shivered.

He half-collapsed over me, head dipping down so that his bangs brushed my face. I could feel the frantic pulse of his body in the side of his neck, the pounding of his heart just above me. He whisper-growled, "You didn't feed."

He was right, I hadn't fed the *ardeur*. I'd forgotten that was why we were making love. With his body still inside mine, a light sheen of sweat on his chest and stomach, my arms letting me know that I'd held this position and us in place a long time, the afterglow of all that good sex still flowing through my body, and all I could say was, "Well, shit."

He laughed then, and he was still too hard inside me, so that it started me writhing and making small noises again, as I laughed with him. We laughed and twitched, and tried to stay on that damn bench, and I still had to feed.

He finally lifted me up into his arms, so that he held me against the front of him, and I wrapped my rubbery legs around his waist. He was still inside me, but growing softer, so that as he picked me up he slipped out, and we were just holding each other, faces inches apart. There was a light dew of sweat on his forehead, too.

His voice was still breathy, his eye still lion-orange. "I love that you enjoyed it so much you forgot the *ardeur*."

I smiled at him, arms around his shoulders, hands clasped at the back of his neck. "You were amazing."

He grinned, a quick baring of teeth, more a cat's snarl than a smile. "I've never had to be this good with anyone else."

"Because you feel you're competing against the other men?" I asked.

"That and I've never been with anyone who likes sex the way you do. I have to keep up with you."

I hugged him with my arms, and my legs that were still around his waist. His hands were supporting my legs and ass, but he held me easily; even with the sweat drying on his body, his breathing still not back to normal, he wasn't straining to hold me. He was strong enough to bench-press small cars, but still I was impressed.

"Right back at you," I said.

He grinned again. "You still need to feed."

"God said he'd send Ethan, or Domino; you want to send them in?"

He shook his head. "No."

I widened eyes at him. "You up to it again?"

"I'm a lion, Anita. Give me a minute, and yeah."

I gave a little frown. "Isn't this fast recovery for you?"

"There's usually a line," he said, "so I step out of the way, usually for Nathaniel."

I smiled. "He does share well."

"He likes to watch," Nicky said. He stood up with me still wrapped around him.

I gave him wide eyes, and tightened my arms and legs around him. "Now I am impressed. I'm not sure I could stand yet."

"In your bed, I'm not the biggest, I'm not the most flexible, I'm not multi-orgasmic, I don't have centuries of practice, I'm not even sure that I have the most stamina. Nathaniel and Jean-Claude are scary impressive there." He stood on one leg as he moved us off the bench completely and started walking toward the showers. "But I'm strong, and I can fight, and my physical recovery time from almost anything is really good. Give me a few more minutes and I'll prove it."

He carried me easily, smoothly, as if I weighed nothing. I was strong for my size, I was damn good, but I'd never be able to return the favor. I would never be a really big, physical man, but in that moment I allowed myself to enjoy that I had one to carry me into the showers, instead of being upset that I could never have carried him.

34

WE CLEANED UP in the shower, and when we'd rinsed the soap and conditioner out, Nicky proved to me that he had more game.

I ended up on the smooth, wet tiles on my knees, the hot water pounding down on us. He shielded me from most of the spray, only rivulets of it tracing down his body so that the water was more decoration to all that smooth skin. I licked the water off the edge of his groin, sipped it off the loose skin that dangled so delicately below. He didn't shave completely like most of the men in my life, so I licked the loose skin, feeling the smoother hardness underneath. We'd already found that my mouth had healed a lot; I wasn't sure it was up to full oral, but I was willing to try, and I'd never met a man who would argue about the offer. If Nicky had been shaved all the way I would have sucked and rolled those delicate balls into my mouth, but hair between the teeth—not my favorite. But either he shaved, or didn't need to, above, and that I took into my mouth completely. He was still small, loose from the heat of the water, so I could take all of him easily, rolling, sucking, licking, enjoying the sensation of him in my mouth when he was still soft enough that I didn't have to fight to breathe, or fight my gag reflex. I could just enjoy myself and I did. He didn't stay small long.

I was even more healed than I had thought. I hadn't remembered concentrating on using Nicky's energy to heal myself, but apparently it had.

I hesitated as he grew bigger, because if I put him in the sides of my mouth he slid over the few wounds that weren't completely healed. I stopped, and thought about the problem, on my knees, staring at Nicky, so hard and perfect.

"If it hurts too much, we can do something else," he said.

I nodded, but decided I'd try avoiding the sides of my mouth. If you can't go around a problem, go straight at it, go straight down it. If I took him straight down, over my teeth, across my tongue, and to the back of my throat, driving him in and out of my mouth so that we were mimicking what he'd done earlier between my legs, it didn't hurt much. It hurt a little, but the worst was to the sides of my mouth, which meant that I'd struggled more in Asher's kiss than I'd thought. I pushed the thought away, and let myself enjoy the man in front of me.

"God," Nicky said.

I rolled my eyes upward to see him staring down at me, face growing frantic. He'd let the water slick his hair completely back from his face. I think it was the first time I'd really seen his face so clean and bare. He was handsome, he really was. I liked the lines of his face without that fall of hair to cover the missing eye. He wasn't less beautiful because he wasn't "perfect"; it was Nicky, it was the way he looked, it was him, and I liked it, loved it. I couldn't smile with my mouth full, but I could put the smile into my eyes. He'd grown long and hard and smooth in my mouth. I loved sliding my mouth down the long shaft of him, until there was that moment when he touched the back of my throat and I could choose whether to go back up or push him down the curve of my throat. He was just long enough that it was an effort to swallow him down. There were some times that bigger was not better.

I wrapped my hand around the base of him, so that I could go down far enough for him to enter my throat, but not so far that it was choking me. I had worked hard to get rid of my gag reflex, and it was a lot less, but there was one reflex that was harder to control, the I-can't-breathe reflex. I slid my mouth over him, and then pushed until my lips touched my hand, and then I let go, put my hands behind him to hold on to his thighs, while I forced myself that last few inches until my lips touched the front of his body completely, my mouth locked around him. I had to calm my pulse, calm my body, it was almost meditative, to stop my body from panicking that we couldn't breathe past him.

I drew back off him slowly, and had to cough. My eyes were tearing up, and my nose was beginning to run. I moved to the side of Nicky's leg and let the spray from the shower hit my face enough to clean the tears and snot away. In movies they clean the actress up between shots, but in real life, it's messy. It was my body trying to get rid of whatever the fuck was down so far, and not being swallowed. The body rebelled against something that large being that far down, and not being swallowed. It was like my body was saying, *Either swallow, or get it out.*

"You okay?" he asked.

"Fine," I said, but my voice sounded hoarse enough that I had to clear my throat. It wasn't sexiness; it was my throat getting a little abused by what we were doing.

"God, Anita, please feed."

"You just want me to use the *ardeur* because I don't have a gag reflex and get even better at deep-throating once I release it."

He nodded, the water misting around him as he moved his shoulders in it. "Yeah," he said, and his voice was a little frantic.

I did what he asked, because honestly I wanted my mouth completely healed, and my stomach was letting me know that there were other hungers that needed feeding besides the *ardeur*. That I noticed it in the middle of good sex meant I was way hungrier than I knew. It was the kind of hunger that if I didn't fix it, my beasts could rise and look for food on their own, and take my body with them while they did it.

Once I'd fought to keep the *ardeur* penned up, but now I had to think about it, find it, call it, unleash it. One minute I was in control, the next the *ardeur* rode me, and spilled out of my skin and into Nicky.

What little gag reflex I had was gone; the small, sharp pains of the wounds in my mouth just added to the desire, everything translated to sex, to want, need, desire. I drove him as deep down my throat as I could, and now there was no need to fight my body. It was on the same side as the *ardeur*, and the *ardeur* wanted to feed.

Nicky put his hand on the back of my head, and I had enough of me left in there somewhere to look up and say, "When I go down, hold me against you."

"You can't breathe," he said.

"I'll tap out, then you let me go. I'll breathe again, then go down again."

"You want me to hold you, force you to stay down on me?" He made it a question.

"Yes."

He raised an eyebrow, and looked totally suspicious.

It made me laugh. "I want you to mouth-fuck me, Nicky, and the *ardeur* will help me do that."

He frowned at me. Naked, wet in the shower, body hard and ready, but he wanted to make sure this wouldn't come back and bite him later. I guess I couldn't blame him.

"I've done it with Nathaniel, and Asher, and Richard."

That made him give me a wide-eyed expression. "Richard, really?"

"Yes," I said.

"Well, fuck, if you can do it with him . . ."

"Yep," I said.

He still looked a little doubtful, but said, "Okay."

I let the *ardeur* rise back up, like heat spilling over my skin, down my fingertips to find Nicky's thigh and pour over us both. I used my other hand to help guide him into my mouth, down my throat, then had to move my hand so I could go all the way down, until my lips were pressed tight to the front of his body. His hand pushed against my head, and I used my free hand to push his hand harder against the back of my head.

He didn't question it this time; he just pressed his big hand against the back of my head and used all that strength to hold me against his body. At first it was exactly what I wanted; it felt so good to be able to just stay there with him impossibly far down my throat, but even with the *ardeur* riding me, eventually I needed to breathe. I tried to come up off him, but his hand pushed harder and I was trapped. Part of me enjoyed that I was trapped, that he could, if he wanted to, keep me there, keep me there until I choked, until my body made me fight for breath. I pushed against his body with my hands, but he pushed back, holding me, forcing me to stay down. I stayed as long as I could, before panic chased back the *ardeur*, and then I tapped against his thigh. There was a moment where I had to trust, utterly trust, that he'd respect the tap-out. I'd admitted to myself a couple of years ago that part of what I enjoyed was that moment of trust, that instant where the person you were with could do something really bad to you, and only their choice to be good kept the bad thing from happening. I liked that moment of not knowing if it was all going to go horribly wrong this time. I hadn't liked that this did it for me, that this kind of moment really, really did it for me, but I'd made peace with it. I'd made peace with myself, and I fucking loved it.

Nicky let me go; he let me draw back off his body. I took a deep, shaking breath.

"Are you okay?" he asked, and he sounded worried.

I nodded, and finally was able to say, "Yes." I looked up at him and said, "We can do this a little more, but the not being able to breathe makes the *ardeur* back off, eventually. It does that when self-preservation is on the line."

"Then we fuck, so you can feed."

"Or we mouth-fuck; with the *ardeur* I can do that, and I enjoy it, too."

He had a moment of indecision so plain on his face it was almost painful, but then he said, "We'll see how we feel when we get there."

I agreed, and we went back to our game of deep-throat bondage, because you don't need ropes and chains for it to be bondage, just to be held and not be able to get away. This game had that in spades.

When we'd done it as long as my throat could take it, even with the *ardeur*, Nicky said, "I want to fuck you again. I love that I'm on your short list of the men you don't make wear a condom."

It hadn't been a front-of-the-head decision; he was just with me when I was with Micah and Nathaniel and Sin so much, and they were on my fluid-bonded list, too, so . . . it had been a recent change to not make Nicky put on that extra layer of protection. I was on the pill, and I was a carrier for lycanthropy so I couldn't catch that even if the rough sex bled me, but I still made most of the other men wear condoms, just in case. I remembered the moment I hadn't made Nicky put one on; Nathaniel and Sin had both been there, but Micah had been out of town. It had just seemed natural, but his mentioning it like that made me think about it. I wasn't always good when I thought about things. I tended to start tearing at my relationships, as if I were trying to break free of some sort of trap. Did I still see love as a trap? Was I still that unhealthy, that once a man reminded me how much he meant to me, I had to fight my way free of it until I destroyed everything? Wasn't that what I was doing with Sin? Was I about to do the same with Nicky?

"I can't hear your thoughts, only feel your emotions, but I don't like that look. It's never good. What did I say wrong?"

I looked up at him. His hair was still slicked back from his face, leaving it bare and wonderful. His body was naked and covered in water, so lickable and yummy. I could still feel the happy ache of him in my throat. He'd been at my side for two years. What did he have to do to prove himself? What did anyone have to do to prove themselves to me? Some of the men in my life would have said a hell of a lot.

I realized that the *ardeur* had receded again. Once I'd been at its mercy, but not now. I controlled the *ardeur* so well that I had to remind myself to feed sometimes. If I didn't feed, my ability to heal was compromised, and I would eventually begin to draw energy off Nathaniel and Damian first, and then move on to Jean-Claude and Richard, but only after Nathaniel and Damian were dead. Jean-Claude had explained that metaphysical math to me when my control got this good, because I'd thought control meant victory. I'd forgotten the *ardeur* was like your stomach; just because you could teach yourself not to want to eat didn't mean your body didn't need the food.

I still needed to feed, but it wasn't the overwhelming control-stealing thing it had been. I had more choices now. I couldn't blame the *ardeur* for the sex I was having. The *ardeur* put some of the men on my plate, but what I did with them was me now. I tried to decide how I felt about that.

"Anita?" Nicky made it a question. His face was closing down, drawing away from me, putting his defenses back in place. He'd been made into a sociopath, which meant some of the emotions were in there. I didn't want him to put them away again. I liked the glimpses I got of his heart.

"Fuck me," I said it softly.

"What?" he asked, like he was having trouble hearing above the pounding water.

"Fuck me," I said, louder.

A smile curled the edges of his mouth, and filled his face with an almost disturbing happiness. There was always the sense that there was darkness inside Nicky that he got to let out thanks to me, but it was still in there, and it always wants out, the dark. It can be controlled, harnessed even, but in the end it just wants to come out and play dark games.

He let me see the happy monster inside him. It had nothing to do with his beast; what I saw in his face wasn't animal, it was all human, just most people didn't like to admit it. Nicky didn't mind. Nathaniel didn't mind. Dev didn't mind. And because they didn't mind, I was beginning not to mind either.

"Fuck me," I said, again.

He didn't make me ask again.

35

NICKY PICKED ME up again, and I wrapped myself around him like a monkey, legs at his waist, and arms around those wide shoulders. He pushed me up against the wall out of the way of the water, while it pounded, hot and steamy, behind us, spraying on the back of his body only when he moved back far enough to try for the hardest, deepest thrust he could get from this angle.

Not every man could do good wall sex. You had to be long enough, and strong enough, and have stamina, not just the regular sex kind, but legs, arms, hips, in a way that regular intercourse didn't demand. He found a hard, fast rhythm, going in and out of me, so that I didn't have time to enjoy one wave of pleasure, before he was thrusting into me again, and one sensation led to the next so fast, so completely that I lost track of everything but the pounding of his hips, his body thrusting into mine. He was going so hard and fast that my body began to bump and scrape against the wall. The tiles were smooth, but it was still a near-bruising rhythm, and I loved it. My eyes started to close, and I had to fight the pleasure to keep my arms and legs tight around him. His hands were on my thighs and hips, but I had to work in this position, too. I had to hold on, and as the pleasure built, that became harder and harder to do. I wanted to give myself over to the feel of his body in mine, the strength of his hands holding me against the wall, the feel of my body rubbing against the wall from the power of his body shoving me against it.

His voice came thin with strain, growling, with effort. "Feed when I go, Anita. I won't have another time in me."

That he admitted it said just how much effort even Nicky was having to expend to do wall sex this forcefully.

"Yes," I said, and my voice sounded breathier than his did.

"Is that yes, yes, great sex, or you heard me?" he asked, in that deep, exercise-rich voice.

"Yes, I heard you," I gasped.

His hips hesitated for a second, and then he went back to that fast, pounding rhythm. I fought between the amazing sensations of him fucking me, and holding on to him, helping him fuck me against the slick cool/warmth of the tiles.

His body shuddered, hesitated, and he gasped, "Soon, real soon."

"Heard you," I whispered, or maybe I shouted above the pounding water, the heat of it, and the cool brush of the tiles as my back rocked up and down on them. I couldn't tell anymore, it was all I could do to keep my grip at his shoulders and waist.

I realized that I'd put the *ardeur* away again, that it had just been me and Nicky against the wall. I had to raise the *ardeur* again, had to call it, and suddenly I was all heat and need, and Nicky cried out, "Oh, God, that feels . . ." Whatever he was about to say was lost between one thrust and the next, but he went in one long, solid thrust between my legs. His body shuddered against me, inside me, as he pinned me to the wall, and I fed.

I fed on the feel of him inside me, the spill of him inside me. I fed on the strength of his hands on my thigh and hip. I fed on the feel of him in my arms, the feel of my legs around his waist. I fed on his eyes closed, head slightly back, and being able to see his face bare and lost to the moment of release. I fed on all of him, and the power rush poured over my skin in a wave of heat like nothing I'd ever felt before.

He put one hand on the wall, and then we were sliding down to his knees. I thought it was just the exhaustion of amazing sex, and then his head bowed, and he began to slump to the side, and I knew something was wrong.

I was able to uncurl myself from him, but he fell completely limp to the floor. I touched his shoulder, and his skin was cool to the touch. I searched for the big pulse in his neck, and couldn't find it. I screamed for help, because I had no idea what was wrong with him.

36

CLAUDIA CAME FROM one entrance and Domino came from the other. He ran a hand through his short black-and-white curls and asked, "What happened?"

I was straddling Nicky's body, pumping on his chest, trying to get his heart to beat. I said, "I don't know."

Claudia used her cell phone to call for the doctor on call. She turned off the water as Domino checked Nicky's neck for a pulse. "Shit," he said.

"I know," I said, and I was on the verge of tears. I screamed his name, and rose up above his body, hands wrapped together to make one bigger fist, and pounded down on that big barrel of a chest. "Breathe, damn you, breathe!"

If it had been any of the other people that I was metaphysically connected to, I could have shared energy with him, but he was my Bride, which meant the energy only went one way. I could draw off him, but I couldn't give him energy automatically. Fuck, fuck, fuck, fuck, fuck!

I opened my link with Jean-Claude. I got a confused glimpse of him and Asher on the bed. He was stroking Asher's hair, cuddling after the sex. I opened myself wide, and I asked wordlessly, letting him feel what was happening, so there wasn't any need to use words. I asked for help, I asked for ideas, I screamed in my mind, "Nicky!"

Jean-Claude rose up in my mind, leaving the bed and Asher lying on his stomach behind him, to sit up, and look at me. *"Ma petite . . ."*

"Help him!"

Claudia said, "We're trying."

I didn't waste time telling her that I wasn't talking to her. Domino was one of my tigers to call; he knew what I was doing, because he could feel it. He knelt by Nicky's head and put his hands on the other man's shoulders.

Jean-Claude gave me memories of Belle Morte straddling a man's body. She damn near glowed with energy, her skin not vampire pale, but almost human-flushed. The vampire under her was paler than death. I knew that Jean-Claude and Asher were seeing her kill one of her Brides.

I knew that they were coming this way, but it didn't matter. Jean-Claude didn't have any idea how to help Nicky.

The medics were here. Domino helped lift me off Nicky, and then helped them move him out of the showers and into the locker room. I followed them, but had to stay in the doorway to the showers, because there wasn't room for more people in the locker room. They laid him on a pad by the bench where we'd made love. The second doctor had the paddles of the defibrillator ready and charged. One of our nurses, who had patched me up before for minor stuff, started putting pads and leads on his chest.

The doc with the paddles called, "Ready!"

Everyone called, "Clear!"

Nicky's body twitched with the charge. The nurse checked for his pulse. The doctor was already charging the paddles again. The male doctor said, "Again."

She hit him again with a stronger jolt. I could smell a little whiff of burning flesh.

"Again!"

I huddled in the doorway and prayed, "Please, God, please save him. Don't let him die, please! Please!"

Nicky gave a huge, gasping breath. His eye opened wide, face frightened, like he'd woken from a nightmare to find it was real. He flailed out at the doctors, knocking one into the wall, but it was as if he had no strength to fight.

I pushed through to him. "Nicky, Nicky, it's me."

He saw me, and I watched the comprehension fill his face. His expression got less frantic, and he tried to reach for my hand, but I had to finish the gesture and take his in mine. He couldn't even wrap his fingers completely around my smaller hand, as if even that were too much. I cradled his big hand in both of mine, and held it against my chest, over my bare breasts.

The doctor was kneeling on the other side of him, listening to his heart with a stethoscope. He seemed to like what he was hearing. "It's slow, but steady; what happened to him?"

I shook my head, and realized tears were sliding down my cheeks. It was more like I was leaking than crying, as if it would happen totally without me. "I don't know. We were having sex, and then he just collapsed. His heart stopped and I couldn't get it started again."

"How do you feel?" the doctor was asking Nicky, but if he heard the doctor it didn't show. Nicky just kept looking at me as if I were the only real thing in the room.

"Nicky," I said, "can you hear me?"

He swallowed as if something hurt, and whispered, "Yes."

"The doctor asked, how do you feel?"

He frowned and looked around as if just now seeing the other people; again, as if I were the only solid thing in the room to him. He wasn't well yet; whatever had happened hadn't been instantly fixed.

"Ask him how he feels," the doctor said.

"How do you feel?" I asked.

He frowned harder. "Bad, weak."

I leaned over and kissed his fingers where they were still too limp in my hand. He gave me a small smile.

"What's the last he remembers?" the doctor asked.

I repeated the question.

"Sex, amazing sex," and this time his smile was wider and happier, but he still looked confused, as if something hurt, or was still not right.

I smiled back at him. "It was a-fucking-mazing sex," I said.

That made him grin, and it was mild compared to his usual, but it was a step in the right direction. Just seeing the grin helped ease a tightness in my chest that I hadn't realized was there.

Jean-Claude came into the room as far as the crowd of medics and guards would let him. I knew he was there before I looked up and saw him with my eyes. His face was beautiful and unreadable, but I knew the set of his shoulders, that particular stillness to his face—he knew something about what had happened to Nicky, and he was afraid I wouldn't like it.

The doctor said, "Can he stand, or do we need a stretcher?"

Nicky said he could stand, but Domino and I had to catch him as his knees buckled. If he'd had a belt to hold on to, it would have been easier to hold him up, but he was still naked. Domino had to take most of his weight, and I struggled to keep up my side. I was just too damn short. Claudia came in on the other side of him, and I let her take my place. She didn't have any problem helping Domino keep Nicky up and moving out of the locker room. I started to follow, but Jean-Claude was standing against the wall just outside. He was wearing the bottoms of silk pajamas in a sky blue that almost matched Asher's eyes. I wondered if Asher was wearing the top part of the jammies. Jean-Claude's curls still had that tousled just-been-fucked look.

"You know something," I said, and I couldn't keep it from sounding accusatory.

"I do," he said, voice as neutral as his face.

"Talk," I said.

"Not here, *ma petite*."

"Where?" I said, and again I knew it sounded angry.

"Asher's room or ours."

"Why Asher's room?" I asked.

"Because I am a fool." It was Asher. He'd been standing in the shadows at the end of the corridor. Either he'd been so still I hadn't seen him, or I was so upset about Nicky that I wasn't noticing things, like vampires standing in the shadows. Good thing I wasn't at work.

"If you want an argument about the fool thing, I'm not in the mood," I said. I crossed my arms under my breasts and realized I was still nude. I'd sort of forgotten. I had a moment of thinking about being embarrassed about it, and then thought, *Screw it*. Nicky had almost died, and the two vampires knew something about what had gone wrong with the *ardeur*, because that had been what happened. I thought I had the *ardeur* all controlled, and now I'd almost killed Nicky by accident. Fuck.

Asher stepped more into the light, his hair a mass of gold that seemed to gather the light to it as he moved closer. He was wearing a robe I'd seen on him before. It was gold threaded with blue and silver embroidery heavy across almost every piece of cloth. Only the edging of pale fur was free of decoration, though I guess the fur was decoration, so did you decorate the decoration? Even as I thought it, it made no sense. My mouth was healed completely; physically I felt energized and almost humming with power. Mentally I was somewhere between angry, depressed, and lost. What the hell had happened between Nicky and me? What had I done wrong?

"Let me get my weapons and something to put on, and then either room. I just want to know what is making you both act like little boys who got caught." Neither of them argued about me calling them little boys who had got caught; it was not a good sign. It meant that there was something for at least one of them to feel guilty about.

37

SINCE WE WEREN'T a hundred percent certain what had happened in the shower, the guards insisted on turning into a crowd. I pointed out that if the *ardeur* decided to eat everyone, then guns, knives, and muscle weren't going to help save anyone, but Claudia stuck by her initial plan of more bodies to guard Jean-Claude and me. All she had to throw at the problem was more muscle, so that was what she did. I knew the look on her face. There was no arguing when she looked like that, so I didn't try. I didn't want to use up energy fighting with Claudia. I was saving it up to fight with Asher, and maybe Jean-Claude.

The clothes I'd worn at the crime scene were still dirty, and I was clean, so I borrowed the silk jammie top that Asher was actually wearing under his robe. It was the match to the bottoms that Jean-Claude was wearing; for some reason that bugged me. The top was wonderful sky-blue silk, soft to the skin, but it also hung to my knees, and I had to roll the sleeves up until they formed a doughnut-sized roll around each arm. I looked like I was a little girl borrowing my father's shirt, but it was better than being naked.

I was able to put the wrist sheaths with their knives back on, but the inner pants holster needed, well, pants. I was able to put the shoulder rig on over the shirt, but it was like putting a more complicated front-opening bra across your shoulders. It was on, but it flapped and shifted, without belt loops to attach to. I carried the things that didn't fit, and was happy that my main gear bags were already in the bedroom.

We had so many guards it was hard for all three of us to walk without bumping into one of them. When we got to the door to Jean-Claude's room I told them to all stay outside.

Godofredo said, "I'm sorry, Anita, but Claudia was very clear. At least two of us have to be on the other side of the door and have eyes on you at all times."

"Why?" I asked.

"Because Asher attacked you earlier tonight and put Sin in the hospital, and now Nicky is hurt. Claudia doesn't want any more problems tonight."

"Asher isn't going to hurt me again, and what happened to Nicky isn't anything that a guard could have helped stop. Claudia being in the room with Nicky and me wouldn't have changed a damn thing, except made her and me uncomfortable with her watching me fuck Nicky."

God's eyes widened a bit. He was never quite comfortable when I talked like a guy about sex. "My orders are clear, Anita, I'm sorry."

"And I'm sorry, too," I said, "but no, none of you come inside. It's just us hashing this out."

He started to protest, but I held up a hand, and he stopped in midsyllable. "Last I checked Jean-Claude and I outrank Claudia, so I'm going to throw down a presidential veto. I don't want or need an audience."

"You aren't hard enough on Asher. That's why he gets out of hand."

I nodded. "That's true, but that's in the past."

God frowned at me. "Anita . . ."

"No, I mean it, Asher doesn't get any more free passes just because I love him . . . just because Jean-Claude loves him and keeps projecting that onto me."

"I don't believe you," God said.

I turned and looked at the two vampires by the door. Jean-Claude had opened the door, and Asher was standing by him. We all looked at each other.

"*Ma petite* is correct. There will be no more free passes for *mon chardonneret*."

"You calling him your goldfinch doesn't exactly makes us believe you," God said.

Domino stepped forward. "Nicky made me promise to stay with you."

"I'm not the one who almost died," I said.

Domino shrugged, brushing his hands through the black-and-white curls again, which I knew was a nervous gesture. His hair was mostly black with white accent curls, showing that he was half white tiger and half black. My only other born tiger that was mixed clan blood, Ethan, also had hair that reflected all his tiger forms. But Domino's hair being mostly black with just a few white curls meant when he'd shifted last he'd been black tiger; if it had been white tiger, then that color would have predominated. Ethan's hair stayed its human color no matter what color of tiger he'd shifted into last. Domino blinked his orange fire-colored eyes at me. Even more than Micah's leopard eyes, Domino's couldn't pass for human, but Domino had been born with his tiger eyes. It was a mark of clan blood to be born with eyes like that, not a punishment like Micah's had been.

"Nicky made me promise that you wouldn't be alone with Asher."

I laughed, but it wasn't a good laugh. "I guess I can't blame him." I looked at Jean-Claude.

"I believe it will be your secrets, not ours, that you may not want Domino to hear."

"I don't even know what that means right now," I said.

"It means let your tiger join us and if you wish him not to hear things, it is your task to make him leave."

I spoke to Domino. "What will you do if I go into the room without you?"

He shook his head. "Did you see what Nicky did to Ares?"

"I did."

Domino looked at me with his fire-colored eyes. The look was eloquent. "I value your safety, Anita, but I really don't want to have to fight Nicky for real." He smiled and shook his head.

"So you're coming in the room with me whether I want you to or not?"

"Anita, Asher cut you up and hurt Sin badly enough that he's in the hospital for the night. Why should your bodyguards trust him alone with anyone?"

It sounded reasonable. I turned back to Asher, still in the doorway. "You going to behave?"

"Nothing I can say will comfort your guards. They will not believe me, and I do not blame them. I have been beyond childish."

"You're always so contrite afterward, but it never lasts, Asher. You do better for a while, and then something pisses you off again, and it's like you forget."

He nodded. "That is fair. I am sorry, truly sorry, but you are right. Apologies that do not lead to better actions are empty things."

"Amen to that," I said.

He bowed his head, all that golden hair spilling around his face. Normally it made me sad that he felt he had to hide the scars that much—it meant he was feeling self-conscious—but tonight it reminded me of Nicky and the way his hair hid his own scars, and it just made me angry at him.

"Fine, Domino can come into the room." I looked at Godofredo. "You can tell Claudia you did what she ordered."

"She wanted two guards in with you."

"Don't push it," I said, and there must have been something in my voice, or in my face, because he literally backed off, hands held sort of out from his body as if he wanted to show that he meant no harm.

"Fine," he said. "As long as you take Domino with you, Claudia won't bitch-slap me."

"More like she'll knock you on your ass," I said.

He smiled, and nodded. "That, too."

I felt a touch on my psychic shielding, the equivalent of a knock. I knew the touch, and dropped shields enough to see Damian. He was still six feet of the whitest skin I'd ever seen on a vampire, because the long hair that spilled over his shoulders was the red of fresh blood, and his eyes the green of grass. He'd been pale when alive, but hundreds of years without sun had paled his skin and let his hair get as red as red could get. I could feel that he had a hand in his, and a thought let me see the woman who was almost as tall as he was at his side. Cardinale's hair was more orangey red and curly to his very straight, but they were both natural redheads, both tall, both slender, though he'd died with muscle over his frame, and she was just model thin, but they were physically very well matched, like a team of beautiful horses chosen because they looked good together.

Damian was manager at Jean-Claude's dance club, Danse Macabre, and Cardinale was one of the dancers. She partnered him for some demonstrations of old dances that had existed when he was alive, but centuries before she was born. She was also one of the taxi dancers, where you paid for the privilege of dancing with a vampire for a song. People loved dancing with the shapeshifters and vampires at Danse Macabre. The club even had a dance master who would work with new customers to teach them the ancient line dances. I'd seen the entire club floor thick with people: human, vampire, shapeshifter, all in neat rows with a hand held here and there, moving to a dance that no one had seen in centuries. It was just plain cool.

Damian let me see the second woman in front of him. She was tiny, shorter than me by inches, short enough that she fit under my arm, when I put my arm across her delicate shoulders. Her shining black hair fell like patent-leather water straight and perfect to her waist. Her uptilted eyes looked brown, but I'd spent enough time looking into them to know they were actually an orange so dark they looked brown. In the right light they were the color of fire when it burns deep into the wood and you think the flame is out, but if you don't douse it with water, it'll flare up and burn the house down. Her Chinese name translated to Black Jade; to me she was just Jade, my Jade. She was my black tiger to call, and the first woman to change me from heterosexual to heteroflexible.

Jade looked frantic, and jerked away from Damian's hand. She started running down the hallway. Damian looked up, as most of us did when we were "seeing" each other in our minds. "Someone told her you were hurt."

"Shit," I said, out loud.

"What's wrong?" God asked.

"Someone told Jade I was hurt. She'll have to see for herself that I'm healed."

"Can't you just tell her mind-to-mind?" God asked.

"She's too scared, and panicking. It makes her head-blind."

"No offense," God said, "but for a ninja assassin super-spy she spooks easy."

Domino said, "You try being abused by a master vampire for centuries and see how you do." His beasts flared enough to raise heat around him like a breath of summer in the cave-cool corridor.

"Hey, no offense," God said.

"None taken," I said, and touched Domino's arm. I was trying to calm him before Jade got here. He was very protective of her. Touching him made the heat of his beasts try to jump to me and call my matching tiger colors, but I understood how to soothe the energy now. Not shut it down, not trap the beasts, but soothe them like you'd pet and cuddle a big kitty. Of course these kitties would have happily torn my body apart so they could be on the outside with their own real fleshy bodies if it had been possible. We'd finally figured out it was Jean-Claude's vampire marks that kept me from being able to shapeshift for real. Modern lycanthropy wasn't contagious to vampires, and I was just too close to being a vampire thanks to his marks, and my own necromancy. Ancient-strain lycanthropy had been contagious to the undead.

"Ease down," I said to Domino.

Jade had paid Domino the highest compliment she had for men; she let him join us in bed. Nathaniel was tolerated in the bed, and Crispin, a white tiger and stripper at Guilty Pleasures, but she seldom slept with me because I kept insisting on all these men being there. Her abuser had been male and it had given her a bad opinion of them; the only thing she disliked more was male vampires. Damian had won her over with tales of his own abuse at the hands of She who made him. His vampire mistress made Jade's master look sane. She'd had to accept that women could abuse, too. Jean-Claude and Asher had enough stories of Belle Morte, and then there'd been the Mother of All Darkness, and Nikolaos the first Master of the City of St. Louis had been one crazy bitch. Crazy didn't discriminate on the basis of gender.

Jean-Claude had won her over by being himself. It had been interesting watching him work to gain her trust. He'd always told me the only woman who ever frustrated his plans was me; watching him charm Jade had made me believe that statement.

Jade came into sight running so fast she was a blur of black and white. I handed the weapons I'd been holding to Domino and then braced. She was small enough and I was strong enough, but running at that speed it was a lot of momentum to stop.

She slowed down enough for me to see the long hair sweeping out behind her, the pale face, eyes frantic, and then she leapt on me like a monkey. Jean-Claude put a hand on my back to help steady me as all that speed and energy leapt into my arms, and stopped. She wrapped her legs around my waist, arms around my neck, and buried her face into my hair and the side of my neck. I put my hands the only place I could to hold her, which was underneath her slender ass. It was the same way Nicky had carried me into the showers. That thought made my stomach clench tight.

She mumbled into my neck, but she was mumbling Chinese. Even after a year, the nuances of the language when muttered into my hair, or neck, escaped me.

I was already making soothing noises to her, but I transferred one hand up to stroke the incredible silkiness of her hair, while the other arm held her weight.

"Jade, sweetie, I can't understand you when you're this upset. Slow down and English, please, dearest, English."

She raised her face up enough to look at me. Her eye makeup was smeared around her eyes, which probably meant I was wearing it on my neck and the blue silk of the shirt.

Her voice came out in a breathy whisper. "They said you were hurt."

"I'm all better; all healed."

She studied my face, serious as a child, as if she thought I might be lying. I'd tried doing that, but found truth worked better than comforting lies. She was way more girly than I would ever be, but liked truth the way that I did, and once lied to, she never forgot. Again, like me.

"Promise," she whispered.

I nodded as solemn as she was. "Promise."

She smiled and her whole face changed from serious beauty to a shining happiness. She glowed, and when someone looks at you like that, what can you do? I kissed her, and she hugged me, wrapping her arms around my neck again, and wriggling happily. I was suddenly glad the shirt hung to my knees; her enthusiastic cuddling had made more than one short skirt ride up and give way too much of a girl-on-girl show for the guards.

"*Ma petite*, should you and the lovely Jade come inside?" He was holding the door and motioning. Asher was already out of sight in the room.

I sighed, but Jean-Claude was right. Jade would never let me just put her down and tell her to go play elsewhere. I had been the one who rescued her from centuries of abuse, by simply being better at metaphysics than her abuser had been; in effect I'd been the better vampire, so he was still alive. The other Harlequin were hunting him and the few rogues left, but he wasn't dead. Jade believed that if I died her old master would take her over again. I wasn't just her rescuer, I was her continued salvation. We couldn't even tell her that she was wrong, because you weren't supposed to be able to cut the bonds between master and animal to call without killing the old master. But what I knew, and he hadn't, was that part of what made it work was Jade's willingness. She had wanted freedom, and when I offered it, she'd thrown her free will into mine. It's so much easier to rescue prisoners if they want to come with you. I'd offered love and safety, he'd offered hate and fear; who wouldn't choose love?

38

JEAN-CLAUDE'S CUSTOM-MADE BED was still a four-poster like his last one, but the heavy wooden posts and crossbeams were too thick for the drapes that used to hang on the bed, making it a cozy nest. The wood also had heavy attachment points scattered here and there. The frame itself was reinforced steel. When you do bondage with shapeshifters and vampires, you need something sturdy to chain them to. The bed was also bigger even than a California king; *orgy-size* was what we'd started calling it. I was sitting with my back against the small mountain of black and white pillows in the middle of the headboard. Jade was snuggled lower on the pillows, so that her head tucked in between my waist and hip; one arm was across my thighs, the other was curled underneath her, the hand touching my calf. I had one hand on her shoulders, touching all that almost slippery shiny hair. Jean-Claude was on the other side of me. He had his arm across my shoulders so I lay back tucked in against the side of his body. My free hand was on his thigh, petting the silk and the muscles underneath it. Asher hadn't even tried to climb on the bed with us. One, I was still mad at him, and he knew it. Two, Jade didn't like him. She didn't trust him, and she shouldn't have. There was something about her extreme victim vibe that made Asher want to do bad things to her, not really hurt her, but dominate her in that bondage-and-submission way, except that Jade wasn't healthy enough for fun and games like that. She might never be. But Jade's very fear of him made Asher want to seduce her, not necessarily tie her up and have his way with her, but make her say yes. Her issues and his: bad mix.

Asher paced at the foot of the bed like a big cat in a cage with too much energy and not enough room. I stroked the warmth of Jade's hair, and then cuddled into the solidness of Jean-Claude. I let their touching me, and my touching them, help dissipate some of the nervous energy that Asher was having to pace away.

"If I had dreamed that you would make love to Nicky more than once so close together, I would have cautioned you," Jean-Claude said.

"I know he's a Bride, but I thought I was a danger to him only if I was gravely hurt; then I might accidentally drain a Bride to death. That's what you told me."

"Yes, *ma petite*, but . . ."

"I wasn't that hurt."

"No, but the Brides have no ability to protect themselves; they are designed to give anything that their master wants from them."

"I didn't use the *ardeur* the first time. It didn't feel like I used it." I tried to think. "I did heal enough to go down on Nicky the second time."

"I cut you badly," Asher said, stopping by the side of the bed. "That is a lot of healing unless the sex was magical."

I frowned at him. "I know that the *ardeur* can drain a lover to death if I feed too often on any one person, but healing from sex has never come with that kind of price unless the *ardeur* is invoked."

Jean-Claude laid his cheek against my hair. "Belle Morte drained her Brides to raise her own power, just before she would take us into a nobleman's court and try to seduce them all."

"I wasn't trying to do anything but heal and feed the *ardeur*," I said.

Asher said, "The first time she killed a Bride and stole all his energy, it was accidental."

We looked at him.

He used his hair to hide almost all of his face, not just the scars, as if he didn't want to see us while he told us. "The first time was like this, just sex, but there was no modern medicine to restart his heart. He died and stayed dead, but she wasn't upset. She loved the power of it, and filed it away in that dark mind of hers. By the time Jean-Claude arrived in court she had made it just another piece of her power."

"You have never mentioned this," Jean-Claude said.

"I did not think that Anita would be able to do it. She is not a true vampire . . . She . . ."

"I am master here, Asher; you should have told me and let me decide what *ma petite* needed to know."

"I see that now," Asher said, and he looked up, letting the shine of his eyes gleam blue, made bluer by the robe he was wearing. "I'm sorry . . ." He reached out to us, a beseeching gesture, and something he'd done leaning against the bed had loosened the sash so that it fell open, giving a glimpse of his body, pale and perfect. The robe fell open only to show the unscarred side, the same way his hair often fell. I knew the hair was deliberate; was the robe? Could he "accidentally" make the robe fall open just so that he gave the perfect glimpse of his body to remind us, no, me, what I was about to give up? Jean-Claude had just finished having sex with him; it wasn't him that Asher needed to re-seduce.

I turned so I could see Jean-Claude's face, which made him have to lean back a little. "Tell me you didn't give in?"

"What do you mean, give in, *ma petite*?"

"I mean tell him he doesn't have to go. He has to go, right? No matter how good the sex is, he has to leave town for at least a month; right?"

"I have not said otherwise."

I didn't like the way he worded that. Jade rubbed her face against my waist like the big cat she was in her other form. She was trying to soothe me.

"Sin could have died tonight. His control over hyenas is better than ours, it's one animal that neither of us has any control over, and Asher used that to make Ares attack another guard. Asher meant for it to be Nicky with his broken arm, et cetera . . . and if Asher hadn't hurt me to begin with, I wouldn't have almost drained Nicky dry. We can't let this slide, Jean-Claude, we can't."

"It is too close to dawn for him to leave tonight, but tomorrow night he will go, as ordered."

"I deserve to be exiled for a month," Asher said, and he had moved down the edge of the bed, so that he was standing opposite us; the robe was so open it was just a beautiful embroidered frame to his body. His hand slid down the edge of the robe so that it was just natural to follow where his hand moved, and his hand moved ever so slowly so that it was like a tour of his chest, the flat plains of his stomach, the edge of his hips, and then the groin, where he lay soft, and waiting. Until he took blood again, that would be all he had to offer, but I actually liked that about vampires. Most men, I started going down on them and they got big too soon, so that I couldn't enjoy the texture and feel that they started with . . .

Jade uncurled herself and began to climb off the other side of the bed. "Where are you going?" I asked.

"I cannot," she said.

"Cannot what?" I asked.

"You like his cruelty. I do not. Please do not order me to stay."

"No one will force you to do anything you don't want to do. I and Jean-Claude have both promised you that."

"I believe you, but . . . May I go?"

I sighed. "Yes, but we're not having sex with Asher."

"You are within your rights to have sex with him if you wish." She was already backing toward the door. One hand was holding her other arm tight enough that her fingers were mottled. It meant she was afraid. She was afraid of men, of sex with men, of vampires, and most especially afraid of male vampires. I was lying in the arms of one vampire with another nearly naked by the bed, and they were both decidedly male; as far as Jade was concerned I was about to do something terrifying.

"We're not having sex," I said.

"But he will try and seduce you, and that is . . ." She backed into Domino, and gave a soft yelp. She startled away from him as he reached to steady her. He dropped his hand to his side. Domino knew better than to push things when she got spooked. It was one of the reasons she could be in bed with him and me when we made love. She'd also allowed Nathaniel that amount of trust. Both of them treated it with all the gentleness they had.

"Walk her back to her room," I said.

"No, he's supposed to guard you from . . . Asher," she said.

"It's okay," Domino said, "I'll get you back to your room, and come right back here."

Jade didn't want him to touch her either, but when she was this shaken she needed someone by her side that she trusted at least a little to keep the panic from growing. She trusted Domino more than any other man. Claudia had no patience with her, and Kelly didn't need to be around Asher tonight, and just like that we were out of female guards to watch over her.

"I'll be back as soon as I can," Domino said. "Don't get hurt. I really don't want to fight Nicky for real."

"We'll be good," I said.

He grinned as he closed the door behind them, and said, just as the door closed, "I know you're good, Anita; just don't hurt each other."

"Domino," I said, but he closed the door to the sound of his soft laughter.

39

THE ROOM WAS very quiet after they left. I don't know what I would have said into that silence, because my phone rang. Did I dive for it a little too eagerly? Maybe, but it was with my pile of weapons beside the bed. That meant that I had to crawl over the acres of black bedspread to grab it. Asher bent down and handed it to me, so that I had to take it from him as I hit the screen and said, "Blake here, talk to me."

"Marshal Blake?" It was the new Marshal, Arlen Brice.

"Yeah, Marshal Blake here, sorry, Brice. What's up?"

"They found bomb-making materials in one of the closets at the house we raided with SWAT."

I was quiet for a second, trying to process it. "Why would they have that? What the hell do vampires need with bombs?"

Asher and Jean-Claude went very still on either side of me. I couldn't explain it, but I knew the stillness was more of a startle reaction than any expression they could have given me. I should not have said the word *bomb* out loud. It was a damn ongoing police investigation, but it had startled me.

"One of the vampires that died at the warehouse was a retired demolitions expert," Brice said.

"Military?" I asked.

"No, civilian, construction, but that just means he knows how to bring down a whole building."

"Not comforting," I said.

"Zerbrowski said that the vamps at the warehouse were talking trash about you and Jean-Claude, so I figured you'd want to know about the bomb stuff."

"Just stuff, not actual devices?"

"No, but the bomb techs are treating this real serious. They seem convinced that some bombs were actually made, which means they may be out there in the city somewhere."

"These guys wanted to be seen as sympathetic in the media. Blowing shit up doesn't gain sympathy from anyone."

"True, but it doesn't stop people from doing it," Brice said.

I wanted to argue, but couldn't, so I let that part go. "Any hint on size of device? What we might want the security details to be looking at?"

"This isn't my area. I can read the preliminary report, but not sure I'm the one you want interpreting it. Talk to"—and he was quiet, as I listened to him riffling papers and clicking keys—"Alvarez, Mark Alvarez, is the lead guy."

"Let me get a pen, and then give me his number."

Jean-Claude got the small notebook and pen that stayed on the bedside table now. There was one by every bed in every room that was "mine."

"You can call Alvarez, but not until you've been informed officially. I mean, I want to help, but don't get us both fired, and you can't tell your boyfriend and his people about what we found."

"Why, because I'm not supposed to know?" I asked.

"They're worried that Jean-Claude could have some of these nuts inside his organization, so if we tell him then we'll be tipping our hand."

"And if someone gets blown up before we share?"

"They actually wouldn't let Zerbrowski leave the big meeting, because they said he'd tell you, and you'd tell the vampires."

"Jesus, Brice, so why are you telling me?"

"They don't think I owe you anything, so they don't think I'll tell you."

"You could get in trouble for this," I said.

"You ready for Alvarez's number?" Brice asked.

"Yeah, shoot."

He gave me Alvarez's contact info. "Got it," I said.

"I just wanted you to have a heads-up as soon as possible."

"I really appreciate that, Brice."

"Hey, as someone who's still looking for true love outside the normal box, I want to support anyone who's found it. I'm not sure if it's prejudice, or if all they're thinking about is the case, but I'm listening to some upper brass make up shitty reasons to justify their actions. Makes me think I'm not coming out anytime soon."

"The new vampire laws make them treat them better, more like people, but new laws don't change how people feel. Thanks again, Brice."

"Not a problem, just don't call Alvarez for a couple of hours. I looked up some of your bodyguards; they've got backgrounds in demolition, military."

"Do my fellow cops have files on my people?"

"Some, but I've been federal longer than you have. I called in a few favors, told them I just wanted to know what I was up against if things went bad. They totally bought it, Blake. I get the idea that certain people are betting when you and your people go off the reservation, not if."

"Sleep with a few vampires and shapeshifters, and people get all weird about it," I said.

"Yep," he said, "gotta go." He hung up.

I hit the button, if *button* is the right word for brushing your thumb across a screen. If I hadn't had years of practice with vampires, and these vamps in particular, I might have thought that they weren't interested in what had just happened, were bored even, but I knew that the stillness, and the pleasant faces, meant they were very interested.

I glanced at Asher, since he was in front of me, but it was Jean-Claude to whom I turned and gave major eye contact. "You heard?"

"Yes," he said simply.

"You know I don't normally share information about ongoing investigations."

"You are very careful about it," he said, and that amazing face was still pleasant, still neutral.

"I have to be if I'm going to be a cop."

"I understand that, *ma petite*." Again, that careful voice.

"I can make both of you promise, word of honor, and all that shit, to tell no one, and I know you'll do it."

"Word of honor, and all that shit," he repeated, but there was a faint edge of his French accent, and that, more than anything else, let me know how upset he was; the accent came out only when he wished it to, or when he was very emotional.

I looked up at Asher, who was still standing by the bed. "You, too, blondie."

"I will do what you and Jean-Claude wish me to do. I have caused enough problems with my childish behavior."

"I wish you meant that," I said.

He looked down, giving me the full weight of those pale blue eyes, through that lace of golden hair. "I mean every word I say."

I sighed. "You do, don't you?"

"*Oui*," he said.

"You are sorry, but you also meant everything you yelled at us earlier, and you meant to hurt me so that no one else could have certain skills from me for a while."

"Can you not forgive me?" he asked.

I waved it away. "Ask me later; right now I'm about to break a rule, one that could cost me my badge. There are people on the force who want to get rid of me for sleeping with you guys, and this could be excuse enough, but if one of these missing bombs blows up and hurts someone I care about, the job won't mean much to me." I thought about it for a few more seconds, but in the end I weighed love higher than my badge, and that meant that Larry and everyone else who thought sleeping with the monsters divided my loyalties were partially right. They were right, because I called Claudia, and told her to tell our security at all of our businesses to look for the damn things. There was a chance that our guards would keep the secret, and they swept for listening devices almost every damn day. They could just accidentally find the bombs when they were looking for electronic bugs. In fact, they probably would have found them, if they were there to be found, either way. But I didn't know much about explosives. I didn't know if searching for bugs would have made them miss bombs, I just didn't know, and I wasn't willing to take the chance.

Yes, I was dating too many people, and taking care of too many people. Yes, I was a little overwhelmed by it sometimes, but I was also happier than I'd ever been in my life, and I didn't want to lose that. I didn't want to lose anyone that I loved. If that eventually cost me my badge, so be it.

Was I a U.S. Marshal, or Jean-Claude's human servant? Was I a Marshal, or Micah's Nimir-Ra? Was I a police officer, or Nathaniel's sweetie? Was I an officer, or Nicky's master? Was I a cop, or the new Mistress of Tigers of Sin, and Dev, and Jade, and Ethan, and Crispin, and . . . Could I keep being a cop and be everything else?

I sat there on the edge of the bed and, for the first time, really thought the answer might be no.

40

WE DIDN'T FIND any bombs, and thanks to the wererats and some of the ex-military in both the werehyenas and wereleopards, we had people who knew what they were doing. If there had been anything to find, I trusted our people to find it. I got the official go-ahead from Dolph about three hours after Brice had called and warned us. Three hours is a long time to wait to warn people.

Dolph ended the conversation with, "I'm sorry, Anita."

"What about?" I asked.

"That some people are more interested in the case than in keeping people safe. Some of these guys are as conflicted about the preternatural community as I was a couple of years back." That was a lot for him to admit.

"Thanks, Dolph, that means a lot coming from you."

"I don't understand the whole fascination with the preternaturals, but I know my son is still happy, and I've never seen you happier than you are right now. The wife says you're not supposed to understand love; if it made complete sense, it wouldn't be love."

"That sounds illogical and absolutely true," I said.

"Illogical and true; sounds about right for love," Dolph said, and he'd hung up.

By the time I knew that everyone was safe and no bombs were anywhere we had looked, dawn had come and gone by hours. I felt Jean-Claude die for the day, and knew that meant Asher had gone before him, because he wasn't powerful enough to stay awake as long as Jean-Claude. They did better in the underground, but the sun came up and the vampires went down, that was just the way it worked. I felt Jean-Claude curl up around the other man, and knew I would find them in the bed together. I didn't like sleeping with vampires once they went cold for the day, so I'd be bunking with Micah and Nathaniel in our room, and maybe Sin, if he was there and not in a hospital bed.

Claudia and I were walking down the midway of the Circus. This close to dawn it was closed tight. One of the things that had made it so hard to search was this section with its booths shuttered tight. There were the usual fairway games, but the stuffed toy prizes hanging from the eaves of the little shopfronts ran high to bats, black cats, Franken-stein's monsters, and strangely cuddly mummies with the glimpses of dead skin through the fuzzy wrappings played for comedy instead of scares. There was scarier stuff from some shops: fake shrunken heads on a stick, monster eyeballs in plastic jars, and a booth that put fake scars and wounds on you. I could smell the sweetness of the cotton candy, the cinnamon of the elephant ears and bear claws booth, renamed "monster ears" and "werewolf claws," and the funnel cakes that always smelled like your grandmother's kitchen was supposed to smell, but never had.

I liked walking the Circus after it was closed. I think it appealed to the little girl in me who had always wondered what happened when the fair closed down. I knew now that it was just like any other job for most of the people. They cleaned up, did prep for the next day, and closed down, but when you're little, the traveling carnival is magical, a mysterious world that you only get to visit. There'd been a time when the midway here seemed ominous; now it seemed homey. If I walked through here, it was usually after closing and I was going to bed: home.

Claudia's phone sounded, and she walked a little away from me to take it. I gave her the privacy. The wererats were primarily our guards in town, but they had business out of town, and it was strictly a don't-ask, don't-tell policy. I carried a badge; I did not need to know details about their mercenary jobs.

She came back to me with a look on her face that I couldn't read, but it wasn't a good look.

"What's wrong?" I asked.

"Mephistopheles is sitting against the wall in the living room, cry-ing," she said.

"Crap," I said.

"You don't even need to ask why, do you?" she said.

"No."

"So it's true you are sending Asher away for what he did last night?"

I nodded.

"About damn time," she said.

"You really don't like him, do you?"

"He's your lover, not mine, Anita. I wouldn't put up with his emo-tional blackmail shit."

"We're sort of through with it, too," I said. I started walking toward the far door and the entrance to the underground. She fell into step beside me.

"It was Graham on the phone." He was one of the few werewolf guards we had, and since he knew nothing about explosives, he'd been kept downstairs to guard the sleeping. He was better at being a bouncer at the clubs than a gun-toting bodyguard.

I shrugged. "So?"

"He called me, to find you, to send to Mephistopheles. If Jean-Claude had been awake for the night, he'd have still sent me to find you."

I could see the door to the underground now. Tonight it had two of the black-dressed guards on it. Usually there were guards only on the inside in the little room behind the doors, but tonight and for the next little bit we were going to put guards on the door. We were going to beef up our security everywhere, hoping to discourage the crazy.

"Dev is my tiger to call."

"It's not that, Anita. Micah is traveling more for the Coalition. Nathaniel takes care of everyone like a 1950s housewife, but he isn't dominant enough to handle comforting Mephistopheles."

"So I'm the go-to person for the hand holding, I get that."

She shook her head hard enough to make her high, tight braid bounce. "We would never call Jean-Claude about this, that's my point."

I stopped walking and looked at her. "Okay, just stop being subtle; you're not good at it, and I'm not good at figuring it out."

She smiled. "You stand there dressed like one of us, and you don't get it."

I glanced down at my clothes and had to smile back. I was in black T-shirt, black jeans, black belt with a blackened belt buckle, and black boots. They had a heel on them, so they were a little more club than guard, but other than that Claudia was right. My holsters and weapons decorated me like every other guard's. Unless it was business hours, we didn't try to hide that we were armed.

"I guess I do have a lot of assassin chic in my closet."

"I know Nathaniel didn't pick the shirt because it doesn't show cleavage, and I'd send a guard back to get lower heels on the boots, but other than that you look like one of us."

"Thanks, I think."

She grinned, and it transformed her face into something beautiful, happy. She didn't smile like that enough. "We trust you to understand whatever we bring to you, Anita. We trust you with the decisions about the guns and violence, and this kind of stuff, too."

"You mean that Dev is crying?"

She nodded, and the grin faded around the edges. "I couldn't date this many people. It's hard enough dealing with just one person at a time. I can't imagine taking care of this many people."

"Are you dating someone right now?" I asked.

She blushed. I'd never seen Claudia blush.

It was my turn to grin. "Who is it?"

She shook her head. "You go take care of your lover, leave mine to me."

"Oooh, *lover* is it, not boyfriend."

She laughed, and it was the kind of laugh I'd never heard from her. "Go talk to the Devil." She walked away, still laughing. I watched her go, and wondered how I'd missed it. It had to be serious for her to mention it at all. Claudia in love; who'd have thunk it? Cool.

I went for the door to the underground, and to take care of my Devil. The thought made my shoulders want to slump a little, as if I were trying to carry something heavy, but I straightened up, took a deep breath, tightened my core, and stood as straight as my five foot three could manage with the help of the three-inch heels. It was a lot of work to take care of all the people I was dating, but there was no one I would trade away. Asher might force us to send him away, but I'd miss him, and I hadn't been his main sweetie for a year like Dev had. He'd wanted to add an extra girl, not lose the man he loved. I sighed, made sure I stayed standing straight, no slumping, and went to take care of my golden tiger to call, my Devil, who was crying over his broken heart. One of the hardest things to learn about being polyamorous was you could be totally heartbroken about relationship B, but still be happy about relationship C, but having C didn't make losing B less painful. It meant you had another established relationship to help you heal over the lost one, but your heart still broke. I'd had this idea that if you loved more people you wouldn't get your heart truly broken unless you lost them all, but like so many theories, reality was different. But as realities went, I wouldn't have traded mine. I hoped I could convince Dev the same. ·

41

I COULDN'T SEE Dev when I first pushed the curtains apart, but I felt him like a brush of heat across my face, which meant his emotions were strong enough that he wasn't shielding well. The golden tigers were masters of control—they'd had to be to hide from the Harlequin for centuries—but now he was leaking through all that practiced control. I followed that hint of energy to find him sitting beside the fireplace, back against the wall, muscular arms hugging his knees to that nice chest, his head bowed over them so that all I could see was the fall of his blond hair with its highlights and lowlights, from nearly white to a deep yellow. The hair was straight and just long enough to spill around his face and hide it completely while he cried. He was inches taller than Nicky, not quite as broad through the shoulders, but he was still a big guy, and yet he'd tucked himself up so tight that he had been completely hidden behind one of the big chairs that bookended the faux stone fireplace. He was wearing a white T-shirt and pale blue jeans, no shoes, so that he was all pale colors to offset the reds and gold of the new living room.

The guards melted away as I crossed the room toward him. It was my problem now. Oh, hell, it had always been my problem. Because of Asher's jealousy, no one else but me was dating Dev, so it was just him and me. I said a quick prayer for wisdom because I didn't know what to say, but I'd learned that it's not really what you say sometimes, it's that you're willing to say something, anything, that you're just there.

I walked over to him and touched the silk of his hair. He took in a ragged breath, loud and painful, and raised his face. I had a moment to see that handsome face tear streaked, his eyes with their amber brown circle around the pupil and the outer edge of rich, pale blue, blinking up at me, and then he grabbed me around the thighs, those strong arms pulling me in against his body, knees opening up so he wrapped as much of himself around me as he could. When he was sitting down, his face still came above my belly button, almost to my sternum. I suddenly felt small.

I stroked his hair and murmured, "It's all right, Dev. It's all right."

He shook his head, rubbing his face against my shirt. He managed to gasp in a breathy voice, thick with tears, "It's not all right. It can't be. It won't be."

"Asher's only going away for a month, then he'll be back."

He pressed his cheek against my stomach. "I love him, Anita, I really do."

"That's great, Dev."

"I've never been in love before."

I bent over him and hugged him back, because the first time can hurt like hell. "It's wonderful and awful, isn't it?" I said.

He turned his head, and I stood back up so we could look at each other. "Yes, because he's wonderful and awful."

I nodded. "Yeah, that's about right—wonderful and awful is very Asher."

"If he heard you say that, he'd assume you meant the scars."

I petted the side of Dev's face, tracing the edge of his profile. "I've offered to try to fix the scars. He won't let me."

"He's afraid."

"I know, I'd have to cut enough flesh away to make a new wound and see if I can heal it with sexual energy. If it doesn't work, then we don't do anything else."

"I think he's afraid to be perfect again."

"Why?" I asked.

He shrugged those big shoulders, arms tightening around my legs, so that my knees had to bend into his chest, so that I would have fallen except he was there to catch me. I wrapped my arms around his neck and shoulders, and his face was suddenly peering at me through my breasts. He snuggled his face so that I could see his whole face framed by my breasts.

I laughed. "I'm here to comfort you."

He rubbed his face against my breasts. "This is comforting."

I gave him narrow eyes. "Is this your way of saying you don't want to talk about this?"

He nuzzled his face against one breast until he found the nipple, then rubbed his lips over it until he felt my body react to his touch. "No, it's me saying that I haven't gotten to touch breasts in a long time, and I miss girls. I do love him, Anita, I really do, but if he wants me to give up everyone but him, loving him isn't enough." He went back to that light caress of lips across my nipple.

The pulse in my neck was jumping, my body beginning to react to him. "Love doesn't conquer all," I said.

"Was it stupid to think it would?" he asked.

"No, not stupid; for some people one person is enough," I said, "but you . . ." He rubbed his face harder against my breast. ". . . You are the most truly bisexual person I've ever met." He licked my nipple through the thin T-shirt material, one long swipe of tongue. My voice was breathy as I said, "You really don't have a preference for boy or girl, you just like the person." He opened his mouth wide and put as much of my breast into his mouth as would fit. My pulse was making it hard to talk. "Someone like you isn't going to be happy without both." His teeth pressed down, slowly, more pressure than anything. "I take it you don't want to talk anymore." My voice sounded strained.

He shook his head with my breast still in his mouth.

"Bedroom?" I asked.

He shook his head again, shaking my breast a little more firmly. It made me have to close my eyes for a minute.

"Here?"

He nodded, biting down on my breast, and letting a slow growl trickle out from between his lips. The growl vibrated across my breast.

"God, Dev," I breathed.

He grinned with my breast still in his mouth. His eyes filled with a mix of mischief, sex, and just him. Dev was short for Devil, and in that moment he earned his nickname. I shivered and he worried my breast with his teeth until I cried out his name.

42

DEV HADN'T TOUCHED a woman in two months. He wanted to touch, fondle, lick, and nibble all the parts that he'd been missing. Who was I to argue? He brought me with his mouth, with me sitting above him, so that I was staring into his eyes when he brought me screaming, my hands searching the air for something to hold on to. He put me on my back and used his fingers between my legs until I screamed his name and sank nails into the one arm I could reach. I was lying on the carpeted floor boneless, breathless, eye-fluttering happy, when I felt the tip of him begin to touch me.

"No," I said.

He stopped, his body pulling back enough so he wasn't touching me. "What's wrong?"

I fought to roll over on my side and fish for a condom in the pile of clothes and weapons. I hadn't had one when I was with Nicky, but I'd started trying to carry some in one of my ammo carriers. I finally rolled back with one of the little foil-wrapped packets in my hand.

He made a pouty face at me, still on his knees. I held the condom in my fingers, and smiled. "Sorry, we aren't fluid bonded."

"Do you use a condom when you're with Asher without me?"

"Yes," I said, and I realized that Jean-Claude had insisted on that. I wondered how long he'd been thinking Asher might have to leave.

"Then that's fair," he said. He got up on his knees and held his hand out for the foil-wrapped condom.

I grinned at him. "If you haven't been with anyone but Asher in two months, then there's something else you've been missing, unless you changed your mind about enjoying pain with your oral sex."

"Asher can open his mouth wide enough to avoid the fangs; just the sucking doesn't work."

I handed him the condom. "Well, if you don't want oral."

He grinned, sudden and wide. "I didn't say that."

He lay back on the floor, and he was already hard and ready. I began to lick the skin around the edges of his groin. "Please, just go down on me. Please, God, just suck me."

"Some of the men in my life complain that I don't do enough preliminaries."

"I won't complain," he said. He gazed down his body at me. I wrapped my hand around the base of him, and licked the tip of him. "Anita, please!" I sealed my mouth over the end of him and began to push my way down slowly, not because I had to, but because I could, and I liked the almost desperate look on his face as I inched my way down him. "Please," he said, again. I plunged my mouth down until my lips met my hand, and then slid back up the long, thick shaft of him. A look of both pleasure and pain crossed his face. It wasn't a good pain, but more as if the way I was doing it were more like teasing than action. I gave up trying to prolong things and rose up on my knees, bending my body forward over his so that I could get a better angle, kept my hand around the base of him, and let myself spill my mouth down and over him in one long, fast movement, until I met my own hand, and then up again, faster this time, until I found a rhythm that was fast, quick, with my mouth so close around the thickness of him that I had to remember to watch that my teeth didn't catch him on the down or up stroke. If we'd had a mattress I'd have used its bounce to help me mouth-fuck him, but

I had to do it all with my legs and one arm for support to the side of his body.

I took my hand away on the next downstroke, and fought to get those last inches down my throat, because to sink my lips against his body, it was down the throat; my mouth alone wouldn't hold all his length. When he was buried as far down my throat as I could get him, my mouth pressed against the front of his body, I drew myself up with my mouth pressed as tight as I could get it, sucking up the length of him, doing what a vampire's delicate fangs wouldn't allow.

Dev made a small eager noise, and when I rolled my eyes up to watch his face, his eyes were closed, head thrown back, and another sound escaped him. I came up off him, and caught my breath, before starting down again. He let me do it twice more and then caught me, his big hands on my arms. His voice was strained and breathy as he said, "If you keep doing that, I'll go, and I want to be inside a different place when I do that."

"We're on carpeting; who gets to be on top?"

"You, me, I don't care. If I last long enough, then we'll change positions."

"Sounds like a plan."

I lowered myself on top of him, and even with all the prep work I was still tight, wet, but tight. "Gods," he said, "I'd forgotten how tight you stay even wet. It feels so . . . damn . . . good."

I sat on top of him with him buried inside me as deep as he could go, our bodies married more intimately than anything else could make us. The feel of him inside me so far, so deep, so big, closed my eyes, bowed my spine above him. I whispered, "Feels so good."

His voice was low, hoarse as he said, "Dance for me."

I danced for him, finding a rhythm that rocked my body over and around his, and he began to push with his thighs, legs, abs, so that we got a lower body workout that no gym could offer. He stared at me as we made love, his eyes getting wider, and then between one dancing movement and another, the orgasm caught me and I writhed and screamed above him. "I won't last if you do that again. Change positions."

"What? Where?"

"Me on top. Couch."

"Okay."

He actually started on his knees with him pinning my left leg against the back of the couch, so the angle was a little deeper, a little more, as he began to push his body in and out of mine. I rose up enough to watch him slide in and out; one moment I was watching our bodies, feeling the pleasure build, and the next stroke pushed me over and I was writhing, shrieking, fingers digging into the red couch, as if holding on tight enough would remind me that I wasn't just boneless, wordless, warm pleasure.

"Anita!" And he began to move faster, harder, his careful rhythm forgotten in the needs of his body, the feel of mine, and my pleasure rode on the almost frantic shoving of his body into mine. I screamed, and tried to move underneath him, but he tightened his hands on my thighs and forced me still as he began to go fast and faster, deep and deeper, until he began to hit the end of me with every other stroke, not pounding, but a tap, a pulse, and then finally he couldn't hold that rhythm either and he drove himself home, burying as deep in me as he could, in one last shuddering push that made him cry out my name, and made me scream one last orgasm that drowned out everything.

He pulled out, which made me writhe again, and then pushed me a little to the front of the couch so he could collapse behind me. He wrapped me in his shaking arms, a dew of sweat on his chest as he hugged me to him, our bodies spooning as he fought to catch his breath. His heart pounded against my back, and I lay there breathless, twitching, my body immobile from the waist down, as the aftershocks shivered and played through my body.

He whispered, "I've missed girls."

I managed to whisper, "I noticed."

That made him give that low, masculine chuckle, and he hugged me close, tucking me in against his body, curling around me. We fell asleep curled in each other's arms, on the couch in the living room where everyone had to walk past to get to anything farther underground. For me to forget we were in semipublic, and both of us to forget to clean up first, meant the sex was good, and we were both tired. Not a tiredness of lack of sleep, but more of too many things happening in too small a space of time. It had been a night and now a day of too much emotion. Dev and I slept all the bad away wrapped in a cocoon of flesh, and sex, and relief. As much as he loved Asher, he was never going to be able to give up women, and he knew I would never ask him to give up men. The sex was Dev's way of saying he was done with Asher, or at least done with the old rules. In trying to keep the Devil to himself, Asher had made certain he wouldn't be able to keep him at all. I slept in the Devil's arms and knew that for this Mephistopheles, the heaven of love had come at too heavy a price, and he was ready to come back to the purgatory of I-like-you-lots-let's-fuck. It wasn't true love, but it wasn't exactly not-love either.

43

SOMEONE WAS STROKING my face, saying softly, "Anita, Anita, wake up, sweetheart."

I cuddled into Micah's hand, and then realized that the body behind me wasn't Nathaniel, too tall, too broad, and all I could feel was Micah's hand, not his whole body pressed to the front of me. It made me blink awake. I saw the living room in the Circus, and remembered sex with Dev, knew it was his arm around my waist, his body pressed against the back of mine.

I raised up enough to realize I'd been lying on a pillow and Dev's arm. He moved in his sleep and made a soft groan.

"How long have we been asleep?" I asked.

"Guards say less than two hours," Micah said.

I looked up at Micah. His hair was loose around his shoulders and he was wearing a pair of jeans, T-shirt untucked, which usually meant he'd dressed in a hurry. He liked his T-shirts tucked in like I did, and he always did something with his hair.

"What's wrong?" I asked, and just like that a spurt of adrenaline washed over me. I was alert, realizing I'd left my weapons in a pile against the far wall, out of reach. Shit, that was careless.

Dev tensed against me and raised that big upper body off the couch, behind me. "My arm is completely asleep; fuck."

"Nothing's wrong," Micah said, "everyone's safe."

I sat up and felt the dried stickiness between our bodies give way. Dev yelled, "Ah, holy shit!"

I froze in midmovement. "What?"

"Condom . . . glued . . . to body . . . and you," he said in a tight, pain-filled voice.

"That's why you clean up afterward," Micah said, but he was laughing.

"Sorry," I said, "I won't move."

"It's okay . . . damage done. Damn!"

"I didn't move," I said.

"I did."

"I thought you said, damage done."

"You're unglued, but I'm stuck to myself."

Micah was laughing full out now. He stood up and offered me a hand. I took it, but I was already looking at my weapons all the way across the room. Technically we were safe, and there were always bodyguards around, but . . . guns are useless if they're out of reach.

He pulled my hand so that I was standing in front of him. He wrapped his arms around me, but kept them a little higher on my back than usual. He was still laughing, his face alight with it, those green-gold eyes sparkling. It made me wonder if a natural leopard would look like that if it laughed like a person.

"Everything is okay, Anita, you don't need the guns."

I wrapped my arms around him and looked into his eyes. Flat-footed we were even, eye to eye. "Am I that easy to read?"

"For me," he said, smiling.

Dev got up carefully from the couch. "I'm going to clean up."

"Anita needs to rinse off, but only rinse off, no shower sex."

I looked at him, and Dev said, "I think I lost skin off my bits, so she's safe; ow."

"Zerbrowski called," Micah said.

I tensed all over again. He hugged me tighter and repeated, "They need you at the station, that's all."

"Why? What's happened?" I couldn't relax into his arms this time. Zerbrowski wouldn't have called if there wasn't something wrong.

"They've got a man who claims to be the human servant to a master vampire named Benjamin. He won't speak to anyone but you."

I started to say I didn't know a master vampire by that name, and then the light dawned. Barney the vampire, Barney Wilcox, our first suspect in the abduction of the girl, had said that the leader of their rebel movement was named Benjamin. Barney had said Benjamin was old school and had a human servant. I hadn't believed him, or I'd thought his "leader" was pretending to be that powerful so the others would follow him. I hadn't believed that any vampire powerful enough to have a servant would buy into such modern ideals as vampires being independent of any master, just good little citizens. I'd assumed any master vampire would know better.

"Is he really a human servant?" I asked.

"They can't tell. You know that one of the points of having a human servant is that they can be the vampire's human presence. If he seemed like anything else, he'd be a bad human servant, right?"

I thought about it, then nodded. "Though by that definition I suck as a human servant, since I so don't hit the radar as human."

"You're a special case," he said.

I nodded. "Sure."

"Were you expecting Benjamin or his representative to show up?" he asked.

"No, I thought the other vampire was lying, or being fooled. I'll get dressed and check him out."

"Clean up first, trust me," he said, smiling.

"The police or the would-be human servant aren't wereanimals; they won't be able to smell anything."

He smiled a little wider. "Anita, rinse off, make it fast, but the police are sitting on your visitor. He'll be waiting when you're ready."

"I didn't hear my phone, did I?" I asked.

"Apparently not," he said.

"So Zerbrowski called you to get me."

"It's daylight, he can't call Jean-Claude."

"True."

"What's wrong? You look way too serious. What are you thinking?"

"That the first time Benjamin's name was mentioned it was a trap to kill me, and now his servant just walks into the police station to talk to me; why? Why not try to contact us in the old vampire tradition of meeting under a white flag to negotiate?"

"Maybe he thought he'd stand a better chance of living through it with the police watching you."

I looked at Micah. "Are you saying that he felt safer with the cops than with us?"

"He's human; that means a lawyer, and a trial if he turns himself in, but if he meets you on a hunt you can kill him. He might wonder what you'd do in private with all your shapeshifter guards around you."

"Good point."

"Clean up, get dressed, get armed, and someone will drive you to talk to him."

"I can drive myself."

"You said the first time was a trap to kill you. They know you're on your way, why not ambush you en route?"

I opened my mouth and then closed it. "Okay, I'll take guards, but they can only go so far into the police station; beyond that they just have to sit and twiddle their thumbs."

"Thank you for just saying okay, and not arguing." He smiled and kissed me, then licked his lips.

I frowned. "You tasted Dev on my lips, didn't you?"

His eyes rolled upward, as if he were thinking, and then I realized he was tasting. "Mm-hm," he said.

"You know, if you weren't a wereleopard that would probably bother you."

He shook his head. "It's not being a wereleopard that makes sharing you okay with me, but I probably wouldn't let you know I could taste another man on your lips if I weren't a wereleopard. If I were just human, I'd pretend more."

Once I would have had to ask questions to understand what he meant, but I totally got it now. Sometimes I thought a little bit more "animal" would help a lot of people be more real and honest in their lives.

"I'll rinse off in the showers. I'll be quick."

"Dev will be there; resist temptation."

I frowned at him. "I have bad guys to catch, I won't get distracted."

He raised an eyebrow.

I grinned, and blushed, then rolled my eyes. "Okay, I won't get distracted today."

He smiled, and kissed me again. "That's my girl."

And I was.

44

WHEN TAKING BODYGUARDS to a police station, you have to make sure that none of them have outstanding warrants. The wererats especially recruited from some rough places. Bram, tall, very dark, and handsome, with the military haircut that he just kept getting redone, waited with the car. He'd been army, rangers, and then a wereleopard had attacked him in some jungle somewhere, and he'd had a medical discharge. The army's loss, our gain.

I purposefully didn't bring anyone that I was dating. I didn't want any more problems with the women at work, or the men for that matter. The multiple gorgeous boyfriends seemed to piss both groups off, just for different reasons. The men got all insecure, and the women got all jealous. So, Godofredo's tall, dark, and very solid muscle stayed at the car with Bram. I took Claudia and Pride in with me.

Claudia was partially to amuse myself. I loved watching the male cops react to such a large, beautiful, and physically imposing woman. It just giggled me, and I was starting to own the things that made me happy, not because it made sense, or was horribly important, but it was just a happy.

Claudia had thrown a black windbreaker over her arsenal, and her arms, so that she didn't frighten the other police too badly. I loved that she was another woman, and she looked as dangerous as she was; I was always too small to scare people just by showing up. Pride stood beside her like a gold shadow to her dark beauty. He was six-one to Mephistopheles' six-three. Pride's hair was short, falling in curls about an inch below his ears. His face was a little more triangular than Dev's, and his eyes were a pale gold that wasn't quite a brown and wasn't dark enough to be wolf or lion amber. I'd asked Pride what he put on his driver's license and he'd said brown, but it was a lie, just like Nathaniel was forced to put blue on his license, because lavender wasn't an option. Standard answers rarely covered the men in my life, or even the ones who worked for me.

Pride was handsome, broad shouldered, athletic, and good enough armed and unarmed that Claudia didn't have a problem with him being her backup. She had no higher praise. But honestly, Pride's two greatest assets for today were that he wasn't my lover, or anyone else's permanent sweetie, and he was gorgeous. I was hoping I could sort of wave him in the direction of Detective Arnet, Millie, and all the women at work, and distract them from my actual boyfriends. Maybe I could even take some pressure off Brice, though honestly my main interest was me. Brice was new, and one of the loves of his life hadn't been threatened by Arnet. She was beginning to spook me, and I wasn't easy to spook.

The only serious downside that Pride had was that he didn't flirt. He could seduce, or date, but he seemed incapable of light flirting. But the other gold tigers that I wasn't sleeping with had other issues; one was a hothead, another was a serious historian and scholar and loved his books more than anything, and the last one was scouting out another vampire kiss where weretigers were the main animal to call of the Master of the City, so Pride was it.

I got up to the two of them, and they fell to either side and slightly back of me. Pride said, "I'm still not happy being your sacrificial lamb for the female wolves at work. Thorn flirts better."

"He's got a temper. I don't want him anywhere near my job."

"Wrath has a very even disposition."

"And he's so deep into his role as historian for the Harlequin that he doesn't remember he's a man, let alone that he likes girls."

"I think he likes his books better than any woman," Claudia said.

Pride and I just nodded, though it made me look at her and ask, "Did you try to date Wrath?"

She blushed, only the second time ever, and both times over me asking about her dating.

"You did," I said.

Pride stumbled in the smooth stride he normally had. "Wrath? Why Wrath?"

And in that moment, I knew that Pride had looked at her and at least thought about it; thought about her as a woman.

"He's not a guard, but he can still handle himself in an emergency. I don't want to date a potential victim, but I don't want to date another bodyguard, or mercenary. They get competitive."

"With you?" I said.

"Yeah."

"I like a woman who can keep up with me," Pride said.

Claudia looked across me at him, and I watched her look at him. "I had you pegged for a competitive bastard," she said.

"I like to be the best, but I don't have to win."

"I'll keep that in mind," she said, and her voice sounded thoughtful.

I had a very alien urge to match-make. I didn't do that, ever, but suddenly it seemed like such fun. If Claudia hadn't hinted that she had a steady lover, I'd have pushed it, but it was too new a thought. I wanted to have more information before I did anything stupid, or helpful. I let it go, as Pride and Claudia both reached for the door at the same time. They glared at each other.

"See," she said.

He gave a small bow and stepped back, letting her hold the door open for me. His handsome face was that arrogant, almost angry, beauty that he wore as his blank cop face. Whatever he was feeling, he didn't want to share.

I went through the door, leaving Claudia looking at him as if she'd never quite seen him before. In the midst of catching bad guys maybe we could have a little romance, and for once, it wouldn't be mine. Cool.

45

CLAUDIA AND PRIDE had to hand their weapons over, and the nice desk officer locked them away for them. Claudia had gone through this once before; that time I'd passed it off as two girls going out for some shopping and range time, and then I got that emergency call. This time I couldn't pretend that they were anything but what they were: bodyguards, my bodyguards.

Zerbrowski pulled out a chair so that Claudia could have a seat by his desk. He made suitably lecherous comments to her. She stood up and looked down on him, way down on him, since he was five-eight. She gave him her best glare, until he grinned and teased her until her mouth quirked and she almost smiled.

She looked across the room at me. "He doesn't mean a damn word of it, does he?"

I shook my head. "Nope."

"Hey," Zerbrowski said, "I resent that, I mean everything I say. I am a pervert, I swear!" He raised his hand like he was about to be sworn into court.

We both laughed at him. He grinned at us, and it was just Zerbrowski.

Pride actually got invited to sit with Detective Tammy Reynolds, Larry's wife. I'd been surprised at first, but Tammy hadn't been as mean to me as Larry was, partly because she'd been gone for a while. Tammy was a natural witch, a psychic, and the Church had made room for people like her as a kind of holy warrior. They used their abilities to help the Church defeat Satan in all his forms. A lot of the witches went into police or social work. She'd taken a year of maternity leave with their daughter, and then gotten transferred to the Preternatural Branch at the FBI. She'd only been back a few weeks.

Her long brown hair was pulled back into a sensible ponytail. Her skirt suit was brown with a white button-down shirt, as sensible as the hair and lack of makeup. She was still pretty, but the clothes wouldn't have flattered anyone. She was five-eight to her husband's five-four, and I'd always liked that she hadn't had a problem being taller than Larry.

Dolph had sort of loomed behind me. Claudia had stood to shake his hand, which made Pride come over and do it, too. It was nice to see a woman who was so close to Dolph's six-eight. Pride looked small beside them, which made me smile. Did I feel tiny standing there with them all? A little, but I was used to it.

Dolph took me back so I could get a look on the video at our supposed human servant, before I went into the interrogation room. "See if you can tell anything from a distance," he said.

I looked at the grainy black-and-white image. The man sat very still, hands folded on the table in front of him. He had short, dark hair, cut very traditionally. His shirt was white and button-down, top button open, no tie. His suit jacket looked black or true navy; either way the clothing was dark and conservative. There was a glass of water sitting by his hand. He never touched it. He sat, he blinked, and he waited.

"He looks almost too ordinary," I said.

"He looks like a thousand businessmen in this country," Dolph said.

I nodded. "Yeah."

"Is he a human servant?"

I shook my head. "The point of a human servant is to appear human. I can't tell from here. I'll need to be physically closer."

"So far almost everyone associated with this group has tried to kill you, Anita."

I glanced up at him. "I can't break through his defenses and tell you if he's human or human servant without getting in the room with him."

"If he is a human servant, will he be faster and stronger than normal?"

"A bit, but mainly he's harder to hurt, harder to kill, just tougher. He shares his master's near-immortality."

"Why do you say near-immortality?" Dolph asked.

"Because anything you can kill with a gun or a blade isn't immortal, just hard to kill."

He smiled and nodded. "Agreed." Then his face went back to being serious. "I don't like you going in there with him."

"You guys searched him for weapons and explosives, right?"

He nodded, again.

"I trust you guys to do your job."

My phone sounded its text noise. I checked it automatically and found a text from Pride that read, "She's trying to convert me to her version of Christianity. Rescue me, or I'm going to be rude."

"Crap," I said.

"What's wrong?"

"Detective Tammy is back to trying to recruit the preternaturally talented for the Church."

Dolph scowled. "Religious freedom allows her to do it, but I have talked to her about concentrating more on saving lives than souls."

"Is she more zealous than she was before she left?" I asked.

"Seems to be," he said.

"I need to go rescue Pride and move him to a different desk, then let's talk to the human servant." I made air quotes around the last two words, a little hampered by the phone in one hand.

"Go save your bodyguard, then I'll walk you in to our businessman."

I didn't even argue that I didn't need Dolph at my back. There were people who would jump me, even with my reputation, who would hesitate at attacking with someone male and Dolph's size beside me. I could hate that it was true, but it was still true.

I went to rescue my tiger. Pride's face was darkening under his pale gold tan. His shoulders, arms, and hands were tight with tension, bordering on anger. Tammy had tried to recruit me to the order of holy witches when she first joined RPIT, and I'd been Episcopalian, so Christian. Pride wasn't, none of the golden tigers were; they all followed a pantheistic religion that had originated in China centuries before Jesus Christ had been a glimmer in the Creator's eye. Their religion had evolved from centuries of being in other countries and having to hide that they hadn't all been slain during the reign of the First Emperor of China in the early two hundreds BC, yeah, as in 259 BC to 210 BC. But the golden tigers were very devout to their faith; they didn't see it as inferior to the upstart religion that had started as a Jewish rebel sect.

I was almost to him when Arnet blocked my path. She spoke low. "Is he another boyfriend?"

"He's not my boyfriend, or my lover, just a guard."

"You swear," she said, arms crossed across her small, neat breasts. I could never do that; my breasts were too big, I had to go under them and sort of lift.

"I swear," I said.

She smiled. "I'll rescue him from the Minister then."

It took me a moment to realize that "the Minister" was Tammy's nickname. Arnet swayed toward them; her skirt suit was cut to show off her ass, and though she was thin, she had a figure. She was also wearing makeup, understated, but Arnet made an effort. She used all that effort as she touched Pride's shoulder and then smiled down at him, and at Tammy. She got him up and moving to her desk. Pride looked at me across the room, and I gave a small nod; he nodded back and let Arnet pull him up a chair. He was safe from Tammy's recruitment drive, and he knew my background with Arnet, so he was as prepared as I could make him.

Zerbrowski was pretending to be scandalizing Claudia, but as I walked by to check on them, I saw that he was actually showing her pictures of his kids on his iPhone, not naughty pictures. He pretended to be a terrible lech, but in reality he was one of the happiest and most devoted family men I'd ever met. Katie, his petite and lovely wife, had told me once at a barbecue at their house that she thought his outrageous flirting was an outlet he needed. Apparently, he'd flirted like that when they first met, and she'd thought he didn't like her because she was the only girl he didn't flirt with; go figure.

Dolph sent two uniforms into the room ahead of us. They took up posts at corners of the room. Dolph said, "Mr. Weiskopf, this is Marshal Blake."

Weiskopf smiled, and it seemed genuine, as if he were really glad to see me. "Marshal Blake, Anita, I didn't expect to see you like this in an interrogation room. My master and I are very disappointed that it's come to this."

I offered him a hand across the table before I sat down. He hesitated, and then took it sort of automatically; most people will, even vampires, but he wasn't a vampire. His hand was just a hand in mine, warm, alive . . . human. I could have put some power into the touch, but he might take that as an insult so I minded my manners.

"What exactly has it come to, Mr. Weiskopf?" I said, as I sat down. Dolph actually pushed my chair in for me, which I'd have preferred he not do, because I still hadn't figured out the timing on that. I sat down too early, as usual, and got the chair shoved into the back of my knees, which sort of hurt. At least Dolph, like most of the men who insisted on the chair thing in my life, was strong enough to push me into place at the table.

Dolph stayed standing at my side, looming over both me and the man at the table. He was trying to be intimidating, and if you weren't used to someone his height, it usually worked.

Weiskopf rolled his eyes upward as if looking all the way to the top of Dolph's head, then back to me. He smiled, hands still clasped on top of the table. "My master does not approve of the violence done in the name of our cause."

"And what cause is that?" I asked. I couldn't think how a crackpot human could have gotten the name Benjamin from our interrogation of Barney the vampire, but I'd learned to never underestimate the crazy. Crazy didn't mean dumb; some insane people were incredibly smart. Sometimes I wondered if you had to be a certain level of intelligent just to go crazy in style.

He smiled at me, his brown eyes filled with a gentle chiding. "Now, Anita, may I call you Anita?"

"If I have a first name to call you?" I smiled back at him. I even made it fill my eyes. The days when I couldn't lie with the best of them were long past.

His smile broadened. "I've been Mr. Weiskopf, or just Weiskopf, for so long that it will do."

"Weiskopf, just that?" I asked.

He nodded, smiling.

"Then you can call me Blake. Last name for last name."

"You think if I give you a first name that you will be able to trace it, and by finding me, you may find my master."

I shrugged. "It's my job to figure things out."

"No," he said, and the smile slipped, "it's your job to kill vampires."

"If they've broken the law, yes."

He shook his head, and he wasn't smiling now. "No, Anita, I mean, Blake, you've killed vampires for petty crimes. Things that humans would never have been executed for."

I nodded. "Three-strikes rules for vampires were very harsh."

He gave a bitter laugh. "Harsh, is that the best you can say?"

"Unfair, inhuman, monstrous, barbaric; stop when you like one of them."

"All of those, and more, but monstrous, I like that one. The human laws against vampires were monstrous; they made the humans into monsters. You became the bogeyman of all little vampires everywhere, Ms. Blake."

"Marshal Blake," I said.

He nodded. "Then I am Mr. Weiskopf."

"I didn't use your name, or title, Mr. Weiskopf."

"No, I suppose you didn't." He seemed to get a handle on himself, smoothing the lapels of his black suit; I could see that it was black, not navy, now. He tried to go back to smiling at me, but it didn't quite fill his eyes now. He was angry, and he didn't like me, or my job.

"My master and I do not believe in an eye for an eye. We advocated nonviolence, though you offered only violence."

"I helped get the three-strikes rule for vamps changed. Petty crimes don't add to the three strikes anymore. A vampire has to harm people to get a warrant of execution now."

"We do appreciate that your testimony in Washington was instrumental in getting the law modified, Marshal Blake. It gave us hope that Jean-Claude would be different from all the ones that have come before him."

Dolph interrupted, "All the what that have gone before Jean-Claude?"

Weiskopf looked up at Dolph, all the way up. "Leaders of the Vampire Council, of course. It's been in the news, Captain Storr; surely you don't want me to believe you are ignorant that there is talk of the first American head of our council."

"I've heard the rumors," Dolph said.

"They are not rumors. They are fact."

I sat there, trying to be very still, trying not to show in any movement, or lack of it, or facial expression that Weiskopf might know things that weren't in the news and that I might not want my fellow police officers to know.

"The fact that Jean-Claude tolerated the Church of Eternal Life, and did not insist they all take oath to him, gave us great hope."

I fought not to relax, because he could have said *blood-oathed*, and I really didn't want to go into details on that with Dolph. He might know, but he might not understand, what it meant for a vampire to take oath to the Master of the City.

"But then, Jean-Claude did demand it, and we lost hope."

"So, you decided to try to kill him," I said.

"No," Weiskopf said, and he looked serious, and shocked. "No, we never advocated violence. On my honor, and the honor of my master, we never encouraged anyone to do violence to anyone. We were most aggrieved to see the dead police officers on the news."

"You chose vampires that looked like children, or the elderly," I said. "You meant to appeal to the media."

"We suggested that we show the media that vampires are not all beautiful and sexy like your vampires. We wanted to show that vampires are truly people in many shapes and sizes, so yes, we chose a group, but we never meant for them to be used in such a vile way."

"Your master, Benjamin, was their master; he had control of them while they did this vile shit."

"No, my master is not theirs. We have purposefully not tried to control any other vampires except through speech and the persuasion that any normal human could use."

"Bullshit," I said.

He let me see that flash of anger again. "I have given you my word of honor."

"He's a master vampire, and they didn't belong to any other master; it means that a powerful enough vampire exerts more control over them than any human ever will."

"Only if the master wills it so, and my Benjamin has been most careful for centuries to control no one but himself."

"Vampires are all about the food chain, the hierarchy; everyone owes allegiance to someone. Your master didn't just spring into being, he came from a bloodline of some vampire, so he owes allegiance to that line, and whoever created him."

"His master was killed by one of the long-ago vampire hunters, the predecessor of you, the Executioner. We were told that if the master of our bloodline died, then we would die with him, but we woke the next night. It had been a lie to keep us from attacking the head of our order."

"I only know one line that had its head wiped out, and only two vampires that survived it."

"Your Wicked and Truth, yes, they survived as my master survived, but our bloodline sprang into being and fled into the wilderness. He did not want to be part of the hierarchy of blood and depravity, but of course, by being a master and acquiring followers he began to value the growing power over his own good intentions, and they were good intentions once. He meant us to live as holy a life as the cursed could."

He was talking of some unknown bloodline that had basically tried to run a monastery in some isolated area. "A vampire monastery?" I made it a question, but couldn't keep the disbelief out of my voice entirely.

"Exactly; as much as the head of my master's bloodline could make it. He was devout, so his very faith made holy objects work around him; it was most distressing to all of us."

I fought not to show surprise, because he was basically saying the vampire had not lost his faith, and his very faith had made holy objects flare around him. I tried to wrap my head around the idea of a vampire that made holy objects work against him, due to his own faith. It was just too weird.

"You may think what you will, Anita Blake, but I am telling the truth."

"Were you there, or is this just what Benjamin tells you?" I asked.

Weiskopf looked at me, very serious eye contact now. "You know as well as I do how complete the memories can be between master and servant. I know the truth, whether this body was present for the events, or the other body was alone for the making of certain memories. We were there. We saw the truth."

I didn't like the way he kept saying *we*; it was creeping me out. Was that what would have happened to Jean-Claude and me if we weren't so very careful about all the psychic connections between us? I thought about the months of learning curve when Richard, Jean-Claude, and I had all intruded on each other emotionally, sensorily, and in dreams. If we hadn't done anything to fight that . . . I remembered moments when I hadn't been sure whose body I was in, and who was seeing what. Yeah, if we hadn't set up rules of psychic etiquette, it could have made us into one mind with three bodies, or that was what Richard and I were afraid of. I wasn't sure if it scared Jean-Claude or not, only that it scared the hell out of me. To the point that I'd run for the hills for six months at a time, and left them both alone physically, emotionally, and as tight as I could shield psychically.

I sat there and listened to Weiskopf say *we*, and knew he meant it. They were a *we*, no longer an *I*. My skin ran cold with the thought of it.

"What has frightened you?" Weiskopf asked.

Fuck, I wasn't doing a very good poker face. Double fuck. I tried to rally and distract him. "So, some long-ago vampire hunter hunted the head of Benjamin's line down and killed him. Killing the master never kills all the little vampires, Mr. Weiskopf. It never has, not a single time, when I've done my job."

He studied me. "But they were small masters, the creator of a blood-line, the fountain of blood, the Fontaine de sangre; slaying that vam-pire is supposed to kill everyone descended from them. But it was a lie to keep us from rebelling against our creators. It was a lie, because we woke the next night. We, alone, woke."

"Benjamin was strong enough to make his own heart beat, simple as that," I said.

"No," Weiskopf said, and he leaned toward me over the table. "No, it's not that simple."

"Then why didn't the other vampires wake that next night? If it was all a lie, they should have all woken up," I said.

"The vampire hunter killed many of them. He murdered them in their caskets, their caves."

"Had they murdered people in the surrounding area?"

He nodded. "Our master had grown depraved with power. You cannot seek to control other vampires without it leading to corrup-tion of your very mind and soul. So we sought to control no one but ourselves."

"And how did that work for you?" I asked.

"We were drawn to make followers, but we resisted. We traveled, al-ways, so that we did not come to the attention of any other master. We did not want to fight for a territory, and we didn't want to be forced to bend our knee to any other vampire. We wanted only to be left alone."

"You had followers. They killed two police officers. One of them was about to kill his pregnant ex-wife when we stopped him."

"Killed him, you mean," Weiskopf said.

I nodded. "Fine, yes, killed him, but if it was him or a pregnant woman who'd done nothing wrong besides leaving her abusive ex-husband, I'd make the same choice again."

"As would we," Weiskopf said. "Saving the woman and the unborn child was the right thing to do."

I couldn't help but frown at him. "Glad you see that."

"Don't be so surprised, Anita Blake. We believe in violence to save the innocent. We are not complete pacifists."

"Good to know," I said.

"We had followers in the way of any human leader, but we did not make them bow to us. We did not make them take an oath to us. We were very careful to use only words."

I shook my head. "Weiskopf, a master vampire exerts control over lesser vampires just by being near them; it's like some kind of preternatural pheromone."

"You lie," he said, and he sounded so sure.

"Don't you understand, that's how a Master of the City knows another master is in his territory. They sense it."

"But your Jean-Claude did not sense us."

I tried to think of a safe way to reply to that. "Which means your Benjamin is very old, and very powerful. Let's say that he truly is trying not to exert control over other vampires. Let's say he honestly believes that he is just talking to them, just telling them that they deserve to be free of any master."

"That is all we want, for us, and for them. Freedom from eons of dictatorial rule, is that so awful a goal?"

"No," I said, and I believed it. "No, Weiskopf, it's a good ideal, it's a great ideal."

It was his turn to look surprised. "I did not expect you to agree."

"I'm just full of surprises," I said.

"I should have known you would be, Anita Blake."

"Anita," I said, "just Anita."

"Being friendly will not fool me," he said.

"I'm just tired of hearing you say Anita Blake. I feel like I'm in trouble with a teacher at school."

He smiled and nodded. "I understand; very well, Anita, and thank you for letting me use your given name."

"You're welcome. So, you and your master decided to try to free the little vampires from the control of the master vampires?"

"Exactly."

"I believe that vampires are people, Weiskopf, or I wouldn't be dating them; I wouldn't be in love with one, or two."

"Then how can you continue to execute them?"

I sighed, and felt my shoulders slump. I made myself sit up straight again. "I've actually been having a little crisis of conscience for a while."

Dolph stirred beside me, a minute involuntary movement. I fought not to glance at him, but to pay attention to the man in front of me.

"So you believe you murder them?"

"Sometimes," I said.

"All the time," he said.

I shook my head. "I've seen vampires do horrible things. I've walked through rooms so thick with the blood of their victims that the carpet squished underfoot and the room smelled like raw hamburger."

He flinched at that.

"I don't believe killing the animals that did that was murder."

He looked down at his hands on the table, then back up at me. "I can see that. Just as the one who tried to kill his wife, Bores, was in the wrong and had to be stopped."

"Yes," I said.

"Would you kill a human who had done awful things?"

"I have," I said.

Weiskopf glanced up at Dolph. "Do your fellow officers know that?"

I nodded. "Sometimes the bad guys aren't all vampires. I've helped the police hunt down and execute them, too."

He narrowed his eyes at me, so cynical. "Humans have more rights; you can't just kill them."

"Do you consider shapeshifters human?" I asked.

"The law gives them the right to trial, unless the warrant has been issued for their deaths. Once the death warrant has been issued, they are as much a pariah of human society as a vampire."

"So, is Benjamin trying to free the wereanimals from their pack leaders?"

He looked startled for a moment, as if the thought had never occurred to him.

I smiled, but knew it wasn't pleasant. "All the old vamps think the shapeshifters are lesser beings. You think of them as animals, not people."

He truly looked disturbed. He opened his mouth, closed it, and then said, "I cannot dispute your accusation. It did not occur to us to try to free them of their oppression, because they are animals, and animals need discipline, a leash of sorts to keep them from running amok and slaughtering the innocent."

"Vampires need the same thing," I said.

He shook his head. "That is not true."

"Bullshit," I said, "the newly risen can be just as animalistic as any first-time shapeshifter." I pulled my shirt collar to one side to expose the collarbone scar.

"That was no vampire," he said.

"You have my word of honor on that." I slipped out of my jacket, and since I'd had to give up all my weapons to enter the interrogation room, I could show off the scars really well, no sheaths to hide them. I showed him the bend of my elbow where the same vampire that did my collarbone had torn at my arm like a terrier with a rat.

"You have a cross-shaped burn scar."

"Yeah, some human Renfields thought it would be funny to brand me with it."

"And the scar that pulls the skin so it's crooked, what made that?"

"A witch that had shape-changed."

"Not a shapeshifter?" he asked.

"No, it was a witch that used magic to steal the animal of a real lycanthrope."

"I was there for that one," Dolph said. "Anita helped save one of my officers."

It had been Zerbrowski with his guts spilling out. I'd held them in with my hands while uniforms refused to help, because they thought the witch was a real lycanthrope and they might catch it. I'd held pressure on his wound, and screamed at them that they were fucking cowards, but Dolph and I had gotten Zerbrowski out of there alive. I'd been the one who held Katie when she fainted at the hospital. There were reasons that Zerbrowski and I partnered, and that Katie made sure I and my sweeties were invited to the barbecues and dinners. She wasn't comfy with the vampires visiting, but she let my furry sweeties come visit. She'd made sure the other cops knew that if they couldn't deal with it, they could leave. Katie seemed so soft, but there was steel under that silk, and she'd used it to defend me and Nathaniel and Micah at the last summer cookout. I loved Katie for that day.

"The vampire that tore at you, he was the newly risen?"

"No," I said.

He shook his head. "No vampire that had been undead for any length of time would do that, unless it was one of the revenants, those poor things that are little better than ghouls."

"The vampire that did this to me was over a hundred years old, and no revenant. He chose to hurt me like this; he wanted to make me suffer."

"Why?" he asked.

"That's something he'd have to answer," I said.

"Is he alive to answer it?"

"No," I said.

"There are bad vampires, as there are bad people, I suppose," he said.

"They're people, Weiskopf, just people, and like all people, some of them are good, and some are bad, but now they're bad people with super-strength, super-senses, and bloodlust. Without a master to hold their leash, they're like most people, power drunk."

"No," he said.

"They've killed two police officers. It was a trap to kill me."

He looked at the table. "They had talked of slaying you and Jean-Claude. We had told them no, but apparently they went ahead without us."

"If you'd really been their master, you could have prevented that, and all of this."

"But that would defeat our purpose, Anita. We wanted them to be free, to prove that vampires did not need to be herded and controlled like animals."

"You mean like the wereanimals," I said.

"They are part animal, Anita."

"I have more lovers who turn furry once a month than sleep in coffins."

He shuddered, actually shuddered, as if it made his skin crawl. "That is your choice, but vampires have no taint of beast in them."

"No, just like human serial killers, they're just people that do unspeakable things."

Dolph said, "We found bombs at the last house we raided."

That was a partial lie; we'd found the makings, or leavings, after bombs had been made, according to Alvarez, but the look of shock and horror on Weiskopf's face made the white lie worth it.

"Oh, no, no."

"What do they plan on doing with the bombs?" Dolph asked.

"How many did you find?"

And there is the problem with lying, you have to keep doing it.

"Two," Dolph said.

Weiskopf looked pale. "No, they can't."

"What are the targets?" Dolph said, and he leaned on the table, using his size to intimidate, but it was lost on Weiskopf. He was truly shaken by the news.

"They spoke of making bombs, but we told them no."

"But you didn't have any real authority over them, because you didn't make them take your oath," I said.

"They were better when we were with them."

"Yeah, the pheromones," I said.

He shook his head. "We worried that our very presence was affecting them, so we began to sleep elsewhere, away from them."

"Fuck, Weiskopf, that lost you and your Benjamin what little control you had over these people."

He looked at me, and there was real anguish in his face. "There has to be a way to be free. There has to be a way to be just human again."

"You're vampires, Weiskopf," I said, and my voice was soft, because I heard the pain in his voice. "That can't be changed, and that means that you need a master."

He shook his head faster, as if trying to shake a thought out. "No, no, that would make everything we've done . . . useless."

"What are the targets for the bombs?" I asked.

He looked at me. "The Church of Eternal Life; they feel that Malcolm betrayed them all by making them take oath to Jean-Claude. Jean-Claude's clubs and businesses. You and Jean-Claude. There were many who felt if they could kill him, and you, that they would be free. We told them that wasn't true, that you were the best and most modern prince that we had ever seen. That you gave us hope."

My pulse had sped, but he wasn't actually telling us anything we hadn't suspected. The guards would triple-check everything. We had good people. I believed that, I did, but I was still scared. "Are there any other human servants in your group?" I asked.

"No."

A little bit of the panic subsided. There was no one to use bombs during the day, and we'd killed their demolitions expert at the warehouse.

"Wait," I said, "are there Renfields; two-biters?"

He made a face of distaste. "*Two-biter* is an insult to humans we are bringing over."

"Renfields, then; do any of the vampires in your group have them?"

"A few," he said.

My pulse was back in my throat. "What are their names?"

He hesitated.

"If the bombs are used, then you and your master will be just as guilty as the rest," I said.

"You can stop this," Dolph said.

"If anyone dies because you didn't tell us, then you are as guilty as they are, and human servants are treated the same as vampires under the law if the vampires in question commit murder and the servants aid them in any way."

"We would never forgive ourselves if more innocent lives are lost," Weiskopf said, staring at his hands where they lay clenching each other on the table.

He told us the names. One of them wasn't in the system at all, but one had a record for assault, and the other was in the system because he'd worked as a court officer before he became a vampire; then he'd lost his job. The government, not just the military branch, didn't want vampires working for them. There was a case before the Supreme Court right now that might change that, but until it did, Clarence Bradley had lost his job, his pension, and over a decade of time in the system. That sounded like an excellent motive for all sorts of bitterness.

We put out an all-points bulletin on the one we had pictures for, and then started working to get the last picture we needed. My phone rang in the middle of it all, and I was only half-surprised when I heard Nicky's voice, "We have a problem."

"What?" I asked, and tried to keep my voice neutral just in case it was a problem that we wanted to handle without the other police.

"We have a Renfield with a bomb strapped to him, and a dead man's switch, so if he dies it blows."

"Where?" I whispered.

"Guilty Pleasures."

"It's closed right now," I said.

"They were here rehearsing the new dance routine."

My mouth was suddenly dry; my pulse couldn't decide it if was going to beat too fast, or stop altogether. "Who's *they*?"

"Our people took out two of them, but the last one, the one with the bomb, he grabbed . . ."

"Nicky, tell me."

"Nathaniel, the bomber has his arms wrapped around Nathaniel. If we shoot the Renfield, the bomb goes off. If we don't shoot him, eventually the bomb goes off."

I had a sudden wave of nausea, and had to sit on the edge of a desk and put my head down. Claudia was there, "Anita, what's wrong?"

So much for me being cool and hiding shit. "Why hasn't he blown it already?" My voice sounded almost normal. I didn't have enough brownie points to give myself for that.

"He wants you to come down. He says he'll let Nathaniel go for you."

"Okay," I said. I gripped the edge of the desk, and lowered myself to the floor with Claudia's help. I was still nauseous, and dizzy, and the room felt hot. Fuck.

"Anita, he may not let Nathaniel go. He may just blow it with both of you there. He's your leopard to call; if he takes you both out, then the chances of you actually dying are better, you know that."

"But *he* doesn't," I said.

"You don't know that, and he may just blow it with both of you because he can, Anita. You can't do this."

"I can't not do it," I said. I added. "Don't sacrifice Nathaniel to keep me safe, I'd never forgive you for it."

There was a crowd gathered around me. Claudia, and Pride, who was kneeling by me. Zerbrowski was there, and Arnet, and Tammy, and Dolph, and . . . I didn't care about any of them. In that moment I just cared about the one person who wasn't there.

"I would never hurt Nathaniel," he said.

"I thought you'd say, now that I told you you couldn't, you couldn't."

"He means something to me, too, Anita. I've had a pride of werelions, but this is the first home I've had since the woman who raised me . . . It doesn't matter. I want him safe, too."

And in that moment I knew that Nicky wasn't nearly as good a sociopath as I'd thought, or maybe as he'd thought.

"Keep him safe for both of us; I'm on my way."

"I will."

"Don't get yourself killed either, okay?"

"I won't on purpose.

"Nicky?"

But he'd hung up. I could have called him back, but what could I have said? *Don't die on me. Don't any of you die on me.* Yeah, I could have said that.

46

GUILTY PLEASURES IS in the Riverfront area of St. Louis. The streets are narrow, designed more for horses than cars, and most of them are still paved with bricks. It's very historic, with very modern clubs in a line that draw in a hell of a lot of tourists. It is one of *the* hot spots on the weekend. There's almost no parking. It sucks as a staging area for SWAT. But we made do, parking everything far enough away that we couldn't see the daylight front of the club.

Lisandro stood by the main truck. His shoulder-length hair was back in a braid. He was still tall, dark, handsome, and happily married. Almost a year ago, in the summer, he'd gotten shot helping us defeat the Mother of All Darkness. There'd been a horrible moment when I thought he'd made the ultimate sacrifice and died, but he was too big a dog, or wererat, for that, and he'd lived. I hadn't had to explain to his wife and kids why I brought their dad back in a box. I was glad of that, but since that moment I'd rejected him from my bodyguard detail. I didn't want the responsibility of making a widow of his wife, or half-orphans of his kids. Standing out in the thin spring sunshine, I remembered that by my side wasn't the only dangerous detail.

We were surrounded by SWAT, with Dolph and Zerbrowski in the mix. All of them were paying me and my people the ultimate compliment by letting them be here.

"How the hell did you let someone wearing a bomb get into the club, and then let them take Nathaniel hostage?" I demanded.

Lisandro looked down, took a deep breath, set his shoulders, then met my eyes and reported. "Clay was on the door; he's never been real military, or seen real violence. With the higher alert I shouldn't have had him on the door. The young man was here with two others to apply as wait staff."

"Were the other two in on it?" I asked.

"They ran like hell, so I don't think so. It seems to have been just the one man."

"How did he get Nathaniel with Nicky and you here?"

Dolph said, "Anita, these aren't the questions you need to be asking."

I looked up at him and started to argue, then swallowed it. I took a deep breath, let it out slow, and nodded.

Hill said, "Let me find out what we need to know, Blake."

I wanted to say that I could do it, but we didn't have time for me to lie to myself. I just nodded.

"We've got blueprints of the club. Blake gave a rundown of the interior on the way in. Who's inside? Where exactly is the hostage being held?"

"Inside: Nicky, Nathaniel, Mephistopheles, and Cynric."

"Wait," I said, "why's Sin here? He's not a guard, or a dancer."

Lisandro looked uncomfortable. "Nathaniel's brought him a couple of times before. He watches the practice, works out some."

"Why is Sin inside, but you're safe out here?"

"He wouldn't leave Nathaniel; neither would Nicky."

"And Dev?"

"He knew Mephistopheles was your golden tiger. He wanted him to stay. I think he plans to take you and two of your cats."

"Sin is one of my cats, too."

"He seemed bothered by how young Cynric is."

"Blake," Hill said, "we don't have time. Is Sin someone important to you, too?"

"Every name he mentioned is a lover, and most of them live with me, most of the time."

The look of sympathy in Hill's eyes almost undid me. "I'm sorry, Blake."

"I've lived with Nathaniel for three years, four in June."

Hill nodded solemnly. "We'll get him out."

"I know," I said, and that was a lie. I didn't know. I hoped, but in this instance, hope didn't seem enough.

Hill and the others began to ask Lisandro questions about the bomb, and he knew way more about it than I would have. I'd have been stopped at *bomb vest*, and I knew what a dead man's switch was, but not exactly what it looked like. Lisandro reported clearly, quickly.

Hill and a couple of the others nodded. They approved. Hell, I approved, but there was a little song playing in my head: *Nathaniel's in there with a bomb. Nicky's in there. Sin is in there. Dev is in there. With a bomb.* That was the refrain in my head while they asked their good questions and got their answers. It was like an evil song stuck in my head, with the beat of *Bomb, bomb, bomb.* Fire was the only thing that wereanimals couldn't heal. Silver could kill them, and other preternaturals' claws and teeth could cut them up, but if they lived they could heal most if not all of the damage. Fire was the only thing that was permanent damage. In fact, some preternaturals burned faster and more completely than a human.

I had an image in my head of a werewolf I'd seen burn last year from being too close to a rocket when it launched. The human form had gone up in flames and tried to shift to animal in an attempt to heal, but it had ended up burned to death, frozen in between both forms, just a blackened, nightmare shape. I did everything I could not to picture Nathaniel like that, or Sin, or Nicky, or Dev.

"Anita can do it." I heard the voice and had to concentrate to realize it was Pride.

I blinked up into his handsome face, so like Dev's; they were cousins, after all. "What? What can I do?"

"You can open your link between you and Mephistopheles, or Nathaniel, or Cynric. You can see the room that way. We don't have to guess."

Hill studied my face. "Can you really do that?"

"If I drop shields and concentrate, yes."

"You'll be able to see inside the club through at least three different sets of eyes, no guesswork?" he asked.

"Yeah, should work exactly that way."

"Damn," he said, "does this work with all of your lovers?"

"No, it won't work with Nicky, just the others."

Hill frowned. "Later, I want to understand how this works, and see if we can use it. Right now, work your magic, Blake. Give us eyes; give us the location of everyone in the room."

"I'll try."

Zerbrowski said, "Try not. Do. Or do not. There is no try."

It took me a second to realize that he had just quoted *Star Wars* to me. It made me smile, and in that moment I loved him, just for that.

47

I SAT ON the shallow curb in the weak spring sunlight in my vest and weapons, and had all the SWAT guys, plus Marshal Arlen Brice, Zerbrowski and Dolph, and a lot more of RPIT than I thought gave a damn, plus my bodyguards, huddling around me to keep everyone else back while I did the psychic dream of every hostage negotiator. We didn't need to call the suspect or get eyes into the club; I had eyes in the club already. I just had to "open" them.

I sat on the curb, and I was small enough that it was like sitting at the bottom of a well of very tall people, but that was okay. I was used to being the smallest kid in school. I opened the blocks I had put in the way of Dev first. Pride had suggested starting with Dev, because he was trained as a warrior, a spy, a guard, and an assassin, though he didn't say all that out loud to the police; he said *guard*, just *guard*. I lowered my shields for Mephistopheles, my Devil. He hadn't come into my life until I'd had a lot of practice keeping my psychic and emotional distance from the people connected to me. I'd never let him in as far as Nathaniel could get, or Micah, or Jean-Claude, or . . . I'd kept him at a distance, because I knew how, because I could. Now, I tore down all that careful work and reached out to him.

I thought about making love to him. The feel of his body in mine, his skin under my hands, his . . . And just like that I was in. Most of the time it was like floating just above the people I was talking to, but the ties that bound me could get closer, much closer. I let that happen now, and I could see out of Dev's eyes for a moment. It was disorienting, and I drew back.

He blinked up at me where he could "see" me above him. He gave his version of blank cop face and then went back to staring across the room. I thought, *What do you see?* And just like that, I could see what Dev was looking at.

Sin was standing just a little farther toward the stage, ahead of everyone else, in the midst of all the little tables, most of them with their chairs put up on the tabletops, waiting for business that night. Nicky was the closest to the door, on the other side of Dev. Nathaniel stood against the wall on the far side of the stage, away from the doors. A man I didn't know had an arm around his neck. His other hand held something that looked like a cylinder with a button that he'd already pressed, and that startled me, except Dev thought at me, *It's armed, but won't blow until he lets go.* Pressing down armed it, letting go blew it.

I moved my perception to Sin. He did startle.

I heard the bomber say, "What's wrong? Where is Anita Blake? Where is she?"

Sin said, "Let my brother go."

"He's not your brother!" He yelled it.

"Yes, he is."

"Shut up! You, lion! Call her again!"

Nathaniel said, "Cynric, leave, please."

I felt Sin shake his head, felt the depth of his stubbornness, and knew he wouldn't leave. It wasn't a death wish, it was just a decision. He wouldn't leave Nathaniel. He just wouldn't.

I thought about Nathaniel, and I could feel the man's arm across my shoulders. I was looking at Sin, seeing his blue eyes too wide, his face pale, visibly scared, but not leaving. I felt Nathaniel's fear for him, tasted his pulse in my own throat, or was it my throat? I had a moment in which I could taste three pulses in my body, and none of them were mine. One of the reasons I had learned to shield like a son of a bitch was that I didn't want to end up like Weiskopf and his master, just one mind in two bodies, or three bodies, or four, or . . . When it had just been Jean-Claude, Richard, and me, we'd had moments of being almost a group mind floating between three bodies. I felt it for the first time with all of them, only Nicky was left out of this level of intimacy, if that was the right word for having someone else's heart beating in your head.

I felt their emotions like cards fanned out in my hand. I caught bits of thought. Dev seemed better at complete sentences, and just thinking about it let me know that the same people who had trained him to fight had trained him psychically. The gold tigers had been raised to be the perfect instrument of whatever master finally claimed them. That master had been me, though technically according to vampire law, Jean-Claude.

Nicky moved closer to Dev; he felt my energy, I knew he did. "I'll call her, just be cool, okay?" he said.

"Call her!" The bomber screamed it this time.

I pulled back, but it was like folding clothes in a suitcase. You never quite got them all put back as neatly and completely the second time. I could feel bits of the connection to all the men inside the club.

My phone rang, and Pride had to help me get it out of its pocket. I was having trouble telling my hands from much bigger ones in that other room. Crap, I had to do better than this, and then I realized I didn't want to close the door completely. If I lost Nathaniel, lost them all, this might be the last touch of them I had. I didn't want to give it up.

Dev thought in my head. *Cut ties, Anita, we can't function like this.*

I did what he asked, but it was Nathaniel I left last, drawing away like

I was caressing him from the inside out. I brought the scent of his hair and skin with me, as I spoke into my phone. "Nicky."

"He wants you inside."

A spurt of fear from Nathaniel broke through the newly raised shields. He was afraid, and I felt a thought in his head that he would set it off before I got there, because he thought the bomber meant to blow him, me, and Dev up; two animals to call and me at the same time upped the chances of my really dying.

"Nathaniel is thinking about blowing the bomb before I get there. He's convinced the bomber is trying to kill me with my two cats, so I'll die for sure."

"Probably true," Nicky said in a very matter-of-fact voice. I could almost picture the smile on his face: pleasant, unreadable.

I thought at Nathaniel, thought hard, *Don't you dare!*

The bomber screamed, "What is that? If you shift, you die!"

"The energy in here just spiked. We're all nervous enough that our human friend here felt it." It was his way of warning me off.

The bomber was more sensitive than I'd hoped. Damn it!

"Where are you?" Nicky asked.

"Just down the road," I said.

"Traffic sucks, huh?"

"You don't want me to come inside," I said.

"No."

"You think he'll blow it as soon as I step inside?"

"I think so."

"Crap."

"Yes."

"Tell him I'll be there as soon as I can."

"Not sure that's a good idea."

The bomber started screaming, "Tell her she has ten minutes, that's it, that's it!"

"Hear that?" Nicky asked.

"I heard. Tell him thirty," I said.

"I'll try." He hung up.

"Tell us what's happening," Hill said.

I told them where everyone was, and that the bomber's nerve seemed to be failing him. "He's starting to panic."

"If it weren't a dead man's switch that'd be good news," Hill said.

"How quick are Nathaniel's reaction times?" Zerbrowski asked.

I glanced at him. "Fast."

"Faster than you were in the warehouse when you stopped Billings from hitting the kid vampire?"

I thought about that. "Yes, he's faster. They all are."

"Everyone in there?" Zerbrowski asked.

I nodded.

Claudia said, "Anita's fast, but she's not as fast we are."

"She's still human," Pride said.

"What are you thinking?" I asked Zerbrowski.

"I think your boyfriend is right. I think this guy will blow you and them up as soon as he thinks you're close enough to die with him."

"Not helpful," I said.

"Hear me out. There was a group of men playing ball in Israel when a guy in a bomber vest with a dead man's switch came in; they jumped him, held his hand pressed on the button until the police got there and shot the bomber."

"He's human," Dolph said, "you can't just kill him."

"He's a human involved with the group that killed two cops. Anita's warrant of execution allows her to kill anyone who is involved in the crime that the warrant pertains to."

"That's when you're on an active hunt," Dolph said. "It was never intended to allow a police officer to shoot a human being in cold blood."

"If it was your wife with an arm around her neck and a bomb pressed to her back, would you be shooting in cold blood?" I asked.

"No," he said, finally.

"Wait," Hill said, "you're saying we let Anita go in there, and hope that all of them figure out that they're supposed to jump the bastard and hold him until we get in and kill him?"

"Yeah," Zerbrowski said.

"Nathaniel isn't trained in hand-to-hand combat," Claudia said.

"Dev and Nicky are," Pride said, "and Sin isn't bad for a beginner, and he's wicked fast."

My pulse was in my throat again, but my skin was cold in the sunshine. "I can 'tell' three of them what we plan to do." I made air quotes for the *tell* part.

"Nicky's good," Claudia said, "he'll move when they do."

"You mean when I do," I said.

"He's human with a couple of vampire bites on him," Pride said. "He won't be stronger than Nathaniel, Sin, Dev, and Nicky."

"You're saying I won't get a piece of him?"

"You won't need to grab him," Pride said.

"I don't understand."

Bram spoke for the first time. "He means you get to blow his brains out so that he can't set off the bomb."

Dolph shook his head. "I'm not sure this is legal."

"I've read those warrants backward and forward," Zerbrowski said, "it's legal by the letter of the law, and there's no trial to worry about, because once a warrant is executed it's done."

We all looked at each other.

"I don't like the idea of you going in there alone," Hill said.

"He never said *no police*," I said.

Hill smiled, and it was a fierce flash of teeth, like showing fangs. "Then I got your back."

"We," Killian said, "we got her back."

And that was what we did. I let Nathaniel and the others know what I needed them to do. I trusted that Nicky would move when Nathaniel did, and I bet his life on his speed and ability to wrestle the bomber long enough for the others to cross the room and help him. They just needed to wait, and then I'd be in the room with full SWAT backup. It all depended on Nathaniel using that same hand-eye coordination and speed that made him so amazing on the dance floor, in the gym, at the shooting range, to keep the bomber's hand pressed tight to the switch.

That was all he had to do, and then the others would be there, and they'd pile on top of the bomber . . . and either they'd have him safe until we got there to finish it, or they'd all blow up together. As plans went, I'd heard better, but Hill, Killian, and the rest were willing to walk in with me. They were willing to trust that if I believed the loves of my life could do this, then they could. I trusted the men in my life, and Hill, Killian, Derry, and the rest, trusted me. Fuck, fuck, fuck.

48

I HAD TO keep my face uncovered so the bomber would be certain I was actually one of the heavily armed people about to come through the door, but other than that I geared up as if it were any other monster hunt. In a way it was, it was just part of an ongoing vampire hunt. I let myself fall into the rhythm of moving with the men in that shuffling movement that looked like it should be slow and awkward, but was anything but.

We were almost there, almost at the door I'd gone through a hundred times, a thousand times. I dropped my shields just enough to let Nathaniel "see" me above him. I was careful to stay further away psychically than I had before, because he needed to be as fast and smooth as only he could be, and I needed to move with precision with the men around me. We both had our jobs, our strengths, and we needed them now. I let Nathaniel know we were coming through the door, and then I cut ties, so everyone was alone in their heads. So, when Derry pushed the door open, and we slipped through in a wedge, the only way I knew Nathaniel hadn't fumbled the first grab was that nothing blew up. In fact, it took a second for our eyes to adjust to the dimness of the interior, to find that all the men were in a pile on the far side of the room. They had dog-piled the bomber.

I ran, I ran the way I had in the warehouse, except this time I wasn't moving to save some stranger from getting hit. I was moving to get to the men I loved, before the man they were struggling with could blow them up. I was across the room, above the pile of them before I'd had time to think. It was like magic, even to me, that I was just suddenly looking down at Nicky's broad back, his one big hand wrapped around everyone else's, like a desperate game of top-of-the-baseball-bat, Dev wrapping himself around the bomber, pinning him to the wall, his hand underneath Nicky's, Sin with his arms around the man's waist like he'd tried to tackle him, and Nathaniel with his hands around the man's one hand, his hair in its braid and the muscles of his shoulders showing through the edges of the cut tank top, and the man's face that I'd seen only through their eyes until that moment, as he looked wide-eyed at me. He had time to yell, "No!" Then I shot him through the forehead, just above his eyebrows. Blood and thicker things exploded out the back of his head, but the entry hole was small, neat even. I put another bullet beside the first one, and the back of his head was just not there anymore. His eyes rolled upward, and now all we had to do was hold on until the bomb techs got inside and told us we could let go.

49

WHEN ALL THE wires had been snipped and the bomb taken away, I sat on the edge of the stage with Nathaniel on one side and Sin on the other. Nicky and Dev were talking to Pride, Claudia, and the rest of the guards on the side of the room. I think they were already trying to figure out what had gone wrong, and how they could keep anything this bad from happening again. I didn't care.

I sat there with Nathaniel's hand in mine, and Sin holding on to the other hand, and just sat there holding them, and being held. That was enough. That was more than enough.

"Is this what it's like at your job?" Sin asked, and his voice sounded odd. I wasn't sure if he sounded odd, or the shock and gunfire in an enclosed space was messing with my hearing.

"Sometimes," I said.

"I don't think I'd want to do this every day," he said.

I smiled and squeezed his hand. "Good, then find some nice and much safer job."

He laid his head on my shoulder, and since he was nearly seven inches taller than I was, it had to be awkward, but he did it anyway. He held to my one hand with both of his, even though his hands were larger enough than mine that he was probably holding more of his own hand than mine.

Nathaniel had one hand on my thigh, the other holding my hand. He kissed my cheek and I cuddled into the kiss. I felt Jean-Claude wake for the day, felt him draw that first breath, and then his voice in my head, asking, "*Ma petite*, what has happened?"

For some reason, that was what made me cry.

50

WEISKOPF GAVE US all the names of the other rogue vampires. He and his master, Benjamin, offered them up in the first-ever successful deal between a vampire and human law. They gave us the names and they were allowed to go free since they had truly not hurt anyone. Benjamin and Weiskopf were very disillusioned about their unblood-oathed vampires. Jean-Claude and I made them promise that they wouldn't try it again. We've pretty much told them that they may be safe from the human police, but if they try for another rebellion they will not be safe from us.

Nicky and Dev had their onstage debut at Guilty Pleasures and were a huge hit. Dev liked performing and may do it again, but Nicky, not so much. Though, watching them both on stage, Nicky seemed just as into it as Dev. Sociopaths are great actors. He refused to leave Nathaniel, not for me, but for him. He said it: He has a family for the first time in his life.

Sin had been at the club because Nathaniel was teaching him how to strip, not for the stage, but for me. He wanted to do a private dance for me, and Nathaniel was showing him how. Sin's reasoning was, "Most of the men you like best are sexy onstage."

"Micah isn't," I'd said.

"But everyone else is," and to that I had no comeback.

Asher left for his month to explore the new city. It would be a good fit for him, and the werehyenas are the major animal group, but . . . he would be hundreds of miles away. He doesn't want to leave, but Dev still wants more girl time, and honestly he'd do other men if he didn't think Asher would go completely apeshit. But Dev's deal breaker is that he needs female lovers, and if Asher can't deal with that, then they have to break up. Asher is trying to put Dev in my bed more; I am a girl, but I have other sweeties, other responsibilities to the other men in my life. Asher is jealous of Jean-Claude, too, and that is totally not cool. We're thinking about a two-month-long trip for Asher to try the new city out for size.

Nathaniel has finally had enough of Asher, and though he was Nathaniel's ideal male dominant, and maybe mine, too, we've both had enough. Nathaniel can't forgive Asher for hurting Sin, and perversely, as Nathaniel has pulled away from Asher, the vampire is chasing him harder. Asher really is one of those people who don't value someone who makes life easy; he only chases the drama llamas, or the people who are more committed to other people. I've told Asher to get therapy. He doesn't want to do it, and you can't do therapy at gunpoint. But I've also told him that if his jealousy and temper get anyone else hurt, I will make sure he hurts, too. I can't threaten to kill him, because he knows that I would do almost anything to avoid that, but there are things he could do where I'd feel I had no choice. I don't want that on my conscience. He should go. But do we have the strength of will to send him away, at least for a month? After that, we'll see.

Does Jean-Claude have the strength to send someone that he has loved for centuries away? I don't know. Do I have the strength to make him do it? Maybe.

Right now we've put a bandage on it. Dev is staying with me more, but he's not Nicky, or Sin, or Micah, or Nathaniel, and I just don't think

I have room in the house or in my heart for another main squeeze. I like sleeping with Dev, but I'm not in love with him. The house is mine, filled with the people I want there, and Dev just isn't one of them, not night after night. I'm told I need one of the gold tigers to be a main sweetheart just for metaphysical reasons, and maybe I do, but maybe my heart is a molecule that has only so many attachment points, and is stable with only so many atoms of oxygen; you go over that limit and it's unstable, unhappy, too active, and finally explodes. Asher isn't the only one with a temper. I think he's forgotten that. If he's not careful, I'll be reminding him—soon. I hope it doesn't come to that, but I'm beginning to try and wrap my head around the thought that no one gets to hurt the people I love, not even another man that I love.

Craving more from Anita Blake?
Look for the steamy outtake

BEAUTY

by Laurell K. Hamilton
Only available digitally as an eSpecial from Penguin Group